Tourist Season

Also by Brenda Novak

THE MESSY LIFE OF JANE TANNER
THE TALK OF COYOTE CANYON
TALULAH'S BACK IN TOWN
THE SEASIDE LIBRARY
SUMMER ON THE ISLAND
KEEP ME WARM AT CHRISTMAS
WHEN I FOUND YOU
THE BOOKSTORE ON THE BEACH
A CALIFORNIA CHRISTMAS
ONE PERFECT SUMMER
CHRISTMAS IN SILVER SPRINGS
UNFORGETTABLE YOU
BEFORE WE WERE STRANGERS
RIGHT WHERE WE BELONG
UNTIL YOU LOVED ME
NO ONE BUT YOU
FINDING OUR FOREVER
THE SECRETS SHE KEPT
A WINTER WEDDING
THE SECRET SISTER
THIS HEART OF MINE
THE HEART OF CHRISTMAS
COME HOME TO ME
TAKE ME HOME FOR CHRISTMAS
HOME TO WHISKEY CREEK
WHEN SUMMER COMES
WHEN SNOW FALLS
WHEN LIGHTNING STRIKES
IN CLOSE
IN SECONDS
INSIDE
KILLER HEAT
BODY HEAT
WHITE HEAT
THE PERFECT MURDER
THE PERFECT LIAR
THE PERFECT COUPLE
WATCH ME
STOP ME
TRUST ME
DEAD RIGHT
DEAD GIVEAWAY
DEAD SILENCE
COLD FEET
TAKING THE HEAT
EVERY WAKING MOMENT

For a full list of Brenda's books,
visit www.brendanovak.com.

Look for Brenda Novak's next novel
available soon from MIRA.

BRENDA NOVAK

Tourist Season

Recycling programs for this product may not exist in your area.

ISBN-13: 978-0-7783-1035-8

Tourist Season

For questions and comments about the quality of this book, please contact us at CustomerService@Harlequin.com.

TM is a trademark of Harlequin Enterprises ULC.

Mira
22 Adelaide St. West, 41st Floor
Toronto, Ontario M5H 4E3, Canada
BookClubbish.com

Printed in U.S.A.

To Roberta Peden, a reader who's followed me from the beginning of my career and has become a friend over the years. Thank you for your sweet, patient, kind and steady support—and the generous donations you've made to the Box Grant Program in Brenda Novak's Book Group on Facebook. You're an inspiration!

1

1

Ismay Chalmers had never faced such terrible weather. A farmer's daughter, born and raised in a small town in northern Utah, she'd seen the occasional blizzard during winter, a twenty-year drought, and scars left by wildfires *once*. But she'd never experienced anything even close to a hurricane. "I can't believe this is happening," she told Remy Windsor, her fiancé, over the phone.

"You have nothing to worry about," he said, but his words sounded hollow. She was alone on an island off Cape Cod that was only ten miles long and five miles wide, facing shrieking gale-force winds that seemed determined to claw the house apart, and dark roiling clouds that blocked out the sun so completely it could've been nighttime instead of midafternoon.

"Easy for you to say. You're sitting in sunny LA," she grumbled. Just imagining the balmy spring weather *he* was experiencing made her wish she'd stayed in California. She would've waited for him, but after passing the bar, there'd been nothing for her to do while he continued to study almost 24/7 for the third and final part of the United States Medical Licensing Exam, which would enable him to become a medical doctor.

Instead, she'd flown to Mariners Island ahead of him to get

settled while he finished up. He was supposed to join her in three weeks. Then they'd spend the rest of May and all of June in paradise, unwinding from the pressure they'd been under, both before they knew each other and after—obtaining their bachelor's degrees at UCLA, passing the exams necessary to get into higher education at the same school, and earning their advanced degrees.

"The storm won't be as bad as it seems," he insisted. "Like Martha's Vineyard and Nantucket, Mariners is an outlier that gets far more nor'easters than hurricanes. Those can be bad enough, of course, but they only come in the winter. And hurricane season doesn't start until August."

When the wind had first come up, she'd checked the internet. She knew what he said was accurate. But there were always exceptions.

"Hurricanes almost always slam into the coast farther south," he continued as she moved to the living room window to be able to watch what was happening outside. "They lessen in severity before moving north, or they curve into the Atlantic."

Feeling the house shudder around her did nothing to build her confidence. Windsor Cottage—a play on Windsor Castle using his family's last name—was located at the end of a lane called "Land's End," because it was on the easternmost tip of the island.

When a jagged bolt of lightning electrified the sky, she could see the angry froth of the sea churning not far away—watched a giant wave rise up and come crashing down on the beach. "It's hard to feel safe when I'm afraid the house will blow down and be swept into the ocean," she said.

"The house won't blow down and be swept into the ocean," he said with a chuckle. "It's been in the family for almost a century. Everything will be fine."

Maybe he was right, and she was overreacting. That wouldn't be *too* surprising, considering she was staying in an unfamiliar house in a part of the world she'd never visited before. "I just wish I'd waited for you. I don't know what I was thinking flying off ahead of you."

"You were thinking of spending your days on the beach, reading escape novels and getting a tan. You've worked so hard. You deserve to celebrate with a sun-drenched vacation on Mariners. That's why my parents insisted we use the cottage."

The word *cottage* was an understatement. *Summer home* would be a more accurate term. The house was worth millions. But she wasn't going to argue over semantics. She'd grown up with seven younger siblings and tired parents who worked from dawn till dusk to provide everything they could for their family, but she'd never known the type of affluence Remy had. His father was a diamond broker in New York City—like his father before him—and thanks to his incredible success, Remy's mother had never had to work. "I just feel so…alone and vulnerable."

"Stop. You'll wake up in the morning, the sun will be shining, and you'll be glad you went ahead of me. You passed the bar in February. You've had to sit around twiddling your thumbs enough while I study."

He was right about that. She'd cracked open her share of textbooks, but she hadn't had to study nearly as hard as he had, and the fact that he was never available was getting old. She was becoming concerned about their relationship. When they met nearly three years ago, she'd been so impressed by his drive and ability, how he always had everything under control. They'd moved in together a year later and gotten engaged, informally for now, nine months ago. But she no longer felt like a priority. Maybe marriage would be a mistake. She'd recently told him she was having a few misgivings, and he'd said things would change once they had their hardest years behind them.

She'd decided to wait and see, when he wasn't so stressed.

"I'll be there before you know it," he promised.

Enough whimpering about the storm, she told herself. He didn't have much patience for weakness—much patience at all, now that she thought of it. She was about to change the subject and ask how confident he was feeling about part three, his upcoming exam, when the lights flickered. "I think I'm going to lose power," she said instead, feeling a fresh burst of panic.

"I'm sure my folks have candles and flashlights and that sort of thing."

"Where?" she asked, suddenly desperate to find them.

"I'll call and ask."

How long would that take? She drew a deep breath. "Okay. Hurry."

As soon as she disconnected, she started rummaging through the cupboards and drawers in the kitchen, thinking she might stumble on what she needed. To prepare for a hurricane—or a bad storm like this—the information online indicated she should have a gallon of water, food, a flashlight, a battery-powered radio, a first-aid kit, extra batteries, and a whistle to use to be able to call for help—although, hopefully, it wouldn't get *that* bad. The list was even more extensive than that, but she figured she'd be happy if she could just gain possession of the top three items.

Fortunately, she'd purchased groceries once she'd landed and bought filtered water.

After she left the kitchen, she managed to locate a flashlight in the mudroom at the back of the house.

Relieved, she turned it on, then groaned. The beam was so weak. It needed new batteries. She was also worried about the battery in her cell phone. She'd been charging it since before the storm started, but it ran down quickly—in a couple of hours. She'd been meaning to do something about that, but she'd been living on student loans and a modest paycheck from the coffee shop where she worked and would need every cent she could scrape together to set up her law practice this summer. She could've joined a firm instead, but she'd chosen to go out on her own so she wouldn't be beholden to the demands—or whims—of those more powerful than she was and could retain control of her own destiny.

She still considered that a good decision. But putting off getting her phone fixed? Not so much. It didn't matter a great deal in LA. There, she was almost always near a working outlet. But what if that wasn't the case here? What if she lost power and it took all night or longer to restore it?

She'd be completely cut off. With everyone having a cell phone these days, Remy's parents had seen no reason to keep a landline when they had the house renovated last fall.

"Shit." After returning to the kitchen, where she'd left her phone, she tapped her fingers on the counter, willing Remy to call back. But he'd been so cavalier and unconcerned, so sure everything would be fine, she wasn't convinced he'd act quickly.

A large boom sounded. She had no idea what it was. It sounded more like something had crashed into the house than thunder. But it convinced her she'd be a fool to waste any more time waiting for him.

Taking only the small flashlight she'd found, she left her charging phone behind to poke through the other rooms.

Surely, she'd find a bevy of stronger flashlights. The house was built on an island, for God's sake. The only way to reach Mariners was by boat or plane, and bad weather routinely cut it off from the mainland. But no one had spent much time at the cottage since it was gutted and remodeled, so a lot of everyday items hadn't yet been replaced.

The lights went out before she could reach the second story. She was only halfway up the stairs when it happened, leaving her in a thick humid darkness that felt like plasma. As she listened to the wind howl through the eaves and the house creak in protest, she realized she was going to have to go ahead and use the weak flashlight.

"What a nightmare," she muttered and hit the switch.

A dim yellow circle illuminated the next step and then the

next. The beam couldn't reach far, which made her nervous. She needed to decide where she'd spend her time until the power came back on, because if she couldn't find another source of light, she wouldn't be able to move about in this unfamiliar place. It wasn't as if she could rely on her phone as a flashlight. She might need what cell power she had for more important things.

Chances were she'd just have to wait out the storm in the dark, hoping the power came back on sooner than later—or that the skies would clear enough by tomorrow morning that she'd be able to see the sun.

Once she reached the landing, she sought out the bathrooms. She was relieved to find several decorative, scented candles by the soaking tub in the master bedroom, but there weren't any matches. Hoping she might run across a lighter in one of the boys' rooms, she brought two candles with her and left them near the wall at the top of the stairs before going into the first door off the hallway.

Although this room had been updated, like the rest of the house, there was a graduation picture of Remy on the dresser from when he got his bachelor's, along with some old baseball and soccer trophies. Remy had insisted she take the master—*might as well be as comfortable as possible, Is. We can always switch rooms if my parents make it out to visit us*—so she wasn't staying in his old room, but she knew this had belonged to him. She'd seen it yesterday when she first arrived and explored the house.

She searched his drawers but most were empty, since the furniture was new. She did find several boxes in the closet filled with old clothes and memorabilia and guessed his mother had asked the workmen to put his belongings there for him to sort through the next time he returned to the island.

After digging through clothes, old schoolwork, and things he'd made as a child, she lost confidence she'd find what she needed in those boxes and started to feel along the top shelf of his closet. Could he have hidden a bong or some marijuana with a lighter? He smoked on occasion, and once told her he'd started young.

Although the closet would be the most likely place to find that type of thing, she couldn't reach all the way to the back, so she climbed up on one of the heaviest boxes and used her flashlight to see.

There was no bong. No lighter or matches, either. She found a ballpoint pen, a random bookmark, and a spiral binder with Remy's name drawn on the cover in colorful graffiti-like letters and pages filled with incredible drawings.

She'd known Remy was talented. He'd done a number of sketches—including a picture of her dog before she had to put him down three months ago—and quite a few human bodies, showing the detailed anatomy of the organs, muscles, and ligaments. He said it was a great way for him to study, and she could see why that might be the case.

But the drawings in this book weren't quite so clinical. These depicted violence—knives dripping with blood, torture devices, and mutilated bodies.

With a grimace, she closed the binder and put it back. She couldn't understand why Remy or anyone else would have the desire to draw such things. But a lot of teenage boys were fascinated with the macabre. Even though *she* found those graphic images unsettling—*disturbing*—especially while her flashlight was fading and she was likely to be left in the dark, stranded alone in this "cottage" by the sea, she shouldn't make too much of it.

Coming to this place had seemed like such a treat before the storm rolled in, she mused. But right now, she'd rather be in the cramped, kitschy, well-loved four-bedroom farmhouse where she'd grown up, even if all her siblings were home and arguing over religion and politics, as they often did.

She was about to scramble down and move on to Remy's

twin brother's room when a loose board along the back of the shelves caught her eye. *There it is.* That had to be where he'd hidden his marijuana, she thought.

Lifting the loose board revealed a hole in the wall that contained a small nylon duffel bag, the kind an athlete would use to carry their equipment. She reached for it, then hesitated. She was already a little shaken by what she'd seen in that notebook. Should she really press on? This wasn't her house. She had no right to invade Remy's privacy. After all, she'd just seen a part of her fiancé—even if it was from when he was much younger—that she didn't find appealing. And they didn't need any more strain on their relationship.

But if this was indeed a bong, and there were matches or a lighter with it, she'd have candles *and* a way to use them.

She wasn't doing anything wrong, she reassured herself, and got down so she could use both hands.

After unzipping the duffel, she pointed her flashlight inside it. But she didn't find what she'd expected. The bag contained several pieces of cheap jewelry, a torn picture of some girl who looked to be eighteen or nineteen, and a handful of women's underwear.

She picked up a pair of yellow bikini briefs—and quickly dropped them again. Why would Remy have a bag of women's jewelry and panties hidden so carefully in his closet?

Her mind raced and her heart began to pound. Like the drawings, the contents of the duffel could fall within the range of what was normal for a young boy to have, couldn't it? Young boys were, of course, notoriously curious about women.

But what she'd found didn't *feel* normal. That was the problem. Whose panties were they? Where had they come from? And how long had they been there?

Whatever the answers to those questions, she wished she'd never found the notebook or the bag. She'd lived with Remy for two of the three years they'd been together, but this made her wonder if she really knew him. He was so…highly focused on school, on himself. He didn't open up a lot. What was going on inside his head?

These items made her wonder like she'd never wondered before.

Intending to get back up on the boxes so she could put the bag away, she turned, but her flashlight died at that moment, leaving her standing in Remy's old room, blinking widely without being able to see a thing—except those horrific drawings and the yellow bikini briefs in the duffel she was holding, both of which were indelibly etched into her brain.

2

Bo Broussard had seen the woman pull into the drive of the main house yesterday. He'd been watching for her. Annabelle Windsor had called to let him know her son and his fiancée, Ismay Chalmers, would be coming to spend the rest of spring and part of summer, and he'd done his job by making sure the cottage was ready.

Bo didn't live directly on the premises, but he lived on the property tucked behind, which was also owned by Mort and Annabelle Windsor. They provided him with a small caretaker's cabin, a Ford F-250 truck, and a modest salary in exchange for looking after the property—keeping teenagers and would-be vandals away when it wasn't in use, maintaining the grounds, and performing minor repairs here and there. His cabin wasn't only smaller, it was located farther from the ocean, and it was mostly hidden by trees. But he preferred it that way. Everyone else wanted to be right on the beach; he just wanted to maintain his privacy.

Glancing down at his phone again, he sighed. He had to go out in the weather. Annabelle had just texted him to say the cottage had lost power—which didn't come as any surprise since he'd lost power, too—and Remy's fiancée was sitting over there in the dark, alone and frightened.

Although he had to make do with a lantern and other emergency supplies, like most regular people in such a situation, the big house had a generator that was supposed to come on. Why hadn't that happened? He'd tested it when he installed it, and it'd worked perfectly.

But it was the first generator he'd ever dealt with. He should've gotten a professional to handle the installation. He would have if it wasn't so damn hard to hire a contractor on the island. The few electricians, plumbers, and other tradesmen they had were booked weeks or months—sometimes years—in advance. Not only had he installed the generator, he'd helped with other aspects of the renovation. Cub Holiday, the most successful contractor on Mariners, was diagnosed with cancer before he could finish the project. Though Cub was in much better health these days, Bo had done the rest of the work for the Windsors—or as much of it as he could, given his lack of experience. Construction was almost second nature to him, but there were still plenty of things he had yet to learn.

On my way, he texted back and yanked on a coat and boots before grabbing his toolbox, a lantern for the stranded woman, and a waterproof flashlight for himself.

"It's all about giving the rich people what they want," he muttered as he stepped outside. But he wasn't bitter. He'd gotten lucky landing his job with the Windsors, and he knew it. When he came to the island looking for a summer gig in the tourist industry, he'd had no idea he'd still be here. But he'd adopted a fake surname and created a bogus work history and, so far, the Windsors hadn't bothered to follow up.

He didn't plan to give them any reason to do so in the future.

It was mid-April, but the weather made it feel like January. Leaning into the wind, he squinted against the rain stinging his face as he stepped over a huge branch that'd been torn from an oak tree and taken part of the fence surrounding the garden down with it. There'd be significant cleanup to do later. But at least that branch hadn't hit the house. It easily could have.

The cottage sat dark and brooding—a hulking giant perched on the last outcropping of land, seemingly staring with resolute determination at the angry sea.

Bo turned a wary eye on the fifteen-foot waves as he made his way to the front walk. The tide seemed dangerously high. But he'd only lived on Mariners for two years. He couldn't imagine this storm was anything notable to those who'd been here a while.

Or...was he assuming too much? There was a first for everything. Who would've expected the strange series of events that'd derailed his life when he was only eighteen...

The wind blew down his hood, but his hands were full, so he couldn't pull it back up. He trudged on doggedly, ignoring the elements raging around him and finally achieving a small reprieve when he climbed up the stairs to the porch, where the deep overhang provided a modicum of protection.

Anxious to start the damn generator so he could return to his own place and get warm again, he pressed the doorbell, then knocked immediately after. "Ms. Chalmers? It's Bo Broussard, the caretaker," he called above the wind. "Annabelle Windsor sent me over. I've got a lantern here you can use until I get the generator going."

He waited what felt like several minutes, but there was no response. Figuring he'd just get the lights on, so she wouldn't need a lantern, he started back down the stairs as the door cracked open.

"Mr. Broussard?"

Ducking back under the overhang, he angled his flashlight below the woman's chin so he could see her without blinding her. From what he could tell, she had flawless dewy-looking skin, the roundest eyes he'd ever seen—though he couldn't make out the color—and curly blond hair that was currently pulled back in a ponytail. She was surprisingly tall, too. He was six-five, so she had to be…five-eleven? Six feet?

Was she some kind of model?

Leave it to Remy to find such a stunning woman to become his wife. That dude had the best of everything. Although Bo had only met Remy three times since he'd started working for the Windsors—the summer he was first hired, Thanksgiving the same year, and the Fourth of July last summer right before they started the renovations—he didn't care for either of Annabelle's boys. They both seemed unashamedly arrogant and spoiled. They couldn't even get along with each other. Weren't identical twins supposed to be close? Almost inseparable?

At least Remy was doing something with his life. He would soon be a medical doctor. Bastian, on the other hand, was supposed to be working in the diamond industry with his father, but Bo got the impression he did more traveling and partying than anything else. Bo had heard Annabelle complain about Bastian's behavior on many occasions. "Money ruins people, Bo," she'd say when she came out to help him in the large garden she left in his care when she wasn't around. "Wealth is a blessing, but it's also a curse."

He wished *he'd* been cursed the way the Windsors had. They'd never been without food on the table, a roof over their heads, that sort of thing. He'd grown up poor, first in Florida and then, when he was orphaned at ten, in a small parish in Louisiana, where he was raised by a great-uncle who lived on Grand Isle with almost nothing—off the grid as Uncle Chester liked to say, which meant he had no government help, taxes, or other normal connections to the rest of society. The bullying Bo had received at school for wearing pants that were too small, or shoes with holes so big the soles flapped as he walked, had been almost unbearable—until he'd learned how to fight. Then the other kids had become too frightened to taunt him. But he'd always known he didn't fit in.

Unfortunately, so had they.

He tried not to remember the years immediately following the incident that'd taken his mother's life. Prison, almost nine years later, after a lengthy trial, had been less traumatic. At least while he was behind bars he'd had three square meals a day, clean clothes, well-established rules, and there'd been a clearly understood pecking order.

And since he'd already learned to fight, he hadn't been scared. That he wouldn't take any shit from *anyone* was something he'd established the day they'd first locked him up. He'd spent the next month in "the hole" as a result, where he'd thought he'd go insane, but he survived, and it was drawing that line that'd made the rest of his time behind bars tolerable. Because of that, and his size, he hadn't had to "click up" with a gang, hadn't gotten involved with anyone he didn't want to. The other inmates quickly learned if they left him alone, he'd mind his own business, too.

Still, the memories he most wanted to avoid—right after his mother had been killed—popped up every now and then. Kids found the damnedest reasons to torment other kids. It was probably thanks to those experiences that he preferred his own company to anyone else's, and that was why this job suited him so well. If he had to get a generator going in the middle of the worst storm he'd seen on Mariners, no big deal. It was a minor inconvenience, all things considered.

He handed the lantern he'd brought to the willowy, slender woman fighting to hang onto the door so it wouldn't blow against the inside wall. "I brought this for you to use while I start the generator."

She used her knee to keep the door in place and switched her cell phone to her other hand so she could accept the lantern. "The *generator*?" she echoed above the storm.

"Yeah, it's supposed to come on automatically once the power goes out. But it's new, since the renovation, and—I'll get it going," he finished, cutting himself off. She needed power, not a fifteen-minute explanation as to why she didn't have any.

"Thank you." She seemed polite and genuinely relieved.

"No problem." He pulled up his hood and started to turn away for the second time, but she stopped him.

"Fixing the generator is something you have to do outside? In this weather? Will you…will you be okay?"

The wind threw her voice around, but he was able to catch the gist of her words. The fact that she'd even consider his well-being told him she was a better person than the man she was going to marry. "I'll be fine."

He got the impression she was watching as he fought his way down the stairs. He wasn't sure why she hadn't simply gone in and shut the door, but he tended to draw attention wherever he went—despite his desire not to. Part of it was his size, he supposed. Not many men were taller than he was. And he was broad, too, especially through the shoulders—something that had only become more pronounced since he started lifting weights in prison, a habit he'd continued after being released because it was like yoga for him. The focus and determination it required quieted his mind.

By the time he reached the ground and looked back, she was gone.

A second later, he saw a dim light appear in the window. She'd turned on the lantern, which made him glad he'd gone to the extra effort of bringing it to her.

Ismay took the lantern the Windsors' caretaker had brought into the living room, with its many sculptures and other expensive art, and sank onto the soft leather couch. She'd have power soon. She no longer had to fear she'd regret using her cell phone, so she called Remy again.

"Did Bo get the power on?" he asked in lieu of a greeting.

Ismay turned the ring on her finger so she could see the tiny diamond. She and Remy had talked a lot about marriage during their time together, but she hadn't let him buy her an official engagement ring yet. She'd known he wasn't really the one who'd be paying for it, not while he was in school, and that bothered her, especially because she knew he'd push her to get something big and expensive. They'd compromised with a dainty promise ring in yellow gold. "Not yet. He's working on it, though. And he brought me a lantern, so I'm no longer stranded in the dark."

"Good. I told you everything would be fine."

An image of the man she'd just met rose in her mind. He had dark distrusting eyes, a strong jaw covered with razor stubble, hollow cheeks, short dark hair that'd been plastered to his head by the rain—and he'd been huge. A mountain of a man. *She* was six-one and he had her by at least four inches, maybe more.

"You did tell me that," she said. "Bo seems capable enough. I'm sure he'll get the lights back on before too long."

"You didn't find any candles?"

He'd never told her where they might be.

Ismay wished she'd never even searched for emergency supplies. Then she wouldn't have discovered what was in Remy's closet. She wanted to at least mention the underwear and jewelry—wanted to hear what he had to say about them. There was a possibility they weren't his. Bo had access to the house, which was more than a little unnerving, considering his size and the fact she hadn't even realized there was a strange man moving about the property. As polite as he'd been at the door, she'd seen enough true crime shows to know what those items in the duffel could signify. The police called them trophies.

Of course, it was the notebook paired with what she'd found in the bag that'd taken her mind down such a dark alley. The items in that duffel could merely be tokens of Remy's past conquests.

Still, what kind of guy would keep a memento from each woman he slept with?

"Ismay?" Remy said.

She blinked and drew her attention back to the phone. "What?"

"Are you going to answer me?"

"Oh, sorry." She cleared her throat. "This storm has me… distracted. I found some candles in the master bathroom, but there was nothing to light them with."

"Good thing you no longer need them. You should ask Bo for a lighter, though, just in case."

"Do you think he'll take the lantern he brought me?"

"Who knows? I doubt the generator will fail once he gets it going, but it's better to be prepared."

"I'll ask him." She nibbled on her bottom lip as she tried to decide what to say—or not say—to Remy about what she'd found. She craved reassurance but the question alone, and what it implied, would upset him.

Should she just assume it was someone else? That it was Bastian, the contractor, or Bo?

She supposed if it wasn't Remy, Bastian was more likely to have hidden that bag than the others. Although she had yet to meet him, Remy often talked about what his brother was like—said he had no direction in his life, couldn't accomplish anything, preferred to live off the family fortune and on and on.

In the end, it was the notebook that stopped her from saying anything. Those drawings had obviously been Remy's—she'd seen his work before and recognized it—which made her believe the other stuff had to be his, too.

"I know you're busy," she said. "I'll let you get back to studying."

"Okay. You're in good hands now."

She almost disconnected, but then she thought of something she wanted to ask. "Remy?"

"Yes?"

"How often have you been here since you graduated from high school?" The last time he'd visited had been a little less than a year ago. She knew that because she'd been in Utah visiting her own family at the time.

"Almost every summer, and some holidays. The islanders make a big deal of Christmas and have Santa come over on a ferry and stuff. Why?"

Wishing the lights would hurry and come back on, she frowned at the shadows Bo's lantern cast on the walls. "Just wondered if you're going to like the renovations."

"You told me yesterday they look great," he said, sounding confused.

"They do," she reassured him. "But I never saw the cottage before, so I don't know how much it's changed. Did your mother have the contractor put the shelves and organizers in the closets—or...or paint them?"

She held her breath, hoping he'd say yes.

"No, it was mostly new siding, a new roof, an open layout for the kitchen, living room, and bar area, and a new master bath along with hardwood floors throughout. Why?"

"No reason," she lied. "I was just...curious how extensive it was."

"It was extensive enough. It cost a fortune and took nine months. But nothing happens fast on Mariners."

She'd heard him say that before. *It's an entirely different pace of life, Is...* He called it *island time.*

"Right. Well, no need to keep you..."

"Okay, I'll talk to you later."

He was gone as soon as he said the last word.

She tossed her phone aside. He hadn't seemed spooked by the mention of closets. Was she letting what she'd found trouble her for no reason?

The lights snapped on, and she heard the heater start soon

after—she'd turned the temperature up to battle the cold. Drawing a deep calming breath, she tried, once again, to shove her misgivings to the back of her mind. In some ways, with the lights and heater on, she felt much safer. But in others, having the power back didn't help at all. Surely, she wasn't about to marry a man who was capable of doing any of the terrible things a collection like that might signify.

Was she?

3

A few minutes after the generator came on, Ismay heard another knock and hurried to open the front door.

Bo stood there. The porch light was now working, but his hood was up, keeping most of his face in shadow.

"Thanks for coming to my rescue," she said. "I'm sorry it meant you had to be dragged into the wet cold."

He kept his flashlight angled at the floor. "No problem. It's my job," he said, shrugging off the credit.

"Still, I appreciate it." She leaned farther outside in an effort to check the progress of the storm. "I've never seen weather like this, have you?"

"I grew up in Florida and Louisiana, so I've been in a hurricane or two, but nothing that bad up here."

He looked to be about her age, maybe a few years older, so she guessed he was around nine or ten when Katrina hit the Gulf Coast in 2005. She'd been six and would never forget her parents being glued to the TV, her mother crying over the lives that were lost. "You weren't in Louisiana for Katrina, were you?"

"No, but I was there immediately after."

"Did you move to New Orleans—or somewhere else?"

"I lived with my great-uncle in a little village in the swampland south of NOLA."

That meant nothing to her. She'd never been there herself. "What brought you to the island?"

"Just…needed a change of pace."

Another big gust came up, blowing down his hood, but he didn't bother putting it back up. He looked impervious to the weather anyway, as if he was made of granite and nothing could hurt him. She wondered if he knew he gave that impression.

"Is there anything else I can do for you before I head back?" he asked.

"I'm set for now—I think. Do you have a generator, too?"

"No."

"Then let me give you your lantern—"

"Keep it," he said before she could turn away. "I've got several flashlights and some candles. I can get by."

She'd have power *and* the good lantern? She'd grown up in a large family, where she'd had to share everything, so she felt guilty taking all the best resources. "I'd rather you have it—"

He interrupted by raising his hand in the classic stop position—apparently in lieu of a refusal because he didn't say anything more about the lantern. "You have food and water, right?"

"I do." Now that she had her basic needs covered—for the immediate future, anyway—her concerns had shifted. What she needed was someone to convince her that Remy had nothing to do with the items she'd found in his closet.

"Can I give you my number, in case anything comes up later?" Bo asked. "I'm just in the bungalow on the property behind this one, so not far away."

Getting his information seemed prudent. Although he was a stranger, and certainly looked as though he'd be a formidable foe if she ever had to fight or resist him in any way, his manner and his help with the generator was making her more grateful than wary. After all, the Windsors knew and trusted him.

That lent him some credibility. And if he had any intention of harming her, he could easily have done so by now. He knew how vulnerable she was.

Instead, he was keeping a respectful distance and trying to help her through a frightening ordeal.

"Of course," she said. "Good idea. Then we won't have to rely on Remy and Annabelle if we need to communicate." Except this time, she hadn't brought her phone to the door. It was back on the charger. She was planning to keep the battery as full as possible in case the generator gave out before the storm. "Can you come in for a second?"

"I'm wet," he said. "I'll wait here."

Her trust in him shot up several more notches. He certainly wasn't trying to get inside the house. "There's no need to stand out in the storm. Never mind if you drip on the floor. I can wipe it up after."

Trying to keep the wind from ripping the door from her grasp, she stepped to one side to make room for him, and after a brief hesitation, he came in and helped her close the door.

"Whew! Now maybe we can hear each other speak without having to yell," she said and went to retrieve her cell from the kitchen counter.

When she returned, she found him exactly where she'd left him, right inside the door. "Here you go," she said and handed him her phone so he could type in his information.

"If something comes up, don't hesitate to call me, even if it's late," he said when he handed it back.

"Thank you." She hit the Call button to ring his phone, so he'd have her number, too. "And I'd like to make you the same offer. If you need something tonight, feel free to reach out. As you can see, I'm pretty comfortable here and have enough groceries and water to share."

After acknowledging her words with a nod, he headed out, and she once again braved the wind and the rain to watch him descend the stairs.

When she couldn't see him anymore, she locked up, then leaned against the door. It felt odd knowing there was a stranger staying not far away, who'd given up his lantern for her. So what if he worked for the Windsors? Why did that mean he had to be the one to go without, especially when *she* had a generator?

"The privileges of money." She wasn't convinced her parents would approve of her letting him sacrifice when he already had less. But then…she wasn't even convinced they approved of *Remy.* Although they hadn't said much, except that they wanted her to be happy, she knew they had to wonder why, since she and Remy had been together for so long, they'd never met him. He'd spoken to them several times over the phone, but every time she thought she might finally bring them together in person—for Christmas, Thanksgiving—Remy would end up having a conflict.

Thinking of her parents made her miss them, the rest of her family, and, more than anything else, the familiar. She'd been excited to come to Mariners for a couple of months. Who wouldn't want to experience such luxury? Staying in a place like this was usually reserved for the very rich. Without Remy and his family, she wouldn't have had the opportunity.

But the storm and what she'd discovered while looking for a lighter had left her feeling a bit like the second Mrs. Maxim de Winter in *Rebecca,* which had been her favorite book as a girl. There were secrets in this cottage. Even after the storm passed, the island recovered, and life carried on with its influx of tanned and beautiful tourists wearing designer sunglasses, she wouldn't be able to forget the duffel bag she'd put back behind the wall in Remy's old closet.

Generator's working. All's good.

Bo sent that message to Annabelle Windsor as soon as he got home and removed his coat. Since he hoped to remain in his current situation for the foreseeable future, he planned to keep her happy.

He peeled off his shirt, which was wet where the rain had seeped down the back of his neck while he'd been working, and tossed it onto the washer. Then, using only a flashlight, he went into the bathroom to dry his face and hair with a towel. Hopefully, Ismay Chalmers was set for the night and he wouldn't have to go out again.

He paused while he pictured the face of the woman he'd just met. She was beautiful. No one could argue with that. But beauty didn't matter much to him. He wouldn't still be thinking about her, except there seemed to be something more to Ismay, something he would hate to see get crushed or turned into a reflection of Remy or even Remy's mother, who was a much better person than her son. Ismay seemed fresh and unjaded, sweet and concerned about others. He wished he could warn her away from the Windsors.

"Money ruins people," he muttered, recalling Annabelle's words yet again. But, like him, Ismay probably thought she could be the exception.

With a sigh, he pulled on a dry shirt and returned to his small living room, where he built a fire to stave off the cold. There wasn't much to do with the rest of the afternoon, except prepare what food he could make without an oven or microwave—and read.

He had extra batteries, and he wasn't hungry quite yet, so he decided to wait until later to have dinner. Using his flashlight to be able to see well enough to read, he opened *Crime and Punishment* by Fyodor Dostoevsky. He didn't have much of an education, had barely attended school after his uncle took him in—most people on their tiny island, the ones he'd associated with, anyway, were uneducated and subsisted on very little other than what they could get from fishing or shrimping—so he'd never had much access to learning materials. He'd certainly never read for pleasure.

But while he was in prison, books had become his salvation, and they were still a huge part of his life. He blitzed through almost any book he could find, craved information the way others craved sex, sugar, praise, or money, and visited the library on the island, which had been established way back in the mid-nineteenth century by the son of the whale-oil merchant who'd founded Mariners. In fact, he went there probably more than anyone else and had devoured hundreds of books since he'd arrived.

He used the internet, too, mostly when he needed to know how to build something or make repairs. Bo could move as fast as he liked and study only what interested him, and he was surprised by how important learning had become to a boy without so much as a high school diploma.

His phone signaled a call.

Reluctantly setting his book aside, he checked to make sure it wasn't his employer or the woman he was supposed to be looking out for during the storm.

It was neither. But his chest constricted when he saw the name. Matilda was calling again. After so long, why was his sister reaching out to him?

He had no answer for that, but just the thought of speaking to her made him feel as though someone had slugged him in the gut. So, once again, he didn't answer. For the third time in as many months, he silenced his phone and put it down. Then he closed his eyes and took a deep cleansing breath as he struggled to bury the pain even deeper before returning to his book.

Ismay curled her feet underneath her on the couch and opened her laptop. She'd never heard of a string of women going missing—or being murdered—on Mariners. But she lived across the country, where the news could've been muted by more local happenings.

She also hadn't paid much attention to current events while growing up. Since she'd become an adult, she liked watching *Dateline* and *Forensic Files* when she had a free minute, which was probably why her mind kept going back to the items in that darn duffel bag. But during the past decade, free minutes had been hard to come by, and she'd never seen an episode that had anything to do with Mariners, other than the case where a twelve-year-old girl went missing in 2000 or 2001, the police couldn't figure out what had happened to her, and then her body turned up—fairly recently—near the lighthouse.

While sad, that case had never concerned her personally. And it still didn't. From what she'd heard and read, the police had finally figured out who killed Emily Hutchins and why, and it had nothing to do with Remy or anyone connected to him.

She told herself the duffel and its contents meant nothing. But she had hours to fill while waiting for the storm to blow over, so she found herself searching the internet for *unsolved cases on Mariners*, *missing women on Mariners*, *rape on Mariners*, and *murder on Mariners.*

Almost every link went to the Emily Hutchins case. *See? You're assuming far too much.*

Except…there had to be a reason, even if it wasn't the one that first came to mind; those items had been hidden so carefully.

She typed in *Mariners, underwear.*

Nothing came up. Just a bunch of information about Mariners in general—its history, its Nantucket-like architecture, its towering elms, its quaint shops and cobbled streets—and a few ads selling underwear.

She changed her search parameters once again—this time to *Mariners, stolen underwear.*

Still nothing.

If there was a string of terrible crimes that'd happened here, there'd be some news piece written about it. The wealthy people who frequented the island would be outraged.

That meant she shouldn't be worried. She'd done her research and turned up nothing.

She started to close her laptop. She wanted to be done with this.

Except…she could've been putting in the wrong information. Could these items be tied to crimes in New York City instead, where Remy and his brother had grown up?

She winced at her uncertainty. It was *completely* far-fetched, way beyond anything Remy would ever consider doing. Of course.

But she had to explore all possibilities. She wouldn't wreck her life by sticking her head in the sand just because she didn't want to face a hard truth. What would police say to the wife who found such a duffel bag and did nothing about it? They'd think she had to know what her husband was up to.

Using keywords to bring up cold cases in New York instead of Mariners, Ismay wound up with the opposite problem. There were so many violent crimes it was overwhelming.

To narrow her results, she tightened her parameters to the period when Remy would've been living at home, but the list was still too long.

"Unbelievable." Setting her laptop aside, she went to his room and got the bag, snapped a picture of the girl's picture she'd found inside it and tried to use Google's facial recognition feature. If it could tell her the identity of the person in the photograph, she'd be able to use that to guide her search. But it was such a blurry old photo, the effort proved futile.

With a sigh, she checked her phone to see if Remy had tried to reach her since she'd let him know the generator was on. She hadn't received a response to her text. He could be *so* caught up in his own goals. There were moments, plenty of them, when she just didn't feel important to him. He assured her she was misreading him. But maybe that tendency to withdraw, to be so aloof, was why she was alarmed about what she'd found. It could be difficult to feel close to him, to feel as though she really knew him.

Certain she'd feel better if she could just hear his voice, she considered calling him. The storm had put her in a strange frame of mind. It was making her see things in their worst possible light. She couldn't imagine she'd be spending so much time scouring the internet if she'd found that bag back at their apartment.

Actually, it would be weird even there, she decided, which was why she didn't call him. What could she say? She certainly wasn't going to tell him what she'd been doing for the past two hours. And she needed to let him study, or he'd blame her if he failed.

She stared at the old photograph she'd found a little longer. The young subject was attractive, with thick blond hair and maybe brown eyes—it was hard to tell. She also had a gorgeous tan and was standing on the beach in front of Windsor Cottage…

"No one's gone missing on Mariners." Determined to stop her imagination, she returned the bag to its hiding place. Then, when she got back on her computer, she changed her search parameters yet again. She was going to forget about what she'd found in that closet and satisfy a far milder curiosity: Who was Bo Broussard?

She no longer entertained the idea that *he* might have something to do with the items in that duffel bag. He'd made no move to harm her even though the storm would've given him the perfect cover. And she felt certain that, were it his, he would've stored it at his own place, where he could reach it whenever he wanted to. Putting that bag in the cottage meant he'd have to worry about the family finding it or getting in the way when he wanted to retrieve it.

There were quite a few Bo Broussards on the internet. But

none of them seemed to be the man she'd met. She couldn't find him on social media, either.

Picking up her phone, she eyed the contact record she'd created when he gave her his information. Then she checked the clock. It was six ten. It'd been two and a half hours since he'd come over to help her.

She wondered what he was doing, if he had food and water, if he still had a working flashlight, if he regretted not accepting the lantern she'd offered him. And just in case he wouldn't reach out even if he needed something, she sent him a message:

It's Ismay—at the cottage. You doing okay over there?

4

Bo had fallen asleep in his chair, but the sound of breaking glass and creaking timbers woke him instantly. Convinced he was still in prison and the siren had gone off because a fight had just broken out in the yard, he brought his head up quickly and his fists, too.

There was no human adversary. But when he sprang to his feet, he dropped his phone and his book, and the book landed on his foot.

"Son of a bitch!" he yelled, shocked that something falling such a short distance could cause so much pain. He didn't have time to focus on it, though. He wasn't in prison, fighting off a shank to the throat. He was in his small cabin on Mariners, looking at the sky and feeling the wind and rain hit him almost as hard as if he were standing outside.

"What the hell?" He blinked. Another tree had gone down, only this one hadn't fallen as propitiously as the one that'd broken the fence surrounding the garden. This tree had crashed through his roof and was lying on top of the house. Because he had only the dying embers of the fire to help him see, it took a moment to realize the extent of the damage. But soon he could make out the wet dripping branches reaching down toward him. Apparently, the wind had only grown stronger since he'd fallen asleep.

He searched where he'd been sitting for his flashlight. It'd rolled off his lap and into the crack between the cushion and frame. He found it with the beam angled into the fabric. But even once he turned it around, it didn't show him much. The light was so dim it'd almost gone out. He needed to replace the batteries, figure out how to get the tree off his house, and patch the hole it'd made before he was facing significant water damage.

But the second that thought went through his mind, he realized he wouldn't be able to do anything until the storm was over. He'd be a fool to even try.

Afraid the frame of the house would give way, and he'd be looking at an even more dangerous problem, he picked up his phone and saw a text he'd missed while sleeping. The woman staying in the cottage had messaged him.

You doing okay over there?

That text had come in three hours ago. And then, more recently, he'd received another message from her. Hey, you haven't answered me. Can you just confirm that you're okay?

And just a few minutes ago: I'm really getting worried.

What should he say in return? That he *wasn't* okay? That a tree had just taken out part of his house?

She'd think he expected her to let him stay in the cottage, and he knew Annabelle and Mort would not like that, never mind Remy. He didn't like the idea, either. What if she accused him of doing something he didn't do, something inappropriate, and he had no way to defend himself?

He was an ex-con. If a question like that ever arose, his conviction and the fact that he'd lied about his past would make him look guilty even if he was innocent.

He wouldn't risk returning to prison. He didn't really know Ismay Chalmers, would be a fool to trust her.

After carefully navigating around the tree and the chunks of wood, Sheetrock, and roofing that were now on the floor, he made it to the kitchen and replaced the batteries in his flashlight before responding. Sorry, fell asleep. He peered around the corner at the hole where the rain was pouring in before adding, I'm fine, and sent the message.

He'd figure out something to survive the night, he told himself—hang out in a back bedroom and hope the rest of the house didn't go down, he supposed. He didn't have any better option.

He was once again edging around the tree so he could make it down the hall when he heard someone banging on the door. At first, he thought it was the storm knocking things around outside. But then he heard his name.

"Bo! Bo Broussard, are you in there?" *Bam, bam, bam.* "Are you hurt? Should I break a window?"

"Oh, my God," he said. "She's at my door!"

Ismay watched Bo out of the corner of her eye. She'd insisted he leave his cabin and come to the cottage with her, but she could tell he wasn't happy about it. Now he was sitting at the kitchen table with a blanket around his shoulders, soaked to the skin, while she made coffee.

She wasn't much drier. She'd borrowed a coat from Annabelle's closet before making the harrowing trek to his place. When she'd packed for Mariners, she'd been expecting a mild spring and part of summer on the beach and brought only a lightweight jacket. But she hadn't taken a hat or gloves or boots, and she definitely should have.

"I can't believe you went out in this mess," he muttered as he shot a disgruntled look at the storm ravaging the island outside the window.

She had a towel draped around her shoulders, which she used

as she moved around the kitchen to dry the water dripping from her hair. "Would you have preferred I didn't?"

She'd been mildly concerned when he didn't respond to her first text, but Bo was a stranger. She had no idea what his habits were like, whether he was good about replying to his messages or not. She'd thought it was also possible he was busy and not checking his phone. So she'd opened a bottle of wine, continued surfing the internet, and called her brother Jack to pass the time. He was the second oldest in the family, next to her in age, and they'd always been close.

It wasn't until Bo didn't answer her second message and then her third that she'd finally set her computer aside so she could go to every room in the cottage that had a window facing the back to see if she could spot his cabin.

There were so many trees in the way that she couldn't catch even a glimpse of another building until she'd reached the master bedroom. Then she could barely make out the corner of what looked like a small cabin in a copse of trees beyond the garden and was fairly certain that had to be where he was living.

Once she'd spotted it, she'd debated whether to go check on him. She'd told herself that he was obviously a strong man and would be safe enough on his own. But something terrible could happen to anyone, strong or not, and when she'd spotted the tree that'd fallen, she'd been glad she'd checked. She'd been terrified she'd find him hurt, possibly bleeding to death, in the freezing dark, pinned beneath a tree branch or debris from the roof. So she'd felt incredibly relieved when he'd answered the door.

"I would've been okay," he said.

"Maybe. Maybe not. But at the very least, you would've been a lot less comfortable." With his shelter compromised the way it was, he would've been cold and miserable. And what if that tree fell any lower? The rest of the roof could cave in! He wouldn't want to be there if that happened…

She poured him some coffee, offered him cream and sugar, which he declined, and set his cup in front of him.

He thanked her but made no response to her comment. She got the impression that if he'd said something, it would've been, "That depends on what you mean by comfortable." Bo Broussard wasn't the most social person in the world. That was becoming obvious. He seemed skeptical of others, including her. She could easily guess he preferred to remain on his own, regardless of the risks.

"You hungry?" she asked.

When he opened his mouth to answer, she put up a hand to stop him. "Never mind. You'll probably say no. You say no to everything."

"Because *yes* can get you into trouble," he said.

"In what way?"

"I won't elaborate."

He'd initially refused to come to the cottage, even though it was safe and dry and had power. And he'd refused to have a glass of wine with her, agreeing only reluctantly to let her make him coffee when she offered that instead.

"Well, *I'm* hungry, so I'm going to make pasta carbonara. If you'd like to have some, there'll be plenty."

"Pasta carbonara?" he echoed.

"Pasta in a white sauce with pancetta—an Italian bacon—parmesan cheese and peas."

He let it go at that but watched her warily, as if she could be as unpredictable as a fox or raccoon or other wild animal.

Where had the Windsors found this man? He certainly wasn't anything like the spoiled, wealthy designer-brand-wearing frat boys who'd gotten off the ferry with her when she'd arrived. Of course, those young men were here to be served; they weren't among those who'd be doing the serving. But still… The difference was marked. "You told me you were from Louisiana," she said as she got out a frying pan for the pancetta. "Did you like it there?"

"It has its attractions."

"What brought you to Mariners?" Although she'd asked once before, she hadn't gotten much of an answer.

He set his cup on the table. "I came for a lot of reasons."

When he left it at that, she chuckled. "A lot of reasons? What? Are they all secret?"

He didn't crack a smile, even though—in her opinion—he couldn't miss that she'd been joking. "Of course not. I have nothing to hide."

She studied him more openly. This man was different from anyone she'd met before. He was polite, hadn't said anything out of line, and yet, he was so guarded. "Okay. So…you came to Mariners because…"

"I knew this place had to have more opportunities than where I come from."

The pancetta she'd put in the frying pan began to sizzle and pop and fill the kitchen with the sublime smell of frying pork. "What about the uncle who raised you?"

"What about him?"

"He still around?"

"He's getting old, but he's still there."

"I bet he hated to see you go."

"I was an adult." He took a drink of his coffee. "I'm sure he expected me to leave at some point."

She got out a pan and filled it with water so she could boil the pasta. "I've never been to a swamp. Are they truly like how they're depicted on TV?"

"Have you read *Where the Crawdads Sing*?"

She paused from cooking to take a sip of her wine. "No."

"You might like it. I did."

"Because…you grew up where that book was set?" she guessed while topping up his coffee.

"No. It's set in the marshes of North Carolina, but there are marked similarities."

With the water on the stove set on high heat, she returned to frying the pancetta. "What's the name of the village where you lived? And how far is it from New Orleans?"

He arched an eyebrow as he looked at her over the rim of his cup. "Do you always ask so many questions?"

"I'm an attorney," she said. "I'll be starting my own practice in July. Talking is a tool of the trade, I guess."

"What kind of attorney?"

"Nothing too glamorous. Wills and trusts."

"You're smart to stay out of the criminal system."

"Why do you say that?"

"It's a tough world."

"Too dark for me. Anyway, since we're both here with nothing except time on our hands, would it be so bad to get to know each other?"

He didn't reassure her. His eyes narrowed a bit, as if he was taking her measure. "That depends…"

"On…?"

He asked a question instead of answering. "Where'd you meet Remy?"

"At UCLA."

"You had a class together?"

"No. I tried to avoid the classes he had to take." She grimaced. "I'd pass out if I had to dissect a cadaver."

"That sort of thing doesn't bother him?"

"Not in the least." As she heard her own answer, she cringed inside. Her fiancé's level of comfort with corpses didn't mean anything, did it? Because when she put that fact together with what she'd found in his closet, and those gruesome pictures, a chill ran down her spine.

"So… I know where you *didn't* meet," Bo said, essentially pointing out that she hadn't answered his question.

"Oh, right." She forced a fresh smile. "I studied in the same place at the library almost every day. One afternoon, he sat down at my table, and we struck up a conversation. Then he returned the next day, and the next, and eventually asked for my number."

The blanket fell from Bo's shoulders as he leaned forward, his large hands cradling his cup. "How long have you been together?"

"Three years."

"You must get along well."

"We do okay." He was so tight-lipped it made her tight-lipped, too—at least on complicated subjects like her relationship with Remy. There was so much she admired about her fiancé. She didn't want to lose him and the good things, the good times. But she definitely had her misgivings...

"When's the wedding?"

"Haven't set a date yet. See?" she joked. "You asked, and I answered."

"Even *you* seem reticent about certain subjects."

Reticent wasn't a word she'd expect a handyman to use. And there'd been other words... Was he well-educated? He seemed intelligent. "I wasn't reticent—just distracted," she explained. She had good reason to be. She wasn't going to mention what was in the closet of Remy's bedroom, but she was keenly aware of having a picture on her phone of the girl whose photograph was in the duffel bag. "Ask me anything. What else would you like to know?" She grinned at him, but he remained wary. She was beginning to wonder what it would take to get him to relax and smile.

"Okay," he said. "Are you really going to marry Remy?"

She froze with the spatula she was using in her hand. He'd said that as if it would be a mistake, which surprised her. Most people considered marrying a handsome athletic young man from a wealthy family—who was going to be a doctor, no less—a major catch. "You don't think I should?"

He pulled his gaze away from her. "I didn't say that."

"It's what you meant, though, wasn't it?" Apparently, when Bo *did* finally speak, he didn't bother with small talk.

"It was merely a question. You were the one who wanted us to get to know each other."

That was a dodge. Bo seemed tempted to open up and really talk to her. But for some reason, he wouldn't. "We're thinking a spring wedding might be nice," she said.

"Next year?"

That suddenly seemed too soon. "Unless I put it off." *Or call it off…*

He held his cup halfway to his mouth. "Are you thinking about doing that?"

She scowled at him.

"What?" he said, spreading out his hands. "It's not as much fun when *you're* the one answering personal questions?"

"I don't mind. It's just…" He didn't know how shaken she was by what she'd found, and she couldn't tell him about it without feeling disloyal to her fiancé. Even if those items didn't signify the worst, they had to mean *something*, and she couldn't think of a good reason for them to be there. "Never mind. It's not your turn anymore. That's all."

"My *turn*?"

"What does your uncle do for a living?" she asked, taking over the questioning.

The way he looked at her suggested he'd allow her the lead but would tolerate only so much of an invasion of his privacy, and she was interested in learning just how far he'd let her go. There was something understated and mysterious about this man. He reminded her of an iceberg. He showed only about 10 percent of who he really was. The other 90 percent remained hidden deep below the surface. "He does what everyone else in the village does. He fishes for crawdads, shrimp, crab. That's how he gets by."

"You don't have any other family?"

"I have a younger sister."

She hadn't expected that. "Where is she?"

"I don't know."

Was he serious? She couldn't even imagine what would cause her to lose touch with *her* siblings to that degree. Despite all the chaos and competition they'd known growing up, they loved and supported each other when times grew hard. "You're not close?"

"My mother died when I was ten." He lifted his cup again. "Things would probably be a lot different if that hadn't happened."

With the generator keeping the lights on, Bo sitting at the table looking powerful enough to protect her from almost anything, and the steam from the water, which was starting to boil, floating up to warm her face, she could almost forget about the storm outside. She felt safe, comfortable, and eager to eat the meal she was preparing. "I'm guessing you'd like me to let it go at that."

"And since you're an attorney, I'm guessing you won't," he said wryly.

She started to laugh. "So you *do* have a sense of humor."

"You were wondering?"

"I'm wondering about a lot of things."

"Where *I'm* concerned?" He pressed a hand to his chest. "Why?"

"Not sure exactly." He preferred to fade into the background, but there was something about this guy she found oddly appealing. He was good-looking, of course. Not many men were as muscular. He also had a beautiful shape to his mouth, with lips that were full, and the longest eyelashes she'd ever seen on a man. Those two features softened a face that probably would've been *too* masculine otherwise.

Still, it wasn't his looks that intrigued her. Remy was probably more handsome, in a classic sense, anyway. It was the intensity of Bo's eyes. There was a fire inside them that burned bright even when he wanted her to believe he was relaxed. He seemed ever alert, ever watchful, always on guard.

The question was why? What kind of threat was he expecting?

"I'm just the handyman who takes care of your rich boyfriend's future inheritance," he said. "There's nothing interesting about me."

"Do you think it's your job that defines you?"

His eyebrows snapped together. "I think Remy's entirely wrong for you. That's what I think."

She felt her jaw drop. "Really? You'll barely say anything, but you'll say *that*?"

When he looked away, she got the impression he regretted the comment. "I have a tendency to focus on what matters."

"Okay, then. What makes you think Remy's wrong for me?"

"You're nothing like him."

"Some say opposites attract."

He cleared his throat. "It's none of my business," he said, clearly backing away from the subject.

The pancetta was nice and crisp. Ismay set it on the back burner while she dropped the pasta into the water and prepared the sauce. "I'm sorry you lost your mother at such a young age. That must've been rough on you and your sister. You said you don't know where she is, but are you assuming she's in Louisiana?"

"Probably Florida, where we were born," he replied with a shrug. "When my mother died, she went to live with my father in Tampa."

Why hadn't *he* gone with his father? What kind of father wouldn't take both of them? "And you went to live with an uncle in the swamps of Louisiana."

"Yeah. I was his favorite."

She got out two big bowls. "I hate to ask about such a painful topic, but—"

"You're going to anyway?" he challenged.

That response would have stopped her, except there was a slight curve to his lips that hinted at his first smile. He liked her in spite of himself. She could tell. "What happened to your mother?"

Ismay expected him to say it was none of her business. He'd be right. But the strange situation they found themselves in seemed to give license to questions she wouldn't ordinarily ask someone she'd barely met. And with that bit about her not being right for Remy, he, too, had said things she couldn't imagine he'd volunteer under normal circumstances.

"She died of a gunshot wound."

Ismay almost dropped the bag of pasta she'd taken from the cupboard. "I assumed you'd say she died of cancer or in a car accident or something. I hope… I hope it wasn't suicide."

"No."

"You're saying she was *murdered*?"

He didn't answer, but a muscle moved in his jaw that seemed to confirm it.

"You must've been devastated! Did the police catch whoever did it?"

He pulled the blanket back around his shoulders. "He got what was coming to him—eventually," he added.

Although she could tell there was much more to the story, he didn't elaborate. She wished she could ask, but she decided she'd found the line he wouldn't let her cross and wouldn't even attempt it. "Where'd you go to school?"

"I didn't have the opportunity."

While cooking frozen peas in the microwave, she grated some parmesan cheese. "No college?"

His cup clicked as it gently came to rest on its saucer. "No high school, either."

"Are you serious?" she asked, putting down the grater. "But… isn't that illegal? I mean…kids in America—at least in most states—have to attend school until they turn eighteen. Or did you drop out and get your GED?"

"I didn't drop out. I made it mostly through middle school, but it was at that point my uncle got sick and couldn't fish, and if we wanted to eat, someone had to put food on the table."

"You had to work?"

"It wasn't quite work. For the most part, it was absolute freedom, and I enjoyed it."

"But…what about when your uncle got better? He didn't make you go back to school?"

"He never fully recovered. I send him money to this day, or he wouldn't make it. Besides, once you start that kind of life, it's almost impossible to go back. I'd missed so much and was so big. Can you imagine being set back three years when you already look three years older than your age?"

"It seems like someone should've made that happen. The police, if no one else."

"There wasn't much oversight where I grew up."

"In the swamp."

"In the swamp," he repeated.

"So you left your uncle's house looking for more opportunity. But I'm still not clear on what made you choose to come to an island off Cape Cod."

"I didn't choose Mariners right away. I rambled around a bit, eventually came up here to see what it was like and…" he shrugged "…never left."

"I see." She strained the pasta and set it aside before mixing some of the water she'd boiled it in with the cheese and peas—all of which she added to the pancetta in the frying pan. "Has it been everything you'd hoped?"

"More or less."

"You don't get island fever in the wintertime?" she asked as she stirred everything together. "Remy told me there're only about fifteen thousand residents year-round, which is a far cry from the number of people who come during the summer. And the nor'easters can be terrible."

"As far as I'm concerned, the fewer people I have to contend with the better. And the nor'easters aren't any worse than the hurricanes in Louisiana."

She could see where crowds of tourists might be a bit much for a person who'd grown up in a backwater village in the swamps of Louisiana. But surely it had to get lonely spending a long cold winter in a cabin in such an isolated situation. "I'm not sure I'm cut out for island life. It's too…unpredictable."

"It's not for everyone."

"But it suits you?"

"For now."

She piled some pasta in a bowl, poured the sauce she'd made on top, and added a spoon and fork before sliding it in front of him. "I hope you're hungry."

"Smells good," he said but waited for her to sit down with her own bowl and glass of wine before taking his first bite.

"How long have you worked for the Windsors?" she asked as they ate.

"Almost two years."

"How well do you know Remy?"

He paused with his fork halfway to his mouth. "Not that well. I've seen him around and spoken to him a few times; I've mostly heard what his mother has to say about him. She comes to the island more often than any other member of the family. I get the impression she needs to be alone sometimes."

Ismay swallowed what was in her mouth. "What does Annabelle say about Remy?"

"She's incredibly proud."

"What about Bastian?"

He'd taken the bite of pasta he'd been holding and was now twirling a new bite against his spoon. "What about him?"

"I've never met him. I've had two chances—when they went

skiing at Vale and when they went to Italy last year over Thanksgiving. I was invited. But I was with my own family both times. Is she proud of Remy's twin, too?"

It took a second for Bo to answer. When he did, his voice was far less strident. "I'm sure she is."

"Just not as much as Remy?" Ismay asked uncertainly.

When he hesitated again, she guessed he was being careful not to say something that could get back to Annabelle.

Leaving her fork and spoon in her bowl, Ismay finished her wine. "There's no need to worry. I won't pass along anything you tell me. You can trust me."

"I hope you won't take this personally," he said. "But I don't trust anyone."

5

The storm continued to rage even after they'd finished dinner and cleaned up the dishes. Bo hated to think of what the wind and rain were doing to the place where he lived. He'd been through hard times before. This was nothing in comparison. He didn't even own the cabin, so the financial fallout wouldn't affect him. But he'd been comfortable there and would be expected to do most of the repair work. And the damage came right when he thought he'd finally gotten his life on a solid footing.

Nothing was ever easy…

They attempted to watch a movie—*Where the Crawdads Sing*, since he'd recommended the book—but the internet was out, and it wouldn't stream correctly on either of their phones. So, seeing the white and black marble chess set on the coffee table, he suggested a game. Anything would be better than continuing to answer Ismay's questions. He'd been careful so far, told her only general information that wouldn't lead anywhere. He wasn't using his real name, anyway. But he couldn't tell her more specifics about the village where he grew up, how far it was from New Orleans, or too many details about his mother's murder. He didn't want what he'd been through holding him back any longer, didn't want the people on Mariners to be afraid of him or assume he was dangerous. He also didn't want to lose his job, and if the truth came out, he probably would, since he'd lied to obtain it.

"I haven't played chess in forever," Ismay said as he carried the board to the kitchen table.

"I play all the time on my phone," he told her. And that was about all he'd done in prison, besides reading and working out. Betting on games with the other inmates, and occasionally a correctional officer, was the only way he could get funds for the cantina. Many of the prisoners had family putting money on their books. He had no one. His uncle had come to visit him twice, but with Chester's health failing and the fact that he didn't own a car, the prison was too hard for him to reach. And he had no money to send.

Ismay gave him a cautious look. "That's worrisome..."

He grinned. "Only if you're afraid of losing."

"The idea of beating me? That's what finally brings a smile to your lips?"

"Someone has to win. Might as well be me," he said jokingly. She'd probably never experienced much loss, certainly not the way he had. She could lose a game of chess. A game of chess was nothing. It wasn't as if they were putting any money on it.

"No way," she said. "I'll just do my best to make sure that doesn't happen."

She put up a good fight, but he beat her handily—and quicker the second time.

"Why don't we play something else?" she asked when he won three games in a row. "This is far too easy for you."

"Like what?"

"Cards?"

"Do we have any?"

"I saw a deck in the drawer earlier when I was searching for a flashlight."

"So…what are you suggesting? Some two-person version of poker?"

"Why not cribbage? I used to play with my brother all the time. It can be a two-player game."

"I've seen cribbage mentioned in a book or two; never played it."

"Good. Maybe I'll beat you for a change," she said, but they were just setting up when she got a call from Remy.

"Give me one sec," she told Bo and stepped away from the table but not from the kitchen. "Hey, babe. Thanks for calling… Yeah, I've got power. The generator's still working. Bo says the propane tank holds three hundred gallons and can last for a couple of days, at least. But you'll never believe this—a tree fell on Bo's cabin and caved in the roof… Yeah, he's okay. He's here at the cottage with me… I have no idea, but it's still going strong right now. We're just hoping it'll blow over by morning… What'd you say?… We're in the middle of a terrible storm, Remy. We're just trying to get through it… Of course not! I can't believe you'd even say that!"

Bo began to feel uncomfortable again. Ismay had insisted that having him come to the cottage was the only logical choice they had, but he could tell Remy wasn't happy about it.

"Where else would you like him to go?… Forget it," she said. "You must be too tired to think straight, or you wouldn't be saying any of this… Who cares what the neighbors will think? This could be life and death!"

"I can leave," Bo murmured after standing up and touching her arm to gain her attention, but she waved emphatically for him to sit back down.

"Go ahead and go to sleep," she said into the phone. "I can't deal with this right now… No, we'll talk about it in the morning… Well, maybe this is one time you won't get your way," she said and disconnected.

"I should go back to the cabin," Bo said and got up again.

"No." She followed him to the door, putting her hand on the panel when he tried to open it. "If you leave, I'll just have to come out in the storm again to check on you. Why keep me up all night, worrying? Remy is safe in California, where it's probably hard to imagine what we're going through over here, especially because he believes I must be exaggerating. He says it's not the season for nor'easters or hurricanes."

She'd told Remy about the tree that'd fallen on the cabin. But Bo didn't point that out. Maybe he *wouldn't* leave. Why give the spoiled Remy what he wanted when they had such a good excuse not to, one they could easily explain to Annabelle so there would be no risk of him losing his job? Why not let Remy worry all night that his fiancée was stranded in the cottage with another man?

It would probably be the greatest adversity Remy Windsor had ever faced… "If you're sure."

"I'm sure. Let's go ahead and play cribbage. I'll teach you how."

Her phone went off again. She looked at it but silenced the ringer.

Bo nodded his head toward it. "That him?"

"He's not used to anyone hanging up on him, especially me," she said ruefully. "But I don't want to get into it with him. You and I are in an unusual situation. If he's not going to be understanding and supportive, it's better I talk to him when this is all over. I mean, it's not like I've ever cheated on him. I don't deserve his distrust."

Maybe she hadn't cheated, would never cheat, but Ismay was a beautiful, smart, engaging person with a kind and generous heart. As far as he could tell, she had it all. Who wouldn't want a woman like that? If she were his fiancée, he'd probably be jealous, too—just because he'd be so afraid of losing her. A man with his background couldn't even hope to attract someone like her.

But Bo was pretty sure Remy's jealousy stemmed more from

control than fear. He wanted to tell her what to do, even though he was three thousand miles away. "Okay," he said. "I guess I'll learn cribbage."

She beat him in the first two games; he beat her in the third. By then, it was getting late, and the storm finally seemed to be waning. But Bo didn't leave. She wouldn't hear of him going back to a house with a tree fallen through it. Instead, they got pillows and blankets from the bedrooms and curled up on separate couches with the lantern he'd brought glowing softly on the coffee table between them.

"It was nice of you to come check on me," he said, breaking the silence before she could drift off to sleep.

"Be careful," she warned with a yawn.

He adjusted his pillow so that he could better see the outline of her shape. "Or…?"

"You might end up with a friend, and I get the impression you're not too keen on letting people get that close to you."

"Is that how I come off?" he asked.

"You didn't know?"

Of course, he knew. But he also regretted it. It wasn't what he'd choose if he had a choice. Some things just couldn't be helped. "It's not a *complete* surprise."

She drew her blanket up higher. "Will you make an allowance for me?"

"Sure," he replied with a chuckle. Why not? She lived clear across the country. He just had to get through the next couple of months without revealing too much about himself. Then he'd probably only see her when she returned now and then with Remy, as Remy's wife—and Bo had no doubt that would be an entirely different experience.

Ismay woke to the smell of coffee and…sausage? She inhaled again. Yes, sausage. "You're up already?" she called out to Bo with a stretch.

"Already?" Bo echoed from the kitchen. "It's nearly eight o'clock."

She chuckled. He'd said that as if it were almost noon. "Clearly, I'm being lazy," she said. "But I've spent the last several years studying until all hours of the night only to get up a few hours later to take a test or attend a class. I plan to sleep in all I can while I'm here."

"Might as well enjoy it," he said, his voice still drifting from near the stove. "You'll have to get back on a stricter schedule when you start your practice in July, won't you?"

"Not necessarily. I'll be in business for myself, so I'm hoping to set my own hours." She pushed the few strands of hair that'd fallen from her ponytail out of her face. "The money and other effort I've put toward getting through college should bring me something."

"Must be nice to be able to call the shots."

She leaned up on one elbow to look over the back of the couch so she could see him. "The lack of a degree doesn't seem to be hurting you."

"Who knows where I'd be if I had an education?" he said. "What you've done means a lot. You should be proud of yourself."

He seemed sincere, as though he truly admired what she'd accomplished. She wasn't used to that. Although Remy was quick to give lip service if the subject ever came up, she could tell he wasn't impressed by law school or even that she'd passed the bar on her first attempt. He thought what he was doing was so much harder—and more admirable. Invariably, he ended up pointing that out. "It's not too late. Will you ever get your GED and maybe a bachelor's?" she asked.

"I doubt it."

Dishes rattled as he cooked. "Why not?"

"That ship has sailed. At this point, I wouldn't have the patience. Did you sleep okay?"

"I did. You?"

"Like a rock."

She'd actually awakened twice and listened to the wind rattling the windows, trying to determine if the storm was truly abating. In the dim light of the lantern, she'd also watched his face, serene in sleep, and wondered why she'd taken such an immediate liking to him. As guarded and defensive as he was, she should probably be more leery of him. But he came across as steady, solid, and reliable—all traits that made her trust him, probably because he reminded her of her father, who was also a strong, hardworking man of few words.

Not like Remy, who loved being the center of attention. He talked a lot, especially when there was someone to impress, and laughed loudly without much care.

It wasn't surprising that Bo would eschew the limelight and always be on the lookout for the next jagged edge he might encounter, Ismay decided. Experience had taught each man different things. Remy, who'd been sheltered and given everything he could possibly dream of, believed the old cliché—the world was his oyster. Bo, whose mother had been murdered when he was ten, leaving him without a protector and a provider, had known only rough seas.

She fell somewhere in between. Part of her identified with Remy. She'd had enough security, love, and opportunity to embrace his optimistic "go get 'em" attitude. It wasn't as if she had much to complain about. But she'd also had to work hard, first helping with her younger siblings and then getting a job at a fast-food joint when she was sixteen. She'd worked ever since, had just quit her job as a barista at a local coffee shop when she passed the bar. Her parents couldn't help too much, not with seven other children.

"What're you making?" she asked.

"Breakfast burritos," he replied. "You cooked dinner, so I figured it was my turn. Hope you're hungry."

"I usually just grab a coffee and call it good until lunch, but whatever you're cooking smells delicious, so I think I'll make an exception."

"I'm happy to hear that since I used your groceries."

She heard the smile in his voice and had to smile, too. Last night, he wouldn't have taken the liberty of so much as opening the cupboards. Maybe he really had accepted her as a friend.

After kicking off her blanket, she instinctively reached for her phone. Remy would be angry with her for hanging up on him last night. No doubt they'd argue today. She hadn't even answered the texts he'd sent afterward, essentially ordering her to call him back.

But it was three hours earlier in California, only 5:00 a.m. He wouldn't be up yet, so she had some time before she had to deal with that.

"Any word from your fiancé?"

She twisted around to see Bo leaning past the corner, looking at her. "Not yet."

"I hope he won't be too mad."

"*I* didn't do anything wrong—he did." She believed Remy should be the one to apologize, but she could easily guess he wouldn't. *Why'd you hang up on me? What guy would want his fiancée spending the night with another dude?*

Never mind that she'd just met Bo, she was only trying to help him, or that Remy should care about his well-being, too. After all, Bo worked for his parents. That should mean something even if he couldn't muster any concern for basic humanitarian reasons.

She got up and went to the bathroom before pulling her hair into a better ponytail and brushing her teeth. Fortunately, she could no longer hear the wind or rain, and what she could see through the small bathroom window showed only a slight drizzle falling on a soggy landscape with driftwood and broken tree branches strewn all over. "I think we're through the worst of it," she told Bo as she entered the kitchen.

He was holding a spatula when he turned away from the stove. "I should go out and check on a few neighbors. See if everyone's okay."

"Do you know many people on the island?"

"Not a lot. Just those who live closest. Only one—a widow named Honey Wellington—lives here year-round. She's who I'm most concerned about."

"How old is she?"

"Seventy, at least."

"Hopefully she didn't lose power. It got pretty cold last night."

"I'll look in on her first." He handed her a plate with a fat burrito on it and nodded toward the coffee maker. "Help yourself."

"Aw, caffeine. I'm eternally grateful," she joked and left her plate on the table while she poured a cup and topped off the one he had sitting on the counter near the stove.

"Are you afraid to see what's left of your house?" she asked as she slid into a seat.

"I'm not looking forward to it. But it is what it is. I'll get it cleaned up and put back together."

"That big a job won't happen all in one day. You should stay here again tonight."

He slanted her a glance. "I doubt Remy would approve."

"I don't care. As far as I'm concerned, we don't even need to tell him."

"What if he finds out?"

"Having you here doesn't hurt a single thing. We're not doing anything wrong."

"I wouldn't want to cause a problem for you," he said. "I can get the tree out of the way so I can patch the roof, at least."

"Well, if it takes longer than you think, you know you have a place."

When he caught and held her gaze, she could tell he was surprised she'd stand by the offer. "Thank you."

Her phone went off before she could respond.

Everyone she knew lived in the west. Who would be calling her at six in the morning California time?

When she retrieved it from the coffee table, a picture of her handsome brother filled the screen, and she had to amend the time in her mind. It was seven in Utah, which wasn't all that early, especially for him. Since he farmed with their father, he got up at the crack of dawn.

Assuming he was calling to check on her since she'd told him about the storm last night, she said to Bo, "Sorry to interrupt breakfast, but it's my brother. Do you mind if I take it?"

As soon as he indicated he didn't, she hit the Talk button. "Hey, Jack."

When there was a long pause before she got a response, she knew something was wrong.

"What is it?" she asked, immediately tensing up. "Are Mom and Dad okay?" Her father had had a heart attack a year ago. She was terrified he'd had another one.

"Everyone..." He cleared his throat. "Everyone's okay." He'd had to choke out those words, which made her suspect him of crying. If he was, it'd be the first time she'd ever known her brother to break down—since he was eight years old, anyway.

"Then...what is it?" she asked.

"Ashleigh never came home last night."

His wife. They'd been high school sweethearts since the ninth grade, gone to Utah State University in Logan, which was only thirty minutes from where they lived, and married when they turned twenty-one. But they had no children. Ashleigh had miscarried three times that Ismay knew about in the past five years. "She hasn't been in an accident..."

"No."

"Then...what is it?"

Bo was watching her. He could tell something wasn't right.

"She left me, Is."

Ismay sat up straighter. "Left you?! You two have been together since you were kids. Were you having problems?" She'd just talked to him last night, for crying out loud. He'd been waiting for Ashleigh to return from running some errands.

"Not that I knew of. I mean…she's been remote lately. Quiet. But she's always been reserved. I just thought…she was upset about our inability to have kids. She's been wanting to try for another baby, but I was hesitant. Each miscarriage takes so much out of her. I was telling her we should adopt instead."

Ismay didn't say it, but she was secretly glad they didn't have any children if they were about to go through a divorce. "Don't tell me there's someone else…"

He had to clear his throat again to be able to speak. "Apparently…there is."

They lived in such a small town. Was it someone she knew—someone *he* knew? That would make the split even harder on him to have to see her with another man at church or around town.

"Who?" she asked, hoping he'd tell her it was someone she'd met online. Then maybe she'd move away from Tremonton, and he wouldn't have to live with the constant reminder.

"Jessica Davidson."

Ismay nearly dropped her phone. Had she heard him correctly? There was no way she could have… "Did you mean *John* Davidson? Jessica went to school with me. She was on my basketball team."

"I mean *Jessica*."

"But… Jessica's married, too. And she has three kids."

"Yeah, her last name is Schultz now, and her husband was just here. He's as devastated as I am."

"I'm sorry, Jack. I really am. I feel so bad for you."

"I've never even considered the possibility she might leave me—for anyone."

"What are you going to do?"

"I don't know," he said. "I—I feel like I'm in the *Twilight Zone*."

Ismay's stomach knotted as she leaned her elbows on the table. "You'll get through it," she heard herself say. "I know it's hard to hear that now, but it's true."

"Do you think… Do you think she ever really loved me?" he asked in bewilderment.

"Of course, she did!"

"She's never even slept with anyone else," he said. "How does she know she's gay?"

"The same way you know you're not. You've never slept with anyone else, either, have you?"

"No. I've never wanted anyone else."

Ismay had never felt more helpless. She could hear his pain—feel it—coming through the phone. "Have you told Mom and Dad?"

"Yeah. Everyone knows."

Her parents and siblings had to be upset, too. What she was about to suggest probably wouldn't make them any happier, but she felt compelled to speak up for her brother's sake. "Jack?"

"What?" He sounded somewhat distracted, as if lost in his own thoughts.

"You once told me you don't want to be a farmer like Dad."

"I never have," he admitted.

"Maybe this is your chance to do something about it."

"What are you talking about?"

"Until you meet someone else, you won't have to worry about stability, being able to afford a house, or kids. You can break away, start over, do something else."

"I can't even think about that right now."

"Why not?" she asked. "It'd be an escape—from everything. You have some savings, don't you?"

"What we were planning on using for a house. But if we divorce, I'll have to give half of that to Ashleigh."

"You'll still have *something*. Use it to come out here and rent a house. Spend the summer with me."

"On Mariners?"

"Why not? It might be a good change for you, help you figure out what you really want in life."

"What about Dad? He needs me, or I wouldn't have started farming to begin with."

"The other kids are older now. Mom and Dad will be okay. Hank likes to farm. He's been helping lately, too, right?"

"He has. It's been more fun having him around."

"Just…think about the possibility," she said. "I don't want you to make a decision right now. But if you need to get away…"

"Sadly, I don't think I'll be able to escape the wreckage she's leaving behind."

"I'm *so* sorry," Ismay said again and felt tears well up in her eyes. "I'd do anything I could to save you from this."

"I know. That's why I called you." He chuckled without mirth. "Big sister to the rescue." She heard something in the background, then he said, "I have to go. Dad's waiting for me to bring the tractor down to the south forty."

"Come to Mariners," she said. "It's time for a fresh start."

She thought he'd turn her down; she was certain he wouldn't be able to pull away while he was going through something as difficult as a divorce. But he shocked her by saying, "Maybe I will."

"What is it?" Bo asked after she disconnected.

She set her phone on the table and watched it like it was a cobra that'd just taken a bite out of her. "My brother's wife left him last night."

"That's too bad. Do you think he'll come to Mariners?"

"Not really. But I wish he would. It'd be good for him."

"If he does, I can probably get him a house-sitting gig. All he'd have to do is look after the place—wouldn't have to pay rent."

She felt a fresh burst of hope. "You think that's a real possibility?"

"I do. You know that widow I mentioned? Her kids have been after her to come to Pennsylvania, where they live. Two of her grandchildren are on a travel softball team, so they can't visit the island like they usually do. She turned them down because she won't leave her house. But if I assure her it'd be in good hands, I bet she'd take the opportunity. As lonely as she is, it'd be good for her, too."

"That would be fabulous!"

He nodded and after being so careful not to get anywhere close to her, he surprised her by lightly touching her shoulder in an obvious act of compassion. "I'll talk to her."

6

At least two inches of brown dirty water covered the floor. It sloshed around as Bo entered his bungalow and stared up at the tree that'd crashed into his living room.

Even with a chainsaw, it was going to take forever to cut that behemoth into small pieces he could haul out of the house. Then he'd have to patch the roof. It would take days for even large fans to handle the drying process, and he needed to get professionals started on that right away, or he risked black mold, which would make the place unlivable.

"Of course, this would happen," he muttered. Things had been going entirely too well.

He lifted some debris that'd caved in from the roof. As confident as he'd pretended to be when he was with Ismay Chalmers, he didn't think he'd be able to get even halfway through such a big project in one day. He had to make sure Honey Wellington had survived the storm before he could even start.

With a sigh, he made his way to his bedroom in rubber boots and managed to get some dry clothes from his closet before wading into the bathroom. He was willing to bet Ismay would've let him shower over there had she thought of it, but he knew Remy wouldn't like that. She'd already been kind enough to him.

Besides, he liked her even more since last night, and that meant he'd be better off keeping his distance. A potential friend would ask more questions than a mere acquaintance and would also remember the things he said. If he wasn't careful, he could easily get tripped up. Ismay was essentially off-limits. All he had to do was avoid her until Remy arrived on the island. Then there'd be no danger.

With a final scowl at the tree that had ruined his next several days, he went back outside. The sky was still dark and ominous, promising more rain. He considered tarping the roof while he had the chance but decided to check on Honey before he did that. If she was in distress, it wouldn't help her if he got there too late.

The trees all around him dripped onto the soggy ground as he made his way down the narrow muddy path that led to her small cottage. Unlike some of the incredible vacation homes on Mariners, her place was nothing to look at. It hadn't been one of the nicer homes on the island even when it was new—and it hadn't been updated since. She could sell it for a lot of money now, though. Whoever bought it would most likely strip it down as far as they'd be allowed before building it back up much bigger and better. But she had no interest in selling. In recent years, her kids had been at her to do just that. They didn't think it was safe for a woman of her age to live alone in a place that could so easily get cut off from the mainland. But she told him she'd lived on Mariners her entire married life and planned to stay until the bitter end, after which she'd be buried next to her late husband in the local cemetery.

Fortunately, although Bo saw some broken branches strewn about as he walked down her long drive, the house didn't seem to be damaged in any way. Did she have power? It didn't look like it—although it was difficult to tell now that the sun was up.

The wooden steps leading to the porch creaked as he climbed them.

"Ms. Wellington?" he called as he knocked.

There was no answer. He was just about to make his way to the back to see if he could rouse her there when she finally opened the door. "Bo, is that you?"

Honey had several layers of clothing on, including a bright red scarf and hat she'd knitted with flowers that had button centers.

Her tabby cat, Clementine, slipped past her feet to come out and circle his.

"Yes, it's me," he said, bending down to give the cat a good scratch. "I just wanted to make sure you weren't getting too cold over here."

"The power's been out for some time, but I've got an electric blanket that runs on batteries. My daughter and her husband gave it to me for Christmas last year, so I'm managing to keep warm, and Clementine snuggles right there in bed with me."

"I'm glad you're both okay. Do you have enough groceries?"

"Oh, yes. Plenty of groceries. I just ate a peanut butter and jelly sandwich for breakfast." She lifted one arthritic hand to smooth a piece of silvery hair out of her eyes. "Probably not what I would've chosen if I'd had a working stove," she admitted, "but it was tasty and filling. At least I was able to open a can of Clementine's favorite—seafood combo."

He straightened and peered into the house behind her. "Any leaks or other problems I should take care of while I'm here?"

"Not that I'm aware of."

"And you have a flashlight?"

"I do—with a fresh set of batteries on hand. I read for hours last night."

He breathed a sigh of relief. "Sounds like you're doing pretty well for yourself." He remembered Ismay's brother. "Have you thought any more about going to visit your family this summer?"

"Not really. They keep trying to convince me, though."

"What if I could recommend someone who would house-sit for you?" he asked. "And Clementine could come stay with me? Would that change anything?"

She pursed her lips as if she was giving the idea serious consideration. "It might. Who do you have in mind?"

"You don't know him. I'm not yet sure he'll be coming to the island. It's just a possibility at this point. But I'll let you know what he decides, and if he comes, you can meet him and see if you can trust him."

"Sounds good." She opened the door wider to let her cat back in. "Where do you know him from?"

"It's Remy's girlfriend's brother."

She made a face. "Is he anything like Remy?"

Bo had already known she wasn't fond of the Windsor boys. She'd once told him they'd both been little devils while growing up. She was actually one of the few people who preferred Bastian to Remy, and it was because she caught Remy kicking the cat she had before Clementine—and when she told his parents about it, he lied and said he hadn't done anything.

They, of course, had taken his side, and that didn't surprise Bo in the least. Remy's parents had a long history of shielding their children from the consequences of their behavior. And with the money and clout they had, they could smooth over almost anything. "I doubt it. If he's like Remy's girlfriend, however, I can almost guarantee he'll be perfect for the job."

"She's that nice?"

"She's that nice," he confirmed.

"Then it might be a possibility."

"Should I take your cell phone and charge it over at the big house and bring it back to you later? Might be smart to go into the night with a full battery." He gazed up at the darkening sky. "Storm doesn't look like it's over quite yet."

"No need. I'm one of the few people around here who still has a landline," she said with a laugh.

"Okay, well, I'll call you later, and if you don't answer, I'll come back to check on you," he said.

She nodded. "You're a good man, Bo Broussard."

He smiled as though he didn't know of anything that could make that statement untrue, but he was thinking, *Proves how little you know.*

He turned and started trudging to his house, battling a stronger wind than when he'd come just a few minutes earlier, but before he could get out of earshot, she called him back and insisted he take a jar of the blackberry jam she'd made up last summer. She was always giving him something; she had to be one of the most generous people he'd ever met.

He was thanking her when his cell phone signaled a call. He hoped it wasn't his sister again. He dreaded seeing her number pop up.

After he pulled his cell from his pocket, he could see that it wasn't Matilda. It was Remy Windsor, but he wasn't any more excited to talk to his boss's son than he was his own sister.

He lifted the jam Honey had given him in lieu of waving goodbye and set out again as he answered. "Hello?"

"Bo? It's Remy."

Caller ID had already established that, but polite convention was polite convention. "Good to hear from you." Bo knew better than to reveal his true feelings. Annabelle would fire a mere caretaker—regardless of how dedicated he was to his job—if Remy demanded it. She did whatever she could to please and indulge her sons. "You must be calling to make sure your fiancée is comfortable and safe." Except Remy could've called Ismay if he was merely looking for reassurance. This was about something else, and considering what Bo had overheard last night, he could easily guess what.

"I'm calling to thank you for looking out for her."

Bo stopped walking. For a second, he thought he'd underestimated Remy—that Remy deserved more credit—but then

Remy continued, "And to make sure you're all set to stay in your own place tonight."

There it was.

Bo pictured the tree that had destroyed most of his living room and the murky water sitting in his house, warping the hardwood floor and creeping up the walls—moving higher the longer the Sheetrock had to soak it up. Remy didn't care about that. He hadn't even asked about the tree or the amount of damage it'd caused, or if Bo would be able to stay warm and dry if he remained at home. He just wanted Bo to keep his distance from Ismay. Period. "Of course. No problem."

"Do you have enough food? Batteries? All of that? If not, it might be smart to stock up while you have the chance, just in case."

So he wouldn't have any excuse to go back to the big house after it got dark…

Bo chuckled humorlessly to himself. As if he didn't have enough to do today, Remy expected him to go to the store. He could've explained that the longer he left the cottage as it was, the worse the damage would be. But Remy didn't care about that, either. His parents would be the ones to pay that price and saving them money had never been a consideration for him. "Good advice," Bo said, as if he weren't smart enough to think of that himself, and hoped he'd managed to keep his tone even so Remy couldn't hear the facetiousness in that statement.

"Great. Just wanted to check in and make sure you're okay."

That was the biggest lie of all. Remy didn't give a shit about him. Annabelle's son was only concerned with getting what *he* wanted. Remy had yet to hit a limit on what he could own, so he felt he could own her. "Couldn't be better," Bo replied.

Fortunately, Remy didn't seem to pick up on the facetiousness of *that* answer, either.

"Wonderful. I'll be there as soon as I finish my last exam."

"Good luck," Bo said, and Remy was gone.

Bo shook his head as he disconnected the call. Remy didn't have to worry about him trying to move in on his fiancée. Bo *wanted* to stay away from Ismay. He was too hungry for the gentle sweetness she seemed to possess, probably because he'd encountered so little of it in his lifetime—and that hunger meant the storm wasn't as much of a threat to him as she was.

While she was on Mariners, Ismay had anticipated shopping, picking out her favorite restaurants to take Remy to when he finally arrived, and spending long lazy afternoons reading on the beach—not huddling inside the house trying to outwait a storm with gale-force winds or worrying incessantly about Jack. She tried calling her brother as soon as Bo left, just to check in, but he didn't answer, so she dialed her mother, who was—not surprisingly—equally distraught.

"I never saw this coming, never dreamed Ashleigh was so unhappy," Betty said. "How'd I miss it?"

"I don't know," Ismay replied. "Have you had the chance to speak to her?"

"No. I—I haven't been able to make myself reach out." Her mother's voice was thick and full of tears. "It's all too new, and… and I'm brokenhearted."

"Where's Jack now?" Ismay asked.

Her mother sniffed. "Out on the farm with your father."

"He's not answering his phone."

"I think he needs a break from it."

Ismay got up off the couch, where she'd been under a blanket, to stretch her legs. "If things don't turn around, I think he should come to Mariners."

"Mariners!" her mother cried. "Why on earth would he go there?"

"To get away from it all."

"But that's clear across the country. What would he do for a living?"

"At first, nothing. He needs a chance to find himself, Mom—to determine what he wants to do with the rest of his life."

There was a brief silence. Then she said, "I didn't realize that hadn't already been decided."

Jack hadn't told them he didn't want to be a farmer, because he didn't want to face their disappointment. He'd told her it was a moot point; he had a wife to support, and they were trying to have a family. He needed to stay and provide. He was now no longer under that yoke, which was the one bright spot Ismay saw in all of this.

"He has the chance to reassess," she said to her mother, trying to state the problem as euphemistically as possible. The last thing anyone in the family needed was more grief. Ismay was just glad her father was old-school and misogynistic enough to believe only his boys could work on the farm. To him, it was *man's work*, and that was the only reason she'd been able to escape Tremonton.

"There's a lot going on," her mother said. "I don't want to talk about that right now."

Ismay frowned at this response. "Okay. We can talk about it later."

"I'd better go," Betty said. "I've got a lot to do."

Her mother hadn't even asked how she liked Mariners, but Ismay understood that Betty was preoccupied and considered the oversight a *tender mercy*, to use her mother's saying.

They said goodbye. Then she was at loose ends as to how to spend the day. Fortunately, because of the generator, she had internet service. So she went online and tried to distract herself from everything—the storm, what she'd found in Remy's closet, and Jack's predicament—by doing some swimsuit shopping.

She ordered a red bikini, hoping the weather would turn around and she'd soon have a nice tan to go with it, and answered some emails from past instructors and fellow students wishing her well as she left UCLA and began her career. When she hadn't heard from Bo by three o'clock, she began to wonder if he'd had lunch. He seemed like the type to work straight through if he had a goal in mind.

She decided to make him a sandwich and take it over before the storm got any worse. If he wasn't hungry now, he could always eat it later, and she wanted to get it to him before the rain made it any more difficult. It'd been drizzling for the past few hours, but there was an ominous feeling on the island—as if it were bracing for another onslaught, possibly worse than the last.

She made him an egg salad sandwich with a touch of honey—her mother's secret ingredient—then put it on a paper plate and wrapped the whole thing in plastic before heading out in the same coat she'd borrowed from Annabelle the day before.

She could hear a chainsaw as she squished through the mud in her running shoes and once she'd cleared the trees, she saw Bo up on the roof wearing a bright yellow slicker. "Hey!" she yelled as she drew closer, waving to get his attention.

The chainsaw was so loud and he was so focused on what he was doing that he didn't notice her. It wasn't until he'd finished cutting off the tree limb he'd been working on and switched off the motor that he realized he had company.

"What are you doing here?" he called down, obviously surprised.

She held up the plate with the sandwich. "I brought you something to eat."

He didn't seem to know what to do—whether to get down or tell her to leave it.

"I can put it inside the house, if you want," she said, gesturing at the front door.

"No. Don't go inside," he said. "It's not safe."

She indicated the hood of his truck. "I can set it here, but you can't leave it there for too long or it'll get soggy in spite of the plastic."

"I'll eat it before then."

"So…you *are* hungry?"

"A little," he admitted, and she guessed she'd been right when she'd assumed he hadn't taken the time to eat.

She continued to squint up at him, sheltering her eyes against the rain. "You won't be able to finish that today, anyway. With these storm clouds moving in again, it's already growing dark. Why not come down, eat, and get warm?"

When he glanced up at the sky, she could tell he already understood he was racing the clock. "The sooner I chop this tree up the better," he called down.

"But is it even safe to run that thing in the rain?"

"It's gas-powered," he replied.

"That makes it safe?" She'd been raised on a farm, but she couldn't remember her brothers or father using a chainsaw in such bad weather. But maybe that was just because they didn't want to be out in it…

"You can use a gas-powered chainsaw in almost any weather," he said. "It's the wet shingles that are *really* dangerous."

"Then get off the roof!" she cried. "I realize you want to fix your house, but it's already wet inside. I can't imagine it will hurt anything to wait one more day." Lightning flashed behind her, adding an exclamation point to her words. "The weather's about to break," she predicted.

He wiped the moisture from his face with one hand before moving carefully so he wouldn't lose his footing, lugging the chainsaw to the ladder.

Everything he'd been doing seemed dangerous. She was glad she'd come over and stopped him. She held her breath while she watched his harrowing descent—the ladder didn't look entirely stable—and relaxed only after he reached the ground.

Skirting the pile of limbs he'd cut off and thrown in the same general spot, she took the sandwich over to him. "You've got to be wet and cold."

"It would be nice if this weather would clear up," he said.

Instead of handing him the sandwich like she'd planned to do, she pulled it back when he reached for it and beckoned him to follow her. "Come on. You're not going to eat this out here in the wind and rain, and you're not taking it into that soggy house, either."

He started to protest, but she lifted her hand. "You just told me not to go inside because it's dangerous," she said.

"It's not as dangerous for me," he responded.

She gave him a skeptical look. "Really?"

"I'll be fine."

"You will if you come over to the main cottage."

"It's my job to take care of this place," he said, gesturing to show he meant the entire Windsor property.

"No one can expect you to work under these conditions. And you *will* take care of everything—when it's safe. Trust me, getting that tree off the bungalow isn't worth your life."

She started out ahead of him, hoping he'd simply fall in step with her. But when she looked back, she saw that he hadn't moved an inch. "Aren't you coming?"

His eyes narrowed. He didn't trust easily. She felt like she was coaxing a skittish animal to take a piece of food from her hand—every time she came close, he backed away. But she didn't see that he had much choice. What she was suggesting was the only thing that made sense.

"You can't really believe the Windsors would rather you were out in this…" she said.

The quizzical expression he gave her suggested he really *did* believe that.

"Come on," she said. "Don't make me stay out in the wet and cold."

"*You* should go in," he said. "I'm fine here."

"I'm not going back without you, so if I get struck by lightning while I'm trying to make you see reason, it'll be your fault."

"What?" he said, obviously surprised she'd take such a hard stand.

She felt her smile widen. There was something about this guy she liked. His prickly, stoic manner seemed to warn her not to assume they were friends, even after the camaraderie they'd shared last night. And yet…she sensed his tough shell harbored a very sensitive heart and he liked her as much as she liked him, in spite of not really wanting to. "You heard me."

"You won't leave…"

She set her jaw. "Nope. So…it's your choice. I can watch you work and probably catch pneumonia out here, or you can come in and save this problem for another day."

Only then, when she made it about *her* welfare, did he reluctantly follow her to the main house.

7

“Is that how you handled growing up with seven siblings?” Bo asked Ismay. “By bulldozing everyone to get what you want?”

“Being the oldest had its advantages,” she quipped, hardly penitent for dragging him back to the big house.

Remy would be furious when he found out Bo wasn’t where he was supposed to be. There was some pleasure in giving him the proverbial finger, but it didn’t come without risk…

Bo could’ve explained to Ismay that her fiancé had called to tell him not to go back to the main house. But he knew she’d feel as though she had to rise to his defense, and he would not put her in the middle.

After he’d stripped off his rain slicker and boots in the mudroom, and she’d kicked off the tennis shoes she’d been wearing—which were no kind of footwear for this weather—she led him into the kitchen and put his sandwich on the table. But then she seemed to think twice. “Why don’t you go take a hot shower first? It’s a cold sandwich, so it can wait.”

He was chilled through. The idea of a steaming hot shower—one where he wouldn’t have to worry about stepping into an inch of brown water on the floor afterward—definitely sounded appealing. But it also felt strange to be making himself so comfortable in the Windsors' expensive vacation home. Although the cottage sat empty quite a bit, he'd never even been tempted to shower or sleep there. He had little interest in taking anything more than what the Windsors owed him. As long as he had his freedom, his health, a place to live, and plenty of books, he figured he was a rich man. "My clothes are wet."

"We could go back to your place and get some dry ones," she suggested.

No. Going to that much effort made him feel even more conscious of defying Remy's wishes. "We just came from there. I'm fine."

"You're freezing. Get in the shower, and I'll just throw your clothes in the dryer."

He tried again to refuse, but she insisted there was no reason to be uncomfortable. "You're making *way* too big a deal out of this," she said, and maybe she was right. If he wasn't who he was—so conscious of every sharp edge in life—this would be nothing.

"Fine. Which bathroom do you want me to use?"

"You can take your pick," she said. "There are four in this house with fresh towels in each. Whichever you choose, I'll be there to get your clothes in a minute."

He wasn't going to use the master, he knew that. There was a suite downstairs, too, but he decided to use the bathroom off the hallway at the top of the stairs. Besides the master, that seemed to put the most distance between him and Remy's fiancée.

But, true to her word, he heard her voice on the other side of the panel just a couple of minutes later. "Are you ready to hand me your clothes?"

He wrapped a towel around his lower half, picked up what he'd dropped on the expensive marble floor, and opened the door.

She was waiting there with a thick white robe she handed over before accepting his clothes. "I realized I should wash this stuff before drying it, and that takes longer than a shower, so this will give you something to wear in the meantime."

He was already regretting making himself at home in his employer's house. "Whose is it?"

"I'm guessing it's Mort's," she said as if it didn't matter. "I found it in the master."

"I don't feel comfortable—" he started, but she broke in.

"It's just a robe, Bo. I'll wash it when you're done and hang it back up. No one will even know you used it."

Reluctantly, he accepted the robe and closed the door. But when he got out of the shower and pulled it on, he couldn't help wondering if the storm was going to cost him his job.

Ismay had left a pair of slippers by the bathroom door after putting Bo's clothes in the laundry. But when he came downstairs, he had nothing on his feet. Apparently, wearing Mort's slippers was crossing the line for him. She could tell he wasn't even happy about wearing Mort's robe, which was too small for him, anyway. Mort was maybe five-nine and not nearly as wide across the shoulders, but she hadn't been able to find a robe of Remy's or Bastian's.

"Coffee?" she said as he came into the kitchen. "Or I bought a six-pack of beer..."

"I'll take a beer," he said and sat down at the table.

"How was the elderly neighbor?" she asked as she got it for him. "Did you have a chance to check on her?"

He accepted the can. "Honey? She was doing great. No problem at all."

"That's nice to hear."

"I mentioned your brother to her." He popped the top and took a drink. "She didn't make any commitments, but she sounded as if she might be willing to have him house-sit."

"It'd be nice to get him a place that easily and that close. I'm so worried about him." Jack had been on her mind all day. She'd tried calling him twice after she'd spoken to her mother, but he hadn't picked up. "Thanks for broaching the subject with her."

Bo took his first bite of the sandwich. "This is delicious," he said after he'd swallowed.

"I love egg salad. That's the way my mother makes it."

"Honey gave me a bottle of blackberry jam. Wish I would've thought to grab it. You might like it on toast."

"You'll just have to have me over for breakfast after all this is over," she teased.

He looked startled, as if that would never happen, and she felt silly for even suggesting it. Once the storm cleared up, they wouldn't be sharing any meals. She was engaged. That didn't necessarily mean she couldn't be Bo's friend, and yet...somehow it did. Something told her he wasn't built for casual relationships. And Remy certainly wouldn't like her associating with his parents' caretaker. So maybe it was partly the fact that Bo worked for the Windsors that made it weird.

"Would you like another sandwich?" she asked when he finished.

"Maybe for dinner," he said.

She glanced at the clock. "That would be in an hour."

"Yeah. Sounds perfect."

"You want to eat again in an hour?" she said as she started to laugh.

"Why not?"

"Okay," she said with a shrug. "Egg salad is easy enough to make." She gave him the once-over. "I wish I had a picture of you in that tiny robe."

His face finally relaxed into a smile. "You must be trying to get me fired."

No wonder he'd left the slippers alone. But could he be right? Certainly, Remy's parents would understand that she and Bo were in a difficult situation and want them to be as warm, dry, and comfortable as possible. Wouldn't they?

Ismay had to admit…she didn't really know the Windsors—not as well as Bo did. "You think Remy's parents would fire you for borrowing a robe?"

His smile disappeared. "I don't think it would take that much."

Jack squinted against the evening sun as he stared out over his father's fields. This farm was all he'd ever known. He'd been born in the house—he'd come quickly in the middle of the night before his mother could make it to the hospital—he'd been baptized and married at the local church, and he'd gone to the closest college. He'd assumed he'd spend the rest of his life here with Ashleigh, who would never be willing to move away from her family. With such a traditional, conservative upbringing, he'd never dreamed he'd be divorced, especially at such a young age—and for a reason like this.

He'd tried so hard to make his wife happy. He'd treated Ashleigh a lot better than his father had ever treated his mother, he thought. Buzz had never been mean to Betty exactly. He treated her with respect, as an equal, but he certainly didn't baby her and try to make things nice the way Jack had with Ashleigh. Buzz expected Betty to be tough, and she'd hung in there and borne him eight children while working just as long and hard as he had.

Although Jack had graduated from Utah State, Ashleigh had dropped out and taken a course that would enable her to become an eyelash technician. Lash extensions had become all the rage in Utah, and she'd decided to cash in on the trend. Problem was…she wasn't the only young woman in the area with the same idea. Competition had been stiff in their small town, so she'd wound up working only a few hours, at most, per day.

Apparently, she'd been getting to know Jessica Davidson the rest of the time. While he was at work…

He rubbed his neck as he watched the plume of dust that followed his father on the tractor. He should be out there plowing, not Buzz. He suspected Buzz had insisted on finishing up himself because he felt sorry about what'd happened with Ashleigh. His father never really addressed emotional issues—certainly not head-on—but there could sometimes be a little give in what Buzz normally expected.

Jack didn't think *anything* could make him feel better, though. He was so shocked, he was numb; it was as if he'd walked out of the house and been struck by a semi.

That didn't stop him from trying to think back and pick through the rubble, however. To look for all the signs he must've missed. And imagine Ashleigh with her new lover. He'd been the one to encourage her to go out and have a good time with Jessica…

"Hey, you okay?"

Jack hadn't heard Hank's approach. Hank had been helping on the farm since he'd finished his bachelor's a couple of weeks ago, so he'd been around a lot lately, but until his brother spoke, Jack hadn't realized there were tears running down his face, either. Embarrassed, he used the back of his hand to quickly wipe his cheeks and turned away without answering. He couldn't deal with having a conversation right now. The pity in his brother's voice was almost as excruciating as the rest of it.

Perhaps he wasn't so different from his father; he was also a private man, preferred to bury his pain. But everyone in town would soon know Ashleigh had left him—for a woman, which would only make it more sensational—and that would mean he'd soon have nowhere to hide.

"Jack?" Hank called uncertainly.

Jack didn't stop. Lifting his hand, he waved to at least acknowledge his brother, climbed in the old Ford he'd bought from their father when Buzz had upgraded, and drove away wondering what he was going to do once he got home. Everything in the house reminded him of Ashleigh. His wife had taken some of her things but not all of them. That would have to happen at some point. When? What was she doing now? Did she regret destroying his life? At least a little? Or was she reveling in the freedom she said she'd been craving to be her *authentic self*?

Had she left him because Jessica could give her children, since she already had three little girls and could probably have more babies? She was still young. All it would take was a sperm bank.

A text came in. He heard the ding. But he left his phone in the seat beside him. Whatever someone was trying to tell him—or ask him—he couldn't face it tonight.

"Still no word from your brother?" Bo asked as he walked back into the kitchen, where they'd been playing chess.

Ismay looked up from her phone. "No."

"Is that normal?"

Since he was so much better at the game than she was, he'd been teaching her various strategies instead of just beating her over and over again. But when he'd excused himself to use the bathroom, she'd immediately thought of Jack and checked to see if her brother had responded to any of her calls or texts. "I don't know. He's never gone through anything like this before," she said, laying her phone back on the table.

"Have you talked to anyone else in the family today?" Bo had changed into his own clothes as soon as they came out of the dryer, and she was washing Mort's robe. She knew he'd hated wearing it, but now he had clean dry clothes, he'd eaten his second egg salad sandwich for the day, as well as a salad, and he was safe instead of risking his life on the roof of a home he didn't even own. Ismay felt good about all of that and refused to consider it meant she was supporting his position over that of the rich family who was hosting her—her prospective in-laws, no less.

"My brother Hank texted me to say he's worried, too," she replied. "And I spoke to my mother this morning."

Bo sat down across from her again. "How's everyone taking the news?"

"They're just as shocked and upset as Jack is."

"Would you say you're a close family?"

"I would. I mean…my parents never had a lot of money, especially when we were little. We had to use our imaginations and get creative to have fun." She remembered playing hide-and-seek in the barn and other outbuildings, driving the tractor and helping to pick whatever fruits or vegetables her father felt he could sell. "A farm is a good place to grow up."

"I bet." He started to move the pawns back to their starting positions on the board. "What does your father grow?"

"Pumpkins, onions, cucumbers, tomatoes, peaches. Brigham City, which is nearby, is known for its peaches. It even has a peach festival that started as a day off from the harvest and has been going since the early 1900s. So he put in an orchard about ten years ago."

"I love peaches," Bo said.

"I'll have to send you a box when they're ripe. There's absolutely nothing better than the ones my father grows."

"Did you work on the farm as a child?"

"Some. But as I grew older, I was relegated to the kitchen to help my mother cook, clean, and can."

"Your folks are traditional."

"Very."

"How old are your siblings?"

She finished the last of her beer. "Jack is twenty-five. Hank is twenty-two and recently graduated from college. Ryan is twenty and chose to attend the University of Utah instead of Utah State, which is as radical as my family gets," she said with a chuckle. "Liam is seventeen and will finish high school next year. Terrence is fifteen, a sophomore. And Oliver and William are twelve and thirteen, only eighteen months apart. They're in middle school."

"That's a big family."

"It is."

"How'd your folks manage having so many kids?"

"My father's strict and can be a bit harsh now and then, but feeding and clothing so many isn't easy, and we know he loves us. That's the important thing, I guess."

As he finished lining up the other chess pieces, Ismay wondered if Bo was comparing her family to his own and couldn't help feeling she should've made hers sound less idyllic. But she had to be fair to her parents at the same time.

"What's Tremonton like?" he asked.

"It's in the Bear River Valley of northern Utah. Has a population of about nine thousand people, which is small, but it's not far from bigger towns like Logan. Low crime rate. Religion is a big part of the culture."

"Are *you* religious?"

"Not anymore. I was never really interested, even when I was young, and became even less so when I went away to college."

"And that's okay with your parents?"

"Not really," she said ruefully. She knew they were disappointed, but to her, what was most important was having integrity and being a good person. "They'd like to see me come back to the church."

"Is Jack still in?"

"He is, and that's going to make what he's going through both better and worse."

"What do you mean?"

"Word of Ashleigh leaving him will spread fast. Almost everyone he sees on Sunday will know what happened by the time he shows up for his church meetings. But many in the congregation will try to reach out to support him, too."

"Double-edged sword," he said. His biceps bulged as he sat back and folded his arms. "That's rough."

"What about you?" she asked as she got up to toss her can in the wastebasket.

"What about me?"

"Why don't you tell me a little more about your family?"

"You don't want to hear about my family," he replied.

She scowled at him. "Everybody's got drama."

He leaned forward again and gestured at the board. "Maybe after we play another game. You can start."

When she just stared at him and didn't make a move, he met her gaze. "What?"

"You just might be the most guarded man I've ever known," she said with a dramatic sigh.

His eyebrows gathered over his topaz-colored eyes. "What are you talking about? I'm an open book."

She could tell he knew better, which made it funny, and she'd had just enough to drink that once she started laughing, she couldn't seem to stop. He didn't laugh with her, but his lips curved into an affectionate, indulgent smile, which made her wonder why she hadn't thought he was the most handsome man she'd ever met the first moment she laid eyes on him.

"What is it?" he asked when she suddenly sobered.

"Nothing." She focused on the game. But the truth was she felt guilty for the first time since she'd met him. Last night, she'd thought it was ridiculous that Remy would demand they not stay together. Because of the storm, it had simply made sense that she give him shelter.

Letting him stay again tonight also made sense; it was storming just as badly and because of the tree that'd fallen on his roof, his house was flooding. And yet…something was different—something that made her slightly short of breath whenever she looked at him.

8

They played chess and then cards until it was late. Last night, they'd stayed in the living room on separate couches with the lantern on the coffee table to offer a soft reassuring light. Doing that had seemed more natural than going to separate bedrooms in such a large house, given the storm raging outside and the fact that the generator supported just the bathrooms and central living areas—the refrigerator/freezer, internet service, air-conditioning/heating, hot water, and TV. It made sense not to change their arrangement, and yet, tonight felt far more intimate to Ismay than the night before.

"Are you sure it's okay to leave the lantern on again?" she asked.

"Should be fine," Bo replied. "Weather report says the storm will be over tomorrow, and the generator should last a couple more days, even if I can't get more gas for it, which really shouldn't be a problem."

She scooted down under the blanket that covered her. He'd told her a little about his days fishing near the small village where he'd gone to live after losing his mother, and his uncle Chester, who seemed like a version of Paul Hogan's character in *Crocodile Dundee*—someone who'd spent his life living off the land.

What Bo had shared made her curious enough to want to visit the village and see it for herself but she couldn't show too much interest. When she did, he shut down. Clearly, there was pain associated with the place that made him reluctant to say too much.

Despite his reticence, or maybe because of it, she was tempted to tell him what she'd found in Remy's bedroom. She thought he might be able to give her some advice on how to interpret the contents of that duffel bag. He knew Remy and the other members of the Windsor family, and he seemed like a wise, quiet observer, who took in far more than he ever shared. She wanted someone to tell her she had nothing to worry about, because as hard as she'd tried to put that stuff out of her mind, she only succeeded for short intervals. As soon as she wasn't preoccupied with something else, the vision of that young girl staring back at her from the torn photograph rose in her mind.

"Do you ever watch true crime?" she asked.

"You mean like documentaries?"

"Yeah."

After a few beats of silence, he said, "Sometimes. Why?"

"I was just wondering if there's much crime here on the island."

"Not really—at least not when it comes to violent crime. I'm guessing there's plenty of theft. I had to chase off some drunk college boys who were trying to break in here once, but I doubt they would've done much more than help themselves to whatever alcohol they could find."

"Is there a good police force on Mariners?"

Again, it took him a second to answer. He was obviously wondering why she'd chosen this topic of conversation. "I think they're decent. They solved the Emily Hutchins murder, which wasn't easy."

"She's the only girl who's ever gone missing from Mariners?"

"That I know of."

Ismay slid her hands under her pillow. If Bo knew anything

about the contents behind the wall of Remy's closet, he certainly didn't let on.

"Ismay?"

She looked over at him.

"Are you scared of me?"

"No!" she said.

He started to get up. "Because I can go back to my own place—"

She motioned for him to lie back down. "If I was scared of you, I wouldn't have insisted you come here. Please don't go. I feel *safer* with you here." And she knew *he* was probably safer, too; what with the state of his house.

He propped his head up on his fist as he relaxed back onto the couch. "So…why are we talking about crime?"

If she was ever going to tell him, now was the time. The words were on the tip of her tongue. But she owed Remy more faith and loyalty than to raise such a potentially compromising question, didn't she? What if he was innocent of any wrongdoing, and she made him look guilty simply by sharing her confusion?

She couldn't risk that. What kind of a fiancée would she be?

"I read about Emily before coming here. It was all over the news."

"As I said, that case has been solved. And even if that weren't true, you don't have anything to worry about—not while I'm here."

"Right. I believe that. So…why do you think some serial killers and rapists keep mementos of their victims?"

"The police and other authorities in the shows I've watched say it's so they can relive their crimes."

"But it also raises the risk of getting caught. I mean, someone could stumble on a cache of those things and bust a case wide open," she said, holding her breath as she waited for his response.

"I guess it shows how twisted they are that they'd be compelled to do it even if it's at their own peril."

She let her breath go. He didn't know anything about the duffel bag. That was clear. His mind had gone in a completely different direction when she'd brought it up.

"Do you think you ever really know somebody?" she asked.

"Somebody who has good reason not to be authentic?" he said. "No. Those people show you only what they want you to see."

"You're probably right," she said and couldn't help thinking how good Remy was at doing exactly that.

The wind had a bite to it. Only Mariners could feel this cold in spring, Bastian thought as he took the early morning ferry to the island—the first ferry to be able to make it over in two days. If it was sunshine he was looking for, he would've been better off heading to Florida. But then his parents would've bitched at him for spending their money on an Airbnb when they had a perfectly good vacation home at one of the most desirable places to visit in America.

This wasn't about a vacation, anyway. He'd heard that Remy had sent his fiancée to Mariners ahead of him and Bastian wanted to meet her when his brother wasn't around. Whoever she was, he felt sorry for her. Remy could be a real dick.

He glanced up at the sky. At least it'd stopped raining. According to the weather report, the storm had left the island saturated and windblown, with fallen limbs, debris, and swollen gutters. But the worst of it was over. He supposed he could tolerate a little discomfort to get away from the city and out from under his father's thumb. His parents had been putting so much pressure on him lately to party less and work more...

He wondered how Mort was going to react when he reached the office and found Bastian's note on his desk. It simply said he hadn't been feeling his best and needed some time off, a chance to gain back his full strength. He didn't indicate where he was going, just that he wouldn't be coming in for a week or two. He didn't want them to tell Remy he was visiting Windsor Cottage. His brother would find out soon enough as it was. This might be his only chance to get to know his prospective sister-in-law—and to warn her about what she was getting into. If he screwed things up for his brother at the same time, even better.

The ferry swayed as it came into contact with the dock, and he went inside to get his suitcase from the table where he'd been sitting when they left Long Island and carried it down the stairs so he could disembark. He hadn't brought a vehicle. He never used one in New York City and his parents kept a Jeep in the garage at the cottage. He just had to take an Uber around the island. Then he'd be set up for the duration of his stay.

He hummed the song playing on his AirPods as he ordered a ride, and a car was waiting for him almost as soon as he stepped off the wharf. When she'd called last night, his mother had told him the power had gone out at Windsor Cottage, but the generator was working, so he assumed he'd be comfortable enough until the power came back on. His future sister-in-law would probably be glad to see him. It had to be scary riding out such a big storm as a stranger to the island, with its temperamental weather.

His Uber driver had to go slower than usual and skirt around piles of driftwood, dirt, and leaves, and Bastian could see where more of the coastline had eroded since he'd been here last, but the cottage looked solid and unshakable in the dawn light. He hadn't seen the renovations yet, so he was looking forward to that; anything his mother did had class and style.

He thanked his driver when he got out, grabbed his suitcase and took a moment to admire the sun peeking through the clouds over a sparkling ocean that was just beginning to settle down.

There was nowhere like Mariners. It was good to be back, he decided, and dragged his suitcase to the front door.

Bo had awakened early, as usual, but the sun hadn't come up yet, so there was nothing he could do to fix his bungalow. He needed light and dry weather. He told himself he'd have to stay where he was for a bit and spent at least an hour studying the beauty of Ismay's face before drifting off again.

It was the sound of the door swinging against the inside wall that jarred him awake and a booming voice that said, "Honey, I'm home!"

Shocked by the sudden intrusion, Bo jumped up, prepared to defend himself and Ismay, if necessary.

"Whoa! Calm down, Buckeroo," the same voice said. "What have we here?"

One of the Windsor twins—Bo hadn't seen them often enough to be able to tell them apart—stood in the doorway. With all the light coming from behind, Bo couldn't make out the expression on his face, but the sound of his voice was a sneer.

Bo immediately began to gather up the bedding he'd been using as Ismay pushed herself up on one elbow, her eyes still filled with sleep. "What—what is it?" she said, blinking at their visitor. *"Remy?"*

"Yeah, it's me, babe. How about a big wet, sloppy kiss before we head back to the bedroom?" Their visitor laughed uproariously, and she scrambled to her feet.

"You're not Remy," she said.

"Darn. You figured it out. You should've taken me up on the offer while you had a good excuse. After all, there is one marked difference between us, and all the ladies we've known can attest to it." He winked before gesturing at the evidence of their sleeping arrangements. "Sorry to ruin your little campout. I had no idea you had company."

"Bo's not company," she said, fixing her tank top since the strap had fallen off her shoulder.

She wasn't wearing a bra. Bo saw Bastian's gaze fall to her chest and knew exactly what he was looking at, because he'd been keenly aware of her breasts beneath that white cotton ever since she'd gone into the bathroom to change for bed. Fortunately, she was still wearing yoga pants, so he didn't think the scene appeared *too* damning.

The Bastian he knew, however, would exploit it for all it was worth. That was the concern. What would he say to Remy? And to Mort and Annabelle?

Bo was as worried for Ismay as he was for himself. Remy had already made it clear, even to her over the phone, that he didn't want Bo at the cottage.

"He's *not* company?" Bastian said. "He lives here, then?"

"The power's out at his house—and a tree fell and crashed into his living room," she explained. "It's currently flooded."

"I see." He looked between them. "Then how nice of you to take him in."

"I would've taken in anyone who didn't have a place to stay," she clarified, obviously hearing the same suggestive tone Bo did. "And I assumed you and your family would want me to share the shelter of this beautiful house with the person who cares for it in your absence."

"Of course, we would," he said, feigning concern.

Bo felt his muscles tense. He hated being beholden to such a little bastard. But it was this bastard's mother he worked for. He had to remind himself of that. And he had a good situation here on Mariners, couldn't do anything to screw it up.

"What—what are you doing here, anyway?" Ismay asked, going on the offensive. "Remy didn't tell me you were coming."

"I didn't know I had to make him—or you—aware of my itinerary."

She looked abashed. "I—I didn't mean that. I'm just so surprised to see you."

He laughed. "Obviously."

"Why are you acting like this?" she asked. "We haven't done anything wrong, and the insinuation is offensive."

"Don't mind me. I'm sure you're both as innocent as the day is long. You just look guilty," he added with a laugh.

Her mouth dropped open. "I… What?"

"I'm kidding." Bastian waved away his words. "You actually look good enough to eat, if you know what I mean."

His laugh was even louder this time. It was all Bo could do to hold himself back. There were guys in prison who'd heckled him, and he'd made them regret it—and they'd deserved to be hit less than this dude. Without Annabelle, Mort, or Remy around to rein Bastian in, Bo had a bad feeling about how the next few days would go. Would he be able to stop himself from decking the little prick?

"The past two days have been quite an ordeal," Bo said, essentially trying to tell him that he wasn't making things any easier. But Bastian didn't care. Bo shouldn't have even bothered to try to make that point.

"Well, fortunately, it's about to get easier. The storm's over, and I'm here now, so you won't have to worry about Ismay's safety. I can be in charge of that." He checked his watch. "By the way, you might want to get started if you plan to remove that tree from your roof by nightfall, Bo."

Ismay's lips formed a firm straight line and her eyes began to glitter, but her voice was surprisingly even when she said, "What time is it?"

"Nearly seven," Bastian responded as if it was noon or later.

Bo had been forcing himself to take the time to fold the blanket he'd been using. He would not let Bastian make him feel as though he had to run off because he'd been caught doing something wrong. But, probably due to the tension, Ismay took the blanket from him before he could finish. "I'll do this," she said. "And I'll bring you some breakfast in a bit."

"You're going to serve him breakfast, *too*?" Bastian said. "My, aren't you accommodating."

"Would *you* like some?" she asked. "Since I have to cook for myself anyway, I don't mind making extra."

"I'd love some. What a woman," Bastian replied with a grin

Bo wished he could wipe off his face. "Remy always did know how to pick 'em."

Bo wished he could stay. He didn't want to leave Ismay alone with this asshole. He didn't trust him. But considering the situation, there was nothing he could do. "Thanks," he muttered to Ismay and stalked out.

Still uncomfortable with having Bastian appear out of the blue, he glanced back before he got so far that the house was out of sight. But he couldn't see either of them through the window.

He'd been afraid the storm would cost him his job. With Remy's twin's arrival, the chances of that happening had just gone up exponentially.

Ashleigh had finally returned his call. She was coming to get her stuff this morning. Jack had spent almost the entire night boxing it up for her. It was a habit to help her whenever he could—a habit he had a hard time breaking even now. But there'd been a selfish element to it, too. Living in a house where everything reminded him of her was difficult. He wanted to remove the rest of her belongings from his sight as soon as possible, just as he wished he could erase her from his mind and heart. So he'd called his father to say he wouldn't be in today, that he had some personal business, and his father hadn't even questioned him. Buzz had said, "Right. See you tomorrow." And then, just before he'd hung up, he'd asked, "Are you okay?"

Jack had claimed he was, but he'd never been in a worse situation. How could he excise Ashleigh from his life? They'd been together since their freshman year. He'd thought he knew her better than any other person on earth…

He winced at the sense of betrayal that welled up. Any thought of her brought fresh pain.

Hearing a vehicle outside, he went to the window and peered through the blinds. Ashleigh was driving the small Toyota he'd bought for her. How would she cover the payments on it? Would Jessica pay it now?

His breath caught in his throat when he saw the passenger door open. She'd brought Jessica!

A few seconds later, there was a timid knock at the door.

He looked down at his hands. They were shaking. He wasn't sure he could do this, after all. He hadn't expected to have to face the woman who'd replaced him.

A second knock rattled the door. "Jack?"

That was Jessica's voice. He closed his eyes. Ashleigh had a key. She could come in if she wanted. This had been her house as much as his. That she was standing on the other side of that panel, waiting for him to greet her as if she'd never lived there with him, showed just how much had changed—in what seemed like no time at all.

Drawing a deep breath, he quit peering through the blinds before they could realize he was doing it and forced his recalcitrant legs to cross over to the door, which he unlocked and opened.

Ashleigh wouldn't quite meet his gaze, but Jessica watched him warily. "We're here to get her things," she said.

He looked at Ashleigh again. Surely, this was just a cruel joke. Any second, she'd start laughing and fall against him, and he'd put his arms around her, press his lips to her head and breathe in the all too familiar scent of her hair.

But that didn't happen. Silence fell until, awkwardly, he stepped back. "It's all…it's all right here."

"You boxed it up?" Ashleigh murmured, her voice barely audible.

"I thought it would be easier for you," he muttered.

"Thank you."

The words were so softly spoken he could barely hear them. Jessica said nothing. She just lifted the first box she came to and started out of the house.

"Do you…do you want to walk through and make sure I got everything?" he asked, unsure of what else to say.

"If you don't mind," she said. "Since I… I didn't get to pack it."

"Did you *want* to pack it?" he asked.

"No. I—that would take too long."

He thought about broaching the subject of the car. They needed to talk about it, but he felt such hostility coming from Jessica—as if she'd expected a fight so she'd come ready to have one—that he just stepped back to clear a path.

Ashleigh walked through every room and, after conferring with Jessica, asked if she could take more of their pots and pans. He thought he'd been generous in what he'd given her, but if she wanted more, he wasn't going to fight over it. What was the point? He'd already lost everything he cared about. "Take whatever you want," he said.

She blinked at him, surprised by his answer. Obviously, she was expecting anger, resistance. She'd brought Jessica with her just in case, hadn't she? But he was too hurt for that. Had she come alone, he would've carried it all out for her, too.

As he watched the pile in the middle of the floor grow smaller, he couldn't help thinking of Jessica's kids. She was six years older than they were, so the oldest two were in school. But what about her four-year-old? Was she at preschool or with Jessica's parents? Or with Jessica's husband?

And if the situation were different, would Jessica have brought them for this? How were *they* feeling about what was going on?

The oldest was probably seven, old enough to understand that something terrible had happened to her family, even if she didn't understand what it all meant and how it was going to change her life.

Donny, Jessica's husband, wasn't only losing his wife, he was losing 24/7 access to his kids. That had to be worse than what

Jack was experiencing, and yet Jack couldn't imagine *anything* being worse.

Ashleigh approached him with their popcorn maker. "Can I have this?"

He remembered when they'd gone to Walmart to buy it. They couldn't afford to go out to a lot of movies, so he'd told her he'd make popcorn at home whenever they watched a series on Netflix. He typically used coconut oil. She liked that best…

"Jack?" she prompted.

He nodded.

"And it was my mother who gave us the drapes." She pointed to the frilly pink curtains at the kitchen window. "Do you mind if I take those?"

What did *he* want with pink curtains? "That's fine." Normally, he would've taken them down for her. She wasn't handy with a screwdriver. But Jessica said she'd brought a tool kit and went out to the car to retrieve it, so he shoved his hands in his pockets and stayed out of the way as Ashleigh's new lover removed the drapes *he'd* put up and then carried them out of the house.

"Your dad doesn't mind that you're not at work today?" Ashleigh asked.

She'd told him she'd come get her stuff when he wasn't there if he preferred it, but he'd said he wanted to be around. Apparently, some masochistic part of him was hanging on to every last second with her, no matter how terrible the experience was. "He didn't say anything about it," he said.

She frowned. "I'm surprised. He works you like a slave."

"He works just as hard," he pointed out but was suddenly tempted to blame how hard his father worked him for the split. Problem was the hours he worked had nothing to do with Ashleigh's sexual orientation, and that was what this came down to.

"I bet he'll have plenty to say about me," she grumbled.

Buzz didn't say much about anyone. He didn't want to be guilty of gossip. But if someone disappointed him, that person typically didn't get a second chance.

"How are *your* parents taking the news?" He'd thought he'd hear from his in-laws. They'd welcomed him into the family with open arms. But they hadn't called, and he hadn't known what to say to them, so he hadn't, either.

"They're upset, of course. They're what got us into this mess. They think sexuality is a choice and that I'm going to hell for being my authentic self."

"They'll come around," he said. "And your sister?" Leila was three years younger and still single. She worked at the only gym in town as a CrossFit instructor.

"Won't speak to me."

"This…this came as a shock to all of us," he said.

Jessica walked back in. "Is that everything?" she asked Ashleigh.

Ashleigh sent him an apologetic look. "Yeah. Except my half of the furniture, but I don't want to talk about that today. There's no way I could fit anything else in the car, anyway."

"You can have whatever you want," he reiterated, which seemed to totally disarm her.

"Thanks for being decent about everything," Jessica said. "Unlike Donny…"

Jack couldn't bring himself to look at her, let alone respond. "I wish you the best," he mumbled to his wife.

Ashleigh glanced at Jessica before meeting his gaze. "Thanks," she said and walked out.

After the door closed, he sank down onto the sofa—which would probably turn out to be *her* sofa—and stared at what was left of the contents of the house. There wasn't much, but that didn't seem to matter because there was *nothing* left of him.

9

Ismay hadn't expected to dislike her prospective brother-in-law quite as much as she did. But he didn't seem to care one way or another. He certainly wasn't trying to impress her. He seemed to enjoy being an asshole and purposely tried to get under her skin.

"So you've been staying in the master?" he'd asked, feigning as though it was an innocent question when he was really intimating that she'd been rudely presumptuous to take that room as a guest—and a first-time guest at that.

"Only because Remy told me to," she'd responded, feeling defensive. "I can move into his room. No problem."

"I'd hate to put you out," he'd said, but it wasn't sincere, and he hadn't protested when she'd packed up her suitcase and carried it to Remy's room.

Had Remy known Bastian was coming to Mariners? Had he asked him to come because he was so upset she was alone with Bo? If so, he could've said something.

Eager to find out, she closed the door as soon as she could and tried to reach him, twice, but her calls transferred to voice mail.

Frustrated, she tossed her phone on the bed and took her time getting situated while waiting to hear back. Moving into Remy's room was the logical choice, the one that wouldn't be questioned, but she wished she could've gone into the downstairs guest room. Not only would that give her more separation from Bastian when she was sleeping—not that she considered him a true risk; she was just uncomfortable—it would put her in a space that didn't remind her of what she'd found in the closet. She thought of those things often enough as it was. Being even closer to them—using that closet while being aware of that hole in the wall—creeped her out.

After she put her things away, she still hadn't heard from Remy. Unwilling to leave the room, she sat on the bed, listening for Bastian's movements in the house. She could hear him downstairs, probably in the kitchen, when she grabbed her phone again.

Remy hadn't even wanted Bo to stay at the cottage one night, and yet she'd let him stay two.

But Bo had been the ultimate gentleman. No one had any reason to complain about his behavior…

She braced herself as the phone signaled a message. It could be that Bastian had shown up completely on his own, as he'd said. But had he let his brother know he'd found Bo in the house?

Either way, she was dying to talk to Remy and make sure everything was okay between them—and with his parents. There'd been an emergency, and maybe they didn't approve of how she'd handled it, but they hadn't been here, didn't know what she and Bo had been up against.

That incoming text had come from Remy.

I saw your call the first time and will get back to you when I can. I'm studying. What's up?

Can you step out of the library for a few minutes? I need to talk to you.

When he didn't respond, she assumed he was doing as she'd

asked—and knew that was the case only after she received a call five minutes later. He could've said, Sure, just a minute. But he was probably irritated by the interruption.

"I checked the weather report when I got up this morning. The storm's moved on," he said without so much as a hello. "Don't tell me the power hasn't come back on and the generator's gone out."

He didn't seem to know about Bo. He didn't seem to be aware that his twin brother was on the island, either. He would've said something right away had either of those things come to his attention. "The power's not back on, but the generator's working."

"So what's wrong? It'd better not be that you're still worried about our caretaker. Bo's resourceful. He'll be fine."

She considered admitting that she'd had Bo stay over again but decided not to bring it up. If Bastian told on her, she could always explain later. "Bastian's here," she said. As far as she was concerned, that was the bigger issue. When she'd decided to come to Mariners ahead of Remy, it was with the understanding that she'd have the house to herself, not that she'd be sharing it with a brother she'd never previously met.

"What'd you say?" Remy sounded surprised.

"I said *Bastian's* here. He just…showed up out of the blue this morning."

"*Why?* What's he doing there?"

"I have no idea. That's why I'm calling you."

"Did he say how long he plans to stay?"

"I didn't ask." She lowered her voice just in case Bastian had come up the stairs. "He seemed pretty put out to find me in the master, so I've moved into your old room."

"Why would he care if you're in the master? Don't tell me he's taking it for himself…"

He didn't seem to be concerned with her being in his old space. Did that mean he didn't know what had been hidden in the wall?

Possibly. But it would also be safe to assume she'd never find it. That no one would. If not for that freak storm, she wouldn't have. It was *behind* the wall.

"I think so," she said. "It sounded like it. But I didn't ask."

"What the hell?! Let me call him and see what's going on."

Afraid Bastian would spin a salacious tale about her and Bo, Ismay cringed. Normally, she wouldn't have cared. Any woman would be glad not to be alone in a strange house on a strange island while facing such a ferocious storm. And with Bo's house the way it was, she couldn't leave him—literally—out in the cold.

She'd chosen the safest option for both of them. That was all. And absolutely nothing untoward had happened.

And yet, as Remy disconnected so he could call his brother, she felt a niggle of guilt. She and Bo could've slept in separate rooms instead of on separate couches.

She could only hope it wouldn't come up—but she didn't think Bastian would miss such a golden opportunity to drive a wedge between her and Remy. He seemed to enjoy stirring up trouble.

She also felt guilty because she'd been glad of such a good excuse to have Bo stay over again. Sharing the cottage hadn't been purely practical, like she wanted them to believe. She'd enjoyed spending time with him.

The weather was dry and clear. But that was the only thing Bo had going for him. Most of the stuff in his refrigerator and freezer had spoiled, and the power was still off when he got home, so he couldn't even make toast. He'd had a peanut butter and jelly sandwich before getting on the roof, but that was probably two hours ago, and he was hungry again.

He was also working at a deficit in other ways. The chainsaw he needed to finish chopping up the tree was out of gas. Since he didn't want to take the time to go to town, he'd been reduced to using a hatchet. That made the process much slower, but at least he had most of the tree off the roof. He was just finishing up when he heard Ismay call his name.

As promised, she'd brought him breakfast. At least, it looked that way. She was holding up a picnic basket.

"You ready to eat?" she called out.

"In a sec. Stand back. Way back!" He gestured until she was at the edge of the surrounding thicket, well out of harm's way. Then he managed to use a branch he'd chopped off as a lever to lift the heavy trunk, which went crashing to the ground.

"Now I am," he called down and wiped his forehead with the sleeve of his jacket as he carefully made his way back to the ladder. The sun hadn't been out long enough to dry the roof, so the shingles were still wet and slippery.

"How are things going with your new friend?" he asked once he'd reached the ground.

"This is probably mean to say about my future brother-in-law, but I don't like him much," she muttered with a grimace.

He almost told her she was in good company but decided that wasn't very smart. Just because it felt like they were friends right now didn't mean that wouldn't change when Remy arrived. "Do you think he's going to try to cause trouble?" he asked instead.

"I'm assuming that's what he usually does."

He beckoned her to the picnic table around back. No way did he want to take her into his soggy house. "Any idea how Remy will react?"

"No. When I called him earlier, he sounded blindsided. He said he wanted to talk to his brother and get back to me, but I haven't heard from him yet. I think they've been fighting. Bastian stepped out of the house, presumably so I couldn't hear what he was saying, but I could tell he was raising his voice, so I know they weren't having a companionable discussion. I took the opportunity to make breakfast while I could be in the kitchen alone, left a plate for him on the table so he can't claim you're the only one I care about here—even though you are—and got out of there." She laughed, then seemed to realize what she'd said and tried to correct it. "I mean, I don't particularly like Bastian, so I wasn't eager to make him breakfast. Not that I wouldn't make Remy's brother breakfast, or that I was eager to…"

He grinned at her when she realized she was just getting herself in deeper.

Letting her words trail off, she finally shoved the basket into his chest. "Here, take this."

"I'm just glad to know you care about me," he said, laughing.

"You're going to get us both in trouble," she muttered but he could tell she was having a hard time hiding her own smile.

He set the basket on the wooden table and started to open it. "I'm starving. What'd you make?"

"French toast with berries."

"I haven't had French toast in ages."

"There are some scrambled eggs, too." She offered him a smile, which he loved because of the way it lit up her eyes. "I've already learned you eat enough for an entire army."

"You're making me sound like a glutton. I guess I won't tell you that I've already had a PBJ this morning."

She rolled her eyes. "Are you going to be able to get the hole patched before nightfall?"

"I think so. According to the weather report, it's not going to rain again—at least not in the next few days—so I'd rather start pumping the water out of the house, but—"

"No power," she broke in.

He lifted out the plate she'd put in the basket and removed the plastic wrap. "Exactly."

"At least your neighbor's okay, and you're not having to deal with that at the same time."

"Thank God for small favors," he muttered as he unrolled his silverware from a napkin.

She sat on the table while he sat on the bench and began to eat. "What if we strung extension cords all the way over here from the cottage?" she asked. "Would that work to pump the water out?"

He made a face to show he wasn't thrilled by the idea. "It would take a lot of extension cords…"

"Well, think about it. If it's possible, maybe that's what you need to do."

He was chewing, so he nodded instead of commenting.

She looked up at the trees overhead. "It's pretty here."

"I like it," he said. "You can't see the ocean like you can from the cottage, but this feels…private."

"I don't know anyone who values his privacy more than you…"

He had good reason for that, but he wasn't about to let on, so he said nothing.

"I can help you clean up after you get the water out," she offered.

"And miss all your time at the beach?"

She could obviously tell he was teasing her. It was apparent in her mock scowl. "Hey, I've earned this vacation," she said, nudging him with her foot.

"I bet it hasn't started out the way you thought it would…"

"No. And I'm not just referring to the storm."

"Bastian?"

"Yeah. It's kind of weird that he'd come on his own. Don't you think?"

"I don't try to make sense out of what other people do anymore," he said with a chuckle.

"He just…makes me uncomfortable."

Again, he chose not to say anything. He had to be careful. It might feel as though she was on his side right now, but…

She got out her phone. He assumed she was going to call Remy and was surprised she'd do it in front of him instead of waiting until she returned home. But she didn't call anyone. She navigated to her pictures and hesitated as she looked at him.

"What?" he said, confused.

A determined expression came over her face, and she turned her screen toward him. "Have you ever seen this girl?"

He studied the picture of an old photograph. "No. Why? Should I?"

She turned her phone back and frowned at it for several seconds before putting it away. "No. Not necessarily."

"Why do you ask?"

She didn't seem as though she wanted to answer the question, which he found odd. "I was just curious."

He was finished with the food she'd brought and had to get back to work, but he wondered why she'd wanted him to see that picture. "Do *you* know that girl?"

"No. I've never seen her before in my life."

"Then why is she on your phone—in your photos?"

"I just thought…maybe she was from around here."

"I haven't lived on the island for very long, don't know a lot of people. But Honey's been here for fifty years, ever since she got married. You might ask her."

She nibbled on her bottom lip. "Since I don't know Honey, that might seem weird."

"Then send that picture to me. I'll ask her."

"That's okay…"

"You don't want her to see it?"

She seemed to consider the question—and go back and forth on it—before ultimately saying, "I guess. Just…don't show it to anyone else."

He studied her, seeing the worry in her eyes. Something about this photograph troubled her. *Why?* "What's going on? Where did you get that photograph?"

She shook her head. "Never mind. Just…forget about it," she said and put his empty plate and silverware in the picnic basket. "I'd better get back."

Remy called while she was walking to the house, so Ismay put the picnic basket on the ground near the stairs to the front door and veered off to walk along the beach, picking her way through the debris left by the storm. "Hello?"

"You're not going to believe this," he said.

She couldn't help but tense. "What?"

"Bastian is staying for at least a week."

She stopped and turned toward the sea. The surf was so tranquil it was difficult to believe it had ever been so rough. "It'll be just him and me for seven days or more?"

"Sounds like it," he replied. "I called my mom, but she said he needs the break."

"In what way?"

"As a stress-reliever, I guess."

"From what you've told me, he doesn't have much to stress out about. It's not as if he could lose his job, or won't be able to pay his rent, or—"

"That's exactly what I said to my mom. But she said we can't judge—just support."

Ismay began rubbing her left temple. This trip wasn't turning out to be anything like she'd envisioned. "I see…"

"But it's a big house," Remy said, his tone conciliatory. "I don't think he'll get in your way."

Get in her way? He'd already gotten in her way. He'd made Bo feel he'd taken advantage simply because she'd convinced him to stay where it was warm and dry. She'd had to change rooms to accommodate Bastian, and now she was using *that* closet. She'd had to hurry to make breakfast before Remy's brother came back down so she could do it in peace—without him baiting her in one way or another. But how did she explain that to Remy? *He* could say terrible things about his brother—and had—but she couldn't. That would never be wise, not if she planned on becoming part of the family. After all, *blood is thicker than water* was a saying for a reason. "Right."

"So…you're okay with it?"

What choice did she have? Unless she wanted to leave and fly clear across the country—back to LA, where he was too busy studying to spend any time with her, or to Utah, to stay with her own family while they were going through the nightmare of what was happening to Jack—she was stuck. If she went to Utah, Remy would just want her to come back out again once he arrived. She couldn't afford to do that. He'd probably offer to pay for it, but she was careful not to let him do too much. It didn't feel right. Her father had always been a stickler about paying her own way, because it was the right thing to do and it meant she wouldn't have to feel indebted to anyone. "Of course."

"It might be a good opportunity for the two of you to get to know each other," Remy said.

Ismay recalled Bastian's smirk when he first entered the house and found Bo sleeping on one couch. "Yeah, I'd like that." It wasn't remotely true, but if nothing else, she owed Remy and his family for letting her stay.

"Okay. I told him he'd better not be a dick."

In Ismay's mind, that was like telling a fish he'd better not breathe through his gills. But she bit her tongue. "I'm sure that won't be a problem."

"Good. I'd better get back to studying."

"Remy?" she said before he could disconnect.

"What?"

"Has Bastian ever used your room?"

"For what?" he asked.

"I mean, was it ever *his* room? Or were you both in there together, maybe back in the old days when the cottage was smaller?"

"No. We've never shared a room. The cottage has never been *that* small. Why?"

She stared off into the distance, at the sun glistening off the water. That last question had been stupid; they would've been too young back then. She was just grasping at straws, hoping against hope that she could find an answer that would satisfy the part of her mind that kept screaming something was wrong. "I was just curious," she said and let him go.

She was turning to make her way—reluctantly—back to the cottage, where she'd have to face Bastian, when a text came in from Bo.

Power's on.

Thank God she wasn't going to have to worry about him staying in that water-logged house with a big hole in the roof.

The day dragged on until Jack got up off the couch and went to work. He'd rather be busy. Lying around only made things worse. But as soon as he parked his truck in his parents' drive, he almost balked. He didn't want to face his whole family and the sympathy he knew he'd see in their eyes. Thinking he'd beg off again and go to bed, even though it was only three thirty in the afternoon, he almost put his transmission in Reverse. But then his father came to the door of the barn and saw him, so he got out and strode over.

In true Buzz fashion, he didn't say much. But Hank was there, too. When Hank started to grill him, Buzz barked an order for his brother to go wash down the tractor.

"How'd it go this morning?" his father asked.

Remembering Jessica marching around his house, hauling boxes and taking down the drapes, Jack stretched his neck. "It's hard to explain," he said. Saying too much went against the loyalty he still felt toward his wife. He wasn't sure why he was still hanging on. Maybe he just couldn't let go.

At this answer, his father nodded once and strode off to the barn where they stored their produce until they could take it to market.

"Dad?" Jack called before he could get too far away.

Buzz turned.

"How do you get through something like this?"

Buzz thought for a moment. Then he said, "You just do, because you don't have any other choice."

Jack drew a deep breath, hoping it would help him withstand the crushing pressure on his chest. "Got it."

"You can't fold," his father said. "Where would that get you?"

Nowhere. It would get him nowhere. There really was no way out, and yet, he didn't see how he could continue to function.

"Your mother and brothers need help harvesting the snap peas. You'd better get out in the field," he said, then added, "The best way to handle what life throws you is to keep fighting."

Jack nodded. He could do it. He could be strong like his father, he told himself, and started out to the acreage closest to the highway.

His youngest brother noticed him first, said his name and pointed. When their mother looked up, he saw the pain and worry in her face he'd been expecting to see, but he no longer dreaded being with her and his siblings. They were the ones who loved him. They were the ones who would never leave.

"Hello, son," his mother said when he got close enough.

She searched his face earnestly, and he manufactured a smile for her sake. When he hurt, so did she, he realized. Besides that, he doubted Ashleigh would have much to do with his family from here on out. Betty had lost someone she considered a daughter. "Hi, Mom. You got a bowl for me?"

"Oliver, give your brother your bowl and go get another one from the barn," she said.

Twelve-year-old Oliver handed him his bowl, then he threw his arms around Jack's waist and squeezed tight for just a second before ducking his head, obviously embarrassed, and running off.

10

Bo was dealing with so much, it seemed stupid to Ismay—not to mention self-indulgent and lazy—to sit around while he managed all the cleanup and repairs on his own.

When she told Bastian she was going over to help, he said Bo was getting paid better than most caretakers—it was a matter of pride for his mother—it was his job and he'd be fine. But she refused to make her decision based on that argument. Besides, she had nothing better to do.

She thought Bastian might call Remy, who'd tell her to stay away from the bungalow, using the excuse that it wasn't safe now that part of the roof had caved in or whatever. But as far as she could tell, Bastian hadn't said anything about finding Bo in the cottage, so she thought there was a chance he wouldn't tell Remy about this, either.

Bo turned, his eyes widening when she knocked on his door, which was already standing open, carrying another picnic basket full of food. "What's going on?" he asked. "You've brought lunch?"

She nodded with a grin. "And I'm here to help with the cleanup. It doesn't make sense that you're the only one working."

He raised his eyebrows. "Bastian didn't try to stop you?"

She set the basket on the counter. "How'd you know?"

"Just an educated guess," he said with a chuckle.

"He said it's your job."

"That's true."

"But you've also just been through a hurricane—or as close to a hurricane as I've ever experienced—and you're racing the clock. I might as well lend a hand."

"This is supposed to be your vacation."

"Yeah, well..." She looked behind her, then lowered her voice. "It's a vacation just to get out of the cottage."

She meant *get away from Bastian*; she just didn't want to say it. But judging by the look on Bo's face, he understood. He opened his mouth as though he wanted to say something along those lines himself but closed it again.

"What?" she prompted.

"Nothing," he replied. "I work for the Windsors. I'm grateful for my job."

"Right. I get that. Don't mind me. I'm just blowing off steam. The storm was difficult enough, and now... I think I'm going to struggle to get along with Bastian. He was pretty rude this morning."

Bo hesitated for a second. But then he said, "He can be like that."

"I guess he's always been the *bad* twin, huh?"

"Not always."

"What do you mean?"

"Believe it or not, it was Remy who was more difficult as a child."

Ismay was surprised Bo would know this information. "Really? In what way?"

He shrugged before he started to sweep the debris on the floor into a pile. "It's just what I've heard. How long's Bastian staying?"

"I don't know. That's the thing."

"And Remy's okay with him being there?"

"Seems like it. Told me it might be a good time for us to get to know each other."

"Maybe it will be. You'll soon be related."

After this morning, that wasn't the most welcome thought… "True. So, how can I help?"

"I've got most of the water dealt with. I'm just sweeping and cleaning now. I'll be okay on my own."

There was still a gaping hole in the roof. She could see a patch of sky through it. "Why don't you cover the roof with a tarp or something and let me take over with the cleaning?"

"Are you really set on doing that?" he asked.

"Of course. I'm a farmer's daughter," she replied. "I'm not afraid of hard work."

Ismay and Bo were sitting, exhausted, at his kitchen table, eating the spicy hummus, cucumber, and sprout pita sandwiches she'd made, with potato salad and some sliced apples on the side, when Bastian knocked. Bo saw him through the peephole, muttered, "It's Bastian," and opened the door.

"What's going on?" Bastian said. "Is Ismay still here?"

Bo swung the door wider, so he could come in, and gestured at the table.

Ismay left her plate and got up. "Is something wrong?"

Bastian looked at the meal they had spread out on the table, along with a couple of beers from Bo's fridge—about all that had survived the power outage—then at each one of them. "I guess I wasn't invited to this little party."

"Party?" Ismay echoed. Did Bastian have to mischaracterize *everything*? He had to be doing it on purpose, just to bug them. There was nothing wrong with helping someone after a storm, but Bastian somehow imbued it with a sleazy quality, as if she shouldn't be over here. "I just finished cleaning the floors, the fridge, and the freezer, and Bo just got off the roof. This is the first chance we've had to eat since I came over. But I left you some potato salad and the pita stuff in the fridge so you could make your own, as I told you earlier. Didn't you eat?"

He wrinkled his nose. "I'm not big on rabbit food."

It was so strange to love a man who looked exactly like Bastian but not care for Bastian at all.

"Tastes great to me," Bo said.

"Just saying, I prefer a juicy burger or some fish and chips," he responded, "which is why I went to Samsons by the Sea. I thought for sure you'd be home by the time I got back..."

What was he implying? That he was judging how she spent her time? Keeping track of her? "Are you saying you were worried about me?" she asked, choosing the most favorable possibility.

"Just wondering what you could be doing over here for so long."

She gestured around them. "If you'd seen this place before, it would be obvious."

"Looks pretty good now."

"Because we've spent hours cleaning it. I wish we could've gotten some fans today. But there's only one restoration company on the island, and it's been overrun."

"Are you saying you have to come back tomorrow because now you need to get the fans up for Bo?"

Although Bo didn't react to Bastian's goading in an overt way, Ismay could see the subtle tightening around his eyes and mouth. He didn't like Bastian any more than she did. She didn't see how anyone could. Did the man have *any* friends?

Maybe that was part of his problem. He'd never learned how to get along with his peers.

"Bastian—" She was finally ready to call him on his behavior, and he could probably tell because he held up a hand and began laughing.

"Don't get bent out of shape, sis. I'm joking. I was just about to watch a movie and wanted to see if you'd like to join me."

Ismay didn't know how to react. She didn't find his kind of humor funny, and to switch gears so quickly was jarring. "I'll head back when we're finished eating," she said and, refusing to succumb to the pressure he was putting on her, she sat back down in front of her meal.

"Got it." Bastian winked at her before swinging his gaze to Bo. "I bet you're glad Ismay's here. This would've been a lot harder without her."

"He didn't ask for my help," Ismay volunteered.

"But I'm grateful for it," Bo said.

Because they were supporting each other, there wasn't much more Bastian could do to cause trouble, and he seemed to recognize that. "Okay, well, see you back at the house," he said and left.

After Bo closed the door, he paused at the kitchen sink—presumably to watch Bastian leave—before returning to the table.

"Sorry about that," Ismay murmured. She knew Bo had to hate Bastian's patronizing tone. Remy's brother was obviously trying to assert his superiority, but the fact that he felt the need to do that told Ismay he had self-esteem issues. Bastian probably felt threatened by Bo's quiet confidence, his self-assured manner, or just that indefinable something that made him so likeable. "He seems to have a problem with you. Has that always been the case?"

"It seems more pronounced than before. But don't worry about it," Bo said. "I've dealt with more than my fair share of assholes."

Ismay suffered through watching a movie with Bastian. He talked over most of it, but she wasn't that interested, anyway. He'd chosen a predictable action flick with exploding cars and men hanging from helicopters, and her mind was on other things. The stuff she'd found in the closet. The girl's picture she'd put on her phone. The comment Bo had made about Remy being the more difficult twin when they were children.

Who had told him that? And more difficult in what way?

Then there was her curiosity as to why Bastian had come to the island. He'd known she'd be here, that he wouldn't have the house to himself. But then, she got the impression he didn't like being alone. Maybe he'd been curious about her and simply wanted to meet her, plus coming here got him out of work. She'd heard plenty about how he avoided any kind of responsibility.

She was also thinking about Jack. Her sensitive, hardworking brother had to be devastated. She'd texted him as she walked back from Bo's, and he'd replied with a text that said he was surviving. He couldn't talk at the time, was currently helping harvest the snow peas on the farm, but she hoped they could speak later. She knew how hard it would be for him to go home to an empty house. Could she get him to come to Mariners for the summer? Could he be honest enough with their parents to admit that he didn't want to follow in their footsteps?

Even if he *did* want to be a farmer, she believed some time away—to meditate, cope with the divorce, and see another part of the country—would be good for him. What Ashleigh had done would be old news by the time he returned, which would take the edge off the spread of that gossip. And if he came right away, she could spend some quality time with him before Remy arrived—no matter where he stayed—and have a good excuse to escape Bastian.

"Can you believe he did that?"

Ismay blinked and looked over at Remy's brother. "I'm sorry. What are you referring to?"

"Aren't you watching?" he asked.

She cleared her throat. "I admit…my mind was wandering.

My brother's currently going through a divorce. I'm worried about him."

"Which brother?" Bastian said. "Remy told me you have like…a hundred."

He laughed, and she forced herself to smile, but in that moment, she knew she had to get away from him. He'd exhausted her patience. "It's Jack, the brother closest to me in age. Listen, I'm pretty tired. With the storm, it was hard to get enough sleep—"

"Even with Bo here?" he broke in.

She gritted her teeth before forcing her jaw to relax. "We were up late, what with the damage to his house and the power going out, and all that. I'm going to turn in. I hope you don't mind."

"You don't want to watch the rest of the movie?"

Hadn't she just said that? "No. I'm going to go call my brother."

"It's nearly eleven. Will he be up at this hour?"

"It's two hours earlier in Utah, and he was working when I tried to reach him earlier. He'll probably just be getting home."

Bastian gestured at the TV. "We can watch something else if you'd rather…"

Ignoring the offer, she got up. "I'll see you in the morning," she said, and felt a rush of relief once she'd climbed the stairs and closed the door to Remy's bedroom behind her.

"Thank God," she murmured and took out her phone. She was just sitting on the bed to call Jack when she received a text from Bo.

Thank you for your help today—and for the food. It was delicious.

You're welcome. Are you okay over there now? Power's still on?

I'm fine. How was the movie?

I would rather have played chess.

With you, she wanted to add, but knew that probably wouldn't sound right, given her relationship with Remy.

I don't think Bastian would be hard to beat.

She chuckled at his response. Not for you.

You don't give yourself enough credit. You're a fast learner.

I'm a good loser. ;) But something tells me he wouldn't be.

I'm guessing he'd be an even worse winner.

That was the worst thing Bo had allowed himself to say about Bastian, and it was a good point. She sent a laughing emoji. But then she felt guilty for talking about her fiancé's brother in such derogatory terms and changed the subject.

What are you doing?

Reading

What book?

Crime & Punishment

She'd been expecting a carpentry book or something like that—even a crime novel—but not one of the old classics.

Are you kidding?

No, why? Have you read it?

I haven't. Should I?

I would recommend it. It's a drama, a thriller. Even has some romance. All set in the back alleyways of Russia during the 1860s.

Sounds irresistible.

Are you serious? If so, I can pass it along to you when I'm done, if you'll turn it in to the library after. That's where I got it.

She hadn't been entirely serious. But why not give it a chance? She'd read a lot of the classics growing up but never that one.

Okay. I can do that.

Would be interested in hearing what you think.

We can discuss it after.

Her friendship with Bo was the only thing that was making her trip to the island tolerable. At least so far. She waited, hoping he'd say good-night. But she didn't receive anything else from him.

With a sigh, she called her brother.

For the first time in his life, Jack had taken a sleep aid. It hadn't been *too* powerful—he'd purchased it over the counter on his way home from the farm—so he hadn't been sure it would work. But miraculously, it had. He fell asleep almost as soon as his head hit the pillow and didn't wake up until the following morning at five thirty, his regular time, since he had to be at the farm at six o'clock.

He felt much better for a moment—clearheaded and free of pain. Then everything he'd been avoiding washed over him, and he groaned. Ashleigh's leaving hadn't just been a nightmare, as he'd hoped in those first few seconds of wakefulness. Living without her—being single and soon divorced—was his new reality.

He grabbed his phone half-hoping she'd tried to reach him. To take it all back. But she hadn't. All he had was a missed call from his sister.

Ismay was worried about him. He felt bad that he hadn't been more responsive. But he had to cope the best way he could, and that was what he'd been doing.

He checked the time on his phone again. It'd be seven thirty on Mariners. She'd probably be up, but just in case she wasn't, he didn't want to risk waking her. This was supposed to be vacation time, her chance to lounge around before starting her law practice.

He climbed out of bed, stood under the spray of a too-hot shower, then hurried to dress.

After he ate some cold cereal, he left his bowl in the sink. That wasn't what he'd normally do. He would've rinsed it and put it in the dishwasher so Ashleigh wouldn't wake up to a mess. But now that he was on his own, what did it really matter?

It was growing light as he pulled into his parents' driveway, but he could see that the barn door stood open. His father—and most likely Hank—were already out of the house, which came as no surprise. Buzz was nothing if not punctual. The rest of his brothers, except Ryan, who was away at college, wouldn't be available to help again until after they got home from school.

He turned off his engine, then sat in his truck staring out at the land on which he'd been born and raised. Did he want to live here his entire life? Die here like his parents would?

His father appeared in the doorway of the barn and looked over at him, so Jack got out.

Buzz waited as he trudged over. "You sleep okay last night?" he asked when Jack was close enough.

Apparently, he didn't look much better than he felt, or his

father probably wouldn't seem quite so worried. "I did." With a little help from the pill he'd taken. He didn't mention that, because he knew his father wouldn't like it. "I can't imagine Ashleigh with Jessica," he said. "I just can't wrap my mind around her being with anyone else."

"*Don't* imagine it," his father recommended and Jack followed him into the barn.

Sure enough, Hank was there, his dark blond hair standing up on one side, a testament to the fact he'd come to work right after rolling out of bed. "You okay, bro?" he said.

This time, Jack was able to meet his brother's gaze and nod.

"I'm sorry. I feel terrible for you. I feel sorry for all of us. We loved Ashleigh, too, you know?"

He nodded. "Thanks. I'm just…hoping I can recover a bit before word starts to spread."

Hank exchanged a look with their father.

"What?" Jack said.

"Word is already starting to spread," Buzz replied.

A sick feeling rose in the pit of Jack's stomach, making him wish he'd skipped breakfast. "How do you know?"

Hank indicated a basket covered with a towel sitting on one of the tables that held bushels of snow peas. "The Sandersons left that on the doorstep last night."

"What's in it?" Jack asked.

"All kinds of baked goods," Hank replied.

Jack walked over to take a look. He found a large loaf of banana nut bread, a dozen or more chocolate chip cookies in a red tin, several jars of peach jam, a jar of local honey, and some homemade fudge. The card read *We are thinking of you at this difficult time with love and support. The Sandersons.*

"That's really nice," he said. "But…how would the Sandersons know?" Although they were members of the same church and attended the same meetings, they weren't related to any of the families involved.

"Who knows?" Hank said. "We knew news would spread fast, and… I guess that's what it's doing."

Jack looked down at his phone and eyed that missed call from his only sister. Ismay had said he should come out to Mariners—escape, get away.

"What is it?" Hank asked when he didn't speak for several long moments.

"I'm leaving for a couple of months," he said.

Buzz had been fixing some broken baskets, fitting them with twine for the handles. At this, his head jerked up. "You're what?"

"I'm going to stay with Ismay on Mariners."

His father spoke carefully, calculatedly—as if he didn't want to set Jack off. "Okay, but…what will you do for work?"

"If I can't get a job there waiting tables or whatever, I guess I'll do nothing. But—" he took one more look at that basket and imagined what it would be like to walk into church for the next several weeks, possibly months, depending on whether Ashleigh and Jessica continued attending, and shook his head "—there's no way in hell I'm staying here."

11

It was a chilly morning with a biting wind, but Ismay had gone to the beach anyway. She wasn't about to hang around the house and have Bastian suggest they do something together. Apparently, he had some friends from college who were on the island for a few days—she'd heard him talking to one of them on the phone—so she was hoping he'd start hanging out with them and forget about her.

But she had a feeling *she* was part of the reason he'd come to the island. She just didn't understand what he was after…

She'd chosen to go to the public beach, since it was farther from him. But even the public area was almost deserted. That didn't bother her, though. In her current frame of mind, she preferred to be alone. Remy had called to see how she was doing, but it was a perfunctory call—one made out of obligation—and, as usual these days, he'd been in a hurry to get off. That final part of his board exams. She understood his need to study, but she couldn't help the nagging feeling that she was just something he'd collected along the way and now took for granted.

She zipped up the windbreaker she'd worn over her swimsuit, figuring she could take it off if the weather warmed up as the day progressed. She wouldn't be getting much of a tan this summer if it was going to be as cold as it had been. But she had bigger worries. Leaving her bag where she'd spread out her towel, she carried her cell phone as she walked along the beach.

It was good to be out, regardless, she told herself. It beat being stuck in the cottage during that terrible storm—or staying there and trying to avoid Bastian. She'd been tempted to stop by Bo's to see how he was doing before coming to the beach. But she knew it was sort of odd that she wanted to see him so soon. It was just that he was her only friend while she was here.

Her phone dinged, signaling a text. She hoped it was from Remy and that he'd say something so sweet and conciliatory she'd be able to let go of some of the resentment that was building up inside her. But it wasn't Remy; it was Jack—at last.

I've decided to come.

Stunned, she stopped walking. Did he mean to Mariners?

Instead of texting back, she called him, and this time he picked up.

"You're serious?" she said.

"Totally," he replied.

"When can you come?"

"If I'm going to cut out of here, I might as well do it right away, when it'll have the biggest benefit."

"As in…this week?"

"As in…as soon as I can make the arrangements. I'll stay in a hotel, if I have to."

But he wouldn't be able to afford a hotel on Mariners. A cheap hotel was three hundred dollars a night, and with Bastian at the cottage, she didn't dare do anything as presumptuous as have her brother join her there.

She thought of Bo and the neighbor Honey. He'd indicated there was a possible opportunity for Jack to house-sit, but she needed to confirm. "I'll figure out someplace for you to stay. Just...get on a plane. I can meet you at the airport."

Silence.

"Jack?" she said.

She heard him suck in a long breath, as if he were finally able to breathe after an extended period of finding it difficult. "That feels good," he said.

She was confused. "What feels good?"

"To know if I make this jump, my big sister will be there to catch me."

"Of course," she said. "Always."

But she was afraid she might have trouble living up to that promise. After they disconnected, she hurried back to where she'd left her stuff, balled up her towel, shoved it in her beach bag, and called an Uber.

Bo was repairing the roof when a car pulled up at the end of his drive. He watched as Ismay got out and hurried across the lawn, her long shapely legs bare beneath an oversized white sweatshirt, her feet in matching flip-flops. She also had her hair pulled up into a ponytail, a colorful beach bag slung over one shoulder and sunglasses resting on top of her head.

She looked good. Too good for a guy who hadn't been with a woman in so long. He'd had a few encounters after he got out of prison, when he was looking for someplace to belong. But that was before he made his way to Mariners. He didn't dare do anything here that might create complications. If he allowed anyone to get too close, it could threaten the secret he guarded, and ultimately mean he'd have to leave the island and the safe haven he'd found here.

Even if he didn't have to keep everyone at arm's length, the last woman he could ever get involved with would be his employer's son's fiancée.

But Ismay not only looked like everything a man in his position would dream about, she acted so happy and eager to see him, with her wide smile and bright eyes, that he couldn't help feeling something he'd rather not feel—a measure of excitement to see her, too.

He'd been too friendly with her, he realized. He needed to back away…

"Hey, what's going on?" he asked, standing.

She shaded her eyes with one hand as she looked up at him. "I just talked to Jack."

"Your brother…"

"Yes. He said he's catching the first flight he can get out of Salt Lake."

"And coming here?"

She nodded, seemed to remember she had a pair of sunglasses, and put them on to help cut the sun's glare. "Is that okay? Do you think that house-sitting gig is still a possibility?"

He'd barely mentioned it to Honey. He doubted she could leave quite this soon, but would definitely follow up. What if she said no? He felt he'd have to find a backup. Or…why couldn't he stay at the cottage? Bastian was there, yes, but there was certainly room for all three of them.

"I'll let Honey know he's coming—and that he's coming right away. But if that doesn't work out, can't he just stay with you at the cottage until we can find something else?"

"If Bastian wasn't there, I'd talk to Remy and possibly risk it. But with Bastian around, taking note of everything I do and painting it in the worst possible light, I'm afraid he'd complain to his parents, and I've never even met them. I don't want them to think I'm abusing their generosity and hospitality by bringing more guests into their home."

Bo considered his second bedroom. He definitely wasn't looking for a roommate. He didn't want someone who might ask nosy questions, then come away feeling he was being cagey or deceptive. Letting *anyone* into his life was a risk, especially letting them get that close. But maybe he could take in Ismay's brother for a night or two…

Except he couldn't say the Windsors would like that any better, worrying it would make them look bad to have their potential daughter-in-law's brother relegated to the caretaker's bungalow.

Still, he couldn't dash the hope that was in Ismay's face. He was pretty certain that surviving the storm together had made her think of him as her ally. "We'll figure something out," he heard himself say.

"Thank you! I hope Honey will be open to this. Tell her… tell her we'll pay some rent besides. Maybe that'll help. Neither one of us has a lot, but this means so much to me. I *have* to help him get out of Tremonton as soon as possible. He's depending on me."

"Right. Just…let me know when he'll be here."

"Okay." Her smile showed her teeth as she waved. "Thank you! I can't tell you how much I appreciate it."

He waved back, then cursed himself as she left. Remy should be the one trying to help her with her brother—not *him*. So why wasn't that happening? Had she even asked him?

If not—or he'd refused—could it be that their relationship wasn't as solid as it should be?

That thought excited Bo. It meant Ismay might also know, on some level, that she wasn't with the best guy. He thought she was asking for heartbreak getting with someone as entitled, spoiled, selfish, and domineering as Remy—and he'd essentially told her so on that very first night.

He couldn't even imagine how good it would feel to take Remy's place—to have her step up to him and slide her arms around his neck as he lowered his mouth to hers.

Jerking his mind away from a precipice that was all too tempting, he swore. He had nothing to offer her. It was dangerous just to let himself entertain the idea.

Quickly blocking her from his mind, he got back to work.

★★★

Ismay sat in the chair swing on the porch as she drank a kombucha and talked to Remy. She was careful not to bother him unless she absolutely had to tell him something, so she had been surprised when he called her just as it was getting dark.

"You done studying for the day?" she asked.

"Yeah. I need a break. I don't think I'm retaining anything anymore."

"Don't stress over it," she said. "You'll do great. You always do."

"I hope you're right. How's the weather there now?"

She gazed out at a tranquil sea. It was so peaceful and calm, it was hard to remember how rough it'd been only a day or two earlier. "Beautiful."

"Awesome. And how are you getting along with Bastian?"

"Fine," she replied, even though she still didn't know how she was going to get through the days Bastian spent on the island with her. "Why?"

"I feel kind of bad you're stranded there with him. He can be…a bit much."

In her opinion, Bastian was someone only a mother could love. But she wouldn't allow herself to say so. "He's out right now with some friends." She hoped he wouldn't get home until late—after she was in bed. He'd invited her to go with him, but she'd said she was planning to wander along the seashore, looking for shells.

"Is Bo going with you?" Bastian had asked.

She'd acted affronted. They had no plans. But once she'd finished her walk, she did find herself wondering what he was doing.

"You might want to stay away from Bastian when he gets back," Remy was saying. "We always fight when he's been drinking."

She rolled her eyes. *Great. More good news.* "I'll steer clear."

"That'd be smart. How's Jack doing?"

She'd texted to tell him what'd happened to her brother's marriage, and he'd responded with the appropriate amount of surprise. But she suspected he didn't truly care.

He'd never even met Jack. So maybe she was expecting too much—especially considering the way she felt about *his* brother. She and Remy probably couldn't have gotten through the last three years without the support they'd given each other. He'd covered some of the expenses she would've been hard-pressed to cover while putting herself through school, and she'd served as an anchor for him—had helped keep him stable under the pressure and had done a lot of the housework so he could focus on his studies. So far, their relationship had been about sticking together and getting through their demanding curriculums. That didn't necessarily mean they cared deeply for each other's families. Not yet. "He's having a hard time."

"That's too bad. What he's going through..." He whistled. "That'd be rough. I mean...*humiliating*, right?"

Whether it was more humiliating than it would be if Ashleigh had left Jack for a guy was a whole other conversation. She didn't want to go there, because she knew it might cause an argument. As far as she was concerned, Remy wasn't as kind or tolerant as he should be.

She considered telling him that Jack was "thinking" about coming to the island, so that he wasn't blindsided when she told him Jack was there. But she also knew he'd resent the added complication when he was already dealing with so much.

She deliberated over that point until they'd discussed a few more things—their future life together, her career plans. These were topics they discussed often because they had yet to arrive at any solid conclusions. So she wasn't all that invested in the conversation. She was too busy trying to decide what to do about Jack.

But she knew if her brother was coming, she had to say something eventually. Deciding to get it over with, she said they'd talk more about when to return to LA and whether she should join an established firm once Remy was on Mariners. Then she steered the conversation back to her brother. "My mom's really broken up about what happened with Jack. It's been hard on the whole family."

"Of course it is," he said, but she couldn't detect much empathy.

"I told him he should get out of Tremonton—out of Utah. He doesn't want to be a farmer, anyway. So why stick around for all the gossip and awkwardness? If he leaves now, he might be able to cut the ties that have held him in place with my parents, freeing him up to do anything he wants."

"That's true," Remy agreed. "With such a big upheaval, now would probably be a good time to raise that issue—get it all over with at once."

"Except he doesn't really have anywhere else to go. So I told him to come out here for the summer and see what it's like on the island."

"Wait…what'd you say?" Remy asked.

She curled her fingernails into her palms. "I told him to come out here. I'd love for the two of you to meet. We could…we could have a lot of fun together."

"While he's busted up over the failure of his marriage? How much fun will *that* be?"

"We could cheer him up, help him get over it."

"But this is our summer off," he argued. "We've worked hard for this. Why would you want to get involved in someone else's divorce, especially now?"

"Because it's not just *someone else's divorce*, Remy. It's my brother's divorce. And he's only twenty-five."

"I don't think having him come to Mariners is the answer. He wouldn't have a job. Wouldn't know anyone else. For God's sake, what would he do all summer?"

"The same things we're going to do," she said. "Meditate. Read. Relax. Go to the beach. Enjoy the food, the art, the shopping. He could catch up on his sleep and think about where he wants his life to go."

Silence. She could tell Remy wasn't pleased. She could even sort of understand. They had *really* been looking forward to a certain experience and having Jack around would change that. But it didn't have to be for the worse. She wasn't happy about his brother showing up out of the blue, either. At least *her* brother wasn't an asshole like Bastian was.

"He's a cool guy," she insisted.

"Ismay, we'll have to entertain him twenty-four/seven. And where will he stay, anyway? With us?"

She was glad she'd been intuitive enough to know Remy wouldn't want her brother at the cottage with them. "There's a neighbor here who wants to travel to the mainland for at least part of the summer and needs someone to house-sit for her. Maybe he could do that. It'd be free, and he wouldn't have to stay with us."

More silence.

"Remy?"

"Surely, he doesn't want to come clear across the country. I mean, your dad's a farmer, and we're going into summer and fall—how will your folks get by without him?"

"Hank just graduated from college, so he's home now. And he likes working the land. This might be the only opportunity Jack has to escape a life he doesn't truly want."

Remy sighed audibly. "It's just that…it won't be the same, Is. I don't have anything against your brother. But this was our big reward, our last hurrah. I'd hate to let anything ruin—er, change it."

"Having Jack here wouldn't ruin anything. It wouldn't even change it that much." She wanted to say she hadn't expected his brother to be around, either. But she couldn't complain because it was his family's vacation home. She was lucky to have the use of it. "Will you give it a chance?" she asked instead.

"Wait." He sounded suspicious. "Don't tell me he's already agreed to come..."

She winced. "He has. He could change his mind, but—"

"So the house-sitting gig is a go?"

She didn't have an answer on that yet, but Remy had confirmed, by his reaction, that she wouldn't be able to offer Jack a room at the cottage. Although...if she handled her brother's lodging and he stayed elsewhere, she didn't see how Remy could be that upset about having him on the island. The Windsors didn't own all of Mariners. "If not, I'll find him a hotel."

"With what money?" he asked. "You're always scraping to get by!"

Because she didn't have rich parents who paid for everything! She opened her mouth to say so but thought better of it. He'd just accuse her of being too sensitive or jealous. "He has some savings."

"Shit," he muttered. "He's going to come, isn't he?"

Finally irritated beyond her ability to hold back, she felt her patience snap. "Why not? Maybe he and Bastian can hang out together," she said and disconnected.

Tossing her phone on the seat of the swing, she got up and began to pace. She shouldn't have agreed to come here. It'd sounded so fun at the time, but she didn't like being at the Windsors' mercy, having to be so grateful to be using the cottage that she couldn't feel free to help her own brother.

She was mumbling all the things she wanted to say to Remy—that she wouldn't let herself—when her phone dinged. That had to be him. No doubt he'd texted her, angry that she'd hung up on him. She could already hear him berating her for not having more understanding when he was under so much stress, saying that if he failed his exams, it'd be because she distracted him and couldn't take care of herself and her own problems for a few weeks.

Reluctantly, she scooped up her phone to see if she was right. Remy had tried calling back—three times. But he hadn't texted her. The text had come from Bo. And there were no words, just a picture of a chess board on his kitchen table.

12

Having Ismay over was a mistake, and Bo knew it. He could've sent her a link to play a digital game of chess, which would've allowed her to stay at the cottage or play from wherever she was. That would've been safer, especially with Bastian around to make a big deal of them getting together again.

But Bo hadn't sent an electronic link. He wanted to see her too badly. He'd wrestled with himself for an hour before giving in and inviting her to play. Then he'd hoped she'd have other plans and turn him down, because it would keep them both safe from spending more time together and, possibly, getting too close.

Instead, she'd accepted his invitation, shown up with a bottle of wine and the groceries to make a cheesy sourdough bread appetizer, which she'd just put in the oven. And now she was sitting across from him, puzzling over her next move in the game they'd started before she'd stopped to make the appetizer.

She touched her knight as if she was going to move it and looked up at him. He shook his head. Then she fingered her rook, and he nodded. She was learning fast, but there was no replacement for experience. He probably helped her more than he should. She'd learn faster if he let her make more mistakes—

but his guidance kept the game interesting, and it made him feel better about beating her. At least he gave her a fighting chance.

"Why shouldn't I have moved my knight?" she asked.

"Because it would've left your queen vulnerable."

"No, it wouldn't." She pointed to the pawn protecting her queen.

He showed her what would've happened two moves down the line, once he'd changed the position of his bishop, and she frowned as she propped her chin on her hand. "Damn. It's frustrating that I don't seem to be improving."

"No one improves that much over the course of a few games. You know what Malcolm Gladwell says."

"What does Malcolm Gladwell say? And where did he say it? In *The Tipping Point*? Because I read that book and—"

"It's in *Outliers*," he said. "Gladwell claims it takes ten thousand hours of intensive practice to get really good at anything."

"You've put ten thousand hours into learning this game?" she asked skeptically.

He remembered the long days in prison, when—other than lifting weights or reading—chess was all he had to fill his time. It was also the only way he could make a few bucks, so he played whenever he could, almost as if it were his job. They weren't supposed to gamble, but that certainly hadn't stopped them. They bet on almost anything and wagered almost anything they could trade—cigarettes, drugs, cash, a cell phone, food, even gum. "Maybe not that many. But close."

"When you were young, or…"

"I've always liked it," he said to avoid a more direct answer. Then he asked her a question—to distract her but also because he'd been curious. "That picture you showed me…"

"What picture?" she asked, preoccupied with the game again since he'd already made his move.

"Of the girl."

Suddenly shifting uncomfortably, she looked up before taking her turn. "What about it?"

"Who is she?"

"I don't know. That's why I asked you if you'd ever seen her."

"But…if you don't know her, why do you have her picture?"

She began to dig at her cuticles.

"Ismay, what is it?" He'd become an expert at reading body language—a very important skill, especially while locked up. His ability to sense what someone else might be thinking and feeling and, consequently, what that person might do, had probably saved his life on more than one occasion. But it didn't take an expert to realize she was uneasy. "Something about that picture troubles you. Why?"

Lines of consternation appeared on her normally smooth forehead. "I don't know what it means."

"What it means?" he repeated. "How do you know it means anything?"

"Maybe it doesn't."

This conversation wasn't making any sense to him. "Where'd you get it?"

"I found it."

"Where?" he persisted.

"I don't… I don't want to talk about it. And please, don't mention it to anyone else."

She'd already asked him for his discretion. Why was she so afraid he might mention it to others? "I won't," he said. "And that's a promise. You believe me, don't you?"

"I do." Her lips curved into a reluctant smile. "Thank you. It's just that… I never should've brought it up. I wouldn't have if I wasn't so worried that—"

"That…" he prompted.

"That I'd be stupid to ignore it."

Now he was *really* curious. They stared at each other for several seconds without speaking. Then he said, "This sounds kind of ominous. I think you should tell me what's going on."

Leaning on her elbows, she pretended to puzzle over the game, but he could tell she wasn't seeing what was right in front of her. She was too deep in her own thoughts.

He guided her hand to the pawn she should move. "This one," he said, and the desire to continue touching her suddenly welled up. She was incredibly beautiful. That and the fact that he genuinely liked her filled him with desire.

Knowing he had to be extra vigilant, he forced himself to withdraw before it seemed odd that his hand was lingering. He took his turn, then the timer on her phone went off.

"The bread," she said, sounding relieved by the interruption, and jumped up to get it out of the oven.

Bo didn't bring up the subject of the picture again. He wanted her to enjoy herself while she was with him, didn't want to put her on edge. He also knew that if he wanted her to trust him, he had to let her arrive at her own decision.

They enjoyed the cheesy bread with butter and garlic and played several more games of chess. Then they played cards, and when they'd finished the wine, and she was sitting on his couch and he was in his chair, they'd talked about the books he'd recently read, her brother's divorce, and her hope that Jack could take care of Honey's house. Until she said, "Remember when I asked you if you could ever really know someone?"

For a second, Bo feared she was talking about him—that she suspected something—and froze. But there was no accusation or anger in her tone. It was just his own guilty conscience that made him feel as if she'd found him out. "I do, and I'd like to know why you were thinking about that," he asked casually.

"It's because everyone has secrets. It's not as if your friend or significant other is going to tell you something he or she knows you won't approve of. With humans, it's all about image and… being accepted, even admired."

Sometimes hiding certain facts was about more than that—it was about being able to make a living and survive outside of prison. "You're referring to Ashleigh?" he guessed, since they'd been talking so much about Jack and his situation.

Ismay had drunk enough wine that she seemed more relaxed than at any other point in the evening. "And Remy," she said. "How do you know if you can really trust someone to be who you think they are? It'd suck to get an unpleasant surprise after you'd spent ten or twenty years of your life with them."

"I guess you look for signs," Bo said. "Notice how they behave in certain situations, especially when they're under stress."

"Remy's always under stress," she said. "It's been a long hard road to get to where he is now. But if people are smart—like he is—they'll know how to behave even if that's not who they really are, right?"

That was what he'd tried to tell her the first night during the storm. She needed to look twice at Remy—at whether she really wanted to tie herself to someone as spoiled and narcissistic as he was. But Bo was so attracted to her he didn't know if he dared to say that. He was afraid those words would make his own admiration of her too transparent.

"Think about serial killers," she continued.

"Serial killers?" he echoed. "That's a big leap. What makes you think of serial killers in the same breath as your fiancé?"

When she didn't answer, he realized she didn't find his comment funny and stopped chuckling. "Ismay?"

"I'm just thinking about how difficult it is to catch a serial killer—because they blend in. Many live regular lives—have wives, kids, jobs. No one suspects them of such heinous crimes. And when the truth comes out, it seems like the family is always shocked."

"There are signs those people aren't like everyone else," he insisted, and he should know. He'd lived among some of the worst human beings. "Someone just has to be paying attention."

She scooted forward, her eyes focused and intense, despite the wine. "But the signs that signal something is wrong could also be completely innocuous. How would you ever tell the difference?"

He rubbed his chin. "From what I've read on the subject, lack of empathy is a big one."

"But a person can lack empathy and *not* be a murderer. You'd hate to falsely accuse someone of a terrible violent act without proof."

"I guess a lack of empathy is just the first sign. Then you have reason to look deeper."

Her gaze fell to the carpet.

"Ismay?"

"What?"

"Are we talking about that photograph again?"

When she covered her mouth in regret, he understood that they were. "Where'd you find it?"

"I can't say. I'd feel too guilty if I was wrong and it meant nothing."

"Did Remy have it somewhere?" That had to be it. Otherwise, she'd be able to say. "If so, that picture could be a girl he knew way back when, a girlfriend. I get the impression there've been a lot of women in his life. I wouldn't worry about it."

She didn't react to the "a lot of women" comment. She seemed genuinely concerned that photograph signified more. "But… what about the other things?"

"What other things?" She hadn't mentioned anything else…

She shook her head. "Never mind. Please. I've already said too much." Picking up her phone, she got to her feet. "I'd better go. I'm hoping to beat Bastian home, so I won't have to lie to him about where I've been."

Bo got up, too. "If you won't tell me where you found that picture, or what you found with it, will you at least tell me *when* you found it?"

At first, he thought she wasn't going to answer. But then she squeezed her eyes closed and said, "The night of the storm. When the power was out."

For years, Bo had been housed with violent men, so he'd come to know some of them quite well. He'd never thought his experience with the criminal element would carry over into life after his release, especially on Mariners. Since he'd come here, there hadn't even been a major crime committed—other than the usual drunken brawl at one of the bars or a domestic dispute. So, even though she was a bit rattled by whatever she'd found, it couldn't mean anything, could it?

A ding sounded, causing Ismay to look down at her phone. "Oh, God," she said.

"What is it?" Bo asked.

"Bastian just sent me a text asking where I am."

"What are you going to say?"

"I'm definitely not going to tell him I'm here."

He nodded. "I think that would be best."

She'd said too much. Bo came across as so solid and easy to trust, and she'd been so worried about her relationship with Remy and what she'd found that she'd given in to the need to confide in someone and chosen him. But she should've chosen Jack or someone else—except Jack was going through enough. She didn't need to get him worried about her. She didn't want to poison anyone in her family against Remy, so maybe telling Bo had been the wisest choice.

Except what about her loyalty to Remy? She was *engaged* to him, for crying out loud, and Bo worked for his family.

Ismay felt nauseous as she slipped out the back door of Bo's bungalow and circled around the property so she could approach the cottage from the road. She hated feeling she had to hide where she'd been—she and Bo had done nothing inappropriate—but there was no way she wanted Bastian to learn they'd been together again, especially when she'd turned down his invitation to accompany him to town. She didn't want that getting back to Remy.

Stop obsessing about it and just get back to the cottage. There'd be plenty of time to kick herself later. She hadn't answered Bastian's message, didn't think she should have to report her whereabouts—and she would tell him so if he complained—but that didn't mean he wouldn't grill her the moment she stepped into the house. She needed to be prepared. If she gave him any reason to doubt her, he'd keep even a closer watch over her.

As soon as she saw the cottage through the trees, she threw back her shoulders and took a deep breath. "Why is Remy's twin even here?" she grumbled but forced a smile, just to get herself in the right frame of mind before climbing the stairs to the front door.

"There you are!" he said when she walked in. "Didn't you get my text?"

Steeling herself against the irritation that immediately reared up, she held her smile firmly in place and spoke as breezily as she could. "I did, but I was already on my way home, so I knew I'd be seeing you shortly."

"Where've you been?"

His imperious tone got under her skin, but still, she smiled. "I went to the beach, like I said."

"And *then*?"

She felt her jaw tighten. "Then I decided to walk to that restaurant about a mile away—Mariners Grill?—and have a glass of wine." She'd almost said *dessert* but was afraid he might ask what kind, and she had no idea what they served. Thankfully, she'd caught herself.

"If you'd answered my text, I could've picked you up in the Jeep," he said.

"It wasn't far."

When she crossed the room behind him and started up the

steps to Remy's bedroom, he got up off the couch and turned to face her. "Where are you going now?"

"To bed," she replied. "I'm tired."

The way he tilted his head and looked at her made her pause. "What is it?" she asked.

"How long have you been dating my brother?"

"Almost three years. We've been living together for two. Why?"

He didn't answer her question. "Then you probably know each other pretty well."

"I'd like to think so." But there was certainly some question about that, which was why she was so worried about what she'd found in Remy's closet—and why she'd finally broken down and told Bo about it.

"And you still want to marry him?" Bastian asked.

"Excuse me?"

A strange expression came over his face—one she could only interpret as…sadness or regret, maybe? "Never mind," he said and turned back to the TV.

Taking the opportunity to escape him, Ismay hurried up the stairs, grabbed her pajamas, and crossed the hall to the bathroom, where she locked the door behind her. She was going to try to relax in a hot bath. Despite what she'd said to Bastian, she wasn't quite ready for bed. Too much was going on in her mind, from the argument she'd had with Remy—she still hadn't called him back—to how much she enjoyed being with Bo even when they weren't doing anything, and the danger she'd created by sharing some of what she'd found in Remy's closet with him. What was going on with her? She should be having the time of her life. She'd just graduated from law school and was supposed to be celebrating. Instead, she was obsessing over a stupid duffel bag filled with underwear and jewelry that could mean nothing, arguing with Remy, and trying to avoid her future brother-in-law.

With a sigh, she stacked her clothes on the closed toilet seat while she filled the tub and was about to step in the water when she paused for a second to text Jack.

Are you still coming?

He answered right away. If you're sure you want me to.

She wanted him to—but Remy had made his reluctance and disappointment plain. Because she didn't have her fiancé's support, it wasn't going to be easy to have her brother on Mariners.

Still, she wrote back with confidence. It wouldn't serve any purpose to make Jack feel hesitancy on her part. Of course I want you to.

Then I'm still coming.

When?

Just told Mom and Dad before I left the farm. So I'm looking for a flight right now.

She could only imagine how surprised her parents were by this development and wondered if they were upset she'd made him such an offer. They had Hank to help with the farm, but more hands were always better. They'd probably been counting on having both their sons. And they might feel as though escaping the situation was taking the coward's way out. Her parents were like that. They lived on principle, and sometimes they chose to take a stand that made no sense to her. How'd they take the news?

They were supportive.

She sagged in relief. At least she wouldn't have her parents to contend with. Just Remy. Thank God, because Jack needed their support now more than ever.

That's wonderful!

I was shocked.

Maybe they understand this is what's best for you.

It's hard enough for them to be the center of town gossip. Did you find out about the house-sitting gig?

Not yet. But I'm working on it.

Okay. I'll let you know when my plane gets in. I can't wait to lock up this empty house and drive away—possibly for good.

I'm looking forward to it.

Setting her phone on the counter, Ismay stepped into the warm water. It wasn't going to be easy making sure Remy had the summer he was looking forward to while trying to entertain and support Jack, especially with Bastian thrown into the mix. But she'd figure out a way to make it all work because her brother needed her. She wasn't going to let him down.

13

Could it be that he wasn't the only person with something to hide?

Bo scratched his neck as he stared up at the cottage from the beach. He'd walked down to the ocean, hoping to get close enough to the Windsors' vacation home to be able to tell if Bastian was giving Ismay a hard time. He figured he'd make up an excuse to knock and interrupt if he had to, say he had to check on the roof or the wiring or some bullshit. Bastian wouldn't know he was lying. He didn't know how to do anything.

But it would seem odd that he'd come by so late. He felt he could potentially cover for it, but it was better that he didn't need to. All was quiet, except his thoughts. What else, besides that photograph, had Ismay discovered at the cottage? Why did it alarm her so much? And where, exactly, had she found it?

It had to be something significant. She'd received that text from Bastian and hurried off before he could press the issue, but he was beginning to think he needed to get her to tell him, in case there *was* something to be worried about. She'd been talking about serial killers, for God's sake. What on earth could've made her go *there*?

After pulling his phone from his pocket, he sent her a text.

I think you should tell me.

Fortunately, she seemed to know what he meant and he didn't have to clarify.

No. I feel bad. I shouldn't have mentioned it.

Why do you feel bad?

Because I don't want to make Remy look like he might be violent or someone he's not.

Violent? What could've alarmed her to that degree?

So you found whatever it is in Remy's room?

No response.

In his mind, that was a yes. She just didn't want to acknowledge it.

Tell me this: is it some kind of rape kit with a rope, zip ties, a knife, a ski mask—stuff like that?

No. None of those.

That came as a relief. And yet she was still worried.

So what could it be?

Again, no response.

Ismay, you can trust me. I'm not going to tell anyone. And I'm not out to hurt Remy. I promise. I won't go to the police or anyone else unless you give the word.

His phone rang, and her name came up on his screen.

"Hi."

"How late do you plan on staying up?" she asked, her voice soft enough to make him believe she didn't want Bastian to overhear.

"As late as I need to in order to figure this thing out. Why?"

There was a long pause. "What you said before about certain signs meaning someone should take a closer look..."

"Yes..."

"Maybe you're right. I'm not out to make a false accusation. I'm just...trying to be cautious, you know?"

He *didn't* know, not exactly. "What does that mean?"

"It means I'm going to show you," she said.

Ismay waited until the TV went off and she heard Bastian walk up the stairs and past her door. Then she waited thirty minutes longer, just to give him more time to fall asleep before she climbed out of bed and texted Bo.

I'm coming.

I'll be waiting for you on the beach.

She'd wanted to meet in the backyard, but he'd made a good point. The window in the master overlooked the backyard.

After she pulled on some sweats, she took the duffel bag from its hiding place in the closet wall, moving as quietly as possible.

She hated even having it in her hands. But she found it comforting that she was going to share the burden of its existence with someone she liked and trusted—even though she hadn't known Bo long. She needed a second opinion. If those items ever turned out to be the warning signal they seemed to be, and someone got hurt, she'd never be able to forgive herself.

Hindsight was always twenty-twenty, she thought wryly. But

she'd been taught to do the right thing, so she hoped she was making the best choice. She hated knowing she might be doing her fiancé a disservice…

Sliding the handles of the duffel bag over her shoulder, she opened the bedroom door and peered into the hall.

Although everything downstairs was quiet and dark, the TV in the master was on. She had no way of knowing if Bastian was still awake, but she felt terrible keeping Bo up, so she decided not to wait any longer.

She checked for a light under Bastian's door but couldn't see anything beyond the shifting pattern of colors coming from the TV, so she drew a measured breath to calm her nerves and moved carefully down the stairs and across the living room to the front door.

She felt the most exposed here, in such a large space with no cover, so she didn't even allow herself to look back. She just unlocked the door and slipped outside, hurrying across the porch and taking the stairs as fast as she could.

Almost before she knew it, she was running across the front yard, through the gate, and down the little walkway to the soft sandy beach.

Bo was waiting for her, as promised. In the light of a full moon, she could see him walking along the shoreline—his head bent, his white shirt rippling softly in the breeze, his khaki shorts low on his hips, and his feet bare despite the cold—and started to have second thoughts. Was she doing the right thing? She'd known Remy longer than she'd known Bo. She'd *lived* with Remy, slept with him. Why would she ever trust a stranger—*this* stranger—over him?

She almost turned back. But then Bo happened to glance up and see her, and she realized she couldn't change her mind now. She'd already told him enough that he knew something was up—possibly something serious. And somehow, she *did* trust him.

"Bastian finally went to bed?" he said as she approached.

"Who knows? That guy's a night owl, never seems to sleep. But he's in his room with the TV on and the light off, so… I figured he couldn't hear me leave the house."

She grimaced as she slid the duffel bag off her arm and handed it to him. "I hope I'm doing the right thing…"

"This is what you found?" he asked.

She nodded.

"And where was it?"

"Hidden in the wall of Remy's closet."

His head came up. *"In the wall?"*

That was part of the reason she was worried. If those things were truly innocuous, why would they be in such a strange place—a place where someone who had something to hide would put them? "Yes. After the power went off, I was looking for a lighter and I noticed a loose board above the high shelf in the closet. I hoped I'd discover pot paraphernalia or something. But it was this duffel bag and its contents."

He seemed concerned and curious as he unzipped the bag and looked inside. Then, because it was probably tough to see with his body creating a shadow, he squatted down, set the bag on the beach in front of him, and pulled out the panties and jewelry that were inside. "Where do you think this stuff came from?" he asked in surprise.

"That's just it," she said. "I don't know."

He held each pair of panties up and checked the size, something she hadn't thought to do, mostly because she'd been loath to even touch them. "They're not from the same person," he said. "At least, they're not all the same size."

That didn't make her feel any more comfortable.

"I've heard of men who like to wear women's underwear. Maybe Remy's one of them. But that doesn't explain the jewelry," he said, looking at a heart necklace.

"What do you think?" she asked.

He seemed as bewildered as she was. "I can't say with any degree of certainty. But… I can tell you what it reminds me of."

The apprehension in his voice caused her heart to sink. She could tell he was reluctant to say, and she could guess why. "Trophies?" she volunteered.

He blanched but nodded. "Maybe it *wasn't* Remy who put this stuff in the wall…"

"That's what I want to believe," she said. "But I found his notebook with it—not inside the wall but very close to the loose board."

"How do you know it was his notebook?"

"His name's on the cover. And I recognize his work."

He pulled the photograph out of the bag, sat on the beach instead of squatting, and used his phone's flashlight to study it.

"This is all so weird, isn't it?" she said as she stood over him and watched. "Do you think whoever owned the cottage before Remy's family might've left this stuff there? It's possible he didn't know what was right behind the wall when he put his notebook on that shelf."

"His family has owned that house for three generations. These panties would look very different if they were from a hundred years ago," he said.

"True." The style and brands looked like those she'd been familiar with growing up. That was partly what alarmed her. The items inside weren't that old. The jewelry made it possible to date them as well. "Who could that girl be? I tried using Google's facial recognition software, but… I couldn't come up with anything."

He didn't respond.

"Bo?"

"Hmm?"

"What're you thinking?"

"I'm thinking I should keep this stuff and try to figure out where it came from."

"No! What if it's Remy's and he tries to look for it?"

"That's a good point. But if we return it to that hole in the wall, you'll need to send me that picture, at least. It's too dark to snap another."

"And what will you do with it?"

"I'll see what I can find out."

A shiver rolled down her spine. What was she getting herself into? Did she really want to dig further? This was a small island. What were the chances that Remy wouldn't hear something about it? "I don't know if we should do anything," she said.

Bo put everything back inside the duffel bag and zipped it before getting up and handing it to her. "Ismay, this stuff raises some serious questions. I think we need to figure out where it came from."

She gripped her forehead. "What if Remy finds out?"

Bo didn't look as though he had a good answer. "I'll do my best to keep it quiet, but I guess there are no guarantees."

Should she just tell her fiancé about what she'd found? She would rather be up front about it. But if she told him, and he was guilty of harming the women who'd owned these panties and jewelry, he'd just deny it. She couldn't see how that would help. She'd just wonder if she could believe him, introducing more tension into their relationship.

The best possible option was to try to determine who the girl was and go from there. She might as well do all she could to quiet her fears. Maybe by the time he arrived, she'd have the answers she needed and would be able to move forward without the nagging doubts and concerns that'd plagued her since finding that duffel.

She'd actually had doubts about marrying Remy *before* she came to Mariners, she reminded herself. That was partly why what she'd found had rattled her so badly. But putting her questions on the contents and placement of that duffel bag to rest would enable her to focus on the smaller problems she'd been expecting to sort out this summer. She'd be relieved just to return to her former anxieties and fears.

"It probably won't come to anything," she said.

"You're right," Bo agreed. "I doubt it will. But..."

"Just in case," she finished for him.

"Just in case," he repeated.

She covered her face with one hand before dropping it so she could text him the image. "Okay. But please...be as discreet as possible."

"Trust me, if anyone in the Windsor family finds out I'm asking questions that could even remotely imply one of them might be guilty of a crime, I'd lose my job. So I'm not eager for them to find out, either."

"Oh, no," Ismay said with a wince. "I probably shouldn't have dragged you into this. I didn't realize it could put *you* at risk. I just... I don't know... I trust you, for some reason. I—I like you."

There was a second when his eyes met hers and she could've sworn he was about to say he liked her, too. She could tell he did. But he straightened instead, and his smile morphed into a scowl. "It's probably better if we don't get too close," he said. "But I'll let you know what I find."

Surprised that he'd suddenly stiff-armed her, she felt her jaw drop. She wanted to make it clear that she hadn't meant *too* much by what she'd said, but he didn't give her the chance. He headed down the beach, no doubt intending to circle around to his house farther up the shoreline.

Stung by his reaction, she dropped the duffel bag on the sand, sank down next to it, and burrowed deeper into her sweatshirt while watching the white foamy waves roll almost all the way up to her feet before falling back into the ocean. Had she been out of line? Had what she'd said sounded as though she was making a play for him?

Maybe so. She'd been too impetuous, spoken directly from the heart, which embarrassed her now. She took out her phone to text him an apology, but she was afraid making a point of that would only turn the incident into a bigger gaffe.

Instead, she messaged her brother. I can't wait until you get here. Maybe then, with his steadying influence, she could find her balance again…

Good because I was just about to let you know I get in tomorrow night.

She dropped her head back to appeal to the moon. *"Tomorrow night?"* That didn't give her much time. But she could see why he'd leave immediately if he was going to leave at all. Why suffer through facing everyone in Tremonton if he didn't have to?

Perfect, she wrote back. But nothing seemed to be perfect at the moment.

Bo was restless when he returned to the cabin. He should've been worried about the items in that duffel bag, and he was. Because of his experience with other inmates, he knew better than most what a stash like that could signify. But it was the way he'd reacted to Ismay's declaration that had him all twisted up inside. He'd never expected to care about anything or anyone Remy liked, but he *definitely* cared for Ismay. He wished he could show her how much better he'd treat her. But he had too much to hide to allow their friendship to grow. He didn't really have anything to offer her, anyway. What would such a lovely woman—an attorney, no less—want with an ex-con?

I trust you, for some reason. Just hearing her say that reminded him he was a fraud. She'd hate him once she learned. But what she'd discovered in the wall of Remy's closet made him think that Remy might be the bigger fraud. And Remy could be far more dangerous. Although Bo couldn't afford to get involved in anything that might drag him under the microscope, he'd known men who'd kept similar trophies, and he knew what they had done, knew firsthand that evil men often appeared to be perfectly normal. If there was a monster like some of the inmates he'd served time with running around free, he had to do something about it.

He pulled up the picture Ismay had sent him and saved it to his photos. He needed to find out who the girl was, and he needed to do it without making any waves. But that wasn't going to be easy. The Windsors had been a prominent family on the island for three generations. They were well-established, well-known, and, because of their money, well-respected. If Remy was hurting others, and he was smart about it, he could operate with impunity for years. Maybe he already had. Digging to find out if there was something serious going on could cost Bo his job or cause others to look deeper into his past, but if *he* didn't take that risk and make sure the items Ismay had discovered were meaningless, who would?

Even if his efforts only saved Ismay from marrying a man like some of those he'd known in prison, it'd be worth it.

After the way their meeting on the beach had ended, Ismay hated to bother Bo again. But with her brother flying in tonight at ten, she had to see if he would talk to Honey. She'd reserved a room for Jack at Hotel Mariners at three hundred and fifty dollars a night. With tourist season upon them, that was the best price she could get, but she knew the financial drain would wear on him so quickly, he'd probably turn around and go home after a few days. That was a lot of money to him—to them both. She needed to be able to promise him that he wouldn't have to pay it for long, and Bo was the only person she knew on the island who could help her find an alternative. She certainly wasn't going to ask Bastian for help.

She'd wanted to bring Bo lunch again. She felt she owed him for all the help he'd given her, including the support he was offering on what she'd found in that duffel bag. But after what she'd said to him last night, she was afraid he'd read too much into another meal. So once she'd showered and told Remy's brother she was going to take an Uber to town to wander through the art galleries and the whaling museum—which he, fortunately, had no interest in doing—she left, and as soon as she was out of sight of the house, veered off the road to go to the bungalow.

Bo was back on the roof, continuing to fix the damage caused by the storm, so she had to yell above his hammer to attract his attention.

Once he heard her voice, he stood. He was wearing a pair of shorts with tennis shoes and no shirt, just a tool belt slung low on his hips.

She tried not to notice how well-defined his arms, shoulders, and chest were. He didn't have a six-pack, but it was close, so his stomach was quite remarkable, too. Although Remy wasn't nearly as muscular, he was certainly attractive. She knew Bo's torso was the last thing she should be admiring.

"Hey, sorry to bother you again," she said when she realized she had his attention. "I was hoping... Is there any chance we could talk for a sec?"

He glanced in the direction of the cottage, as if he was wary that Bastian might've followed her. But then he crossed over to the ladder and came down. "Is everything okay?" he asked. "Did you get that stuff...put away?"

He was obviously referring to the duffel bag. "I did. It's back behind the wall."

"Good."

"This is about something else."

"Bastian?"

"Jack. He's coming in tonight. I have a room for him over at

Hotel Mariners, but I'm afraid those prices will make him want to leave almost as soon as he gets here, and I'd hate for him to spend the money on the flight to come out here only to feel he has to go right back to the farm."

"You need me to talk to Honey sooner rather than later."

"If you would. I hate to ask you, but when Remy found out Jack was coming, he wasn't happy about it. I can't have Jack stay at the cottage."

"I can't believe any of the Windsors would mind."

"Really?" she said skeptically.

"Surely, your fiancé can help out your brother," he insisted.

It was saying something that she felt more comfortable asking Bo for *his* understanding and help than Remy's. But she didn't want to examine that too closely. "If Remy hadn't set his expectations for a great summer so high—and didn't feel it was a reward for his hard work—he probably wouldn't mind letting Jack stay. But..." Hearing how selfish that sounded in the face of what Jack was going through, she stopped and tried again. "I don't want to feel as though I'm taking advantage of his family's generosity, and if Honey needs someone to house-sit anyway—"

Bo lifted a hand. "I know Remy and—well, you've said enough. So just give me a minute. I'll grab a shirt."

"Now?" she asked. Wasn't he going to finish what he was doing?

"I'll take you over to Honey's. I think it will help to have you meet her."

"It doesn't have to happen *that* fast. I feel terrible interrupting you. I just...wanted to let you know, as soon as possible, that he's coming tonight."

"I don't mind," he said. "You'll rest easier once we have this handled."

"I will, but I'm not trying to turn my problems into your problems. I seem to be coming to you for everything."

He looked down before meeting her gaze again. "That's what friends are for."

She felt a smile stretch across her face. She liked this man entirely too much.

14

Bastian stopped in the hallway as he passed Remy's room, closed his eyes, and breathed deeply. He could smell Ismay in the air—her perfume or shampoo or whatever. God, she smelled good. How she couldn't see through Remy, he had no idea. But then, Remy could certainly put on a front. He was a chameleon, could blend in wherever or whenever he wanted to.

Eager to get something to eat, he started toward the stairs again, but the temptation of that scent drew him into Remy's room first. For a moment, he just stood in the doorway, surprised to see that she'd made her bed. He didn't know many people who bothered with that these days; he certainly didn't. But her tidiness somehow fit her and made her even more appealing to him. He could see why Remy had decided to marry her. What man wouldn't be happy with such a fresh-faced, sensitive, kind, and intelligent woman?

And that was before he got to her beauty…

Glancing down the stairs to make sure the coast was still clear and she wasn't about to return for something she'd forgotten, he walked farther inside and lifted the suitcase she'd placed in the closet. Empty, of course. Any woman who was going to make her bed each day wouldn't live out of a suitcase.

He fingered the blouses she'd hung up—the light silk of an off-white button-up, the coarse linen of a black oversized shirt, and the soft red cotton of a tank top—then counted the chinos, jeans, and shorts on the lower rack before checking the labels. She didn't spend a lot on clothes. Remy probably didn't like that. He'd expect his woman to match him. But that was the thing—Ismay made even cheap clothes look expensive. She had the tall, lean body of a model.

He crossed to the drawers and sorted through her panties. Most were thongs. He'd wondered what she'd choose. He lifted a pair to his nose, just in case any trace of her lingered, but he was disappointed. All he could smell was laundry soap.

He started to put them away. But at the last second, he shoved one in his pocket, smiled at himself in the mirror, and whistled as he walked out.

Jack was packing when he got a call from Donny. He'd been tempted to reach out to Jessica's soon-to-be ex, if only to compare notes and commiserate. Nothing drew people together like suffering. But he hadn't been sure he could withstand the other man's grief. He was having enough trouble dealing with his own.

He almost let the call transfer to voice mail. But just in case Donny had something important to say, something he needed to hear before he left, he picked up at the last second.

"'Lo?"

"Jack?"

They knew each other. They'd watched their wives play in pickleball tournaments, played board games together on an occasional game night, gone out to the movies when the Schultzs could get a babysitter. He and Donny even texted each other occasionally about sports or borrowing a tool here and there—stuff like that.

"It's Donny."

"I know."

"How are you doing?"

Jack's head prickled, making him want to scratch it harder and harder. "I could be better."

Donny's voice dropped. "Can you believe what those bitches did to us?"

Jack winced. As angry and hurt as he was, he had trouble calling Ashleigh names. They'd been together for so long—since they were kids, really. But the way Donny was slurring his words suggested he'd been drinking, so he probably wasn't thinking clearly. "It's not an easy situation," he hedged.

"It's not an easy situation?" he repeated with a bitter laugh. "I hope they get some kind of venereal disease."

Jack pressed a thumb and finger against his closed eyelids. "Donny, I don't want to hear this."

"What, you're just going to let her ruin your life?"

"What can I do? Drinking certainly won't help."

"That's where you're wrong, buddy," he said. "It's sure as hell making me feel better."

"Really? Because you sound pretty angry to me."

"And you're not?" he snapped.

He was. He'd never felt such rage. He'd loved Ashleigh so much. He didn't feel he deserved what'd happened to him, so the injustice cut almost as deeply as the rejection. "I am, of course. But it's her life and her choice. It's not as if she's leaving because of something I can change."

"You've got to be kidding me!"

"What?"

"Maybe you can just throw up your hands and say, oh, well, but I can't. I've lost my kids, man. Half my net worth. And in the most public and humiliating way imaginable. Ashleigh and Jessica are stupid if they think I'm going to take all that lying down."

"You need to be careful with that kind of thinking," Jack said, but Donny didn't respond. He just called him a fucking loser and hung up. Jack threw his phone on the bed as if it were a poisonous snake.

He'd texted Ashleigh to tell her he was leaving town and that he'd given their landlord notice. His brother Hank said he'd pack up his stuff and move it all to the farm before the end of the month—what was left of it, anyway. And his mother had said she'd clean the place to make sure he received his deposit, which made him eternally grateful to both of them. He'd also told Ashleigh that since she had the car, it was now her responsibility to make the payments. But she hadn't responded to either text.

If she didn't pay, he figured he'd have to, and he might have to pay their credit card bills, too, until they could divvy up their obligations in the divorce proceedings. He couldn't allow her to ruin his credit. That was the only thing he had left. But right now, there were certainly bigger things to worry about than money—like his sanity.

Don't think about Ashleigh. Don't think about Donny. Don't think about any of it. Just keep packing.

If he didn't, he'd miss his plane to Boston, and if he had to catch a later one, he'd miss his connection to the island.

Ismay couldn't help feeling a little anxious as she stood at the neighbor's door with Bo at her side. She figured she could possibly find her brother a room to rent, but the people who lived on Mariners weren't really the type to need the income, so she wasn't very hopeful she'd come across that kind of situation. This opportunity was an anomaly. So it felt like there was a lot riding on this visit.

The elderly woman who opened the door was tall and thin, if a little stooped, and she had her nails manicured into a point with bright red polish. She was wearing a colorful housedress with an even more colorful apron over it, and orthopedic shoes, and she had her silver hair swept up and pinned back. The smile lines around her mouth and eyes creased as soon as she spotted Bo. "Bo, what are you doing back here already? You don't need to worry about me—I'm doing fine," she said as soon as she'd opened the door. Then, while he caught and held it for her, she bent to pick up a yellow tabby cat. "And so is Clementine."

"I haven't been as worried since the power came back on," Bo said.

"It's definitely nice to have some heat." She smiled at Ismay. "And who do we have here?"

Bo gestured in Ismay's direction. "Honey, this is Ismay Chalmers, Remy's fiancée. Ismay, this is Honey Wellington, who makes the best dill pickles, canned beets, and jellies this side of the country."

"It's very nice to meet you," Ismay said.

Honey's eyes were kind but shrewd at the same time. "Aren't you beautiful?"

Ismay felt her face heat. "Thank you."

"How do you like Mariners?" Honey asked.

"It's a lovely day today, but…it wasn't so accommodating right after I got here," she said jokingly.

"This island is certainly unpredictable," Honey said. "But I've always loved wild things. Bo told me your brother might be joining you."

"Yes. He's going through a terrible divorce and needs to get away, so I suggested he come visit. He's a farm boy from northern Utah—he's never experienced anything like this."

"How old is he?"

Ismay stroked the cat Honey was holding, which started to purr. "Only twenty-five."

"And he's already going through a divorce?" she asked in surprise.

"I'm afraid so. The poor guy is heartbroken, never saw it coming. He and his wife have been together since the ninth grade."

"Did she find someone else, or…"

"She did," Ismay said.

"I see." She nuzzled her cat. "When does your brother arrive?"

"He's coming in tonight, actually."

Her eyes widened. "So soon?"

"I figured if he was going to get away, he might as well do it immediately. Then he won't have to face the gossip."

"Does he need a place to stay?" she asked.

"He can stay with me," Bo said, causing Ismay to glance at him.

"No," she said. "I'm not asking for anything like that. I've reserved a room at the Hotel Mariners for now. But Bo mentioned you might like him to house-sit at some point—there's certainly no pressure."

"I just thought I'd bring Ismay by so you could meet her and see if you might also like to meet Jack," Bo volunteered.

"Yes, I would. I spoke to Frankie today—that's my daughter," she explained for Ismay's benefit, "and she said I should definitely come for a few weeks, at least."

Bo lifted his hands. "Well, we're not trying to hurry you on your way. Merely wanted you to know that Jack would be an option, if you're interested."

"That's good to know." She turned to Ismay. "Why don't you bring him by tomorrow so we can talk?"

"I'll do that," Ismay said. "Is there any particular time you'd like to see us?"

"Why don't all three of you come for lunch?" she asked.

"Oh, I wouldn't want to put you out," Ismay replied.

Honey scowled at this response. "You won't be putting me out. It'll be my pleasure."

"Thank you. Thank you so much." Ismay turned to Bo. "Can you make it for lunch?"

"I don't know. I've a lot to get done, so I—" he started to say, but Honey broke in almost immediately.

"We all have to eat, Bo," she said. "And you know I can cook."

"I do know that," he agreed. "I guess I'll be able to take an hour or so."

She put her cat down and nudged it to go back into the house. "You're always doing things for me. It's nice that I can do a little something for you."

"I appreciate it," he said. "We'll see you tomorrow."

"I'm already looking forward to it." She winked at Bo. "And you were right, you know. She *is* special."

Bo looked as if she'd just punched him in the face, which made Honey chuckle as she went back inside and closed the door.

"You told her I'm special?" Ismay teased as they walked back.

"I was exaggerating," he muttered, and she started to laugh.

It was difficult to finish patching the roof knowing Ismay was inside the house. Bo had told her she should go to town or head to the beach—enjoy herself while she was on vacation—but she'd insisted on staying to help clean up, even though she'd already done so much. He was grateful to her, but he was also concerned that Bastian might come looking for her again. Where was Remy's twin today?

Once he finished and could go inside, he was intent on telling her he'd take it from there. But it'd been four hours, and he couldn't see much more to do. She'd used the wet/dry vac he'd provided to suck up what remained of the water and mopped all the floors. It looked as if she'd also scrubbed down the baseboards.

When he found her, she was making food in the kitchen.

"The floors look great," he said.

She peered around the corner at the hardwood in the living room. "I did my best. The rest will be up to the restoration company."

"They've been slammed but promised me they'd at least drop

off some bigger fans." He checked the time. "They claimed it'd be today, but it's nearly five, so…maybe it's not going to happen."

"Are you hungry?" she asked.

He grinned. "What do you think?"

She indicated the table. "Sit down. I've almost finished a salad made of quinoa, spinach, and avocado with a fried egg on top. It's delicious, especially if you add some sriracha."

"Sounds good."

She piled two plates high and brought them over before getting silverware and napkins.

He got up and selected a bottle of wine from a small rack he'd built himself. "This okay?"

"Looks good to me."

He poured them each a glass and sat down with her. Eating together was becoming a habit. On the one hand, it made him uncomfortable. He knew Remy wouldn't like it. On the other… it was difficult to stay away from Ismay. They'd fallen into this situation that made it all too easy to hang out together.

"What do you think Honey will decide?" she asked while they ate.

"I think she'll go to Pennsylvania. The question is when. But Jack can stay here until then. I've got an extra room. I just need to move my weights out of it."

"I don't expect *you* to take him in," she said. "I feel bad that I've leaned on you as much as I have."

"You've helped me, too," he pointed out.

"That's what friends are for," she said, echoing what he'd told her earlier.

"Exactly." He just had to be careful. He couldn't get close to Jack, either. Letting her brother stay was risky. But the dude was probably so caught up in his own misery that he wouldn't pay much attention to Bo. And if he started getting too inquisitive… Bo would just have to figure out something else. Hopefully, Honey would be gone by then and Jack could move to her place. He couldn't make the poor guy pay nearly four hundred dollars a night when he had an empty room.

"What do you think Remy will say when he learns Jack is staying here?" Ismay asked.

"The Windsors may own this place, but it's up to me what I do with it—within reason, of course. Taking on a roommate should be within my prerogative."

"But my brother of all people?"

He swallowed his food. "Maybe it'll shame Remy into doing the right thing and inviting Jack to stay at the cottage."

"That would be nice, except even if he did, he'd just resent it, and I'd certainly be aware of the big favor he was doing for me."

Bo stopped eating and leaned back. "Why are you even with Remy?"

"He has his good traits," she said, immediately defensive.

"And they are..."

She pushed her food around her plate with her fork. "He's clever, driven, smart, talented, handsome, funny—"

"Rich?" he added, watching her closely.

She scowled at him. "That has nothing to do with it. Honestly."

He studied her for several seconds. Then he said, "But can you live with all the things he's not?"

She'd just opened her mouth to answer when a knock sounded at the door.

Bo got up and peered through the window. He was expecting the restoration company, but he couldn't see their truck in the drive.

"Who is it?" Ismay asked, holding her wineglass loosely.

When Bo reached the door, he caught sight of a slim dark-haired man through the peephole and cursed softly. "It's Bastian."

15

Ismay held her breath as she heard Bo and Bastian at the door. She didn't want to let on that she was in the house again—and yet, if she didn't speak up and Bastian later realized she'd been there, it wouldn't look good.

She sat warring with herself for several seconds and eventually decided she had to get up and say hello. But she couldn't make herself do it. Bastian would almost certainly get the wrong idea when she popped up behind Bo at the door. That he kept finding them together would make them appear to be far closer than would seem justified by the length of time they'd known each other. She knew that because he'd insinuated she had no right to be at Bo's when he caught her here the last time. So if there was a chance her presence could slip by unnoticed, she should probably take it. Why open herself up to Bastian's judgment all over again? Remy's brother might even be offended, like he was before, that she'd chosen to spend her time with Bo instead of him, a decision that would be hard for her to defend to Remy, especially since it kept happening.

Once she'd sunk back into her seat at the table, she scooted lower to hide herself a little more, should he peer in the window before he left—she wouldn't put that kind of nosiness past him; since his family owned the bungalow, he'd feel entitled—and could only hope that Bo wouldn't say anything about her being there. It wasn't as if she had any way of communicating her thoughts to him at this point…

"My mother's been trying to reach you and hasn't heard back," Bastian was saying.

"I've been up on the roof, haven't had my phone on me," Bo responded. "I'll give her a call after I eat. Or…is this some sort of emergency?"

"It's not an emergency. She just wanted to see if your house was okay. The restoration company called to tell her they can't get out until tomorrow."

"Not sure why they bothered her. I had it all lined up. But I've been wondering why they didn't show."

"They probably called her because she'll be the one paying their bill, right?"

Ismay bristled at the arrogance in Bastian's tone. Did he have to be so rude to Bo?

"I work for my compensation, and this house is part of it," Bo stated, obviously feeling some antagonism himself.

"Whoa! No need to snap at me," Bastian said. "You asked why they'd call her. I was just pointing out the obvious."

"I'm aware of the obvious," Bo bit out.

The hostility between the two men—which had so far remained under the surface—was starting to ooze through the cracks. Actually, Bastian hadn't changed. It was Bo. He had to be tired of taking Bastian's shit because he wasn't allowing Bastian to push him any further.

Ismay couldn't help being concerned for him. Bo wasn't in as strong of a position as the spoiled son of the rich family who employed him. She desperately hoped Bastian wouldn't become aware of the fact that she'd spent much of the day with Bo and even cooked him dinner. That wouldn't help matters.

“Great. Give her a call. When it’s convenient for you, of course,” Bastian added, as if Bo had been needlessly testy.

Bo said nothing. He just shut the door. Then he walked to the sink where he stopped and stared out, presumably watching Bastian leave.

“Do you think he knows I’m here?” Ismay asked, keeping her voice down.

“No way. That would’ve gone much worse if he did, especially because you were here the last time he came over.”

“I don’t think it went very well as it was,” she said.

He shrugged. “He likes to push my buttons.”

“He likes to push everyone’s buttons.”

“Especially if he feels he can get away with it,” Bo pointed out. “I’ve met guys like him before...”

“Where you grew up?” she asked.

“No, not there,” he replied. “But plenty of other places.”

Other places. He never got specific, didn’t like to talk about his past, but given the violence that’d claimed his mother’s life, she supposed she could understand.

Once she felt safe Bastian wouldn’t be able to see her, she got up and peered through the window, too, just in time to see Remy’s brother disappear behind the hedge between this property and Windsor Cottage. “It was nice of you to offer to let Jack stay here. But now I know we can’t take you up on the offer.”

His eyes focused on her. “You’re not saying that because of Bastian...”

“I *am* saying it because of Bastian. You don’t need another source of friction between you and your employer’s sons.”

“I can’t help it if Remy and Bastian have been overly indulged and turned out to be arrogant assholes. I’m sorry if that offends you, but I’m not going to let either one of them dictate what I do—beyond what I’m getting paid to do, of course.”

She shoved her hands in the pockets of her faded jeans. “The

Windsors own this house. What if they say you can't charge rent for a roommate?"

"I wasn't going to charge Jack."

"There's no way he'd stay for free, Bo. He wouldn't be comfortable if he wasn't compensating you in some way."

"Then we'll work out a trade—the room in exchange for cooking or something."

That sounded fair. As far as the Windsors knew, he'd be a guest, and she couldn't see how they could object to Bo having a temporary guest—even if it was her brother. And with Jack staying in the bungalow, she'd have some time to make other arrangements, even if Honey decided not to go visit her family. "I have no doubt he'd help with whatever you need. He's a handy guy to have around. He could even chop down the tree that fell in the garden and repair the fence."

"We'll get along fine. Sounds like you'd better cancel his stay at Hotel Mariners, if you can."

Her eyebrows shot up. "You're okay with him coming *tonight*?"

"As long as *he's* okay with the fact that this place isn't in the best shape at the moment..."

"He won't care about that. As I said, he'd be happy to help you get it pulled back together."

"Fine. I'm looking forward to meeting him. There's no need to make him pay for a hotel."

"Are you sure?" she asked. "I don't want to take advantage of your kindness or put you in a bad situation. You barely know me—and you don't know Jack at all."

A mock scowl creased his face. "What do you mean? We've spent two nights together."

She smiled at his joke. "And you've taught me to play chess. We've covered a lot of ground in just a few days."

She thought he might mention their secret meeting on the

beach and the stuff she'd shown him from the duffel bag. In some ways, she felt closer to him than to most people she knew.

He gestured at their food. "Let's finish eating."

With a nod, she followed him back to the table. So far, her trip to Mariners hadn't been anything like she'd envisioned. Instead of enjoying the carefree vacation she'd been hoping for—a chance to rest up and play before having Remy join her, at which point they'd work to fix the cracks in their relationship—she felt more stressed than ever. But she was glad she'd met Bo. She wished she could stay with him and Jack instead of having to go back to the cottage…and Bastian.

Ismay found Bastian sprawled on the couch watching a movie and drinking whiskey from a nearby bottle. He was drunk, and she could tell the moment she walked in.

"There you are!" he bellowed. "I didn't expect you to be gone all day. Where've you been?"

His imperious tone immediately got on her nerves. "I told you where I was going," she said, fighting to keep the irritation out of her voice. "I went to town."

"All day? What were you doing?"

She hated having to lie and resented the fact that he was questioning her so closely in the first place. "A lot of things," she replied.

He pushed himself up. "You don't have any bags. Must not have done much shopping."

"I looked around, but I didn't buy anything. I have to be careful with my money. I'll be starting my own law practice in the fall."

"How will you open a law practice if you don't have any money?" he asked skeptically. Then suspicion dawned on his face and he tipped his glass toward her as if he'd figured out the answer to his own question. "Or is that where Remy comes in?"

She felt her spine stiffen. "Remy doesn't have anything to do with it. I can take on work without having an office and grow from there." She pointed to her head. "I have my mind, and I have a computer. That's all I really need to be able to work."

"Might not impress your clients to meet you at the public library..."

"I'm barely out of law school, Bastian. Everyone has to start somewhere."

"My parents know a lot of people," he said. "They can probably throw a few clients your way."

"Not unless the people they know live in California, because that's where I'm licensed."

He seemed startled by this declaration. "You and Remy won't be moving to New York?"

She blinked at him. "No."

"Interesting..."

"Why's it interesting?"

"I'm pretty sure that's what my parents are expecting."

Had Remy led them to believe that? Because he'd never mentioned it to her. And he'd also be licensed in California. "I'm sorry to hear that, because it's not in our plans."

He tossed back what was left in his glass. "You don't like me very much, do you?"

A denial rushed to her lips. But the tension between them was so thick she knew he'd be able to tell she was lying as soon as the words came out of her mouth. So she decided to be honest. "You've done everything you can to make me *not* like you."

He set his empty glass on the table. "If I stop acting like a prick, will it help?"

She dropped her purse on the table next to the couch opposite his. "It certainly could."

"Fine. Why don't we start over? Get things right this time? What do you say? Otherwise, it's going to be a long summer."

Summer? Did he plan to stay? Before she could ask, he said,

"Let's go out to dinner tonight to signify the beginning of a brand-new beautiful relationship."

She didn't trust his sudden change of heart. She didn't understand what had instigated it or how long it would last. "I already ate."

"Oh, come on," he said. "You're far too leery of me. I'm not that bad. Really. And you don't have to eat. Just order a drink or dessert or something. We don't even have to go to town. We can walk over to the restaurant you went to last night."

Except she'd never visited that restaurant. Was there some way he'd be able to figure that out?

She couldn't see how. If he asked what kind of wine she'd had, she'd say she didn't remember unless she had the menu in front of her, in which case, she'd just pick one. It would be difficult to turn him down. It was only seven o'clock and she had to pick up her brother with the Jeep, if it was available, at ten o'clock. Her alternative was to sit with Bastian and watch TV until Jack arrived.

She preferred to go to the restaurant. At least there'd be other people around. And he was watching some horror flick she had zero interest in. "Fine. Let me grab a sweater."

He was waiting for her at the foot of the stairs when she came down. She'd changed, pulled her hair into a messy bun on top of her head, and applied some lip gloss. He'd cleaned up a little, too. She could smell his cologne before she even reached him.

"All set?" he asked.

She was impressed by how well he held his liquor. She guessed he'd had quite a bit, but he didn't sway or slur his words. He'd combed his hair and pulled on some chinos with a simple cashmere sweater. That sweater had probably cost five hundred dollars, but he wore it as casually as a holey T-shirt.

"I've never seen identical twins quite as identical as you and Remy," she said. "It's uncanny. I'm not sure I'll ever get used to it."

"Are you kidding me? I'm so much better-looking than he is."

She smiled—grudgingly. She *did* like the way Bastian wore his hair. It was longer than Remy's and slightly curly in front, reminding her of the actor Timothée Chalamet.

"You might be too pretty to go out with me," she said jokingly.

He made a face. "I'm not buying that. You're gorgeous. With any luck, you'll decide to marry me instead of my brother."

He laughed as though he was joking, but she still found that an odd thing to say. "Wow, you really are turning over a new leaf."

"It might seem like he's the better man—" he winked "—but you haven't gotten to know me yet."

Charming Bastian should've bothered her as much as the former version. But it was hard not to soften, at least a little, since he was finally making an effort to be nice. And it wasn't just that. For the first time, she noticed a hollowness in his eyes that made her wonder if he acted the way he did because he was miserable. And that begged the question—what could possibly be wrong?

Bo had searched the internet for the girl who matched the picture Ismay had given him—and, like Ismay, had come up empty-handed. But without a name, he couldn't perform a very thorough search. He felt she had to have lived on the island, wasn't just a tourist. But really, she could be anyone. And the stuff in the duffel bag could have no meaning. But he had little doubt some of the rapists and murderers who'd been behind bars with him had taken trophies that resembled what Ismay had found. He was aware of that behavior in an up close and personal way.

Bottom line, it was a safe bet that anyone who'd hidden such items—in the wall of a closet no less—was trouble, which was why he was so alarmed.

But it wasn't in just anyone's closet. It was in *Remy's* closet—

someone who was supposedly a law-abiding soon-to-be doctor. Did that change anything?

Bo sure as hell hoped so.

He checked the clock. He had some time before Jack would be arriving—time he could use to attempt to solve this mystery.

He grabbed a jacket and pulled it on before stepping outside and locking the door behind him. He thought about asking Ivy Hawthorne, who'd worked at the public library since she was a teenager, and kept abreast of what happened on the island better than almost anyone. But the library had closed for the day.

He could pay Honey another visit, though. It was probably risky to create a potential connection between him and the girl in the photo, but he trusted that Honey would never try to make trouble for him.

When he reached the road, he couldn't help glancing toward Windsor Cottage and wondering how Ismay was doing with Bastian. Knowing Remy's brother was alone in the house with her made him feel he needed to figure out what the items in the duffel bag signified as soon as possible.

The porch light was on at Honey's, even though it wasn't quite dark. He'd put her lights on a timer, just to help keep her safe, and had set them for thirty minutes before sundown so they'd be glowing even before she needed them.

"Hi, Bo," she said when she answered his knock. "Don't tell me you've come to cancel our lunch tomorrow..."

"No. I just wanted to make sure the timer on the lights was still working."

"It's been working perfectly. Just like magic," she said. "Why don't you come in?" She pushed the screen door wider. "I'll give you a piece of the coffee cake I just baked for our lunch tomorrow."

He could smell it from the door. "Sounds great."

Her place was getting a bit threadbare since she didn't replace anything as it grew older, but it was always clean and tidy. He sat at her small kitchenette, where she offered him a cup of coffee with the cake, which he gladly accepted. There was a small TV on the counter. She had a classic black-and-white movie on, and Clementine immediately jumped into his lap and twitched her tail back and forth. "Can I bring anything for lunch tomorrow?"

"Good Lord, no," she said. "I can certainly manage a meal for four."

"It's nice of you to do it—and to consider letting Jack house-sit if you go to Pennsylvania."

"Divorce is so hard," she said, shaking her head.

He wouldn't know, but he could imagine it wasn't easy.

While he ate the cake, Honey pulled Clementine into her own lap, and they talked about the historical society and the house Honey had been helping them save—the oldest house on the island—which they'd moved to safer ground before it could be lost to erosion. He was finished with his cake and his coffee by the time he brought the conversation around to the real reason he'd come. "Have you ever seen this girl?" he asked, showing her the picture Ismay had sent him on his phone.

Honey nudged Clementine so the cat would jump down, and got her reading glasses from a stack of magazines she'd pushed off to one side of the table. "She's not familiar to me. Why do you ask?"

"I found this photograph tucked inside one of the library books I have and wanted to find its owner," he said, using the lie he'd prepared in advance.

"That's so nice of you. Old photographs can be priceless treasures. But—" Honey shook her head "—I can't say she's from around here."

"No worries. At least I tried." He thanked her for dessert and said he'd better get back and prepare for Jack's arrival. It was getting late, and he still needed to remove his weights from that room and make up the bed.

He was already on his way to the door when she called him back.

"Bo?"

"What?"

"I just thought of something," she said. "Can I see that picture again?"

He took out his phone and turned the screen toward her.

She pursed her lips as she took it and studied it closely. "This could be the girl who died in that fire..."

"What fire?" he asked.

"The one at the McMurtry place over by the golf course."

"I don't remember a fire."

"It happened before you got here, probably eight, nine years ago. Sean McMurtry was a prominent artist who lived here half the year. His stuff is still in some of the galleries in town. Anyway, his son and some friends were partying one night when he and his wife were off the island. The power went out, so they were using candles and... I don't remember exactly what happened. Two kids started fighting or something, a liquor bottle fell and smashed on the floor, and a candle got knocked over."

"That's what started the fire?"

"If memory serves. And if this girl is the one I'm thinking of, everyone got out except her."

"Do the McMurtrys still live on Mariners?"

"No. Once the insurance money rebuilt the house, they sold it. I don't think any of them have been back since. Who'd want to face that memory?"

"What about *her* family?"

She gave his phone back. "If I remember right, they were locals who lived here year-round. Her father managed one of the hotels in town. I doubt they're still here, though."

"Do you remember their name?"

She shook her head. "But you could probably look it up. There must've been an article or two written about it—maybe not in the national news but something local. The incident rocked the whole island. The McMurtrys were criticized for leaving their son unchaperoned, and the boy had a rough go of it, too. It was a tragedy for everyone concerned."

"Sounds like it." Bo slipped his phone back in his pocket. "I'll look for an article. Considering the circumstances, this picture might be important to the girl's family."

"That's a strong possibility. It's nice of you to go to the trouble. You're so good to everyone."

Since he didn't deserve the praise—not in regard to this—he chafed at it. "See you tomorrow."

She walked him to the door and called out, "Good night," as he left, and he moved as if he weren't in any particular hurry. But once he reached the darkness outside the circle of her porch light, he picked up the pace. He was eager to learn if the girl in the photograph was, indeed, the one who'd lost her life in that house fire. Because if he could establish who she was, he might also be able to figure out why Remy would have a picture of her in a duffel bag hidden in the wall of his closet with some underwear and jewelry...

16

The restaurant was open to the outside with seating on the beach, but the weather was cool enough that only a few stragglers accepted those tables. Most preferred to eat inside, then walk out for a picture.

Ismay sat with Bastian at one of the best tables, which had warmth *and* a view—and she knew it was because the maître d' had recognized Bastian, who'd also slipped him a few bills. Remy did the same type of thing. He expected the very best wherever they went, but it wasn't quite so easy to obtain preferential treatment in LA, where there were a lot of rich and famous people. On Mariners, his family's name and wealth made more of a difference.

Bastian ordered a whiskey and then bluefin tuna. The waiter said it was unusual to have tuna this early in the season, so Bastian tried to convince her to order it, too, but she got a seared scallop appetizer with butternut squash puree and a mojito.

"Are you sure you don't want anything else?" Bastian asked as they surrendered their menus.

"No. I'm not hungry."

"Well, save room for dessert. This is a celebration."

"Of what?" she asked in surprise.

"My reformation," he teased. "What else?"

His self-deprecation could be disarming, but Ismay was still wary. "I have to admit, I'm starting to like you better."

"I knew you would." He laughed. That he could turn on the charm so easily begged the question—why didn't he make the effort more often? And what had finally convinced him to try with her?

"So…tell me about you and Remy," he said.

"What about us?" she asked.

"How'd you meet? What attracted you to him? How are you still together despite his neglect while he's studying? And when do you plan to get married?"

Since she lived with Remy, she knew the two brothers didn't speak very often. They'd never gotten along, preferred to avoid each other. But they'd traveled to Vale and Italy together since Ismay had been with Remy. Certainly, Remy must've mentioned her. Or at least some of what he'd told his parents should've filtered through. "You don't know any of this?"

"I'd like to hear it from your perspective."

She leaned back as the waiter delivered her mojito and his whiskey served "up."

"We met at the school library. I don't know why he sat down next to me, but—"

"Quit being so modest," he broke in. "You have to know why any single man would sit next to you. It's obvious to everyone else."

She felt herself blush. Now he was lavishing her with compliments to the point she was embarrassed they still flattered her. "Well, I guess he found me attractive. And then he struck up a conversation and returned the next day and the day after until, a few days later, he asked me out."

"Where'd he take you on your first date?"

"To a fancy place called APL Restaurant on Hollywood Boulevard. He said Jake Gyllenhaal and other celebrities had been spotted there."

She'd told Bo that Remy's money had nothing to do with her attraction to him, but that wasn't entirely true. She wasn't after his money, but there was something about the confidence money could give—the safety and security—that helped her relax. Her parents had to stretch every dollar, especially while she was growing up, so it was a relief to have more than enough, even if it she could only enjoy it through someone who was close to her. Remy liked good food, fine wine, and doing fun things, and shared all of that with her.

"Why haven't you joined for any of the family trips he's invited you on?" Bastian asked.

"There've only been two, and they both fell on holidays."

He looked confused. "When you were out of school..."

"Yes, but that was also when I'd promised my own family I'd be home."

He took a sip of his whiskey. "So you're loyal, even if it means missing Europe or a fabulous ski trip to Vale..."

"You could put it that way, I guess. I didn't want to disappoint my parents. These days, I rarely get to see them and my siblings." She didn't volunteer that she already felt slightly disconnected from her family since leaving the religion that was such a big part of their lives. She didn't want to do anything to separate herself further.

"What do they think of you spending the summer on Mariners?"

"I think they wish I'd come home instead, but they've accepted it." The topic of this conversation had created a perfect opportunity to tell him about Jack. She was afraid "nice" Bastian would disappear, and he'd revert to the man she'd first met, but it would seem strange if she didn't speak up now that they were discussing her family. "I don't know if Remy's told you, but Jack, the brother closest to me in age, has decided to come here." She checked the time on her phone. "He actually arrives tonight."

Bastian rocked back. "Your brother's coming here? *Tonight?* For how long?"

"That's yet to be determined. He's going through a hard time—a divorce—so nothing's for sure. It's a chance to escape all the gossip, as well as his estranged wife, and spend some time meditating on what he really wants for his future."

A contemplative expression crept over Bastian's face. "Is he staying at the cottage?"

She was glad she could say no. But she didn't want to tell him Jack was staying with Bo, either. He'd find it strange, which was why she hadn't even told Remy yet. "I got him a room at Hotel Mariners," she said and left it there. Technically, that wasn't a lie. She *did* get Jack a room at Hotel Mariners, but she'd already given it up. Still, it would seem more natural if Bastian and Remy thought staying with Bo was something that'd cropped up *after* her brother had been at the hotel for a few days.

"Interesting," he said.

She shifted in her seat. "In what way?"

"In a lot of ways." Finished with his third—or was it fourth—whiskey, he flagged down the waiter to get him another one.

He'd already had plenty to drink. She was afraid he wouldn't be able to walk home, but she didn't say anything. At least they were finally getting along. "I hope you don't mind that's he's coming…"

His lips curved into a smile that showed such perfect teeth, she wondered if they were veneers. Maybe that was one way she could tell the brothers apart, she realized. Remy's teeth were more natural in color. "Me?" he said. "No way. The more the merrier. I'm just surprised he's not staying with us."

"I didn't want to take advantage of your parents' generosity. And Remy's looking forward to a certain kind of summer. I think it'll be better—for everyone—if Jack stays somewhere else."

He spun his glass around on the table. "Remy knows your brother's coming and didn't insist he stay at the cottage?"

She didn't want to make her fiancé look selfish, especially to someone who already seemed to think the worst of him. So she said, "Jack insisted. He doesn't mind."

"That's got to be expensive. But...okay. I can't wait to see how he and Remy get along."

What did Bastian mean by that? "Jack can get along with anyone."

He chuckled softly. "I wish I could say the same for Remy."

He'd found it. Bo studied the image that'd come up when he performed a Google search for *house fire kills girl on Mariners* and compared it to the photograph on his phone. They looked so similar it had to be the same person.

Her name was Lyssa Helberg, and she died nine years ago in June, only a year or so after her family had moved to Mariners from Boulder, Colorado. It'd been long enough that people wouldn't still be talking about the incident, which was why he hadn't heard anything about it.

"Thank God for Honey," he murmured as he read the articles attached to the various headlines.

Girl, 19, Dies in House Fire

Power Outage, Candles, Booze—Recipe for Death

McMurtrys Sell Home for $2 Million Less Than True Value

No Charges Filed in McMurtry Case

Bo searched every article he could find for mentions of the Windsor boys. The girl would've been a couple of years younger than they were when she lost her life, but the party hadn't been exclusive. While the articles included statements from several of the partygoers, neither Remy nor Bastian was one of them.

It was possible Remy had known her. Cared about her.

But that didn't explain the underwear and jewelry. Nothing Bo could think of explained the underwear and jewelry, certainly not better than what seemed to be the most logical answer—that Remy, or someone, was peeping on women, assaulting women, or worse.

That was what his experience as an ex-convict suggested, and it was downright terrifying—so terrifying he couldn't accept it. What were the chances?

Next to nil, he told himself. He wanted to keep focusing on this problem, keep searching to find the people quoted in those articles. One of them might be able to tell him if Remy or Bastian had been there that night.

But if word got back to any of the Windsors that he was digging up the past—questioning people about Remy's and Bastian's whereabouts that night—it might not go over well. They'd certainly wonder what he was after, and he couldn't imagine they'd take it as a friendly gesture.

Dare he push the issue?

Time was getting away from him, he realized. He needed to get the spare bedroom ready for Jack. Ismay was probably on her way to get him right now.

Bastian insisted on paying for dinner, and Ismay let him because he was the one who'd extended the invitation and insisted she go, even though she'd told him she wasn't hungry.

Afterward, he acted as if he'd accompany her to the airport. But she managed to sidestep that—barely—by saying it would be better if she had a little time alone with Jack. She could tell Bastian didn't like not getting what he wanted, making it awkward having to insist, especially since she was using the Windsors' Jeep. But she had no idea what shape her brother would be in emotionally and could easily guess he wouldn't be excited to meet anyone, especially one of the Windsors, as soon as he walked off the plane. Beyond that, Jack didn't know he couldn't tell Bastian he was staying with Bo. She didn't want him to feel uncomfortable about it.

If she could just keep Remy's brother and Jack separated for a few days—long enough to create a believable story on how Jack came to be staying in Bo's bungalow—everything would be okay. She hoped she'd be able to say that Jack had needed something to keep himself occupied while he was on the island, and she'd known Bo could use his help. Then she'd explain that after a day of working together, Bo had invited him to stay since he had an extra bedroom. She felt that would be her best chance of ensuring no one, including Remy, had a problem with the arrangement.

The cobblestone streets caused the Jeep to shimmy as she passed the quaint shops and restaurants downtown, with their mid-nineteenth century architecture and sidewalk dining beneath the tall leafy elm trees that lined most major streets. She wanted to take Jack out to eat before going to Bo's so they could have some time to talk. But it would be rude to arrive at Bo's too late, so she thought she'd order some food while Jack was deplaning and take it over to Bo's. With any luck, by the time she returned to Windsor Cottage, Bastian would be asleep—or if he continued to drink, maybe he'd just pass out. She'd never seen anyone consume so much alcohol in one night.

The parking lot was nearly full, but she managed to find a space along the perimeter. Then she used her phone to place an order for three meals of fish and chips at a restaurant that had fabulous Yelp reviews and hurried inside the small airport, where Boeing Business Jets, carrying sixteen people, took off and landed—weather permitting—several times a day.

While she waited in the crowded room for Jack's plane to come in, she received a text from her mother. Has he arrived yet?

Not yet, she wrote back. I'll let you know when I've got him.

Good. I'm worried about him. But I'm glad you convinced him to leave this place. Tongues here are already wagging.

Ismay had known they would be, but she was still surprised her mother would admit she was glad Jack had the opportunity to leave. She'd thought her parents would be angry she'd tempted him away from the farm.

I'll take good care of him. Have you talked to Ashleigh?

I tried calling her. She won't pick up.

Ismay was going to leave it there, but her mother sent another message.

Ashleigh's mother called me today, though.

Marie? What'd she have to say?

She was in tears. Said she couldn't understand what had possessed her daughter to do what she did.

She doesn't believe Ashleigh's gay?

You know what she believes.

That sexuality was a choice—despite all the scientific research indicating otherwise.

What do *you* believe?

Don't bait me, Ismay. I don't know what to believe anymore. I'm just glad you're there to help us get through this.

Ismay smiled at her mother's message. Suddenly, the gulf between them didn't seem quite so wide. Maybe the tragedy of Jack's divorce would pull them back together, so there'd be a silver lining to all the pain.

Travelers coming from the tarmac began to stream into the building. Ismay waited anxiously until she saw her brother, who was easy to spot because of his height, even though he was at the back of the line. He wore a world-weary expression that made him look much older than when she'd seen him last, with hollow eyes and tousled hair.

"You okay?" she murmured as he reached her and bent to give her a hug.

"I'm breathing," he said.

"You're going to get through this."

His mouth twisted into an approximation of a smile. "I'm glad *you're* confident."

"I am." She drew him toward the baggage claim area. "How was it, flying for your first time?"

"If I had more fight in me, I would've been scared to death," he said with the same wry note in his voice. "Instead, I was praying we'd just go down, and it'd all be over."

She swatted his arm. "Don't talk like that."

"It was a joke," he mumbled, but she didn't fully believe him.

As soon as his bag showed up, he wheeled it out while she led him to the Jeep. "I got your text when I landed," he said. "So… I won't be at the hotel, after all?"

"No. You'll have a room in the bungalow, where the Windsors' caretaker lives, which will be free."

"The free part's nice. I was a little stressed about how much it'll cost. So I'm staying with the caretaker, and you're staying with Remy's brother?"

"Yes. But the cottage is very close."

"I'm not worried about that. It's just…isn't it sort of weird that it's just the two of you?"

"To be honest? Yes," she said. "No one knew Bastian was going to show up. And I'm hoping he won't be here long. Then you can hang out at the cottage with me until Remy arrives, and by then, I'm hoping the house-sitting gig will materialize."

"Remy doesn't want me at the cottage?"

"I didn't say that."

"Nothing else explains it. Seems like a welcoming brother-in-law, sis."

Ismay couldn't miss the sarcasm. Jack had always had a dry sense of humor. "Stop. He's just…a little spoiled," she admitted.

"A little?" he echoed, and when they both laughed, Ismay felt a measure of relief. Thank God she'd been able to convince Jack to leave Utah. With time, she felt her brother would be okay. He had a long road ahead of him, though.

"You're going to love Bo," she said with confidence.

He looked askance at her as he deposited his bag in the back of the Jeep. "How well do you know this guy?"

"He helped me get through the storm."

"And is that affection I detect in your voice?"

Hoping the darkness hid her burning face, Ismay refused to meet his gaze. "No. He's just…a cool guy."

"Cooler than Remy?"

In some ways, yes. But she wasn't about to admit that. "They're very different. I like them both."

He froze. "Did you just say you *like* Remy?"

Growing flustered, she gestured for him to get in the car. "I don't remember you being this difficult."

"I can't pretend I'll be any fun while I'm here. I feel like the living dead."

"Sometimes terrible things turn out to be what's best in the end."

He sighed as if he couldn't believe that could apply to him. "That's just what everyone says when they don't know how to fix something."

"You'll see," she promised and reached out to cover his large hand, already calloused from years of work on the farm, with hers.

17

There was nothing as claustrophobic as two grown men sharing a six-by-eight-foot cell. The bungalow wasn't big, but it still had a hell of a lot more room than that, so Bo didn't consider having Jack in the extra bedroom a major sacrifice. Besides, Ismay's brother wasn't meant to be there very long. Bo was more worried about the time they'd spend together each day—and any telltale signs he might unwittingly give away to indicate his past wasn't exactly as he'd represented it.

Fortunately, he was able to relax a little once he met Jack, who came off as immanently likeable.

"You hungry?" Ismay asked, lifting a sack from a local restaurant after she'd made the introductions. "I brought food, thought you might like to have dinner with us."

"At eleven o'clock?" he said with a laugh.

"Jack's been traveling all day, so he didn't get much to eat. And I know how much *you* like food. I didn't think the time would matter."

He took the sack she handed him. "Thanks. You're right, it doesn't."

He gestured to the table, indicating they should sit, and offered them each a beer. Jack declined, said he didn't drink. And

Ismay said she preferred water. "After seeing how much Bastian put down tonight, this might be a dry summer for me," she said ruefully.

"What was he drinking?" Bo asked.

"Mostly whiskey," she replied. "When I left him, I couldn't believe he was still standing."

Bo got them each a glass of water before bringing his beer to the table. "Hopefully, he's sleeping it off by now."

Ismay's phone dinged, and he watched her pull it out of her purse.

"Don't tell me that's Bastian," he said dryly.

"No. Remy. I told him Jack was arriving tonight, but from this text I don't think it registered. He's not keeping close track of anything until his exams are over."

"Then what does he want?" Jack asked.

"He's just wondering if I had fun today. I'll reply in the morning. For all he knows, I'm asleep."

Bo swallowed the fries he'd put in his mouth. "When will Remy be finished with his exams?"

"Not for a couple more weeks," Ismay replied.

"I wonder if Bastian plans to stay that long," he said, dipping more fries in ketchup.

She sprinkled malt vinegar on her battered fish. "So do I."

Jack should've been the hungriest as Ismay had indicated, but he was barely touching his meal. "Are you sure you don't mind me staying here?" he asked. "I *really* don't want to put you out."

Bo guessed he was having second thoughts about coming to Mariners. It couldn't be easy for him to be in a foreign place right after his life had been turned upside down. But Bo felt it had to beat staying in Utah amid the rubble of his marriage. "You're welcome to stay as long as you'd like. Won't bother me," Bo said and was surprised to realize he meant it. Maybe he'd feel differently later on, if Jack did something to get on his nerves. But Ismay's brother seemed subdued, easy to get along with, and quiet. In a word—solid.

"I'll pay for my stay, of course," Jack said.

"Your sister's already promised me you'll pay with your labor," he said with a grin. "The storm that just passed through here did some damage. I could use an extra pair of hands for the next few days."

"Happy to help," he said and sounded completely sincere.

Bo hadn't been looking for free labor when he agreed to let Ismay's brother use the spare bedroom, but it was kind of Jack to return the favor. "You won't have to do too much. You should have plenty of time to be lazy like your sister," he added jokingly.

"Lazy! I've earned a summer off!" Ismay gave him a mock scowl, but another ding from her phone drew her attention before the conversation could continue.

"Remy again?" Jack said as she checked it.

She frowned. "Bastian."

"What does *he* want?" Bo asked.

"Says he's just checking to see if Jack arrived safely. But he's probably wondering what could be taking me so long."

As far as Bo was concerned, Bastian had far too much interest in his brother's fiancée. "Does he know Jack's staying with me?"

She sent a message back before replying. "Not yet."

Bo finished the last of his fish. "When are you going to tell him?"

"Not for a few days."

Immediately picking up on the undercurrent of the conversation, Jack looked from him to Ismay and back again. "Why not?"

"It's none of his business, for one," she said.

"He won't like it?" Jack guessed.

"He doesn't have any say in it," Bo clarified. "It'll just be…less of a focal point if he thinks you're staying at the hotel for now."

Jack's eyes widened. "So…what do I say if he asks me?"

"With any luck, he won't even see you," Ismay replied. "And if he does, just say you're helping Bo out."

Jack didn't respond, but he shoved the rest of his food away as if he couldn't finish it, and Bo knew he was probably wondering why he'd come.

"Everything's going to be fine," Ismay said, trying to reassure him.

"You'll love the island," Bo added and, assuming Jack had to be exhausted, Bo got up to show him his room.

"We'll share this bathroom," he explained after he'd led Jack down the hall and opened a cabinet so he'd know where to find the towels and extra toilet paper.

"I'm glad to be here," Jack said, but Bo figured it would take a while until Ismay's brother felt comfortable.

Jack put his suitcase in the room. Then he came out to say good-night to his sister before turning in.

"Do you think he'll be okay?" Ismay whispered after his door closed, obviously concerned.

"He just needs to adjust, and that takes time," Bo replied.

She looked up at him with an earnest expression. "This is so nice of you. I can't tell you how much I appreciate it."

He shrugged. "It's no big deal."

"But you barely know us."

Wanting to smooth the hair out of her worried eyes, he lifted his hand. She was so beautiful. He'd never touched a woman quite like her. But he caught himself at the last second and, hoping his intention hadn't been obvious, raked his fingers through his own hair. "I guess that's true, but..."

"What?" she prompted.

"Somehow, it feels as though I've known you a lot longer," he admitted.

The sweetest smile curved her lips before she leaned forward and pulled him in for a hug. "Thank you."

Bo breathed deeply as she brought her body into contact

with his and closed his eyes as he allowed himself to tighten his arms around her. The embrace lasted only for a moment. It was something friends often did when saying hello or goodbye. But for him, it wasn't nearly that casual. He wished he could hold her longer, move his hand up her back, and bury his face in her warm neck…

"Good night," he said instead and released her.

"Good night," she murmured and looked slightly embarrassed.

Once he'd closed the door, he stood at the window over the sink, watching her get into the Jeep, and knew this summer might prove to be his hardest yet. Just seeing her with Remy, and knowing he was unworthy of her, would be difficult. The existence of that hidden duffel bag and its contents—and knowing that photograph was of a young woman who'd died on the island—only gave him more reason for concern.

He needed to keep Ismay safe.

But the biggest challenge to overcome would be wanting her for himself.

Bastian had left the porch light on for her, which was decent of him, but when she got back, Ismay was even happier to find he wasn't up and moving around. She didn't want him to question her about Jack.

She moved quietly so she wouldn't wake him and managed to get into bed without an encounter. The TV was playing in the master again. For all she knew, he slept with it on. Regardless, she was grateful for the ambient noise; it helped cover her movements.

She hoped bringing Jack to the island wouldn't turn out to be a mistake. He'd looked so shell-shocked when she first saw him that it'd made her realize how dependent he would be on her—at least at first. She just hoped being on the island would really do him some good…

Her mind shifted to the hug she'd given Bo. He'd felt so solid in her arms. She closed her eyes as she relived that moment and wished she hadn't enjoyed it quite so much. It made her feel guilty, as if she'd done something wrong.

It was just a simple hug, she told herself—the kind she gave a lot of people. Except she'd wanted to remain in his arms and was beginning to fantasize about what it might be like to kiss him…

"Shit," she muttered. Even if Remy weren't in the picture, she couldn't allow herself to become infatuated with a guy who lived three thousand miles away from where she was now licensed to practice law.

She was being ridiculous. She barely even knew Bo. It was just that the unusual circumstances she'd found herself in since coming to the island were messing with her mind.

She eventually fell into a fitful sleep. She'd wake up, start obsessing about the growing desire she felt to touch Bo in a way that was decidedly *not* within the bounds of friendship, and after several minutes, drift off again. So at first, she thought she had to be dreaming when she heard a creak outside her door.

Lifting her head, she looked at the alarm clock, which read three thirty. That was when she realized she was indeed awake, and someone was in the hall.

Her heartbeat sounded like a bass drum in her ears as she slid up to lean against the headboard. It had to be Bastian. He was the only other person in the house.

She heard the hardwood floor creak again. Then the handle of her door began to turn.

She covered her mouth so she wouldn't make any sound. Her mind went to that stuff hidden in the wall. Did he know about it? Was *he* the one who'd put it there?

Even if it was him, he wouldn't dare touch *her*—would he?

Maybe he would. But if he hurt her, he couldn't let her live to tell Remy. He'd have to kill her and dispose of her body.

She'd just had dinner with him. Something like being murdered by him was beyond imagination. But he could easily say she'd gone for a late swim in the ocean as he was going to bed, and he didn't realize until the next morning that she'd never come back.

The knob jiggled more insistently when he couldn't gain access. Fortunately, she'd felt uncomfortable enough that she'd locked her door. The question was…how far would he go to get in? And if he tried to force his way in, would she be able to stop him?

Her hand was shaking when she grabbed her cell phone from the nightstand. She could call for help. But she didn't dare do it too soon. What could she say right now? That her prospective brother-in-law was trying to open her door? She doubted the police would rush to her rescue—especially here on Mariners, where the Windsors had such influence.

She held her breath as she waited, and the jiggling stopped. Then she heard some rustling and, finally, his footsteps retreated.

What was that all about? What was he even doing up at this hour?

She remained tense, gripping her phone while waiting to see if he'd come back. But she didn't hear anything—other than a toilet flushing probably an hour later—and eventually the sudden adrenaline rush she'd experienced being awakened like that took its toll.

The next thing she knew, she still had her phone in her hand but it was morning.

Bastian had always struggled to sleep—even as a young boy, which was why he'd started drinking at fourteen. Sometimes liquor helped. He'd just drink until he passed out. Other times, it didn't seem to make any difference. If he passed out, he'd just wake up again a few hours later.

He tried to trick his mind by watching TV. The noise kept him from being awakened by other sounds in the night if he did happen to nod off, but he'd become a regular night owl, always wide-awake and staring around while the rest of the world slept. He hated it; those long hours could be interminable.

When he heard Ismay downstairs, he rubbed his face and reached for the remote so he could finally turn off the damn TV. He'd managed to grab a few hours, but he still felt like roadkill. And he had a terrible hangover to boot. He couldn't continue to live like this, he decided. He needed to see a doctor. Afraid the doctor would say something was wrong with his head and send him to a shrink—his parents had dragged him to enough of those when he was younger—he'd put off seeking that kind of help for as long as he could. But it was getting to the point that he had to do something, or he was going to lose his fucking mind.

With a yawn, he climbed out of bed and went to the bathroom. The scent of bacon was beginning to permeate the entire cottage, but his head was pounding too hard, and he was too nauseous to find it appetizing. He thought about going right back to bed to sleep off the worst effects of his drinking—he found it easier to rest during the day—but he was afraid Ismay would leave, and he wanted to see her. He wouldn't have all that long until Remy showed up, and he was going to need every possible opportunity to win her trust.

Shoving the hair out of his eyes, he brushed his teeth, pulled on a sweatshirt along with a pair of Nike shorts, and, moving carefully, eased his way down the stairs.

When she heard him approach, she turned but didn't say anything.

"Morning," he said, wondering why the look she shot him was filled with hostility.

"Morning," she responded but her voice was so low he could barely hear her.

"How'd you sleep?"

She'd gone back to frying her bacon and didn't look up again. "Not so good. You?"

"Good enough," he replied.

"Do you want some breakfast?"

Just the idea of food made him grimace. He went to the fridge and pulled out a beer. "No. I think I'll start with this."

"Already?"

The irritation in her voice nearly made him snap back, but he managed to overcome that impulse. "It takes the edge off."

She fell silent as she finished the bacon, made toast, and created a BLT.

"Did your brother get in okay?" he asked when she brought it to the table.

"Yeah."

"How does he like the hotel?"

Her chair scraped the floor as she pulled it out. "It's comfortable there."

Was she mad that Jack hadn't been invited to stay in the cottage?

After popping the top of his beer, he took a long drink and sank into the chair across from her. "What are your plans for today? Any chance you'd like me to show you around? Jack could come along if he wants."

She opened her mouth to respond but gave him another hostile look instead.

"Is something wrong?" he asked. "Because you're acting like you're upset."

She'd just picked up her sandwich. At this, she lowered it again. "I am upset. What do you think you were doing last night?"

He spread his hands to show she had him at a loss. "You mean…besides drinking?"

"Someone tried to get into my room in the middle of the night. It could only have been you."

"It *was* me," he said.

She seemed taken aback that he'd admit it so readily. *"Why?"*

"I couldn't sleep. I was just going to peek in and make sure you were back safe."

"Peek into my bedroom? That's an invasion of my privacy, Bastian!"

With a wince at the caustic edge in her voice, he put up a hand to ask her to keep it down. "I'm sorry. I hadn't heard you come in, so I was worried. But when I found the door locked, I knew you must've made it home safely and went back to bed."

She gaped at him as if she didn't quite know how to respond. "What if I'd been undressed?"

"It was the middle of the night, Ismay! I knew you'd be covered."

"And if I wasn't?" she persisted.

"It was dark! How much would I be able to see? I wasn't being a lecherous bastard. I was just going to make sure there was a human-sized lump in the bed!"

She sighed and seemed to relax. "Don't check on me like that in the future."

"Okay, but… I wouldn't want anything to happen to you while I'm here."

"I'll take my chances."

He hadn't seen any real fire in her before, but he liked it. A good challenge was always more tantalizing.

"You could've checked the garage for the Jeep…" she continued.

"You wanted me to go outside to look in the garage at three thirty in the morning?"

That must've seemed unreasonable even to her because she didn't answer.

"It was just a quick *is she here*," he said. "If you were awake, why didn't you say something?"

"I don't know," she grumbled. "It…took me by surprise."

"I'm sorry if I scared you."

She finally started to eat. "Let's just forget about it."

"I'm certainly willing to do that. So…what do you say? Do you want me to show you and your brother around the island?"

"Jack's not here on vacation. I don't think he'll be in the right frame of mind to act like a tourist. He might not even be willing to get out of bed. But if he's interested, I'll give you a call."

It was going to be hard to get close to her if she wouldn't let him. He'd thought he'd made some progress at dinner last night, so he couldn't help being disappointed by this setback. The fact that he'd awakened her when he tried to open her door had cost him a lot of credibility. He'd have to be more careful. "Sounds good."

After she'd finished eating and cleaned up her mess, she took his empty beer can and threw it away. Then she poured him a cup of coffee and put it down in front of him before walking out of the kitchen.

18

Ismay showered and got ready for the day before calling Remy. Although it was eight thirty in California, not all that early, she wasn't overly optimistic that she'd be able to reach him. He usually studied until late. But she'd never answered his last text, so she was eager to talk to him. She also thought it might help keep her mind where it should be, remind herself of her commitment to him.

"Hey," he said, his voice filled with sleep.

"I didn't mean to wake you. Just…wanted to touch base."

"No problem. I need to get up, anyway. How are things on Mariners?"

"Jack got in last night."

"Great. Now both our brothers are there."

At least he wasn't excited about Bastian being around, either. He wanted it to be just the two of them, and she could understand why.

She thought about telling him that Bastian had tried to get into her room last night, but Bastian's explanation was plausible enough—especially for someone who was drunk. She didn't think her future in-laws would be pleased if she were to complain about a little drunken fumbling at her door, especially since nothing had come of it.

"It'll be fine," she said. "We'll make the most of it."

"I guess we'll have to. No matter what happens, it'll be better than spending more time at the library. God, I'm tired of studying."

"You're almost at the end of it."

"Two more weeks of this sounds like an eternity."

"It'll be worth it."

"What do you have planned today?"

She thought of lunch with Honey, Bo, and Jack. But Honey's consent wasn't a given, and she didn't want to saddle Remy with the worry that she might not be able to find Jack a place, so she decided not to mention it. "I'll probably take Jack to the beach."

She heard his alarm go off. "Must be time for you to get up."

"Yeah. And I'm meeting a study partner, so I can't be late."

"Mitch?"

"Sam."

Although lately he studied with Sam more than Mitch, Ismay had never met him. "Okay, I'll let you go."

"Have fun today."

"I will," she said and disconnected.

After he was gone, she remained on her bed, waiting to feel… something. That she missed him. That she couldn't wait for him to arrive. That he cared about her. But those feelings didn't come.

What was wrong? she asked herself. And how could she fix it?

She fell back on the bed and stared up at the ceiling. Maybe she'd been so busy finishing school and taking the bar that she hadn't realized how much things had changed between them. She'd accepted her own excuses—told herself that things would get better when they got out of school and started their post-grad lives together.

But if Remy was caught up in what he was doing now, it

would only get worse during his residency. Those hours were notoriously long. Although she had several hard years ahead getting her practice started, his would likely be worse. At least she could set her own hours. Did she want to feel alone and neglected when she got home at night?

He was preoccupied trying to accomplish something great, she reminded herself, and that was no reason to give up on him. She wasn't that kind of person. He said he loved her, that he needed her to be patient and support him, and she didn't want to let him down. Once he got to the island, they'd be able to work things out.

Gathering her energy, she got up and texted Jack. You awake? How are you feeling?

She didn't get a response, so when she came back downstairs, she told Bastian, who was hanging out on the porch wearing a tank top and swim trunks and drinking another beer, that she was going to see her brother.

"You taking the Jeep?" he asked.

Her mind raced as she paused on the steps of the porch. She didn't need a vehicle. If she took the Jeep, where would she park it so he wouldn't be able to see it? "I…um, no. I think I'll walk."

"*To town?* That'll take an hour, at least."

"I'll call an Uber if I get tired," she said. "Have a great day!"

The restoration company had finally come and set up some giant fans, and Bo and Jack were ripping the baseboards off the walls when Ismay reached the bungalow. She'd walked beyond the turnoff, then doubled back so Bastian wouldn't see her heading to the caretaker's. She didn't think he was following her, but she thought it wise to be cautious all the same. "Wow. You guys are working already?" she said when she walked in.

"I tried to tell your brother he should spend his first day with you, going out to see the island, but he said there'd be time for that later."

"Now is when you need me," Jack clarified. "Ismay can show me around later. Maybe by then I'll be better company, anyway," he added.

"I'm not expecting you to pretend to be happy and go out with me," Ismay said. "I know how you're feeling. I just wanted to get you away from the situation at home."

There was a loud popping sound as he pulled off more of the baseboard. "And I appreciate it. I just need to stay busy right now. It helps."

Ismay indicated the growing refuse pile. "That's a lot of trim."

Bo tossed another piece onto the pile. "Some of the Sheetrock will have to go, too."

"Are you going to replace it yourself or hire someone?" she asked.

"We might as well replace it ourselves," Jack said. "Together, we can do it fairly quickly."

Ismay rested her hands on her hips. "Since when have *you* done anything like this?" she asked her brother.

"Who do you think helped Dad remodel the kitchen a couple of years ago?" he asked.

"And there's always YouTube," Bo joked.

"Whatever the Windsors are paying you, it isn't enough," she told him. "Are all caretakers as capable as you are?"

He shrugged. "I like knowing I'm earning my keep."

Trim work was specialized enough that he could easily have told Annabelle it was beyond his skill level and forced her to hire a contractor. But going above and beyond by doing the work himself seemed to be a matter of pride to Bo, which made Ismay like him all the more. He wasn't lazy, he didn't complain, and he didn't think only about himself. He just stepped up and made a difference, whether that was helping to repair a house, getting a generator started for someone during a terrible storm, or letting a complete stranger stay with him.

"You're certainly unusual," Ismay said.

His lips slanted into a crooked grin. "I prefer to think of it as being one of a kind."

She returned his smile. "Can I help, too?"

"You bet." Jack pulled off his gloves and tossed them over to her. "Use these, though."

"What will you use?" she asked.

"*I* know what I'm doing," he replied, and it felt good to hear him make a joke.

"You haven't seen what *I* can do yet," she said, then helped them remove baseboards for the next two hours. The work was so laborious she was exhausted by the time they decided to stop and get showered and ready to go to Honey's.

"Can I ask you something?" Ismay said to Bo once they were ready and walking over.

"Maybe..." He grinned, but she could tell he wasn't entirely joking. The answer probably depended on the question.

"How does Honey know it was Remy and not Bastian who was kicking her cat?"

"Maybe they were easier to tell apart when they were younger," he said. "I don't know. Why?"

Because she couldn't help thinking that it would've been all too easy for Bastian to say he was Remy. If twins could get away with that type of thing, they did—at least occasionally—didn't they? Especially if it meant getting out of trouble...

When she didn't respond right away, Bo slowed his step. "Ismay?"

She was tempted to tell him about Bastian trying to open her bedroom door in the middle of the night. She was still a little freaked out by that. But she felt she'd already done too much to pit him against his employer. She'd feel terrible if he quit his job or was fired because of her.

Besides, Jack was listening to the conversation. She didn't see how there was anything to be gained by giving him more things to worry about, especially because Bastian's intentions could've been exactly as he'd described them.

"I was just thinking," she said. "After getting to know Bastian, I could certainly see him kicking a cat."

Bo looked over at her in concern, and she knew it was because he'd seen the contents of that duffel bag. He knew where her mind had been going with the question about the cat. A lot of psychopaths started out by harming animals. But she shot a pointed glance toward her brother when he wasn't looking, to let Bo know she didn't want to bring Jack in on what she'd found in the wall of Remy's closet, and he gave her a slight nod to signify he understood.

Honey served homemade chicken potpie that was so delicious Bo nearly moaned. He knew Honey was a good cook—she'd made him a few meals in the past—and after prison food, it didn't take much to impress him, but this went above and beyond anything he'd ever eaten before.

Ismay must have agreed with him, because she said, "Wow! Where'd you get this recipe?"

Honey filled their glasses with more sweet tea garnished with fresh mint leaves. "Oh, that's been in the family for generations."

Ismay used her knife to cut a chunk of potato in half. "Is it something you're willing to share, or—"

"Of course, I'll share," Honey broke in. "Good recipes are meant to be enjoyed. I'll copy it onto a card before you go."

"Thank you." Ismay took another sip of her tea. "I haven't done much cooking since I've been in school, but I hope I'll have more time for it this fall. Or maybe I'll get more serious about it this summer—if I ever get tired of reading on the beach," she added with a laugh.

Clementine had been passing back and forth under the table while they ate. The cat wound around Bo's leg, brushing him with her tail, but since they were in the middle of a meal, he refrained from picking her up.

"I love time-tested recipes," Honey said as she put the pitcher down again. "But I enjoy trying new ones, too. I collect magazines for just that reason. I cut them out and paste them on a card. I have more recipes now than I know what to do with, but it's sort of my thing to include a different one with each greeting card I send at Christmas or for birthdays or whatever—a recipe for something I think that person would particularly enjoy."

"What a clever idea," Ismay said.

"Does your daughter like to cook?" Bo asked.

"Are you kidding me?" Honey rolled her eyes. "Frankie orders out for every meal. I keep telling her all that rich food can't be good for her or her family, but she won't listen."

Bo stabbed a piece of gravy-covered carrot, cooked to perfection, with his fork. "It's a different era."

"My granddaughters love to come here because I'll actually make them a meal," Honey said.

"I'd rather have a home-cooked meal, too," Ismay said. "Like you, my mother is an excellent cook."

"Maybe one or both of your granddaughters will take after you," Bo said to Honey.

"I certainly hope so." She turned to Jack, who hadn't said more than a few words since they'd arrived.

"Jack, I hate to bring up a painful subject, but… I hear you're going through a divorce."

He swallowed. "Yeah."

"I'm sorry to hear it. Love is such a two-edged sword, isn't it?"

He nodded. "I never dreamed…" he started to say but fell silent.

Bo could tell that an upwelling of emotion had tied his tongue and felt for the guy. He was liking him more all the time and felt terrible for what he was going through.

Honey must've heard the same thickness in his voice. Wearing a compassionate expression, she studied him for a moment. "You know, it might be hard to hear this now, but I've lived quite a few years longer than you have and would like to give you the benefit of my experience—if you wouldn't mind."

"I don't mind," he managed to say but his gaze lowered to his plate again.

"I went through an early divorce, too," she said.

Jack dragged his gaze back up to her face. "You did?"

"Oh, yes. I had my oldest child and no help. I could barely eke out a living. On top of that, I thought I'd never love again. I had to take it one day at a time, but eventually those days started getting just a bit easier—and then I met my late husband. So have faith."

"One day at a time," he said.

She gave him a kind smile. "Yes. That divorce turned out to be the best thing for me. Maybe it'll turn out to be the same with you. You're clear across the country on an island you've never visited before. Who can say what possibilities will open to you?"

"True," Jack responded. "But I feel like a burden, like I shouldn't have come."

Bo would've assured him, but Ismay beat him to it. "You're not a burden!" she exclaimed.

"Your sister's right," Honey said. "You'll be doing me a big favor. I wouldn't have left the island this summer if you hadn't come, but sometimes we have to get out of our comfort zone."

"So you're going to go to Pennsylvania?" Bo asked.

"I am," she said decisively. "I figure the universe is telling me I'd be a fool to miss this opportunity to be with my family while I can still travel." She took a sip of her tea. "I'll leave in two weeks. That'll give me time to make all the arrangements. And I'll be gone at least a month, maybe two."

"Sounds as if this summer will hold something different for all three of you," Bo said.

Honey put down her fork and knife. "Maybe even you, Bo."

He thought the same thing. Just having someone like Ismay around created a big change. He'd never met anyone like her. But he didn't care to explain that, which was why he hadn't included himself in the comment.

"Did you ever find out if the girl in that picture you showed me was the one who lost her life in that tragic fire?" Honey asked.

Suddenly uncomfortable, Bo shifted. He hadn't had a chance to tell Ismay about the information he'd found or how he'd found it. He'd been hoping to learn more first. Not wanting the subject to become the focus of their lunch, especially given its sensitive nature, he shook his head. "Not yet."

"Well, I don't know how to use a computer," she said. "I don't even have one. But I went over to the library this morning while I was out getting the whipping cream for our dessert and found this. I thought it might help."

Bo could see Ismay tense as Honey got up and took her purse off the counter. She knew exactly what Honey was referring to, and he could tell it made her nervous. She'd trusted him, clearly indicated she didn't want anyone else to know about what she'd found. But he *had* drawn someone else into the situation, which wouldn't be interpreted as a good thing.

Fortunately, she remained silent. For that, he was grateful.

When Honey sat back down, she pulled a photocopy of an article out of her purse, unfolded it, and handed it to him.

At first, he thought it contained all the information he'd already found online. Who Lyssa Helberg was. What had happened to her. How hard her death had hit the entire island. But as he finished reading and looked more carefully at the picture that'd been published with it, he caught his breath. Lyssa's casket sat in the foreground with a huge spray of flowers on top and a semicircle of funeral attendees gathered around.

And right there, in the front row, stood Bastian, Remy, and their parents.

Remy had known the girl. But in what capacity? And had he been at the party that night?

"This is great," he told Honey. "Do you mind if I keep it?"

"Not at all. I also spoke with Ivy Hawthorne at the library about where Lyssa's folks are living these days. Seems they moved away shortly after this tragedy, and I don't blame them." She pulled out another slip—one on which she'd written a name and address in her spidery script.

"They're back in Boulder?" he said when he saw the address.

"That's what Ivy said."

"Did she think it was odd that you'd inquire about Lyssa all this time later?" he asked.

"I don't think so," Honey replied. "I told her you'd found a picture in a library book you wanted to return to the family, and she called a mutual friend to get permission to give me Lyssa's father's office address. He's a developer in the area."

Bo took the paper and folded it inside the article before slipping both in his back pocket.

Ismay sent him another glance. He could feel it, but he didn't look back at her. He wanted Honey to feel her job was complete, so she'd forget about the picture and leave the rest to him.

"I'll get it off to them," he said as if that was that. "Thanks for your help."

"Of course." She clapped her hands. "Now, who's ready for dessert?"

Working. That was the only thing that helped. The sound of the hammer was more comforting than anything else, Jack thought, as he helped Bo tear out the ruined Sheetrock and replace it. The sound of the saw, which blocked out all other noise, was even better as he mitered piece after piece of baseboard so Bo could attach it to the wall.

They'd paint last. Probably tomorrow, since it was getting late. That would be a quieter job, but at least he'd still be busy.

It was when he had nothing to do that the reality of his situation hit him. Then he'd ask himself what the hell he was doing clear across the country working with a dude he'd barely met to repair a storm-damaged house he'd never seen before when, just days ago, he'd been married and hoping to start a family with Ashleigh.

At lunch, the neighbor for whom he'd soon be house-sitting had suggested he'd eventually heal. But it was hard to believe that was true.

He was dying to call Ashleigh, to hear her voice. She'd been an integral part of his life for so long. But something about how she'd behaved the day she came to pick up her things stopped him. She'd asked for more of their belongings than what was fair. That showed how little she really cared about what was left of him, because she didn't care if there was anything left *for* him.

At six o'clock, Bo set aside his hammer. "That's it for the day. Let's go to town and grab dinner. I'll take you to my favorite place. You've earned it."

The only thing Jack wanted to do was lie down and curl into a tight ball. But constantly being with Bo, who expected him to react as though he *weren't* a hairsbreadth away from buckling under the pain he felt, kept him going through the motions of working, eating, showering, and attempting to sleep, even though he'd only stared at the ceiling last night. Part of him was tempted to bolt—to fly home right away. But the other part wanted to do anything *except* face the reality of what he'd left in Tremonton.

So he felt frozen in space and time with something terrible going through his gut. "Should I call Ismay to see if she wants to join us?" he asked.

Bo hesitated for a brief second. His reaction was subtle, but somehow—despite being so caught up in his own misery—Jack noticed. "Maybe the two of you would like to be alone," he said. "You've had hardly any time together since you arrived."

"I'm sure she'd be happy to come along. She likes you. I can tell."

"But I just remembered I have to put together some receipts and other stuff for the family who pays me, so… I'll grab a sandwich here, and you two go out."

Jack didn't know how to respond. It seemed as though his suggestion that Ismay join them was what had made Bo decide not to come. But he knew Bo would deny it if he suggested she was the reason he'd changed his mind, so he simply nodded and texted his sister. We ever going to eat?

You're already done? she wrote back. You sure you don't want to work around the clock?

She was teasing him, trying hard to do or say anything to lift his spirits.

I'd be fine with that. It's Bo. He's the lightweight. ;) He was making an attempt to joke around with her like he normally would, but it was weird that something like that suddenly required effort.

Good. I'm glad one of you finally made the other stop. Let's go get some dinner.

Where?

Bo's coming, right? I bet he knows of a good place.

This was proof she didn't mind if Bo joined them. But Jack had no energy to cajole either one of them. He was barely handling his own problems.

He's not planning on joining us.

Why not?

Has something to do.

Then maybe I should let Bastian come along. Is that okay with you? Or would you rather it's just the two of us?

He hated small talk, but meeting Remy's brother might prove to be a good distraction—like working was. At any rate, it'd probably be better than probing what he was currently feeling, which was what would happen if they went alone.

Sure, bring him. It's kind of funny that I'm meeting him before I meet my future brother-in-law, but…

What can I say? Remy's trying to set the world on fire. That doesn't leave room for much else.

What does Bastian do for a living?

We'll let him explain it to us tonight.

19

Ismay could tell that Bastian was out to show Jack a good time. Instead of letting her spend time alone with her brother, he'd insisted they all go to an expensive restaurant neither she nor Jack would've chosen, made a big show of picking up the check, and then coerced them into going to a different restaurant to cap off the night with a final drink—or in Jack's case, dessert. Ismay was glad Remy's brother was on his best behavior and seemed to be welcoming Jack to the island, but she was anxious about Bastian discovering Jack was staying with Bo. She'd had her brother meet them at the first restaurant as though he'd just walked down the street from Hotel Mariners, so if Bastian found out, she'd look pretty ridiculous.

The possibility kept Ismay from enjoying herself. But it wasn't just that. All afternoon, she'd been uneasy about the exchange between Bo and Honey at lunch. She wanted to talk to him about what it meant that the girl in the picture had died in a house fire. With Jack at Bo's side almost every moment, however, she hadn't had the opportunity. She hoped they could talk later tonight, that maybe he'd meet her on the beach again.

So she laughed and talked and went through the motions of enjoying herself while Bastian reveled in the attention. He loved having an audience, did most of the talking, and didn't seem to realize that she and Jack were growing tired of listening. Afraid he might go on all night, regaling them with story after story, she yawned and stretched before he could order yet another drink. "I think I'm ready to call it a night, Bastian. Jack must still be jet-lagged, too."

"We can drop him by his hotel on our way back to the cottage," Bastian said.

"Actually, we'd like to call our parents and check in with them, so if you don't mind, I'm going to hang out with him for a bit."

He didn't seem happy she wasn't planning to go back with him. He liked to be the one in charge.

Somewhat reluctantly, Bastian drained his glass, tossed some cash on the table, and stood. But he was unsteady enough she decided it wouldn't be safe to let him drive. "Why don't you take an Uber, and I'll bring the Jeep?"

"Why?" he countered.

She used the app on her phone to request a ride. "You've had much more to drink than I have."

"I'm fine," he insisted, wearing a skeptical expression. "I can drive."

"There's no need for you to." She showed him her phone. "Look, I've already called for a ride."

She guessed he would've given her more of an argument but having the Uber on its way put a decisive end to the question, and she was grateful he accepted it. She didn't want him to get belligerent and cause a scene at the restaurant as she tried to fight him for the keys.

Fortunately, he handed them over without further dispute.

"You'll be coming back soon?" he asked as they waited on the curb for his ride.

"Pretty soon," she replied. She wasn't going to let him hold her to anything.

"See you when you get home."

With any luck he'd be asleep, but she nodded and smiled as she sent him off. Then she turned to her brother. "Thank God."

"No kidding," Jack grumbled. "That dude's a pompous ass. Don't tell me Remy is anything like him."

"No, they're very different." At least in most regards. Remy wasn't a braggart, but he could be selfish—not that she wanted to get that specific.

Jack jerked his head toward the Windsors' vehicle. "Nice move on getting the Jeep."

She pressed the fob that would unlock the doors. "I couldn't let him drive like that."

"Dude thinks he can do anything," Jack said.

Ismay didn't comment. She felt bad disparaging her future brother-in-law, but he was pretty darn insufferable.

"So where are we going now?" her brother asked. "We should probably wait a while before heading over to that side of the island."

"Yeah. Just in case he doesn't go in right away or walks over to Bo's to check on the repairs. You never know."

"Should we go ahead and check in with Mom and Dad?"

That had been an excuse, but Ismay thought it was a pretty good idea. While they sat in the Jeep, they called them on Bluetooth.

Their mother answered right away. "How are you enjoying the island?" she asked after they'd said their hellos.

"It's beautiful here," Jack said.

There wasn't much enthusiasm behind her brother's words, but Ismay had to respect that he was trying. "He's lucky he got here after the storm."

"What storm?" Betty asked.

"We had a bad one."

"It felled a lot of trees and that sort of thing," Jack explained.

"I've been helping the Windsors' caretaker fix his bungalow. There was a significant amount of water damage."

"I'm glad you're doing your part," Betty said.

Jack moved the seat back to accommodate his long legs. "Can you get Dad on the phone, too?"

Ismay got the impression her brother was homesick and wasn't surprised. Other than leaving for college, which was only a half hour away, or maybe driving down to Salt Lake or up to Boise to see friends, he'd never been away from Tremonton.

"What's it like there?" Buzz asked when Betty used her speaker function to allow their father to participate in the conversation.

"It's different. Feels almost like colonial New England to me," Jack said with a laugh.

"I'd like to see it one day."

That comment took Ismay by surprise. Her father wasn't much for travel. "You two should come out," she said.

"Can't do it right now," Buzz told her. "Too much work to be done here."

Ismay had expected a refusal. It was harvest time. And her parents kept a tight budget. They still had a lot of children to support.

"I'll send plenty of pictures," Jack said.

Their parents asked about Remy and when he'd arrive, where Jack was staying and what he planned to do with his time. He said he'd try to find a job after the bungalow was finished and the fence surrounding the garden was mended. Then Jack asked what he'd probably wanted to ask from the very beginning.

"Any word from Ashleigh?"

There was a brief silence before his mother answered. "I saw her in the grocery store the other day. But she wouldn't acknowledge me."

He shoved a hand through his thick dark hair. "Was she alone?"

"No, Jessica and the kids were with her."

"Did she seem happy?"

"I couldn't tell, Jack," Betty said. "As soon as she spotted me, she grabbed their cart and shot down a different aisle."

He let his head fall back on the headrest. "Wow. They're out grocery shopping together…"

Ismay knew he was still hoping Ashleigh would come back to him, that he wouldn't really be stuck in the nightmare in which he found himself.

Reaching over, she squeezed his forearm. "Everything's going to be okay," she murmured, then spoke up for the sake of their parents. "We'd better go. Jack's worked hard all day. He's got to be tired."

"We're heading to bed, too," Buzz said.

"Good night," Ismay said, but her mother caught her before she could hang up.

"Ismay?"

"What?"

"Remy's brother sure seems like a great guy. It's a relief to know you're in good hands."

Ismay moved her purse from her lap to the floor of the passenger side. "What'd you say?"

"I said I like Bastian. It was considerate of him to call and assure us that he's looking out for you."

"Bastian called *you*? How? When?"

Her mother sounded confused when she responded. "It was just this morning. I—I thought you'd given him our number."

"No, I… Why would he feel the need to call *you*?"

"I don't know, but it was very thoughtful."

"What'd he say, exactly?"

"Just that he could tell we raised you right, that you're a very nice girl, and it must be hard having you so far from home. He wanted to assure us that he's looking out for you while you're there."

"Why would I need someone to look out for me?" she asked.

"What do you mean?" her father responded. "Why would it hurt?"

Ismay began to rub her forehead. She couldn't really fault Bastian for what he'd done. She supposed, on the face of it, his call was polite. And yet…like so many other things about him, it was odd.

"He's…different," she said.

"In what way?" Betty asked. "Because he seemed perfectly genuine to us. To be honest, we wish…"

"What?" Ismay prodded when her words fell off.

"We wish Remy would show a little interest in us. We've never even spoken to him, so imagine our surprise to hear from his twin brother!" her mother finished.

Ismay had made many excuses for the fact that Remy seemed so indifferent toward her family. She'd be grateful if she didn't have to deal with his brother, so maybe she was just as bad. But at least she'd met Bastian before making that determination.

"Aren't you glad he's there?" her father asked.

She remembered her doorknob jiggling in the middle of the night and the fear that'd welled up. She wasn't glad Bastian was there. She'd felt much safer *before* he arrived.

Bo never thought he'd have to sneak out of his own bungalow, but Ismay had texted him to see if he'd meet her on the beach, and he didn't want Jack to know he was leaving the house. Jack probably wouldn't care; he wasn't intrusive like that. But it was late enough that Bo knew Ismay's brother would wonder where he could be going. If he was careful, Jack wouldn't even have to know he'd left.

The front door clicked as he shut it behind him, so he waited a few seconds to see if any of the lights went on. When they didn't, he decided he was in the clear and hurried down the walkway before circling around the cottage to the beach.

Ismay was already there, sitting on the soft sand with the wind ruffling her hair as she stared out to sea. Hearing him approach, she looked over and scrambled to her feet.

"That girl in the picture died in a house fire?" she said.

"Apparently." Finally able to show her the article Honey had given him, he pulled it from his pocket and turned on his phone's flashlight.

"What do you think?" he asked when he could tell she was getting to the end. "Did you see the picture?"

She held it closer to her face before looking up. "Remy's in the front row."

"Along with his family."

"So…maybe their families were friends?"

"I haven't been able to determine that yet. I'm sorry if my asking Honey made you feel as though I didn't keep my word."

"It's okay. You covered for it well. It just…took me by surprise."

"She's lived on the island for a long time. I didn't know how else to go about finding out who was in that photograph."

"It worked," she said.

"It did. Now we just need to figure out why that photograph was in the duffel bag."

With a sigh, she sat down again, and he sat beside her. "Coming here has been nothing like I anticipated," she said. "I'm worried about Jack. And Bastian. And, most of all, that damn duffel bag."

He could see her point. "It's not turning out to be much of a vacation so far."

"There've been a few highlights."

The sound of the surf had always been comforting to Bo. That was part of what kept him on Mariners. "Such as?"

"You're one of them," she said.

He didn't know how to respond. Meeting her had been a highlight for him, too—but it had also introduced some risk and uncertainty into his life right when he'd begun to feel he could quit looking over his shoulder. "I'm glad it hasn't been *all* bad." Making light of it would keep them from drifting too close, he hoped.

"I'll have to figure out a way to ask Bastian, and maybe Remy, about Lyssa Helberg," she said. "See how they react, what they have to say."

"I can talk to the librarian, Ivy Hawthorne, in the morning. She knows a lot about what goes on here."

Ismay hugged her knees to her chest. "How will you bring it up?"

"Just by following up on what Honey told her—that I found Lyssa's picture in a library book."

She heaved another sigh. "That'll be good."

"Shouldn't raise too many alarms," he added.

"Do you think we're worried for no good reason?" she asked. "Sometimes it feels ridiculous that I'm even trying to figure this stuff out. Maybe I should just ask Remy about it."

From what Bo had seen, most normal, good people struggled to believe psychopaths truly existed. Or rather, they knew psychopaths existed on a cognitive level, but they couldn't imagine ever being victimized themselves. "I wouldn't," he said.

The look on her face when she glanced over at him suggested she'd heard the caution in his voice. "Why not?"

He refused to meet her gaze, because he couldn't tell her why—at least he couldn't say what he really wanted to say. "I just wouldn't."

"You think that duffel bag could indicate something terrible?"

"Don't you? Isn't that the problem?"

She didn't answer.

"I think it could also mean nothing," Bo continued. "But we won't know until we learn more."

She let go of her knees and began to push the sand into a pile. "Bastian called my parents this morning."

"What for?"

"To tell them he's looking out for me while I'm here."

"What would make him do that?"

"I have no idea. He didn't tell me he was going to do it. I don't even know how he got their number."

"Do they have a landline?"

"Yeah. They've had the same number for years—since I can remember."

"Then he was probably able to look it up online."

"But why would he go to the trouble?" she asked. "That's what has me boggled. He was such an asshole when he first got here. And now he's trying so hard to be *the man*. It's just…weird."

Bo shrugged. "He gets off on doing weird things," he said, but he was willing to bet the way Bastian had acted at first had more to do with Bo than Ismay. Bastian hadn't liked finding them together, hadn't wanted to be one-upped by a mere caretaker.

"I guess so," she said. "But… I've been feeling strange ever since I got here. Everything I thought I knew… Never mind."

He helped her pile more sand on top of the mound she was creating. "Are you having second thoughts about spending the summer here?"

"It's not that exactly. It's… Oh, never mind. I shouldn't have brought it up."

"There's a lot going on."

"And I don't really know where to turn," she admitted.

He wanted to tell her she could turn to him. He also wanted to put his arm around her and pull her close. But he resisted—so he was surprised when her hand slid into his.

He knew he shouldn't accept the overture, but he wasn't about to reject it. He stared down at their clasped hands, his heart pounding far harder than it should as he threaded his fingers through hers.

Ismay wasn't sure what she was doing. To second-guess everything she'd thought was a given—that Remy was a wonderful person who would go on to do great things in the medical field, that they'd overcome the problems they'd been having in their relationship and find a way to stay together, that she'd enjoy a leisurely couple of months on Mariners and go back to California a new woman ready to tackle her own career—made her feel as though she'd been suddenly cast adrift. She certainly couldn't lean on anyone in her family. They were going through enough with the implosion of her brother's marriage. She couldn't lean on Remy or his brother, who were also the reason for most of her concerns. That left Bo as the closest and most accessible friend, the one who'd been supporting her since she'd arrived on Mariners. It didn't matter that they hadn't known each other long. When she was with him, everything felt better.

"I don't think this is a good idea," he said, obviously referring to the contact.

"We're just holding hands," she told him. "There's nothing wrong with that. Lots of friends do it."

"That's fine, I guess. Except..."

"Except..." she prompted.

"What I'm feeling is definitely not platonic."

As guarded and cautious as he was, this admission took her by surprise. But he was a person who called everything the way he saw it and, apparently, this was no different.

Knowing he was right, she pulled her hand away and opened her mouth to say she hadn't meant anything by it. But that would be a lie. And she couldn't lie to Bo. She felt like she was always pretending lately. Pretending not to feel estranged from her family, even though she did, probably because she was the only girl and had chosen a different path. Pretending not to feel strange about staying with Bastian when he made her so uncomfortable. Pretending all was well with Remy so that he could get through his exams when she'd been having serious misgivings about their relationship for quite some time. And, of course, she was pretending she hadn't found what she'd discovered in Remy's closet. So, instead of telling Bo the contact hadn't meant anything, she simply said, "I'm sorry."

He said nothing. They sat in silence, listening to the churning of the ocean and watching the waves wash up the beach toward them. But then she heard him mutter, "Aw, what the hell," and he put his arm around her and pulled her into the warmth and shelter of his body. "Don't be worried," he said. "Everything's going to be okay."

She closed her eyes as she rested her head on his shoulder. She had only a second before she had to pull away again, or she really would cross the line, but she was going to take this chance to imprint the feel of him on her brain. If all things remained the same, this summer could be the only time their lives would ever overlap, and there was something tragic about that.

20

Somehow, Ismay managed to fall asleep, but half dreams and troubling thoughts bothered her all night. Bo played a major role in what was going through her mind, which made her uncomfortable. So did the way she justified wanting to spend more time with him. She was engaged to Remy; she needed to get her head and her heart back where they should be. But before she could move in that direction with any degree of confidence, she had to know whether her fiancé was the man she'd always assumed he was.

That was what it came down to, wasn't it? That was the cause of her confusion and uncertainty. If she felt she *really* knew Remy—completely believed in him—she'd be able to put forth more of a dedicated effort to make the relationship work. Then even the contents of that duffel bag wouldn't shake her.

But she hadn't even had the nerve to tell Remy what she'd discovered. She'd been afraid he'd react in a way that would only create more doubt—because she feared her intuition had been trying to tell her something for quite a while. She'd certainly seen personality traits in Remy that concerned her. And those traits, taken together with the panties and jewelry in that bag, were—

"There you are!"

Although she couldn't see who'd just spoken, Ismay recognized the voice. She twisted around to see Bastian coming up behind her, wearing swim trunks and carrying a towel, and nearly groaned. She'd chosen the public beach for a reason, had never dreamed he'd follow her here—not when he'd insisted the private stretch of beautiful white sand at the cottage was so much better. Apparently, he was more interested in company than privacy; he was always eager to put on a show.

"I thought you were going to see your friends today," she said, covering her irritation and disappointment with a friendly voice.

"It's such a gorgeous day I decided to put them off until tomorrow. Maybe then I can convince you to join us." He winked as he laid out his towel and dropped down on it. "What are you reading?"

Crime and Punishment sat next to her. After waking up to a text from Bo this morning, telling her he'd finished the book and left it under the cottage porch for her, she'd gone out to retrieve it and added it to the contents of her beach bag. As he'd mentioned, it was a library book, so she needed to read it sooner rather than later but she hadn't been able to sink into the story. She was too preoccupied with how she was going to track down Remy's connection to the girl who'd lost her life in the fire and determine if it meant anything.

"Just an old classic," she told Bastian as she watched three kids toss around a beach ball nearby.

He lifted his sunglasses as he picked up the book. "I've read this."

From what she'd heard, he never really applied himself to anything, so she was somewhat skeptical that he'd actually read such a tome. "Did you like it?"

He thumbed through the book before setting it back down. "I did, actually."

She suspected he was lying, but she didn't press him. She'd

moved on to *The Psychopath Test* by Jon Ronson, anyway, something she'd downloaded to her e-reader a couple of hours ago. At the moment, she was much more interested in the subject of that book and various facts she'd been looking up on the internet via her phone.

According to what she'd read, up to 30 percent of the population had some level of psychopathic traits. Most were *subclinical*, meaning they weren't violent offenders, but they were callous and selfish enough to lie, cheat, steal, manipulate, and hurt people in other ways. She found it interesting that such individuals gravitated toward jobs that held some respect and power—like police, clergy, and CEOs. *Doctor* was also on the list, but so was *lawyer.*

Maybe none of it had any real meaning. The whole point of Ronson's book was how dangerous it could be to classify someone as a psychopath according to some standardized test that could easily be too simplistic a measure for anything as complex as human thought and behavior—and therefore prone to error.

Still, psychologists had to work with something to try to protect the general population. Most used the Hare Psychopathy Checklist, or PCL-R, the *R* standing for the revised edition, which a Canadian forensic psychologist had developed in 1985. It listed twenty traits—everything from lack of emotional depth to parasitic lifestyle to grandiose sense of self-worth—to measure traits of psychopathic personality disorder.

If she were being brutally honest, Ismay could imagine Remy fitting within the 30 percent. That was what her intuition seemed to be telling her—that he had some traits that might cause problems down the line. But she couldn't imagine him actually hurting someone, could she? Could he also fall within the 1.2 percent of US men who had enough psychopathic traits to be clinically significant?

Supposedly, 20 to 30 percent of US prison populations were psychopaths—but the smartest ones never got caught, and Remy was certainly smart. She'd read that psychopathy also tended to run in families, which didn't surprise her. Bastian seemed to possess far more of the characteristics on the checklist than Remy—lack of emotional depth, callousness, poor behavioral controls. He also abused alcohol, which was listed as an indicator.

"How long do you plan to stay out here?" he asked when she went right back to reading. Obviously, he'd been hoping she'd entertain him—or, more accurately, let him entertain her.

"I'm waiting for Jack to join me," she said without lowering her e-reader.

"Why isn't he here now? What's he doing?"

She figured she might as well tell Bastian that Jack was helping Bo. If he found out on his own, it'd look like they were trying to hide it. And once Bo and Jack started fixing the fence around the garden, they'd be in plain sight of the cottage. "He's helping Bo."

Bastian's eyes widened. "Helping Bo do what?"

"Fix the roof and water damage at the bungalow. Jack's good with his hands, and he was looking for something to keep his mind off his troubles." She was tempted to elaborate, but she'd learned in law school that sometimes less was more, or at least the smarter way to go.

"We're paying Bo enough that he can hire other people?" Bastian asked.

Ismay was tempted to take issue with the *we* in that statement. His parents were paying Bo. Bo didn't work for him or Remy. But she bit her tongue. What she needed to do was act like she wasn't all that involved, so that Bastian would drop his guard. "Jack's doing it for free."

He scowled at her. "That doesn't make any sense."

"Of course it does," she replied mildly. "Like I said, he needs something to do. And Bo could use the help."

His dark eyebrows slammed together. "Does Remy know?"

"I haven't told him yet. I've been trying to leave him alone as much as possible so he can study. Besides, I can't see why he'd care what Jack does."

"It's just...weird."

She pulled her knees in and hugged them to her chest. "What's weird about wanting to help? Jack grew up on a farm. He's used to working hard."

A skeptical expression settled over Bastian's face. "Are you sure you aren't trying to help Bo instead of your brother?"

"What do you mean?" she asked, even though she knew exactly what he meant.

"You really like our caretaker. I can tell."

She busied herself putting *Crime and Punishment* back in her beach bag so she could return it to the library later. "I'm grateful for the way he looked out for me during the storm. That's all."

"You realize my mother *told* him to do that. He wasn't some knight in shining armor riding to the rescue. It was his job."

She could see a distorted version of herself in the reflection of his sunglasses as she took her hair down, raked her fingers through it, and pulled it up again. "So? It was still nice."

With a sigh to demonstrate his exasperation, he stretched out on his towel but rose up almost immediately onto his elbows. "Nothing happened between you and Bo before I got here, did it?"

The question was wildly inappropriate and should've made her angry. But Bastian was like that—hot then cold, sometimes acerbic, sometimes unexpectedly magnanimous, always unpredictable, and...shallow. That was her assessment of him so far, anyway. But her anger was immediately quashed when the memory of taking Bo's hand last night landed on her conscience like an anvil. She shouldn't have done that. She wouldn't want Remy to do the same thing with another woman. What had she been thinking? She still loved her fiancé. At least...she'd been fairly certain of that only a week or so ago, and real love couldn't change that fast. "I hope you're not asking what I think you're asking," she said, trying to sound offended enough to beat back his suspicion.

"No, never mind."

Although he'd finally broken eye contact with her, Ismay felt a sudden impulse to call Remy and confess to taking Bo's hand. But she couldn't. That would only distract him at the worst possible moment and make him feel justified for acting like a jealous ass *before* there was any good reason to. It might also cause the Windsors to turn on Bo.

What she had to do was stay in better control of herself in the future. That would be easier if she could just keep her distance from Bo. But he was letting her brother stay with him, and helping her determine what that stash in the closet might mean. She couldn't avoid him altogether.

Which reminded her of Lyssa Helberg. She wanted to casually bring up the topic of the past to see how Bastian reacted. So she asked him what spending summers on the island was like, whether he'd made any lasting friends here, and, eventually, if he'd known the family of the girl whose remains had been discovered at the lighthouse last year.

He told her he'd always loved summers on the island, they were some of his fondest memories, but most of the people he'd met through the years weren't his age and they didn't stay in touch. He said the girl who'd been killed had come to the island with her family as a tourist, so he'd never met her. He'd merely heard about her when she went missing and again when her body was found.

But bringing up Emily's case allowed Ismay to work the conversation around to the subject of crime on the island, which opened up a small opportunity. She just had to handle it well. "What happened to her is terrifying," she said. "Is there a lot of crime on the island?"

A beach ball came bouncing over to them, and he tossed it

back to the kids. "No. You don't have to worry about anything like that."

She slid her sunglasses farther up the bridge of her nose. "Then why'd you call my parents and tell them you'd look out for me while I was here?"

A sly smile slanted his lips. "They told you about that, did they?"

"They did."

"I just wanted to let them know you're in good hands now that I'm here. That there's no reason to worry about you."

Could his motive really have been that altruistic? Somehow, Ismay couldn't believe Bastian was so thoughtful. His call to her parents felt orchestrated, designed to impress her—or them. She didn't know which.

Maybe he'd done it just to bug Remy. Remy claimed his brother did whatever he could to get under his skin. "That was nice of you," she said, smiling despite her true feelings.

He seemed to revel in the praise. He also seemed to accept what she'd said as sincere, even though her true opinion was that he'd overstepped. "I have my moments."

"But why did you feel the need?" she pressed. "If the island is so safe?"

He seemed to be searching for an answer when she added, "Wasn't there another girl? Lyssa Something? Who died at a party?"

His mouth fell open—proof he was shocked to hear Lyssa's name. "That was something else entirely," he said. "An accident that happened years ago."

Although mentioning Lyssa caused a much stronger reaction than mentioning Emily, Ismay had already figured out that the Windsors had known Lyssa. "But isn't it sort of weird that everyone else got out?"

"It was tragic, not weird. I really liked Lyssa." He scooped up a handful of sand and let it drain through his fingers as he added sullenly, "I can't believe Remy told you about her."

Remy hadn't mentioned Lyssa, but she went along with the assumption, since it was a logical one. "He didn't say much, just that a girl died in a fire at a party he went to once." She was pressing her luck assuming Remy had been there, but she couldn't get the information she needed without risk. "And that it was something he'd never forget."

She couldn't see Bastian's eyes behind his dark lenses, but it seemed as though he were looking right through her. Had she screwed up? Given herself away? It was obvious he didn't like this subject. "Remy never cared about Lyssa," he said when he finally spoke again. "And she certainly didn't care about him. She didn't want anything to do with him."

Then why had Remy—if it was Remy—hung on to her picture? And what was it doing in that duffel bag with the other items?

"What happened? How'd the fire get started?"

"I don't want to talk about it," he snapped and got up and grabbed his towel.

Despite having sunglasses on, too, she raised a hand to block the sun. "You're leaving? But…you just got here."

"I'm going back to the cottage. It's too damn hot for the beach today," he said, but she got the distinct impression that his leaving had nothing to do with the temperature.

"You told her about Lyssa?" Bastian knew he probably shouldn't have called his brother. This wouldn't end well. Most of their conversations didn't. But he'd had enough to drink since he'd come back from the beach that he was aching for a fight.

"What are you talking about?" Remy sounded confused.

"Lyssa Helberg. I know you remember her, so don't pretend."

"Bastian, I'm studying. I don't have time for this."

"You'd better make time, brother," he said, pivoting at the fireplace to head back across the living room. "After all, I'm here alone with your fiancée."

There was a long pause. Bastian almost thought his brother had hung up—until Remy spoke again. "Is that some sort of threat?"

"What would you do if it was? Go to Mom and Dad?" Bastian peered through the window toward the walkway leading to the front porch. It'd been two hours since he'd left Ismay at the public beach. He didn't expect her to come back yet, not with her brother joining her at some point. They'd probably hang out all afternoon and have dinner together. But he also didn't want her to walk in on this conversation.

"I might. You know how you get."

Did he have to be so damn patronizing? Bastian could never have a legitimate complaint. Remy passed off whatever he had to say as his own fault because he wasn't *right in the head*, which was so fucked up it made Bastian instantly angry. "Stop with the bullshit! Don't pass this off like you do everything else, saying it must be me because it's always me."

"Will you calm down?"

"Don't tell me to calm down!" Bastian warned. "You think you're so superior, just because you've been through med school. But you're not a doctor yet, even though you act like you are."

"I don't have to be a doctor to know you need mood stabilizers or something, buddy. Anyone who's around you for five minutes can tell you that."

"Fuck you!" he said.

"I don't remember telling Ismay anything about Lyssa," Remy said, ignoring Bastian's foul language. "I can't imagine why I ever would."

"You must have. She just asked me about her."

"What would make her ask about Lyssa?"

"She heard about Emily Hutchins, and…never mind. It doesn't matter how it came up. It just did. And she said you told her Lyssa died in a fire."

"She *did* die in a fire."

"Because of *you*!"

"Not because of me." His brother remained calm, but his words were velvet over steel.

"She was the only girl I ever loved!" Bastian railed. "I don't want you talking about her. Ever! Do you hear? Not to anyone."

"Fine," Remy responded wearily. "Like I said, I don't remember doing it in the first place. Maybe Bo told her."

"He didn't live on the island back then. But there's something about that son of a bitch. He watches everything. Listens to everything. I don't trust him. Neither should you. He acts respectful, but… I think he hates us."

"He doesn't hate us," Remy said. "Don't get paranoid—I'm not worried about Bo. Now I have to go. My exams are coming up, and I'm running out of time to study."

"There's something going on between him and Ismay, Remy."

The silence that followed was all too satisfying, so satisfying that Bastian was tempted to reinforce his statement—to tell Remy that he was losing her to Bo, that he'd found them sleeping in the same room even though the storm no longer made that necessary, that her brother had just arrived and yet he was helping Bo fix the place up after the storm *for free*.

Still, he held off, so he wouldn't make Remy defensive. He'd said enough; he just needed to let the seed of suspicion he'd planted take root and grow on its own…

"What makes you say that?" Remy's voice was low when he spoke again.

"You might think my head is screwed up, but I'm not so screwed up that I could miss something like that."

"What would she want with a caretaker?"

"Maybe she doesn't want anything long-term. Maybe she's after what a lot of tourists are—one hell of a fun summer."

After another long pause, his brother said, "I'll take care of it," and then he was gone.

21

Jack had been in a fog since Ashleigh dropped the bombshell that she was leaving him for her best friend. Actually, it'd been more of a red haze. But something about the fresh ocean air ruffling his hair, the soft warm sand beneath his feet, and all the smiling swimsuit-clad people enjoying the beauty and warmth made him feel like a small semblance of the man he used to be. He'd never been to a place like this.

Closing his eyes, he turned his face up to the sun, breathed in a huge breath, and slowly let it go. The call of seagulls punctuated the laughter, and he could hear the group closest to him and Ismay talking about ordering hot dogs from one of the vendors nearby. Mention of the food helped him separate that scent from the various suntan lotions that filled his nostrils, and he felt the stirring of hunger.

"Let's get a hot dog," he said, opening his eyes and looking at his sister, who was sitting on the towel next to his.

She was reading again. She'd been reading pretty much since he got here, but he didn't mind. He didn't want to have to carry on a conversation, to answer any questions about how he was feeling or if he'd heard from Ashleigh. He preferred to just live in the moment and enjoy this brief cessation of pain.

"They have burgers, too," she said.

"I'll get you one, if that's what you prefer. But I'm sticking with a hot dog. And maybe some cotton candy."

"I'll definitely skip the cotton candy. And the hot dog. But I'll take some of that astronaut ice cream."

When he got up and turned toward the concession stand, he nearly ran into Bo. "Hey, man. I thought you weren't coming."

Bo peered around him at Ismay before meeting his gaze. "Changed my mind. I haven't been to the beach yet this year. Figured it might be fun."

"It's a nice day for it," Jack said. "I was about to get a hot dog. You want one?"

Bo didn't seem eager to accept things. He was always wary, reserved, as if he were afraid there might be strings attached. So Jack felt somewhat gratified, as if Bo was beginning to trust him, when he nodded. "Sure, I'll take one."

"Relish?"

"Onions, no relish."

"Got it. Ismay's right there." He gestured, even though he knew Bo had already seen her. "Why don't you join her, and I'll be right back."

Bo nodded and Jack got in line. While he waited, he turned to watch the other people on the beach, and Ismay and Bo caught his attention. There was something going on between them, he decided. It was subtle, but the way Ismay looked at Bo made him think—

No, he told himself. He had to be wrong. She'd already chosen the partner she wanted to spend her life with. She'd come here to be with Remy for the summer. And yet...

"Can I help you?"

Jack shifted his attention to the little window of the food truck and placed his order. But while the food was being prepared, he looked back and saw the expression on his sister's face as she talked to Bo. She admired him, all right. He knew her well enough to be able to read that easily.

Would she be happier with Bo? He wasn't rich like Remy, but Jack really liked him. And he knew his parents had concerns about Remy, who'd shown zero interest in their family. Ismay insisted he was just busy, that it took a superhuman effort to get through med school, and maybe that was it. But Jack couldn't help wondering if this summer might turn out to be an inflection point for both of them, spinning them off the trajectory they were currently on and flinging them in a direction they never saw coming.

Ismay was much more excited to see Bo than she'd been to see Bastian. She knew that wasn't how things should be. But she couldn't help smiling every time Bo looked at her. And the way he looked at her… It made her feel breathless, which was odd. She was acting completely out of character. She'd never been the type to become infatuated with someone so easily.

"How's Jack handling the work?" she asked while her brother was getting the hot dogs.

"He's a hard worker," Bo replied. "Knows what he's doing. And if he doesn't know, he's eager to learn."

"I hope it hasn't been too inconvenient having him stay with you."

"Nah. I like him. Makes it easy. But Bastian came snooping around today."

She'd told Bastian that Jack was working with Bo. That had to be what'd instigated the visit. "What'd he say?"

After straightening out his towel, Bo crossed his legs in front of him and leaned back, supporting himself with his hands. "Made a few snide comments."

She craned her neck to be able to see his face since it was turned away from her. "Like…"

"We *must've gotten pretty close during the storm*," he muttered. "Stuff like that."

"How did you respond?"

"Didn't. I think that's why he gave up and left. He couldn't goad me into a fight."

Ismay began to draw in the sand beside her towel. "You don't think he's figured out that Jack's staying with you..."

"No. I'm sure he would've made a big deal about that."

"So what do you think he'll tell his parents?"

"What can he tell them?" Bo countered. "That your brother is visiting the island and helping me while he's here? I don't see how they can get mad about that, especially because I'm handling the reconstruction instead of waiting for a contractor. Not only does that save them money, it means their property will be put to rights that much sooner."

Bringing in her knees, she folded her arms on them and rested her chin on top. "I mentioned Lyssa Helberg to him."

Bo wasn't wearing sunglasses, so she could easily see the concern in his eyes when he looked over. "And? What'd he say?"

"Basically, he confirmed that he and Remy were at the party when she died."

"How'd you bring it up?"

Checking to make sure she had time to explain before her brother returned, she saw Jack at the small table near the food truck adding ketchup and mustard to the hot dogs. "He assumed Remy mentioned her, and I let him. It made him mad that Remy would talk about it. It was obviously a touchy subject."

"That's interesting. You don't think he'll tell Remy about your conversation, do you?"

"I'm almost certain he will. But Remy and I have been together long enough that it's believable he *did* mention Lyssa and simply forgot—maybe one night when he was drunk."

"So Bastian and Lyssa were friends, or were they something more?"

"I got the impression he liked her as more than a friend. Not sure if she felt the same. He told me Remy never cared about her, and she didn't want anything to do with him. But knowing the two of them…"

"You can't imagine anyone not preferring Remy."

"There's that. But I also detected some…jealousy or something."

"You think they both wanted the same girl?"

"Maybe."

"Remy's never mentioned the party, the fire, or Lyssa?"

"Not that I can remember."

Jack was approaching with the food. She gave a subtle signal with her head to let Bo know they were out of time and changed the subject. "So how long will it take to mend the fence around the garden?"

"Day and a half," Bo replied. "We'll get the posts in tomorrow, then let the cement harden before adding the slats. Won't be too difficult."

"What are we going to do after that?" Jack asked, handing Bo his hot dog.

"At that point, you're going to have to start acting a little more like a tourist," Bo joked.

Jack sat down beside Bo as he took his first bite and spoke around it. "I thought I'd get bored sitting on a beach all summer. But—" he finished chewing and swallowed "—there's something cathartic about being on this island, isn't there."

It was a statement, not a question. "I think this place is just what you need," Ismay said. "Maybe you'll finally have the chance to decide what you want to do instead of letting the current of life continue to just…carry you along."

A contemplative expression came over his face. "There's a lot to discover outside of Tremonton."

The worry she'd been feeling for him eased ever so slightly. "Exactly."

* * *

At first, Ismay couldn't tell what the pictures she'd just received on her phone were all about. They'd been taken at a crowded restaurant, from a distance. But once she enlarged the first shot, she recognized Remy sitting at a table in the corner. She couldn't tell who he was with, though. It looked like a woman.

What was this about?

She moved on to the second picture, taken from a closer angle. He was *definitely* with a woman. Ismay could see that clearly now. She was wearing a little black cocktail dress. Actually, they were both dressed up. The restaurant looked like a fancy one, the kind Remy preferred.

When were these photographs taken? Remy loved going out. But he wouldn't be going to a place like this when he couldn't even take five minutes to talk on the phone.

She studied the number from which she'd received these photos. There was no contact name attached, and they'd come without an explanation. Who was this?

The sound of Bastian coming up the stairs caught her attention. He stopped outside her door, which made her freeze. Would he say something? Try to come in again?

She breathed a sigh of relief when his footsteps receded as he continued to his own room. After going to the beach, she'd had dinner with Bo and Jack at a sidewalk café not far from the old-world mansions that lined Elm Street—built by the owners of various vessels during Mariners's whaling heyday—and they'd laughed and talked until it'd grown too dark. She'd only had a pair of loose-fitting cutoffs to wear over her swimsuit and a towel to sling around her bare shoulders.

She'd hoped she'd find Bastian gone when she got home—visiting his "friends," if he really had any—but she'd found him in the living room, so inebriated she'd gotten him a blanket and suggested he sleep on the couch.

Apparently, he hadn't taken her advice.

At least he'd made it safely up the stairs.

When she heard the TV go on in the master bedroom, she knew she was probably safe from bother and returned to the mysterious pictures she'd received. A third one had just come in. This one showed Remy holding the woman's hand across the table as they seemed to talk earnestly.

Then a short video arrived.

Ismay knew she shouldn't click on it. This wasn't going in a good direction. But she couldn't stop herself. The video showed fifteen seconds of Remy kissing the woman so passionately it left little doubt in her mind what would come next, since they were obviously leaving together.

Was he cheating on her? Could this be happening *tonight*?

She felt shaky as she navigated to Remy's last text. He'd sent a message to her earlier to say he was heading to the library and would be up most of the night studying with Sam again.

This was definitely *not* the library…

She switched back to the video. Maybe it was masochistic, but she couldn't keep from watching it again. He'd been so busy, so worried about his exams. Could it be that whoever was in this video wasn't really him? After all, the lighting was so dim…

A second later, she caught sight of the gold ID bracelet he always wore with his Rolex—a gift from his parents when he got his bachelor's degree. She didn't know one other man who wore an ID bracelet, let alone one who was the spitting image of her fiancé.

She swallowed hard as she sat up and focused once again on the number of the person who was sending her this stuff.

Who are you? she wrote and held her breath, hoping to get a response.

Fortunately, she did.

A friend.

Of mine? Or Remy's?

I think this makes that plain.

When was this taken?

Just a few minutes ago.

Who's he with?

Samantha Something. I don't know her last name.

Samantha. Sam. Could this be whom Remy had been studying with? He'd acted as though *Sam* were a guy…

Ismay threw her legs over the side of the bed and got up.

How do you know her first name?

I heard him say it.

And how do you know me? How'd you get my number?

We had a class together once—and did a group project not long after you got with Remy.

Ismay was feeling a bit sick to her stomach.

What's your name?

I don't want to say.

Why not?

Because Remy can be a vindictive bastard.

Was that true?

How would you know?

When he got me pregnant, you should've seen how he acted.

The word *pregnant* stood out as the other words melted into the background.

You were pregnant with his baby? When?

Before you came along. When he was with Noelle Poole.

Ismay recognized the name of Remy's former girlfriend. They'd run into her occasionally on campus or various local eateries, but the relationship had ended badly, and Remy always circled wide to avoid her.

You're saying he was cheating on her with you?

Isn't that obvious? This is my revenge. And God, does he deserve it.

Ismay tried to get this woman to engage with her again. She'd revealed enough with the pregnancy that Remy would be able to identify her. Didn't she realize that? Ismay pointed it out. And asked if she'd had the baby. Did Remy have a child out there he hadn't told her about? That possibility was mind-blowing. But after a few minutes of nothing, someone else answered—she got the impression it was a man—who said not to bother him again. He claimed to have let a friend borrow his phone, and that he'd never reveal her name. He left Ismay with: If you have half a brain, you'll get away from Remy Windsor and stay away.

After that, she guessed he blocked her, because she couldn't get him to respond again.

★★★

Fortunately, Ivy was at the library when Bo went in the following morning to return his books.

"Hey," she said when he approached the circulation desk.

He smiled. "Hey."

"Haven't seen you for a couple weeks. I've been wondering if everything's okay."

"The storm wreaked some havoc on the other side of the island, setting me back a bit. And with the cottage now in use, I've got more to do."

"The Windsors are in town, are they?"

"No, it's just Remy's fiancée and Bastian."

"Bastian's there alone with Remy's fiancée? That's a bit odd, isn't it?"

He almost mentioned that Ismay's brother was also on the island but decided that was another tangent he'd avoid. "Maybe a little."

"Where's Remy?" she asked.

"Still in LA. Has to take some exams before he can leave."

"Is he really going to become a doctor?"

He put down the books he'd brought in. "Sounds that way."

"I thought he'd go into the diamond business, like his father."

"I guess Bastian's got that covered."

"Guess so." She started scanning the books in. "What are you looking for this week?"

"I'm considering *The Good Earth* and maybe *The Grapes of Wrath*. With summer here, I won't have as much time to read, so I'll probably stop there."

"For so long, you were reading every business book on the shelves, now you've switched to the classics?"

He curved his lips in a wry smile. "The business stuff got a bit dry, and it was becoming repetitive. I needed to change things up."

"Well, you can't go wrong with the classics."

"Figured it's about time I read them." He looked around at the mahogany shelves, the brass accoutrements, the elaborate winding staircase leading to the second floor, and the heavy-framed picture of Ivy's great-grandfather hanging behind her. "I love having access to so many books."

She gave him a funny look. "There was no library where you lived before?"

"It wasn't very…accessible," he said and thought truer words had never been spoken. In prison, it wasn't easy to get the books he'd wanted to read. Almost all the money he earned hustling chess went to Amazon—inmates could order books as long as they came from a recognized publisher or a third-party business. He probably should've saved more of his winnings; he'd had very little to start with when he was finally released. But he'd left the prison library far better stocked than it had been when he was first incarcerated. At the beginning of his sentence, there'd been only a bunch of old tattered paperback novels—castoffs from God knew where.

When he'd left, there'd been enough books to create categories for business, religion, philosophy, popular fiction, and self-help. He hadn't had a chance to collect any of the classics before he was released, and he regretted that now—wished he'd started with them. Although most of the guys behind bars preferred genre fiction, he believed it was only because they didn't know what they were missing. *He* certainly hadn't.

Instead of walking over to the shelves, he remained where he was. "I lent *Crime and Punishment* to Remy's fiancée. But she'll get it back—to me or to you—before the due date."

"No problem."

He'd thought Ivy might bring up the fact that Honey had asked her about Lyssa Helberg, if only to make sure he'd sent off the photograph he'd "found." He sort of hoped she would—to create a natural transition. But she didn't, so he had to bring it up himself.

He started walking away before turning as if he'd had an afterthought. "By the way, thanks for giving Honey the address for Lyssa Helberg's father. I was able to get that photograph off to him."

"I'm surprised you found it in the first place," she said. "You'd think someone else would've run across it by now. It's been…what…nine years since that tragic fire?"

"I don't know how long it's been. Until I found that picture, I hadn't even heard of it."

"I can see why. Emily Hutchins's body being discovered at the lighthouse last year gave everyone something even worse to talk about."

"So what happened with the fire, exactly?"

"Remy and Bastian got into a fight at some party—"

"Wait," he broke in, holding up a hand. "Remy and Bastian were there?" He knew they'd been there; Ismay had told him as much. But he wanted Ivy to elaborate as much as possible, and he felt he had a better chance of that happening if he played dumb.

"They were. The girl who died was Bastian's girlfriend."

A chill rolled down Bo's spine. "Really?" The articles he'd read hadn't made any reference to the Windsors. There was only that picture of the whole family—along with everyone else—at the funeral. "Honey didn't say anything about that."

Ivy checked in another book. "Maybe she doesn't know. The Windsors managed to keep their name out of the papers."

So Annabelle had stepped in to protect them. Bo doubted it was Mort. Mort was too busy with his business. It was Annabelle who looked out for the boys—unless she had to get Mort involved. She brought in the big guns when she had to, and her husband relied on her to let him know when it was that time. "What were Bastian and Remy fighting about that night?"

"According to the gossip that was flying around at the time, they were fighting over Lyssa. Bastian was claiming Remy made a move on her. But who knows if that's true? Word has it they fought over everything."

"I don't get the impression that's changed," he said dryly.

She chuckled as she glanced up. "Somehow that doesn't surprise me."

"So…if they were fighting over Bastian's girlfriend, how was it that she was the only one who didn't survive? You know how it is when someone yells *fight!* Everyone gathers around. Where was she?"

"I heard she started crying and locked herself in an upstairs bathroom when it got nasty between Remy and Bastian. Once the fire broke out, with all the panic and screaming and confusion, it wasn't until the whole house was engulfed that Remy or Bastian or anyone else realized she wasn't out. That was why Remy attempted to go back in."

"He tried to rescue her?"

"That's the story. But the fire was already out of control. Bastian held him back and made him wait for the fire department to arrive, and by then, it was too late."

Remy didn't seem like the type who'd risk his own safety for the sake of someone else. But maybe Bo had him all wrong. The dude wanted to be a doctor, didn't he? "That's rough. Remy and Bastian must've been destroyed. Especially Bastian."

When Ivy didn't answer right away, he prodded her. "Don't you think?"

"I'd hate to guess," she said. "They're…unusual. Nothing seems to bother them."

"What do you mean?"

"I saw them at the coffee shop with some friends only days later, and…"

"It seemed as if nothing had happened?" he guessed.

Although he could tell she didn't want to admit it, she ultimately nodded.

"Do you find it odd that Bastian was the one holding Remy

back, and not the other way around?" he asked. "Since it was Bastian who was in love with Lyssa?"

"That occurred to me, too," she admitted. "I also found it kind of weird that Bastian would flip-flop so quickly and become Remy's defender when they'd just been fighting. But who can say what was going through their heads? An emergency like that probably brings what's most important into focus pretty fast."

"No doubt," he said. "I'm sure they felt terrible. And I'm sorry for her family."

"How would you ever get over that?" She shook her head. "I'm glad you inquired about that picture and were able to get it back to them."

"Me, too. So…you didn't know Lyssa?" he asked.

"I knew of her. I'd seen her around the island. But she was a decade or so younger. It wasn't as if we'd ever hung out." Finished checking in the books he'd returned, she pushed her chair out so she could get up. "Do you need some help finding *The Good Earth*?"

Apparently, she didn't want to talk about the incident anymore. They'd established a certain rapport, mostly over their love of books, but she probably thought she'd said too much. The Windsors were pretty influential. They could even be among the benefactors of the library.

"No, I've got it," he said. "Thanks again."

22

Ismay was grateful Jack was busy building the fence around the garden today because she didn't feel she could entertain him. She was too caught up in her own problems. She'd spent another miserable night watching that video of Remy with "Sam" at the restaurant over and over. After holding Bo's hand and leaning into him for a few moments the night before last on the beach, she wasn't exactly filled with righteous indignation. She felt a degree of guilt herself. But she decided it was time for them to have a talk, whether Remy had exams or not. She couldn't put her life on hold any longer. The emotions churning in her gut were consuming her.

She held her breath as she tried to call him. It was early in California, but she was hoping to catch him before he left for the day.

Maybe he was at Sam's house, and the two of them were still in bed…

The mental image that created made her nauseous, but she knew they'd been together last night, and if she wasn't there to give him a reason to come home, why would he? No doubt, he felt he was in the clear. She could now understand why he was so adamant that she travel to Mariners ahead of him. It enabled him to have a last hurrah before he joined her.

Or that was what she suspected…

His voice mail came on, but she didn't leave a message. She texted him instead.

I need to talk to you. It's important.

She had a shower and put on her makeup, but got no response, so she sent him the video she'd received. Then he called her immediately.

"Where did you get that?" he asked.

The defensiveness in his tone made her curl her fingernails into the palm of her free hand. "Someone sent it to me last night."

Silence. She was the one who eventually broke it. "Is that Sam?"

"No."

"Sam isn't short for Samantha?" she pressed. "There's another Sam in your life? A male one?"

He wouldn't want to admit there wasn't. Then she'd know he'd been cheating for months. He'd been talking about Sam since the start of winter semester. But he must've realized that if he stuck by his initial answer, she'd just challenge him to introduce her to his male study partner, because he backtracked right away. "It's not what you think."

Her knees turned to jelly. She had to leave the bathroom so she could sit on the bed, because she could tell it was exactly what she thought. "You *haven't* been sleeping with her?"

"No, we—"

"Don't," she said, cutting him off immediately. "Don't lie to me on top of everything."

"It's the pressure," he said, changing tactics. "She's in med school, too, and understands what it's like. I guess… I guess I started leaning on her, and…and it went too far."

"You insisted we'd mend our relationship while we were here on the island."

"And I meant that. I still do. After I pass my exams, what happened here won't matter. I'll fly to Mariners, and we can start over."

Her heart was racing so fast she could hardly catch her breath. She closed her eyes as she struggled to get enough air.

"Ismay?" he said. "I'm sorry."

Her mind went to Bo. She wasn't guiltless. She hadn't gone nearly as far as Remy had, and she'd been true until the day she arrived on Mariners. Some would say holding hands and one brief hug was nothing. But she'd felt something while touching Bo, and to her, that counted.

"Can you forgive me?" he asked.

Could she? *Should* she?

If you have half a brain, you'll get away from Remy Windsor and stay away.

Those words ran through her head as she searched her heart.

"We've been through so much together," he said. "Don't give up on me now. It was one mistake."

That'd started at least five months ago. That was a hell of a long mistake. He hadn't seemed to mind lying to her for the duration of that time. And what about the woman who'd outed him? She'd said he'd gotten her pregnant, which meant he'd cheated on his former girlfriend, too. That kind of infidelity made him a serial cheater. "The woman who sent me those pictures claims you got her pregnant."

"It was *Kathleen*?" he said in disgust. "Don't listen to her. She's a goddamn liar."

So was he. Obviously. She opened her mouth to say so but pressed her lips together as he continued.

"We had one encounter, Is. She wanted it to continue, but I

wasn't interested, so she tried to trap me by saying she was going to have my baby. It was all bullshit."

"She was never pregnant?"

"No! Or she would've produced a positive pregnancy test. I asked her for one."

It was plenty warm in the room and yet Ismay's hands and feet were blocks of ice. She'd felt Remy pulling away from her these past several months, felt him taking her for granted more and more—and she'd allowed him to blame it all on the pressure he was under.

"Is?" he said.

A tear rolled down her cheek. She didn't know how to respond. Was he a bastard for doing what he'd done? Or was she just as bad because of how attracted she was to Bo?

"Can you forgive me, babe?" he said. "I never meant to stray. It was just the stress of what I'm going through. I can hardly function."

He hadn't looked as though he was too stressed last night.

"Maybe you'd rather be with her," she said woodenly. "Have you asked yourself that? It might be she's a better fit."

"No! God, no," he said. "You're the one for me. I know I could never find a better person to share my life with, to start a family with."

Once again, she thought of how excited she was every time she saw Bo. That was a form of cheating, too. She could forgive Remy, couldn't she? They'd have to forgive each other. Except… she couldn't tell him that she was attracted to Bo. If she did, Bo could lose his job. Remy wouldn't want him around anymore, especially if he couldn't be on the island to defend what he believed was his.

Considering what Remy had done, she hadn't done enough to worry about confessing, she decided. But before she could even suggest that she might be able to get beyond this, she needed to know that what she'd found in his closet wasn't anything to worry about. She *had* to have that reassurance. "There's something else," she said.

"What is it?" he asked right away.

"The night of the storm? That first night?"

"Yes..."

"I found something hidden in the wall of your closet."

"Did you say *in the wall of my closet*?" he repeated incredulously.

"Yes." She drew a shaky breath. "The power was out, so I was looking for some matches. There was nothing on the shelf except an old notebook of your drawings. But then I felt something unexpected—a loose board—and when I pulled it away, I discovered a duffel bag filled with women's panties, some cheap women's jewelry, and a picture of Lyssa Helberg."

"No way."

"You think I'd make that up?"

"I guess not, but... I have no idea what you're talking about. I didn't even know there was a loose board up there, let alone put that stuff in the wall."

Was he telling the truth? Could she convince herself to believe him?

"And how do *you* know Lyssa?" he added.

"I was curious about who she could be so I did a little digging," she replied. "I also learned you were at the party the night she died."

"I knew her, but... I'm speechless, have no idea where that stuff could've come from."

"You didn't put it there—"

"Of course not!"

"Who else could've done it?"

"Honest to God, Bastian is the only one I can think of. He loved Lyssa. He's never gotten over her. But... I'm not sure what the underwear could mean. Maybe they were hers?"

"I doubt it. They're different sizes and styles," she pointed out.

"Then I don't know what to say."

She let her head fall into her free hand. *Damn it!* This was exactly what she'd been afraid of—that telling him would only introduce more doubt. Was he playing dumb? Could she freaking trust him?

"Babe, I know you must be hurt. But I promise you, things will be different when I get there. I'll make it up to you, prove my love. Just…just hang on that long, okay?"

Another tear slid down her cheek.

"Will you answer me?" he said.

She was staying in his family's cottage. And now she had her brother on Mariners with her. It wasn't as if she could just buy a ticket and fly home. She had to be here for Jack. And what she'd had with Remy was at least worth digging through the embers to see if the flame was really dead, wasn't it?

"I don't know what to do," she said.

"Wait until I get there. Then we can have a heart-to-heart, and I'll prove to you how much I love you—that I'll never do anything like this again."

She began to massage her left temple. The best indicator of future behavior was past behavior. Her parents preached that all the time. Would she be a fool to give him another chance?

Did she have any choice? She was stuck on the island for the summer. And she wouldn't want to pull the plug on a three-year-long relationship too soon. He *had* been under a lot of pressure, and her heart had wandered a bit, too. "I… I'll do my best," she said numbly.

Ismay's door was still closed when Bastian approached it. He hadn't seen her come out yet this morning. But he'd heard the shower. "Good morning!" he called, giving the panel a brisk knock.

There was no answer.

"Ismay?" He thought he heard movement. "Hello?"

"Just…just a minute," she called back.

Her voice had a nasal quality, and when she opened the door, he could see why. She'd been crying. There were no tears now, but her eyes were red and puffy. "Is everything okay?" he asked.

"Fine," she replied.

"Does this…have anything to do with Jack?"

"No."

"Remy?"

"I don't want to talk about it," she said wearily.

So it *was* Remy. Otherwise, she probably would've said no again. "I'm sorry you're upset."

"It's nothing," she said. "Really. What's going on with you today?"

"I'm about to head out to lunch with my friends and was hoping you'd join us."

She shook her head. "I don't feel like going out."

"Oh, come on," he said. "I know you'll love them. And they'll love you. Moping around here won't help whatever you're going through."

After an extended pause, she said, "Okay. Just…give me a minute."

"I'll wait downstairs," he told her.

Surprised and a bit encouraged, he went down to the front entryway—and smiled when she eventually came out and descended the stairs. Remy had caught himself a real beauty, someone who seemed sincere, kind, fair.

This was really going to be good, he thought with a smile.

Matilda was calling again. Bo silenced his ringer before mopping the sweat from his forehead with the bottom of his T-shirt. But only a minute later, his phone dinged with a text. He hadn't picked up, so she'd messaged him.

It's about Uncle Chester.

Shit. She had him. Since Chester didn't have a phone of any kind—refused the cell Bo had tried to give him—it was difficult to check on him. Bo wrote him snail mail letters, but it'd been probably two months since Chester had responded. Bo had written to a neighbor but hadn't heard from him, either. Had they all been flooded out again? Global warming certainly wasn't treating those who lived in that area very well.

"Everything okay?" Jack asked.

Bo's expression must've betrayed him. He quickly schooled his features to mask the emotions flooding through him. "It's nothing," he said. "I just have to call my sister. Mind if we take a few minutes?"

Jack stood his shovel against one of the fence posts they'd put in and removed the leather gloves he was wearing. "Not at all." He bent to retrieve his water bottle. "Ran out of water about an hour ago. I'm going to the house to fill up. You need anything?"

"No, I'm good." Bo waited until Jack was halfway to the house before returning Matilda's call.

As the phone started to ring, he steeled himself for the sound of her voice.

"I have to make you believe something's wrong with Chester to get you to call me back?" she said without so much as a hello.

"*Is* something wrong with Chester?" he asked.

"Maybe, maybe not. First, you're going to listen to me. Then I'll tell you what I know."

"You probably don't know anything." He almost hung up. He hated to let her back into his life. He knew it would bring pain. But she must've sensed she was about to lose the opportunity to speak to him, because she said, "Wait!" And for some reason he listened long enough to hear, "You haven't heard from him recently, have ya?"

He hadn't. He hoped that didn't mean what he thought it meant. "If you know something, tell me. And make it quick."

"First, I want to tell you that Dad's sister asked about you."

"Why?" Like Matilda, his father's family had sided with the prosecutor.

"She didn't say. She just asked if I had a way to reach you."

Matilda wouldn't have had any way to contact him herself if Chester hadn't caved in and given her his number. Chester was obviously getting soft in his old age. And his mind wasn't what it used to be. "What'd you tell her?"

"I said no. I was afraid if I said yes, she'd call you and then you'd change your number to be rid of both of us."

"If you don't leave me alone, I just might do that."

"Are you never going to forgive me?"

As far as he was concerned, she didn't deserve forgiveness. "You're the one who said you'd never forgive *me*, remember?" he reminded her.

"That was a long time ago," she said. "I—I'm not so sure anymore."

"Yeah, well, the damage has been done. It's too late to second-guess the situation now."

"It was a difficult time for everyone."

"You don't say." After she'd helped put him in prison, she hadn't even come to visit him—hadn't so much as sent him a Christmas card. He'd never felt so alone in his life.

She cleared her throat. "So…where are you these days?"

"Nowhere close to you."

"How do you know where I am?"

"If you're still in Florida."

"That doesn't tell me much."

"I'm nowhere close to Chester, either, if that helps. Are you going to tell me what's wrong with him?"

"You only want to hear about Chester? You're not even going to ask how *I'm* doing? If I'm happy? Healthy? I'm married and have two kids now, you know."

His chest tightened. Closing his eyes, he dropped his head back as he battled the demons that'd haunted him for so long.

"Considering what you think of me, I can't believe you'd want them around me anyway."

"Did you do it?" she asked.

How many times was she going to ask that? And how many times would he have to tell her before she believed him? "I have work to do," he said.

"Please." She barely caught him before he hung up. "Can't I know *anything* about you?"

As far as he was concerned, he didn't have any family. Except his great-uncle, of course, who'd stuck by him through thick and thin. "I'll get home to visit Chester as soon as I can," he said and disconnected.

23

Ismay hadn't wanted to join Bastian and his friends for lunch. But she'd had no other plans. And it'd seemed too self-indulgent and maudlin to continue to sit around crying. In that moment, she'd decided she should make more of an effort with Remy's brother.

So far, she was glad she'd come. Bastian's friends seemed to genuinely like him. He'd gone to college with Jace and Terrell, the two guys. Holly, who was a few years younger, maybe twenty-five, was Jace's girlfriend. Like Ismay, Bastian was meeting her for the first time.

Ismay learned a lot by listening to the conversation. While Remy had gone to UCLA for even his undergrad years, Bastian had attended San Diego State, where he'd stayed long enough to get a degree but didn't actually accumulate many credits. He freely admitted he'd spent most of his time on Mission Beach playing sand volleyball with Jace and Terrell, among all the other enthusiasts who hung out there looking for a pickup game. Ismay got the impression Bastian wasn't close enough to these people to invite them to stay at the cottage or show them around during their visit, but he knew them well enough to have a meal with them while they were on Mariners—and maybe see them once or twice more before they left.

Ismay liked Terrell the best. He'd played football for the Aztecs, had a close-cropped Afro, an engaging smile, and warm brown eyes. Jace wasn't quite as tall as Terrell, but he was almost as muscular. He looked like so many of the other people who came to the island—affluent—with his blond hair pushed up off his forehead using a bit too much gel and a pair of designer sunglasses on his chiseled face. He'd played on the football team, too. That was how he and Terrell met, and they'd started rooming together their sophomore year. Despite the lure of Mission Beach, they'd both managed to graduate.

They still lived together in San Diego, despite being from other places, and worked in marketing, Terrell for a local investment firm and Jace for a beer company. Holly, a petite brunette, was an Instagrammer, an aspiring actress, and an exotic dancer. Ismay got the impression she'd attained some success on Instagram, maybe had a lot of followers, but it was mostly the dancing that paid her bills.

"What made you decide to visit Mariners?" Ismay asked Terrell, Jace, and Holly while Bastian placed his order last.

Jace lifted his water glass. "Hearing Bastian talk about it, I guess. To be honest, I wanted to go to Mexico, where our money would stretch a bit further. It was Terrell who was stuck on crossing the entire country to visit this place."

"You hear about Long Island, Martha's Vineyard, Nantucket, and Mariners all the time," Terrell said. "I wanted to see what it's like."

They were sitting out on the sidewalk under a bright yellow-and-blue-striped umbrella with flowers pouring out of pots hanging on poles that also supported a string of lights. Ismay gestured around them. "Well? What do you think?"

"I think it's nice here—Old-world—but as expensive as we were told," Terrell said with a laugh.

"Good thing you make the big bucks," Jace said.

Terrell grimaced. "I don't make that much more than you, bro."

"Well, this meal won't cost you anything," Bastian said, joining the conversation again as the waitress, who now had all their orders, left. "It's on me."

"Damn. Then call her back so I can order some more," Terrell joked.

"You can order whatever you want," Bastian said magnanimously.

Ismay knew he honestly didn't care. He wasn't paying for it. He had his parents' credit card. Remy had one, too, and used it just as freely. "Where are you staying?" she asked the three of them.

"At the Hotel Mariners," Holly replied, and that was when Ismay recognized her error. There were so many other hotels in town. She hadn't expected them to be staying at the one where her brother was supposed to be.

"Ismay's brother Jack is at that hotel, too," Bastian piped up, right on cue.

"For a short time," Ismay added. "There's a neighbor who's leaving for the mainland to see her kids and grandkids for most of the summer. He'll soon be house-sitting for her."

"What neighbor?" Bastian asked.

"Honey Wellington."

"You know Honey?"

"Not really, but when I learned Jack was coming, I asked Bo if he knew of any places Jack could stay, and he told me Honey might need someone to house-sit."

"Wow," he said. "Bo does look after you, doesn't he?"

Terrell and Jace glanced at each other over Holly's head. Hearing the sour note in Bastian's voice seemed to make everyone uncomfortable.

"It was nice of him," she mumbled.

"Why didn't your brother join us for lunch?" Terrell asked.

Ismay was grateful to him for jumping in. "He's helping to rebuild a fence that was blown down in the recent storm."

Holly moved back as the waitress arrived with their mimosas. "I'm glad we missed that."

"It was bad," Ismay told her. "Felt like a hurricane."

Bastian rolled his eyes. "It wasn't a hurricane. It's not even hurricane season."

That didn't mean one couldn't come up, not with all the changes in weather patterns that were happening all over the globe. Besides, he wasn't even on the island at the time. He didn't know what it had been like. But Ismay wasn't interested in arguing about it.

"Ismay's brother's wife just left him for another woman," Bastian announced.

"No way…" Jace said, properly scandalized.

Bastian took a sip of his drink. "Yes, way."

Jace turned to Ismay. "Was that a surprise? Or did he know something was going on?"

"It was a total surprise," she admitted.

"That sucks," Terrell said, shaking his head. "Do they have kids?"

"No." She didn't elaborate, didn't feel her brother's situation was any of their business. It wasn't Bastian's place to tell them about it, either, especially because he was using it simply for the sake of entertainment.

Their meals arrived, putting an end to the topic. Ismay was happy to focus on her food. The restaurant served gourmet burgers and fries, as well as a variety of large salads and sandwiches. She'd ordered a smoked salmon salad with balsamic and pesto dressing, and she enjoyed it while listening to the others talk about their lives, their plans for the summer, and the good old days at SDU.

Eventually, Terrell asked Ismay what she did for a living, and she told them about law school.

"Can you believe she's going to marry my brother?" Bastian said. "She hasn't yet figured out he's a total dick."

"Remy's starting his residency this fall?" Terrell asked, ignoring the comment.

Finished with her salad, Ismay put down her fork. "Actually, his residency starts July 1st. He's still in LA, taking the last part of the United States Medical Licensing Exam. Then he'll be joining me here on the island, and we'll go back to California at the end of June."

"What kind of doctor is he going to be?" Holly asked.

Bastian answered before Ismay could. "He's going into emergency medicine, which should be perfect for him." He snapped his fingers three times in quick succession. "He likes it when things are hopping."

"He'll be doing his residency at Prime West Consortium in West Anaheim," Ismay added.

"How long will that take?" Terrell asked.

The check arrived. Bastian signed for it before saying he had to go to the bathroom and leaving the table.

"Four years," she told Terrell.

Jace finished off his second mimosa. "So you couldn't leave LA even if you wanted to—not for a while."

"Fortunately, I don't want to," she said. "I like it there."

"Even though you're a farm girl from northern Utah?" Terrell teased.

She'd told them where she was from earlier and, of course, Bastian had tied it back to Jack, saying he'd probably never even met a gay person, and then his wife had turned out to be gay. "Maybe *because* I'm a farm girl from northern Utah," she joked.

It wasn't until the waitress came to clear away some of the plates while Bastian was gone that Ismay realized she had an opportunity. These people hadn't known Bastian that well—hadn't lived with him or anything—but they'd known him when Lyssa Helberg was killed in that fire. There was a chance Bastian had talked about her…

"Did either of you ever meet Lyssa Helberg?" she asked as though they should recognize the name—and was gratified when they did.

"The woman who died in the fire?" Terrell said. "She came out to SD once and watched while we played some volleyball."

"Terrible what happened to her," Jace added.

Ismay braved a quick glance toward the restrooms. "I bet Bastian took it hard."

"I think that's what really came between him and finishing school," Terrell said. "He was never the same after that."

Jace seemed confused. "He told you what Remy did that night, didn't he?"

"What *Remy* did?" she said.

Jace and Terrell looked at each other. "Yeah," Terrell said. "You don't know?"

"I know Remy and Bastian got into a fight over something and knocked over a candle. That's how the fire got started."

"That's not what we heard," Jace said.

Bastian came out of the bathroom. "Let's forget it," Ismay said, lowering her voice because she didn't want Bastian to know what they were talking about.

But Terrell didn't let it go. He turned to Bastian as soon as Bastian reached them and said, "You're going to let her marry Remy without telling her what happened to Lyssa?"

A deep scowl etched itself into Bastian's face. "Why would you have anything to say about Lyssa? You didn't even know her!"

Terrell's eyes widened as he leaned back. "I met her once and clearly remember what you told me," he snapped. Then he got up and walked out.

Ismay's heart was racing. She felt bad she'd caused a sudden blowup. But she was also curious—and frightened—about what

Terrell had said. What didn't she know about Lyssa? And Remy's involvement?

"Thanks for lunch," Jace mumbled tersely and, taking Holly's hand, led her out of the dining area to join Terrell before heading down the street toward the hotel.

"Why'd you go off on Terrell like that?" Ismay asked Bastian once they were gone.

"Because it's none of his business, that's why. What makes him think he knows anything? I just bought the bastard lunch, and he calls me down like that, as if I've done something wrong?"

He was almost shouting, so everyone was staring at them, including the waitress who'd come out to finish cleaning off their table. There was a lot Ismay wanted to say. She needed clarity. But Bastian didn't seem to care that he was disrupting a business and disturbing everyone's lunch. "We can talk about it later," she said softly. "Let's go."

"You can take the Jeep. I'll call an Uber," he said and threw the keys at her.

She could hear the people around her murmuring as she rubbed her arm where the keys had struck her before bending to pick them up, and he stalked out.

Ismay was so shaken by Bastian's outburst she didn't want to go back to the cottage for fear that was where he'd gone. She didn't want to call Remy, either—not after learning about Sam. It wasn't just that he'd slept with another woman, although that was bad enough. It was more that he'd been seeing Samantha Whoever She Was since early January, and Ismay had never suspected a thing. Everything he'd told her during the past several months was now suspect in her mind.

That he could hide an affair that easily said something about his ability to compartmentalize and deceive. She could no longer trust him.

As she climbed into the Jeep, she thought about calling her

mother. Whenever something upsetting happened, it was a natural inclination to want to call home, she supposed. She adored Betty. But she knew she wouldn't get the consolation and advice she needed. Her mother would only hate Remy if she learned he'd been cheating. And she'd think Ismay was suffering the consequences of her choices—for leaving the church, getting involved with a man who wasn't a member, and becoming *worldly.*

Bo was whom she wanted to talk to, anyway.

She started the Jeep and drove around the corner so the people at the restaurant could no longer stare at her. Then she parked again and messaged Bo.

How's the fence-building going?

He didn't answer, which meant he was probably still digging holes and mixing cement for the posts. She got out and meandered down the street—from shop to shop to restaurant to art gallery—until she heard her phone ding.

It'd taken nearly an hour—it was three thirty—but Bo had finally gotten back to her.

Just finished. Heading inside to shower. We'll add the slats tomorrow.

What are you doing after you shower?

The dots that came on the screen when someone was typing appeared and then disappeared twice, as if he couldn't decide how to respond.

Eventually, she got a message from him.

No plans. Do you want me to take your brother somewhere?

I was hoping you'd be able to get away alone. I need to talk to you.

Is something wrong? Just tell me where to meet you, and I'll be there in thirty.

There'd been no equivocating on his answer. She wiped the tears that'd started rolling down her face.

I don't know where to go. I just need to see you for a few minutes.

Let's meet at the lighthouse.

She sniffed as she wiped away more tears. She could find the lighthouse easily enough.

After sending him a thumbs-up, she drove to the beach and took her time walking along the shore to the lighthouse, where she sat on a big rock and waited for him.

As he approached, Bo could see Ismay staring pensively out at the ocean and couldn't help thinking how beautiful she was. He needed to be careful with her, couldn't let his feelings—or hers—get out of control. But he hadn't been able to forget about that moment when she'd taken his hand at the beach. That was something he'd never expected—and should never have allowed. While he didn't want to see her with someone like Remy, he couldn't get involved with her himself. She didn't even know who he really was. And she deserved much better than he could offer—better than a man lying about his past and struggling to live with the scars.

As he approached, he steeled himself for the moment she turned those gorgeous green eyes on him. But it didn't do any good. When she looked over, the desire he'd begun to feel for her only grew more acute. Maybe there was a silver lining in having to go to Louisiana to see his uncle. Maybe he'd be gone long enough to stop himself from destroying her future.

"Thanks for coming," she said as she got up.

"No problem. What's—"

He didn't even get his question out before she threw her arms around his neck. He told himself to set her away from him, but he was pretty sure she was crying and that disarmed him enough that he couldn't bring himself to do it. "What is it?" he murmured, his lips against her hair as he let his arms close around her.

"I don't even know where to start," she said.

He'd thought she'd release him after the embrace. But she didn't. She just stood there, squeezing him tight, and before he could stop himself, he slid his hands up her back and kissed her temple. God, she felt better than anything he'd ever experienced. She smelled like heaven, too. Everything about her seemed perfect. "Why don't we start with the reason you're crying?"

"I don't know what to do," she replied.

"About…"

With a sniff, she pulled away and found something on her phone she apparently wanted to show him because she handed it to him.

It was a video taken in a dark restaurant. At first, he couldn't make out what was happening, but then he realized. "This is Remy?" He glanced up to catch her nod before he finished watching—and then watched again. "When was this?"

"Last night."

"Who's he with?"

"He's been telling me since January that he's studying with a partner named Sam. Well, that's Sam—or Samantha."

"This doesn't look good," he admitted, cringing at the pain and humiliation it must've caused her.

"I'm fairly certain they've been seeing each other for months and I had no clue."

He lifted the phone. "Where'd you get this?" Obviously, Remy wouldn't have sent it to her.

"That's where things get worse," she said with a grimace.

"The woman who texted it to me claims he was cheating on his former girlfriend with her—and got her pregnant."

Bo felt himself stiffen in surprise. "He has a child?"

"I don't think she had the child. But she wouldn't tell me much." She gestured at her phone. "You can read the exchange."

He took a few minutes to do that. "Wow," he said when he was done.

"Yeah."

"So…what are you going to do? Does he know that you know?"

"He does. I called and told him."

Bo wished he could've heard that conversation. "And?"

"He claims it's nothing. A mistake caused by all the stress he's been under. Swears he doesn't want to lose me. Insists no one can compare to me."

He was right about that, but Bo couldn't admit it.

"I also asked him about the panties in his closet."

The hair on the back of Bo's neck stood up. "You did?"

"I had to hear him tell me why those things were there."

"Did he?"

"Claims he doesn't know anything about them."

Bo's stomach sank. Of course, Remy would deny it. "Do you believe him?"

"How can I?" She took back her phone. "After this?"

"So…what are you going to do?" He wanted to believe she wasn't in danger, but his life had taught him the worst *could* occur.

"Remy made me promise I wouldn't do anything until he could get here, and we could talk. I don't want to throw away the past three years any more than he does. And yet…"

"And yet?" Bo prompted.

"I was second-guessing our relationship before I ever arrived. This past year, he's shown little interest in supporting me. It was always more about him—what he likes to do, when he has time to do it, if he's ready to give me some attention—but it's gotten so much worse over time. And yet, I felt like I was a bad partner for not being more understanding. He always claimed his classes were so much harder than mine. But if he's had time to carry on an entire second relationship..."

Bo could hear the emotion in her voice and understood that she'd stopped talking because she was struggling to get the words out. "He doesn't deserve you," he said. "You know I've felt that way since day one."

A tear slipped down her cheek. He reached up to wipe it away with his thumb and somehow ended up cupping her face with both hands and gently pulling it toward his. He expected her to push him away. Part of him wanted her to. He needed her to set the boundary he was having such a hard time maintaining himself. But she didn't. Her arms went around his neck and her lips parted as their mouths touched—and then he was completely lost.

Bo's kiss was unlike anything Ismay had ever experienced. She'd never really believed a kiss could be *intoxicating*, had never experienced that for herself, but now she understood. When he raised his head, she gazed up at him for several seconds—feeling slightly dazed—and could see that he was as taken aback by the impact of their kiss as she was, and that only made her want more. Lifting herself on tiptoe, she pressed her lips to his again, and he kissed her more deeply.

When his palm came up to rest on the back of her head and he groaned in surrender, she felt completely swept away. She would've gone on kissing him until—she didn't know what—if he hadn't finally broken it off.

"Ismay, we can't do this," he said, but he didn't extract himself. He spoke earnestly as he gazed down at her, his hands gripping her shoulders.

"Why not?" she asked. "I don't owe Remy anything. He certainly hasn't been fair to me."

"And I'd hate to see you stay with him. I don't trust him to treat you right. But...you don't want to get involved with me."

"I understand. I'd feel terrible if it cost you your job—"

"My job has nothing to do with it," he broke in. Well, almost nothing. His job mattered; it wouldn't be easy to replace the situation he'd found here on Mariners. But for her, he'd take the risk if that was all there was to it.

She blinked several times. "Then...is there someone else?"

"No. But you and I live a continent apart," he said, choosing that excuse instead. "There's no future in it."

"I know. But...does that mean we don't even take advantage of the time we could have together?"

"What are you saying?" he asked.

She raked her fingers through her long hair. "I don't know. I'm heartbroken, but I'm not sure it's for the right reasons. I feel like a fool for being so oblivious. I'm afraid I never really knew Remy, and yet I was prepared to marry him. And here I am, craving your touch when we haven't known each other very long and before things are entirely over with Remy, which makes me think I may not be any better than he is."

He pulled her against him and rested his chin on her head. "Trust me. You're *way* better than he is."

"Except... I wanted you even before I learned about Sam," she admitted.

There was a moment of silence before he said, "You didn't act on it."

She'd held his hand. So, there was that. It didn't sound like a lot, but there'd been plenty of emotion in it, so what she'd done was potentially worse. "With more time, who knows how far I would've gone?"

"You would've broken up with Remy before you did anything."

She'd been on the verge of breaking off the engagement for the past couple of weeks, so she hoped that was true. "I'm off balance," she said. "None of it really makes any sense."

He pulled back enough to peer into her face again. "Which is why we need to be careful. I don't want to make what you're going through any worse."

"Okay," she said, but quickly, impetuously, kissed him again. It was just a peck; she had to have one last taste. But then he lowered his head and kissed her soundly, and it was even more satisfying than before. She'd thought maybe he'd changed his mind—until he wrenched away.

"Damn, this is going to be hard," he said and stalked off.

24

"Where've you been?" Bastian asked as soon as she walked into the cottage.

His words were slurred, and Ismay assumed he was drunk again. He was always drinking. He didn't seem to have anything else to do, which made her wonder why he'd come to the island in the first place.

She'd had enough. If she had to move out of the cottage, she would. She felt that was probably the wisest thing to do, anyway. Then she wouldn't be beholden to Remy, Bastian, or their folks. "None of your business," she replied.

Obviously surprised by her terse response, he tossed the remote onto the coffee table and got off the couch. "So we're not playing nice anymore, huh?"

"I'm tired of letting you be rude to me," she said. "I won't allow it in the future."

"Oh, you won't?" He started laughing. "What are you going to do about it?"

He had all the power here… "I could fly back to California."

"What about Remy? And your brother?"

She purposely ignored the part about Remy. "If it comes to that, Jack could head home, too," she said, but she'd texted Bo almost as soon as he'd left her at the beach to tell him not to let her brother know about Remy and the woman he'd been with. She didn't want Jack to feel his time on the island was going to be cut short, or that he'd made a mistake trusting her enough to come. She planned to manage her own affairs so he'd be able to get back on his feet. "Or we could both move into Honey's house while she's gone and enjoy the rest of our summer vacation," she said.

He gave her an "as if" look. "Remy would never stand for that."

"It's not up to Remy," she responded.

"Something's changed." He cocked his head to the side. "Something between you two."

"Yeah. I don't consider us engaged anymore. That's what's changed."

His eyes lit up. "You broke it off?"

"Not officially, but I will."

She hadn't been quite as decisive when she'd talked to Remy as she was now, but she certainly planned to make it clear that he no longer had any claim on her fidelity.

He gestured at her left hand. "You're still wearing his ring."

"I'm about to take it off."

Bastian followed her as she crossed the room to the stairs. "What does that mean? Is it over for good? Or..."

"You'll have to ask him."

"Does this have anything to do with Bo?"

The mention of Bo's name sent a shot of adrenaline through her. There was no way she could let Bastian—or Remy—make this about him. Turning on the second step, she said, "*Absolutely* not."

The grin that stretched across his face was so gleeful it almost made him look like Tim Burton's version of the Mad Hatter. "Methinks thou dost protest too much," he said.

Terrified her problems would lap over onto Bo, she lifted her chin. “You want to blame what’s happening between Remy and me on your caretaker?” she said. “Take a look at this.”

Navigating to the video where Remy was kissing his date last night, she turned the screen on her phone to face him. He tried to take it, but she pulled her hand back. “No. Just watch.”

He bent closer as he did. Then he started to laugh almost maniacally and couldn’t seem to stop.

“There’s something seriously wrong with you,” she said and stomped up the stairs before slamming and locking her door.

You’re losing her. You realize that, don’t you?

After what’d happened with Lyssa, Bastian couldn’t help taking great satisfaction in the trouble between Remy and Ismay. He knew he shouldn’t goad his brother. No one could be more vindictive. But it was such perfect revenge that he couldn’t stop himself from gloating, especially since he hadn’t even had to do anything to break them up. Remy had handled that himself.

What are you talking about? his brother texted back. She’s not going anywhere.

You might want to tell her that.

Is she moving out?

Not right now, but I believe she’s thinking about it.

We’re going through a rough patch. That’s all. Once I get there, everything will be okay.

Not if Bo has anything to say about it.

Quit trying to make me jealous! Bo can’t offer her what I can.

I have everything you do, he pointed out.

No, you don't. We might look the same, but we're not.

Thank God.

She would never be interested in a rich derelict like you, and she would never be interested in a mere *caretaker.*

Bastian glared at his brother's words. Remy had always acted so fucking superior. The shrink their mother had taken Bastian to years ago said Remy was just trying to establish his own identity. But it was more than that. *Way* more.

Tamping down the anger that'd welled up and ruined his buzz, he took another shot of whiskey before responding.

I don't think you know her that well. Or you don't understand her.

His fingers fumbled with the keys. He had to go back to correct several words, but he took the time to do it because he didn't want to create an even easier target for his brother. Remy had always made him feel like he was the dumber twin.

You've got her all wrong. She's not materialistic.

Every woman wants security, bro, especially Ismay. She was raised with very little. She appreciates what I can provide.

Okay, Bastian wrote back. Forget I said anything. He knew acting as though he were throwing up his hands would bother his brother even more than if he kept arguing. And, sure enough, Remy wrote him right back.

You've known her how long—a few days? And you think you can tell me what she's really like?

"Sometimes you miss the obvious," he said, speaking aloud. "It's always been that way. Just like with Lyssa."

She showed me the video, Rem. How long have you been seeing that other woman?

That wasn't what it looked like.

There could be no confusion. It was right on the video! Only Remy could try to sell such an outrageous lie.

Well, she believes you were cheating. That's the problem.

I've got this, Remy wrote back. Just stay out of it.

Okay. Bastian filled his glass before plopping back on the couch. "You haven't *got* anything," he said to the room and flipped to the golf channel. But he could've been watching anything. All he could think about was that, for once, Remy wouldn't get everything he wanted.

Remy called before Ismay could decide what, exactly, she wanted to text him. She stared at his picture on her phone, wondering if she should pick up. He could be so persuasive and persistent; she didn't want him to talk her out of what she was going to do. But avoiding him for that reason seemed a little sophomoric, so she forced herself to answer.

"Hey, babe," he said.

She rolled her eyes at the saccharine in his voice. He wasn't going to win her back that easily. "Don't you need to be studying?"

"How can I study when you're upset with me?"

"I'm more than upset, Remy."

"And I can see why. I feel terrible."

Would how she was acting impact his ability to prepare for the last part of his medical boards? She hated being responsible for setting anyone back. But she always took on too much responsibility. *She* was merely reacting as anyone would, she reminded herself. It was a natural consequence of *his* actions. *He* was the one who'd caused the rift between them. "I think… I think we need to call off the engagement."

"Why? We have time to work this out. And we will. I swear I'll prove myself. I'll be a different man, a much better one, once I clear this hurdle and start my residency."

But his residency would present its own challenges. Was she going to have to worry about him continuing to sleep with Sam or the female nurses and/or doctors where he worked? Would she be at her office, trying to concentrate on her own work when he called to say he wouldn't be home for dinner and get a sick feeling in her stomach as she wondered if he was hiding away in a closet at the hospital with an intern?

"I'm happy to hear that," she said. "And maybe it'll be true. But until I can heal and rebuild my trust—*if* I can heal and rebuild my trust—I'm taking marriage off the table."

"Ismay, come on. Don't be a bitch. I told you, Sam doesn't mean anything to me."

The irritation and impatience in his voice absolutely confounded her. How dare he act as though *she* were doing something wrong simply because she'd been hurt by his actions? "Call me a bitch if you want to, but I've already taken off your ring. You'll find it on your dresser when you get here."

"And where will *you* be?"

"I don't know," she said and hung up.

A text came in from Jack before she could even gather her thoughts after that call.

Want to go for a walk along the beach? Weather is perfect.

She did want to go. She felt she was suffocating in the cottage with Remy's things surrounding her, that duffel bag lurking in the closet, and his drunk brother parked on the couch downstairs.

Yes.

Private beach or public one?

She didn't only want to get out of the house; she wanted to get off the property.

Public.

Want me to meet you there?

She no longer cared if Bastian knew her brother was staying with Bo, not for her own sake. But she didn't want it to cause any problems for Bo, so they still had to be careful.

Okay if we walk? I don't want to ask Bastian if I can take the Jeep.

Sure. Meet you at the turnoff to Bo's in ten minutes?

Perfect.

By the way, I have some good news.

She could really use some.

What is it?

I'll tell you when I see you.

Ismay climbed off the bed, brushed her teeth, pulled her hair into a ponytail, and grabbed a jacket, in case it chilled off. She didn't want anything forcing her back to the house before she was ready.

She'd opened her door and was about to walk into the hall

when she realized she hadn't yet taken off her promise ring, although she'd told Remy she had. Taking a few seconds to twist it off her finger, she put it in a monogrammed leather dish-like holder Remy had on the dresser and walked out.

As soon as her feet hit the main level, Bastian leaned up over the couch. "Where are you going?"

She didn't even look at him, let alone reply.

Ismay was happy to see her brother when she found him waiting for her down the road. There was strength in numbers. They would support each other and manage to make the most of their once-in-a-lifetime stay on Mariners, she told herself, even if this summer was far different than what they'd both expected.

"How'd it go today?" she asked as she came even with him.

"Good. One more day and the fence will be fixed."

"Bo told me he's really grateful for all the help you've given him."

"He's a cool dude—sort of like working with Dad, except without all the criticism if I do something wrong."

She laughed. "He's the strong silent type?"

"Pretty much. I can't help liking him."

Ismay couldn't help it, either. She quickly turned her face away, because the memory of kissing Bo earlier immediately came to mind, and she didn't want a silly smile or dreamlike expression to give her away. "What's the good news?"

"Honey called Bo just before I texted you."

"What for?"

"To tell him that her daughter has broken her ankle."

"Ouch!" Ismay sent him a sharp look. "That's *good* news?"

"No, sorry. Not that part. Honey's taking the first flight out tomorrow. She's needed to help take the girls where they need to go for softball and their other activities."

"I hope her daughter's foot heals quickly, but I bet it feels good for Honey to know she's needed."

"She's certainly anxious to get there. She said I can move in tomorrow. She asked me to come by at eight thirty tonight, so she can go over how to take care of the cat and her plants and get the mail and whatever else she wants me to do."

"That's wonderful! Bo will have his bungalow back, so we'll no longer have to worry about getting him in trouble with the Windsors, and you'll have a place of your own," she said and then came to a sudden stop.

"What is it?" he asked, turning back to see why she'd quit walking.

Ismay thought of how uncomfortable she was staying with Bastian, despite the size and elegance of the cottage. "Do you mind if I move in with you?" she asked.

He seemed taken aback. "Of course not. You're the one who found me this place. And I'm sure there are at least two bedrooms. I can ask Honey tonight if it's okay. But why would you want to leave the cottage?"

She raised her eyebrows.

"All right," he said, immediately backing away from the question. "Bastian's a good reason. But what about Remy? Will you move back when he arrives?"

She started walking again and he fell right in step with her. "Maybe. We'll have to see what happens."

Jack said you're moving in with him. Does that mean you broke things off with Remy?

Bo's message came in late, as if he'd been trying not to text her after what'd happened between them at the lighthouse, but he ultimately couldn't stop himself.

Or maybe it was just that he couldn't sleep. Ismay was having trouble nodding off herself. She'd struggled to rest ever since she'd arrived on Mariners—first with the storm and then Bastian showing up. That she was getting more and more frazzled was pretty ironic, since she'd come to the island to relax.

Tonight, Bastian couldn't seem to shut down and go to bed. He'd been wandering around the house muttering to himself ever since she'd told him she'd be moving out in the morning. There were moments she could've sworn he was standing right outside her door, as if to intimidate her. Maybe he was angry and had something to say? Or worse, wanted to indulge in some twisted fantasy that had to do with the contents of that damn duffel bag?

That was what truly frightened her. Whenever she heard a creak on the stairs or in the hall—even if it was just the house settling—her skin would prickle and she'd hold her breath. What was he doing? Why didn't he pass out from all the alcohol, or turn on the TV and shut himself in the master like he usually did?

Thank goodness she'd soon be out of the cottage. Honey had agreed she could stay with Jack, and she'd feel a lot better when they were together.

When she heard the cupboards opening and closing in the kitchen and knew Bastian was downstairs, she drew a deep breath and turned her attention to answering Bo.

Yes. I'm not going to remain engaged to a serial cheater. He insists there's never been another woman besides Sam—no one he got pregnant before—but he doesn't have a lot of credibility right now.

I'm sorry. You've come so far from California and were expecting such a different experience when you got here. How'd he take the news?

Bastian seems more upset than Remy.

What makes you say that?

He's acting strange. He's been drinking again—a lot—but I don't think it's just that. It's almost like he's tripping on a psychedelic or something.

What's he doing?

Wandering around the house. Talking to himself. Laughing loudly for no reason—at least that I can hear. Just weird stuff.

Sounds like you might be right.

She thought about mentioning that he kept coming to her door, but she wasn't entirely certain of that, and she didn't want to falsely accuse him.

I can't believe Remy took the breakup in stride, Bo wrote.

Only because he hasn't given up yet. His last text said everything would be okay once he gets to Mariners. He's not used to losing anything, probably doesn't believe the breakup will last.

How do you feel about that?

I don't know how I feel. I can't focus on the future. I'm just trying to get through this night.

Bastian's making you that uneasy?

I guess so, what with that stuff hidden in the wall of the closet and Remy claiming he knows nothing about it. What if it's Bastian's? After getting to know him, I could easily believe that.

Strange place to put it, no? In his brother's bedroom?

Except then, if anyone finds it, Remy looks bad instead of him.

Good point. From what I can tell, they've had plenty of sibling rivalry. Bastian would probably love to make Remy look guilty of something twisted and serious—to finally be the best twin.

Exactly.

If you're scared of him, why don't you come over here?

If he finds out I went to your place, it wouldn't be good for you. I think he feels threatened by the man you are, feels he can't compete but should be able to.

He has no reason to be envious of me.

That wasn't true. Ismay could easily tell Bo was twice the man Bastian was, and Bastian didn't like being outdone by anybody, especially someone he considered so obviously inferior. Ismay knew that simply from the way he made himself the hero of every story he told.

He has issues with you and Remy, she wrote, maybe every man he doesn't compare favorably to.

Your safety is more important than how he feels about me. I'm worried about that stuff in the closet. Maybe it does belong to him. We know he was in love with Lyssa. It'd be like him to keep that photograph.

True. I don't want to drag it out again, but I've been thinking that maybe I should take pictures of all of it, not just Lyssa's photograph, in case something ever comes of it—or happens to it.

That would probably be smart. A little documentation couldn't hurt.

And tonight would be her last chance to do it.

Okay, she wrote, but don't go anywhere. It creeps me out to have to touch it again.

I'll be right here.

Once again listening for Bastian, to determine his whereabouts, she held her breath, but the house was silent. Had he gone to bed while she was texting with Bo?

She hadn't heard him in the hall…

Maybe he'd finally passed out on the couch downstairs.

Hoping that was the case, she climbed out of bed and crept across the floor. The boxes were still there—she hadn't moved anything—so she used them once again as the step stool she needed to reach above the shelf.

Putting a hand on the lintel to steady herself, she used the video feature of her camera to show the shelf, Remy's notebook, the loose panel, and how it came out—and the hole behind it. But when she reached in, planning to pull the duffel bag out for the camera, there was nothing there.

25

Was Bastian some kind of pervert?

He was certainly odd. Bo paced in his bedroom while waiting for Ismay to get back to him. He didn't like that she was at the cottage alone with Bastian, not with the way things were going. Actually, he'd never liked it. He hated to step in—it really wasn't his place and risked his job—but who else was going to do it?

Tomorrow she'd be out of the cottage and away from Remy's brother, he told himself. Surely, she'd be safe until then. But after he received her text, he was no longer so confident.

It's not there.

Too impatient to bother continuing to write, he called her.

"Hello?" she said, her voice barely audible.

"What do you mean it's not there?"

"It's not there," she reiterated.

"Where could it have gone?"

"Bastian has to have taken it. He's the only one here."

"Shit."

"Maybe he realized the danger of me finding it, since I'm staying in this room. Or maybe all the talk about Lyssa spooked him, and he decided to get rid of it. I don't know. My mind's racing."

So was Bo's.

"And something else is weird," she said.

"What's that?"

"I'm pretty sure a pair of my underwear's gone missing."

This was more alarming than all the rest. "Are you kidding me?" he said, leaving out the expletive that nearly wound up in that question.

"No. I… I didn't keep a strict count when I packed. I just brought a lot since I knew I'd be here all summer. That's probably why I didn't notice until now. But after I found that duffel bag gone, I knew Bastian had been in my room, so I started looking through everything."

"Considering what was in that duffel bag, your underwear would be a good place to start."

"I'm pretty sure he took a white pair with lace around the top. I know I brought those, because I just bought them and remember packing them, but they're not in here and I haven't taken anything down to the laundry yet."

Bo had lived with violent criminals for twelve years. He'd met all kinds of men—some who were downright perverts. But he'd never expected to run into something like this *after* he was released, especially here on Mariners. "You should come over. Right away."

"I'm scared to unlock my door, to be honest. I don't want to have to talk to him."

Bo wasn't worried about what Bastian might *say*. He didn't want to let his background cause his imagination to run wild. Neither did he want to spook Ismay. But the dude probably thought he could get away with anything. "He'd be stupid to hurt you. You're Remy's fiancée."

"*Was* Remy's fiancée."

"Yeah, but…"

"He holds a grudge against Remy for whatever happened with Lyssa," she said. "Maybe he blames him for the fight, which caused the fire that took her life. I don't know. But having something happen to me could be his idea of the perfect revenge."

"God, I hope not."

"He's been in the kitchen for a while. You don't think he'll try to burn this place down..."

"You're scaring the hell out of me," Bo said. "I'm getting dressed and walking over there. If you're not at the back door when I arrive, I'm coming in to get you."

"What about all my stuff?" she asked.

"Bring what you absolutely need and leave the rest. I'll make sure you get it back."

"I don't want to keep pitting you against your employer! I'm worried that...that I'm messing up your life."

He scratched his head. Feeling he had to protect Ismay was the last thing he'd expected, but he didn't trust Bastian any more than she did and wouldn't leave her vulnerable. "Let me worry about that. Just do as I say, all right?"

She didn't answer.

"Ismay?"

"Bastian's coming up the stairs," she whispered.

"All the more reason for you to get out of there!"

Silence. Then he heard her talking to someone else, presumably Bastian. "What do you want?"

Bastian's response was loud enough that he could pick that up, too, since Remy's brother was yelling through the door.

"I'd just like to talk to you. Even if you're not engaged to Remy anymore, you don't have to leave the cottage. There's plenty of room here for both of us."

"You knocked on my door at nearly one o'clock in the morning to tell me that?" Ismay said.

"Is it that late?" Bastian replied. "I didn't even realize."

"We'll talk in the morning, okay?"

"If you're already awake, why can't we talk now? Why won't you open the door?"

"I'm in bed, Bastian."

"Are you scared of me, Ismay?"

There was a slight pause, but then Ismay said, "Of course not."

"You don't trust me," he said.

Bo held his breath as he awaited Ismay's response.

"Don't create a problem that doesn't exist. I'm just trying to get some sleep," she finally said. He didn't hear anything more from Bastian afterward.

Bo waited two or three minutes, during which there was only silence, before asking, "Is he gone?"

"I think so," she whispered.

"Good. Slip out of the house as soon as you can. I'll be waiting for you."

He thought she might refuse, say she'd be fine until morning. Given the late hour, she probably believed she'd successfully navigated her final encounter of the night with Bastian. But as erratically as he was behaving, Bo wasn't convinced he wouldn't come back, and this time, he might be angrier—angry enough to force her door open.

So he was relieved when she said, "I'll be there in ten minutes."

Ismay slung the bag that held a change of clothes, her toothbrush, and makeup over her shoulder and pressed her ear to the door. She could hear the TV in the master but nothing else.

Still nervous because Bastian had seemed so agitated tonight, she checked her watch. One twenty. Surely, he'd gone to bed by now. Even if he hadn't, she couldn't keep Bo waiting. She had to take her chances, leave now.

Grabbing her purse, she carefully twisted the knob until it clicked and peered out through a narrow crack. The light was on in the master. Some of it spilled into the hallway, indicating the door stood open. But she couldn't hear any movement.

The floor creaked as she stepped into the hall, and she cursed to herself.

Was Bastian, who was probably in bed, still awake? Or was he going through that duffel bag and fantasizing about what was inside it? Were those panties of hers that'd gone missing now part of his collection?

She grimaced in distaste. He'd been in her room. Imagining him fondling her belongings made her angry and tied her stomach in knots at the same time. She didn't want to see him. She was afraid of what she might say—about her panties, Lyssa, the duffel bag, all of it. But she was more afraid of what a man like that might do…

If he was in the master, he was behind her at the end of the hall, so she was probably in the clear. He might call out to her if he heard her tread on the stairs, but she didn't plan to answer. She was just going to duck her head and go straight through the living room to the kitchen, the mudroom, the screened-in porch—and, finally, the stairs down to the garden, where Bo would be waiting for her.

She made it to the living room before realizing that Bastian wasn't in the master—and he wasn't asleep. He'd probably been on the couch, and the moment he heard her come out of her room, he got up to intercept her at the foot of the stairs.

"Is something wrong?" he asked.

Although it was mostly dark, there was enough light streaming through the large windows from the moon—in addition to the light from his bedroom falling into the hallway above—that they could see each other. "N-no," she stammered.

His eyes immediately locked onto the bag she was carrying. "What's that? Where are you going?"

She tried to skirt around him, but he cut her off.

"Ismay? What're you doing?"

"Isn't it obvious?" she said. "I'm leaving."

"Why?"

"Because I can't sleep."

"Where will you go?"

"To see my brother."

"At the hotel?"

"Yes." She didn't want him to know she was going to Bo's, didn't want to take the risk that Bo would be penalized for trying to help her.

"Do you know how far that is?" he asked.

She eyed the front door, but she'd have to go around him to reach that, too. "Of course. I can get an Uber."

"Why don't we sit down and talk for a few minutes?" He tried to take her bag, but she jerked it out of his hold.

"I don't want to talk. My brother's expecting me. I have to go."

"Is something wrong?"

She wouldn't be leaving in the middle of the night if there wasn't, so she didn't bother denying it. "You know what's wrong."

"Remy," he guessed.

She nodded. "Now...if you'll excuse me."

"He won't like it that you're leaving," he said, his voice a warning. "He always has to be on top, the one to say goodbye."

"I don't care," she said.

"You think he'll just let you go?"

She was more afraid of Bastian trying to stop her. Was he projecting his own controlling nature onto Remy? She'd known her former fiancé wasn't the most nurturing person, but he'd never given her reason to be afraid of him. "I'm not asking for permission."

There was a noise at the back door, after which they heard movement in the kitchen and Bo came into the room. He had a bat in one hand, which made him look even more formidable than he usually did. "You ready?" he said as soon as he saw her.

Shit. She hated that Bastian had held her up long enough that Bo felt he had to come in. "Yeah. I'm… I was on my way," she said.

"You used your key to let yourself into this house in the middle of the night?" Bastian said to Bo. "While *I'm* here?"

Bo's gaze shifted from Ismay to Bastian. "You've been acting a little unpredictable lately, Bastian. Your behavior tonight—with all the drinking and wandering around and muttering to yourself—spooked her. So I said she could come stay with me."

Ismay had just told him something different, and he immediately called her on it. "The hotel, huh?" he said. "You're not going to the hotel. You're going to stay in the bungalow *I* fucking own!" Bastian gestured at the bat. "And what, exactly, were you going to do with that?"

Bo lowered the arm that carried it, but his expression suggested he'd use whatever he needed to—if it came right down to it. "Just making sure there won't be any problems."

"How dare you?!" Bastian cried. "You work for me! You're only staying on this property because of the kindness and generosity of my family—"

"It's not a handout," Bo interrupted, his voice almost a growl. "I'm staying on the property because it's a good place for a caretaker to be, and it's part of my compensation package, which I earn, by the way, so don't act like you're doing me any fucking favors."

Bastian seemed shocked that Bo would come back at him so strongly. "Whoa! The real Bo comes out."

"That's right," Bo snapped. "So don't push me." He gestured with his free hand for Ismay to walk over to him. "Let's go."

"You two are making a big mistake," Bastian said. "I keep trying to warn you, but you won't listen."

"We have the right to live our lives as we see fit," Bo said. "The fact that I'm working for your parents doesn't change that."

"And are you going to live your lives together?" Bastian asked.

"That's nothing you need to worry about." Ismay spoke up so Bo wouldn't have to take all the heat. "We're both single adults. We can do what we want."

"Oh, boy!" Bastian clapped his hands. "I can barely wait for Remy to get here."

Bo's hand closed around her wrist as soon as she reached him, and he led her out while Bastian started to whoop and holler, saying all hell was going to break loose.

"This is going to be one hell of a summer!" he yelled after them, but Ismay didn't reply and neither did Bo. Bo's hand slipped down to catch hers, and they laced their fingers together as they jogged down the porch steps to the damp earth.

"You okay?" he murmured when they reached the ground.

"I'm fine," she replied. "Just sorry Bastian caught me before I could get out. I really didn't want you to have to come inside. I feel terrible that I've dragged you into this when it isn't your fight."

"I guess it's my fight now," Bo said. "Because there's no way I'm going to let that douchebag, or his douchebag brother, give you any trouble."

Ismay was out of breath from all the excitement. "Everything that's happened since I left LA has been…" She shook her head, unable to find the words.

"I'm sorry," he said as they reached his front door.

"Don't apologize. Because the thing is…"

"What?" He'd lowered his voice as he let them in so they wouldn't disturb Jack, and she followed suit.

"It hasn't *all* been bad."

"It hasn't been very good," he said as he set the bat aside.

She caught him before he could advance any farther into the house. "We could always make it better," she whispered and kissed him.

* * *

He didn't want to do it, but Bo managed to make himself set Ismay aside. He told her she was on the rebound at the moment and in no position to get involved with him or anyone else, and he made himself a bed on the couch, so she could have the privacy of his room. But then he lay there, his senses filled with the smell of her hair and the taste of her kiss—until enough minutes passed that he began to fear she'd go to sleep and he'd miss his opportunity, which propelled him to his feet.

When he knocked on the door, he wasn't sure if she'd heard him—he'd done it softly so he wouldn't wake her brother—and was just ordering himself to go back to the couch where he belonged, when she opened the door a few inches and looked out at him.

He rubbed a hand over his face. "I don't know if—I don't know what, exactly, you were offering out there, but..."

She didn't help him by clarifying. Her eyebrows arched as she gave him an innocent expression. "But?"

"Whatever it is, I want it too badly to turn it away." He lowered his voice even more. "You'd be wise to say no," he added.

A sexy smile curved her lips. "You're advising me against getting physical with you, but you'll take it if I'm still offering?"

Feeling a bit sheepish, he stretched his neck. "I guess that about sums it up."

She'd been teasing him, obviously. She sobered as her eyes met his, but she didn't make a move to let him in, so he nodded and turned to go.

"Wait," she whispered, and caught his hand.

His heart started to race as she pulled him into the room with her. Now that she was no longer behind the door, he could see that she wasn't fully dressed. "You're gorgeous," he said as he slid a hand inside the white tank top she was wearing with nothing but a pair of panties. "You should really send me away."

Her eyes closed as his palm reached her breast. "You said that already," she whispered.

"Because it's true."

"Why would I do that?"

"For all the reasons I gave you before. And I don't have any birth control."

She chuckled breathlessly as he slid his other hand up under her shirt. "I'm on the pill. And you gave me *one* reason. You said I was on the rebound."

"Isn't that true?"

"Who can say? I know my future looks a lot different than it did just a couple of weeks ago. But Remy and I have been struggling for a while. This summer was supposed to bring us back together. Instead, it's broken us apart—before he could even get here. All I can tell you right now is that I'm completely untethered and have no idea where I might drift. It's frightening, but it's also…liberating."

"I don't want to add to your confusion—" He started to pull away, but she caught his hands and kept them on her breasts.

"The only thing I *know* I want is to feel your mouth on mine, your skin against mine, your arms and legs intertwined with mine as we make love, which is shocking, because I should be too hurt to be thinking of that."

"Maybe you're looking for revenge."

"I don't think so. I feel relieved, set free. Not angry."

"You just made it impossible for me to stop," he said. "You realize that?"

She smiled as she pulled her shirt over her head. "Why would you stop?"

As he gazed down at what she'd revealed, he couldn't help bringing his mouth to her breast. Maybe she was looking for an escape from what she was going through, a few moments to feel good and receive some emotional support. He was happy to provide that. It was everything that might come afterward that could become a problem…

But he'd already screwed up his job. He was pretty sure there'd be no saving it, not once Annabelle heard what Bastian had to say. And he couldn't believe an educated beautiful woman like Ismay would be interested in him long-term. So what was he really worried about? If he was about to be fired, he wouldn't be on the island much longer. He needed to go back to Louisiana, anyway.

She tugged on the T-shirt he was wearing with a pair of basketball shorts, so he took it off. Then she slid her arms around his neck, bringing her breasts in contact with his chest, and he thought he might climax before he even made it to the bed.

What the hell, he thought. Something like this didn't come along every day. After what he'd been through, no one knew better than he did how important it was to savor the good times.

26

The way Bo touched her and kissed her and encouraged Ismay to relax and trust him was both tender and reassuring—and kept any second thoughts from creeping in. Being with him was more fulfilling than being with Remy had been, at least in a long time. That she'd even have such a thought shocked her. There was just something about him. It'd been there almost from the beginning, when he'd knocked on her door during that terrible storm. He was just so calm and seemed immanently reliable. She knew he was a good person, knew he'd take her feelings into consideration every step of the way. That was what Remy often neglected to do. He didn't pay enough attention to what she was experiencing, because he was too focused on what *he* was experiencing—something that extended beyond their sexual relationship.

"I haven't been with many women," Bo admitted, when he climaxed almost as soon as he pressed inside her. "Even then, it's been quite some time."

She could tell he was embarrassed that he hadn't been able to last as long as he wanted. But she didn't mind. There was a level of intimacy in what they were sharing that had nothing to do with whether she came, too. She felt safe in his arms, enjoyed the solid weight of his body while he was resting on her and the comfort and security she felt while resting on him.

So falling asleep with him afterward was probably the best part—until he woke up a few hours later and started touching her again. Then he seemed determined to take her all the way, and since they were past any initial uncertainty regarding whether they should allow themselves to have sex, she was able to cast aside any remaining inhibitions and thoroughly enjoy herself.

As the pleasure built, she loved that the moon was bright enough outside the window that she could see Bo's face. There was so much intensity there—not because he was trying to hold back; she got the impression he was in control this time—but because he was obviously enjoying what he was doing for her.

Still, when she felt that incredible release and groaned, he let go and came only seconds behind her.

"You're incredibly good in bed," she said as he slumped over her while trying to catch his breath.

"Are you kidding?" he said, a smile in his voice. "You can say that after I botched the first time?"

"It wasn't botched. It was…real. Honest. Raw. I loved it."

"It was certainly better than anything *I've* ever had," he said.

That statement was something she'd never expected him to say. "I don't know much about your life before you came here."

He didn't respond. His eyes were closed. She didn't know if he was thinking or falling asleep, but one of them had to move out to the couch. She was afraid if they dropped off again, it would be morning by the time they woke up, and then there'd be no way to avoid her brother realizing they'd been together.

She preferred not to have that happen. "You said you haven't been with many women, but have you had any long-term relationships?"

He roused himself enough to say no.

He didn't elaborate, so she said, "Why not?"

"I just haven't been in the right situation."

"I'd love to hear more about your life—what it was like living in lowland swamps, what you did after you left that area."

Opening his eyes, he lifted his wrist and checked his watch. "Wow, it's late. Or, rather, it's early. I'd better get out of here. Jack will be up before we know it."

"He *is* an early riser," she pointed out.

"And we're supposed to finish the fence."

"You won't have the strength for that kind of physical labor after being up with me most of the night, will you?"

"I'll do what I can. We could always put it off a day and finish tomorrow. Or not at all. Who knows what the Windsors have in store for me."

She caught his arm before he could leave the bed and pulled him in for a final kiss. "I'll feel terrible if they fire you. I'm really hoping that won't happen."

He studied her for several seconds as he smoothed the hair out of her eyes. "Whatever they do, it was worth it."

"Why are you on the couch?"

Bo squinted as he looked up at Ismay's brother. It felt like he'd barely fallen asleep after leaving Ismay in his bed, but it'd probably been an hour—long enough to fall into a deep sleep. "Your sister's in my room."

"She is?" he exclaimed. "Why's that?"

Bo didn't know how much Ismay wanted her brother to know, so he deferred to her. "You'll have to ask her. I'm a bit groggy right now."

"Don't tell me she and Bastian got into an argument," Jack said. "Dude's insufferable! I'd love to punch him in the face."

This was the most emotion Bo had ever seen from Jack and he took it as a good sign. Hopefully, he was beginning to bounce back. "I think a lot of people would like that opportunity, including me."

"So you were up late helping her? Why didn't she call me?"

Bo's eyes felt like sandpaper. He blinked as he tried to get more moisture in them. "Maybe she did. I don't know."

"I don't have any missed calls."

"She probably didn't want to bother you."

"She called you instead?"

Again, he didn't know how much she wanted to tell her brother about their relationship. "Bastian's been so unpredictable that I reached out to see if she was okay."

Jack opened his mouth to say something else, but Ismay came into the room, her eyes filled with sleep, her long hair tousled and knotted, drawing their attention. "You two are up already?"

There was a certain electricity in the air when she was around. Bo wanted to touch her, say good morning, and ask how she was. He hoped she didn't regret last night. She pulled on a NASA T-shirt and some cutoffs, but he couldn't help wondering if she was wearing the white tank top and panties underneath, and just the memory of seeing her in her underwear sent a jolt of testosterone through him. He already knew he'd never forget last night.

"We need to finish the fence today," Jack said. "Then we can get moved."

Bo waved him off. "Don't worry about the fence. I think we should focus on getting you and Ismay into Honey's house first. The fence can wait."

"I just need to pack up my bag and haul it over there," Jack said. "Shouldn't take long."

"We also need to get Ismay's stuff from the cottage," Bo said.

"Does Bastian know you're gone?" Jack asked his sister.

Ismay used her fingers to get some of the tangles out of her hair. "He does, and he's not happy about it."

Jack frowned. "You don't think Bastian will give us any trouble when we go back, do you?"

"I hope not," Ismay said. "But if he does, I'll just have to get by without the rest of my clothes. Buy new ones or something."

She looked up at Bo and blushed slightly, and he couldn't help lowering his gaze to her mouth. God, he wanted to kiss her.

He shook off the temptation. "Bastian will give you your things," he said. He planned to make sure of it.

"Now might actually be the best time to get it," Ismay said. "It's eight. I bet he's finally asleep. He's a night owl, so he doesn't get up until at least noon."

Bo kicked off his blanket. "Good point. Just in case, I'll go with you."

"We'll all go," Jack said. "I doubt he'll pick a fight if there are three of us."

If it came to a fight, Bo certainly wouldn't need the two of them, but he didn't say so. He nodded and went to put on a fresh T-shirt and jeans.

"You're not worried about going over to the cottage, are you?" Jack asked Ismay when they stepped out into the morning air.

"Maybe a little," she admitted.

"Why?" he asked. "You'll have both of us with you."

Bo could hear the scowl in her voice when she said, "I don't trust Bastian. There's something seriously wrong with him."

Shockingly, Ismay was able to gather her things and get out of the cottage without incident. The TV was still on in the master bedroom, which came in handy because it covered the noise of their movements. Ismay guessed Bastian needed it to make him feel less alone. She never wanted to see him again.

Bo stood in the hall, watching her pack. Jack came in and grabbed some of the clothes she'd stuck in the drawers to make it quicker. While they were there, she motioned them to the closet and showed them the hole behind the board where the duffel bag had been. Jack gave her a perplexed look. He didn't understand why it was there, but she indicated she'd tell him later.

Then she went into the bathroom and gathered her toiletries while Jack carried her suitcase out of the house.

Bo stayed, though, waiting for her.

When she had everything else, she whispered, "Let's get out of here."

But he didn't move. He leaned in and lifted her chin with one finger before he kissed her, and when he broke off the kiss, she grabbed him by the shirt so she could pull him back for another.

He grinned when she finally let him go—seemed tempted to laugh—but sobered as he cast a glance at Bastian's door and motioned her ahead of him.

They didn't talk until they were outside with Jack, well away from the cottage.

"Will Bastian be mad when he sees that all your stuff is gone?" Jack asked. There were wheels on her suitcase, but the ground was so uneven he had to carry it.

Ismay looked back at what she could see of the cottage through the trees. "Who knows? He's been all up in my business from the beginning."

Jack switched her suitcase to his other hand. "Have you heard from Remy?"

Ismay hadn't had anything to put the last of her toiletries in, since she'd already taken her smaller bag to Bo's. She hugged her deodorant, face cleanser, and razor to her body while getting her phone from her back pocket. "Nothing yet this morning. But he sends random little messages."

"Like…" Jack prodded.

"I love you… I could never live without you… I could never replace you…"

He gave her a funny look. "I could never replace you? That's kind of a weird thing to say, isn't it? What happened to, 'I miss you'?"

Remy had good reason to be so conciliatory, but Jack didn't know she'd caught him cheating. She'd only told him that she and Remy were taking a break, that she was starting to have second thoughts about marrying him because he was so aloof and hard to reach on a deep level. "He's…different."

"It's a good thing he's got a big exam," Jack said, letting Bo take a turn with her suitcase. "That'll keep him busy until you're back on your feet emotionally."

She wanted to ask him if he'd heard from Ashleigh, but was afraid that would only reopen the wound. "That'd be nice."

They reached Bo's bungalow and piled what they'd brought from the cottage in the back of Bo's truck. "I don't think Mom and Dad'll be too upset when you tell them that you broke it off with Remy," Jack said.

It certainly wouldn't hit them the way the split between Jack and Ashleigh had. "Probably not. They've never even met him," she said dryly, and Jack went inside to get his suitcase so they could haul everything over to Honey's.

Jack took a seat by the large window in the living room and pulled Clementine into his lap. The cat started to purr the moment he began stroking her soft fur as if she was more than content to settle in with him, even though he was mostly a stranger to her. As vulnerable as he was feeling, that quick acceptance meant far more than it should have.

He'd enjoyed his stay with Bo. Bo was easy to get along with and the work had kept him busy during his toughest days. But even though Ismay was here with him, having Honey's house gave him his own space again, and that put him at ease, made it seem as though he could slow down, take a deep breath, and simply recuperate.

With the sun streaming in—and not a cloud in the sky—he felt warmer, even on the inside, than he had since Ashleigh left, almost human again.

Although he'd doubted it at first, coming to Mariners was going to be a good thing. He was already changing, didn't have to stay quite so busy all the time. It was as if Ashleigh had made him short circuit, but he was slowly rebooting and his systems were coming back up, one after another. Not being back home amid the gossip came as a relief. Ismay had yanked him out of that situation and given him a retreat.

Closing his eyes, he leaned his head back on the chair so the sun could hit his face more directly. In a little while, Bo was coming to get them for lunch. He was taking them to a little dive off the beaten path, which he said was the best-kept secret in town.

Hanging out with him and Ismay, having some good food, and decompressing even more sounded cathartic. And after lunch, Bo said he'd show them the library, since Ismay still had to return a book Bo had loaned her. Then they were going back to the beach. Jack hadn't felt like swimming when he'd been there before, but today he was looking forward to barreling into the waves and being completely engulfed by all that churning energy. He knew he'd feel one with the anger of it as he swam—as hard as he could—against the current.

The bedroom door opened, and Ismay came into the living room. "What're you doing?" she asked. "You didn't take a nap?"

He lifted his head as he continued to stroke Clementine. "Didn't need a nap. Unlike you, I wasn't trying to escape Bastian in the middle of the night."

She rubbed her face. "Lucky you."

"That stuff you found in Remy's closet is weird," he said. He'd been thinking a lot about that too since Ismay and Bo had filled him in as they'd carried their stuff into Honey's house. "Bo made it clear he's concerned."

"Having that hidden the way it was doesn't look good, especially when the woman in the picture died such a tragic death."

"Are you going to talk to the police about it?"

She sighed. "Do you think I should?"

"Someone should see if there's any reason to be alarmed."

Although she didn't seem happy about it, she nodded. "I

know. I just… It feels terrible to tell on somebody, especially when you're not sure—"

"If there's nothing to it, you can apologize after," he broke in.

"I doubt the Windsors will ever accept an apology. I know Remy won't tolerate that kind of betrayal."

"So you have to decide if you're completely finished with Remy first."

"I don't know about that," she admitted.

"Having second thoughts?"

"Just need time to work through all my feelings—and what I want for the future. Everything turned around on me so fast."

"Got it. We'll leave it there, then." In his mind, they were taking a day off from regular life and all the worries that went with it. "Did you get enough rest?"

"I think so. I don't want the day to slip away. Things have been so crazy—I'm looking forward to feeling like I'm on vacation."

"Thanks for inviting me out here," he said.

She curled her legs underneath her as she took a seat on the sofa. "Do you mean that? For a while there, I was afraid you regretted it."

"For a while there, I did. I wanted to be back home—but only if I could be with Ashleigh. Now I feel a sense of freedom I've never experienced before."

She looked surprised by this revelation. "That's probably both welcome…and terrifying. I was hoping you might be able to imagine a different life eventually."

Clementine saw a butterfly outside the window and jumped down to bat a paw at it. "I'm getting there," he said. "Now when I imagine the duplex where we lived, it doesn't look nearly as nice as it did in my mind even a few days ago. When I imagine going to work on the farm, I suddenly remember the drudgery that made me feel trapped. When everything was taken away from me, panic welled up, and I desperately wanted it all back.

Now the loss still hurts, but—" he stretched "—I actually *want* to go to the beach today."

"That's a start," she said with a chuckle. "Recovery is often two steps forward, one step back. But we'll get there. We're going to have a great summer."

He would never have believed that before. He still couldn't see how he could actually be *happy* in the near future. But it felt as though a small candle of hope had been lit inside him and was burning way down deep. "What about you?" he asked. "How are you doing? You're going through a breakup, too."

"Mine's very different from yours."

"Don't minimize it. You've been with Remy for three years. You thought you'd spend the rest of your life with him."

"But I've had doubts about our relationship for a while. I just didn't want to examine it too closely. We were doing everything we could just to finish our last year of school."

"And now?" He grimaced. "You don't think you'll go back to him…"

"I'd be lying if I said it was easy to let go," she admitted.

He sat forward. "That's it! That's how I feel. What you have may not even be what you really want, but it's so damn frightening to let go."

"Change can be daunting," she agreed.

He watched Clementine sitting close to the window, studying the world beyond it, probably hoping the butterfly would come back. "I see the way Bo looks at you," he said.

Ismay's face flushed, but she gave him a shy smile.

"And I see the way you look at him."

"Maybe that's why my breakup isn't as painful as it should be," she said. "I'm infatuated with someone else."

"*Infatuated* is an interesting word choice."

"It happened so fast. What else could it be?"

"Maybe it's chemistry," he said. "Fate. Destiny. Kismet. Whatever you want to call it."

"Whoa!" She put up a hand in the classic stop position. "Let's not get carried away."

"He's single. You're single."

She raised her eyebrows. "He lives on the east coast. I live on the west coast."

"Is that a deal killer?" he asked.

She didn't get a chance to respond before her phone went off. She looked down at it. "Damn."

"That's Remy?" he guessed.

She nodded.

"Are you going to take his call?" When she'd told him about the duffel bag, she'd finally told him that she'd caught Remy with another woman. "After what he did, you don't owe him anything."

"He'll be coming here soon. I won't be able to avoid him indefinitely."

"You can avoid him until then. Even after he arrives, it doesn't have to be terrible. A lot of people come to the island. We'll be fine here, minding our own business, until Honey gets back. Then, if there's much summer left, we can see if there's somewhere else to stay for a while or you could go back to California, and I could go back to Utah."

"Sounds good. Regardless, I'm not going to let him ruin this day." She silenced her phone before giving Jack a grateful smile. "When I invited you out here, I didn't realize how important it would be to have you around."

He smiled. "Somehow, we'll both be okay—*eventually*," he added with a laugh.

27

Bo woke to the sound of his phone going off. He'd had to schedule his flight to Louisiana, so he hadn't been napping long. But once he closed his eyes, he'd dropped into a dreamless sleep and felt lethargic, almost drugged, as he was jolted into consciousness by the jingle of his phone. He assumed he'd overslept, that it was Ismay or Jack calling to ask where he was. But when he grabbed his phone off the nightstand, he saw that it was Annabelle Windsor.

No doubt Bastian had called his mother and said Bo had used his key to enter the cottage in the middle of the night with a baseball bat. Bo hadn't actually planned on hitting anyone with that bat. He didn't need a weapon to take care of Bastian if it had come to that.

But, of course, Annabelle wouldn't know his intentions at that moment. Fortunately, she didn't know his background, either, or she'd be even more upset.

Trying to rid his mind of the cobwebs so he could think straight, he got up as he hit the answer button. He didn't want to sound as though he'd been sleeping. He put in plenty of hours—he didn't owe the Windsors every second—but Annabelle was off-island and had no idea how hard he'd worked to fix all the storm damage.

"'Lo?"

"Bo?" she said, her voice full of alarm. "What's going on? Bastian said you threatened him with a bat last night!"

Bo rolled his eyes. "I didn't threaten him. There's been a lot of drama since he arrived. It was to help *avoid* a fight, not cause one."

"With Bastian?" she said, sounding properly horrified.

"I think he was on something last night. He was acting erratic, scaring Ismay. She texted me in the middle of the night, saying she didn't feel safe, and I helped her get out of the situation."

Silence.

"Mrs. Windsor? I knew you wouldn't be happy about what happened, but if Bastian had hurt Ismay, whether he truly meant to or not... Well, I would've felt responsible if I could've done something and didn't."

"I see," she said, suddenly much calmer. "Ismay is with you, then?"

"No. Honey's daughter broke her ankle, so she had to go to the mainland to help with her granddaughters. Ismay is house-sitting for her." He didn't see any point in mentioning Jack. There was enough to explain as it was.

"Then the situation's been defused."

"Fortunately."

"Bastian told me you're getting involved with Ismay...romantically. Is that true?"

"I've barely met Ismay," he said to avoid a more direct answer. "I've only tried to keep her safe while she's here."

"Then you're not the reason she's broken off her engagement with Remy?"

"Absolutely not," he said. "That has to do with a video Ismay was sent from a third party showing Remy with another woman."

She gasped. "You mean…*cheating* on her?"

He knew Remy wouldn't appreciate what he was divulging, but it was about time the would-be doctor had to account for his behavior. "Yes."

"That can't be true!" she said, raising her voice again.

"She showed it to me. If you want to call her, she can probably send it to you."

"I don't want to see it," she said, sounding as though news of Remy's infidelity had punched the last of the fight out of her. "She must be heartbroken," she added softly.

"She is. And then to have Bastian wandering around, coming to her door and trying to get in after one in the morning… It was unnerving."

"I bet," she agreed. Then she got quiet, and Bo thought she might be weeping.

"Mrs. Windsor? Are you okay?"

He heard her sniff. "Yeah. I—I just don't know what to do."

"Don't worry. I have things under control here. I've repaired all the water damage, and I'm just about done with the fence—"

"I appreciate that," she said, but she hadn't even let him finish, so obviously she didn't want to hear about it right now. Her mind was elsewhere.

"I hope you're not upset about what I did. I couldn't see any other way around it."

"I'm grateful to you for handling things as well as you did," she said. "But…that's only a small part of the problem."

"What do you mean?" he asked.

"I just… I don't know what I ever did to deserve the children I got," she replied. Then she disconnected, because she'd probably already said more than she intended.

Stunned that she seemed to believe him over Bastian, he sank back onto the bed. He half expected her to call again, take it all back. But that didn't happen. He received no calls and just one text. From Matilda.

When will you be in Louisiana?

He was taking the first flight off the island in the morning. He'd had to put together a patchwork of travel plans in order to arrive by nightfall, but he wouldn't let Chester, the one person who'd looked out for him, go without help if he needed it. But Bo wasn't going to tell her that. He was afraid he'd show up at Grand Isle and she'd be there waiting for him.

Ignoring her message, he shoved his phone in his pocket and went into the bathroom. He had to pick up Ismay and Jack in fifteen minutes.

"Jack's doing better," Ismay said, obviously relieved.

Bo watched her brother dive into the surf. It was the warmest day they'd had so far on Mariners; the storm that'd hit the island felt like a distant memory. "I'm happy to hear it. Hopefully, that trend will continue. Has he heard anything from Ashleigh?"

"I haven't asked. He seems better able to cope if we don't talk about it."

Bo straightened his towel over the soft warm sand. There was something else they hadn't talked about, and that was what they'd done in his bed last night. Bo thought she might want to address it now that they had a few minutes alone, but so far, she'd avoided the subject. "Annabelle called earlier," he said.

Her lips parted in apparent surprise as she looked over at him. "You picked us up almost an hour ago, and you're just mentioning this now? *Please* don't tell me she fired you..."

"Surprisingly, no. She was upset, but once I explained what happened, she just got...quiet and sad. I think she's coming to realize she can't always stick up for her sons, that her loyalty and desire to protect them has maybe been misplaced."

"What makes you say that?"

He told her about the conversation, how Annabelle had started to cry and what she said right before she got off the phone.

"That's not like her, right? To be that self-aware?"

"Not really. It felt like she made a bleak realization, that she could no longer pretend her sons were admirable or even that she could trust them to behave as they should."

"Did you tell her about the duffel bag?"

Jack came up for air and went back under the waves as Bo locked his arms around his knees. "I didn't. I wasn't going to base that decision on one uncharacteristically honest and transparent reaction."

"You're afraid if she learns what's inside that bag, she might try to protect Bastian from…whatever should be coming to him?"

"Damn right," he said. "Especially when she has a history of covering for his inadequacies and bad behavior."

She adjusted her sunglasses. "So do we go to the cops?"

"I think we have to, don't you? Then whatever happens next will be up to them. At least we would've done our part."

She pursed her lips. "You can't get involved. The police are going to need to talk to me anyway, since I found it. There's no reason to drag you into it."

She made a good point. But going to the police meant alienating herself from her prospective in-laws for good. And who could say how Remy—or even more concerning, Bastian—would react.

Jack was breathing heavily as he walked up the beach and shook the water out of his hair before dropping down on his towel on the other side of Ismay. "That felt good," he said.

"Is this the first time you've ever been in the ocean?" Bo asked.

"Yeah." Jack leaned up on his elbows as he watched all the activity around them—the sunbathers, swimmers, dog walkers, joggers, and children playing in the sand. "But I now know one thing—I want to live by the ocean. Maybe move out to California, near Is. But I'm not sure what I'd do there."

"We could live together," Ismay said. "You could get a job while I start my practice."

"I think I'd like that," he stated matter-of-factly and got up again. "Anyone want a hot dog?"

"We just ate," Ismay pointed out.

"I know, but I'm starving again." He grabbed his towel and dried his hair before dropping it and trotting off to the food trucks.

"Appetite's coming back," Bo said.

"Another good sign," Ismay responded.

They watched a boy playing fetch with his dog for a few seconds. Then Bo said, "I have to go out of town first thing in the morning."

Ismay's eyes widened. "You do?"

He nodded. "Just came up. I made my travel plans after taking you and Jack to Honey's this morning."

"Is something going on?"

"That uncle I told you about? He might not be well."

"So you're going to Louisiana..."

He nodded.

She adjusted her bracelet to bring the little jewel around to the front. "How long will you be gone?"

"It'll depend on what I find when I get there."

"The Windsors won't give you any trouble for leaving, will they?"

"I don't think so, especially if Jack will finish the fence for me. I'll pay him, of course."

"I bet he wouldn't mind doing that at all, and he won't let you pay him. Not with all you've done for us. Anyway, he said the hard part's already been finished."

"I'll ask him. I texted Annabelle, and she didn't seem to have a problem with it. But I've never used any vacation days. Or sick days, for that matter. So it's not like she can accuse me of taking advantage of her." He'd had nowhere else to go. It was easiest to hide from his past right here.

"Considering how mad Bastian must be, maybe it's a good time for you to be gone."

"He's the reason I wish I didn't have to go," Bo said. "I don't want him harassing you."

"I'll be okay. Jack's here. I don't think he'd dare bother me."

He nodded, but if Bastian was what Bo thought he might be…

He couldn't even let his mind go in that direction. His uncle Chester needed him.

"Will you take an Uber to the airport? Or would you like me to drive you?"

"If you want to drive me, you could use my truck while I'm gone."

"You wouldn't mind?"

"Not at all." He'd actually feel better knowing she had some wheels.

Bo searched the crowd near the hot dog stand for Jack and saw that he'd already eaten his hot dog and was in line for an ice-cream bar. "About last night…" he said, thinking he'd better tackle that subject while they still had a few minutes alone.

Ismay immediately started playing in the sand. "I'd rather not talk about it. Not yet."

"Okay." He figured he'd given her the opportunity; she didn't want to talk, so he'd let it go. But in the very next moment, he heard himself say, "Is there any chance you'd like to come back tonight?"

When she twisted around, he could tell she was checking to make sure Jack wasn't within earshot. "Okay," she whispered. "I don't see how it could hurt anything now."

Ismay waited until the house was quiet before slipping out. Even though it wasn't far, Bo had insisted she not walk to his place alone, so he was waiting for her, but he didn't speak when he saw her. He just took her hand and kissed her knuckles before leading her silently through the warm night to his place.

Once he let them both in and they were no longer out in the hushed stillness of the night, that hesitancy to speak was broken. "Are you all packed?" she asked when she saw a suitcase set off to the side by the entryway.

He moved it so they could get into the kitchen. "Packed and ready to go."

Bo took out two glasses, filled them with a white zinfandel and handed her one. "I wish I weren't leaving," he said, leaning against the counter. "The Windsors are used to getting whatever they want. I don't trust Remy to let you go without a fight."

"I'll be fine," she insisted. "If he's been cheating on me, he can't care too much about me."

"With people like Remy, it's not about caring. It's about owning, controlling. He might feel as though *you* wronged *him* by not letting him have everything he wanted—or fly into a rage for holding him accountable instead of accepting his excuses."

Ismay was beginning to worry about staying on the island herself. Remy could be so persistent. Bo didn't know him nearly as well as she did, and yet…it seemed, in some ways, as if he knew him better. What was Remy going to do when she finally drew a line? "I'll get through it," she said. "And hopefully you won't be gone too long."

"I'll get back as soon as I can."

She was eager to feel his hands on her body again, his mouth on hers, but he lingered over his wine.

"There's just one other thing…" he said.

She set down her glass. "And that is…"

He grimaced. "You know I'm not a viable alternative for… for a serious relationship, right? I'm a loner. And my job is here. Or I might have to move back to Louisiana. California isn't a possibility."

It was a big dose of reality, one she hadn't expected to come at this particular time. "Right. And you're saying this now because…"

"Because I think it's only right. The last thing I'd ever want to do is hurt you."

"Got it." She stood. "You should probably get a good night's rest, anyway. I think I'll go back to Honey's."

His stricken expression told her that was the last thing he wanted. "I'm sorry."

"No problem."

"I wouldn't have said anything but… I didn't think it would be fair."

She slipped past him to get to the door. "I appreciate the honesty. I really do."

She opened the door to go, but he said, "I don't want you out there alone. I'll walk you." He put down his glass, but once he met her in the open doorway, he took both her hands and looked down at them without making any move to go out.

"What?" she said.

"I care about you," he murmured. "And I want you. There's no question about that. I just…don't want to be the worst thing for you."

He'd been ultra-cautious even the first time. She remembered how he kept telling her she should turn him away. That, along with his sincerity, made her soften. "I can't make any promises, either," she admitted. "So maybe we should just take it one day at a time."

He nodded, seemingly relieved that she wasn't angry, and kissed her forehead before stepping onto the landing. She knew she should probably follow him out. She could still take him to the airport in the morning if she stayed at Honey's. And if she didn't, Jack would probably realize they'd been together. But she didn't want to squander any of the time they could spend together, especially if it was so limited. So she tugged on his hand to stop him, and when he turned back, she leaned forward and pressed her lips to his.

28

Their clothes were off by the time they reached the bedroom. They'd dropped article after article as they moved through the living room and hallway, kissing while trying to avoid hitting the furniture and knocking over the lamps. Bo had been looking forward to this moment since they'd been at the beach, but nearly losing the opportunity to touch Ismay so intimately again added a huge amount of relief to the pleasure. He couldn't have enjoyed himself, though, not if he hadn't been up front with her.

"You're unlike anyone I've ever met," he murmured.

They fell onto his bed, and he began kissing the elegant line of her neck, moving down toward her breasts. She wasn't particularly curvy, but he thought everything about her was perfect.

"I felt something for you the moment we met," she admitted.

He lifted his head to look down at her. "When I was being pummeled by the wind and rain trying to get that damn generator started?"

She laughed. "You stood way out on the porch whenever you had to talk to me, wouldn't even come close to the door."

"I didn't want you to think I was some kind of threat, especially with all you were dealing with."

“I think it was that you’re a little shy,” she said, giving him an endearing smile.

She was probably right. He *was* a little shy when it came to women. He’d never had a steady girlfriend. Didn’t socialize much. “I’ll show you how shy I am now,” he teased and went back to kissing and tasting her wherever he wanted.

He felt her hands in his hair as he moved lower. He’d never gone down on a woman before, but he was enjoying himself so much he didn’t want their lovemaking to end. The more he could do to draw it out, the better. The memories might have to last him for a long time. And he loved making her feel good.

He lifted her legs over his shoulders and heard her gasp as his mouth closed over her.

“I’m glad I stayed,” she joked breathlessly, and he would’ve laughed, except he wasn’t about to pull away.

As her breathing grew labored, he became more and more excited—until her body gave an involuntary jerk, and she moaned. He knew then that she’d reached climax and couldn’t help lifting his body over hers so he could drive inside her.

They’d fallen asleep almost immediately after making love. Far too soon it seemed, the alarm went off. Ismay yawned as Bo reached over to silence his phone, then smiled groggily as he scooped her up, hauled her back a foot or so in the bed, and spooned her.

“I wish we had more time,” he mumbled as he kissed her shoulder.

“Do you need to shower?”

“I do. It’ll be a long day of travel. I think that would be a welcome courtesy for the people I’ll encounter,” he joked.

“Then that will buy us some time. Turn on the water and let me know when it’s hot.”

“You’re getting in with me?” he asked, leaning over to see her face.

"You need someone to scrub your back, don't you?" she teased.

"This is going to be fun," he said. "I've never showered with a woman before."

She almost couldn't believe that statement. "You've got to be…what? Thirty-two?"

"Thirty-three."

"Then how is it you've never showered with a woman?"

His teeth flashed in a sexy grin. "I guess I've led a sheltered life."

She could tell by the way he said that sentence there was a deeper meaning to it, a joke of some kind, but he was already en route to the bathroom, so she didn't stop him to ask about it.

"It's hot," he called a second later, and she kicked off the covers before joining him.

Steam rolled out when he opened the shower door, but he turned the temperature down so it wouldn't be too hot for her. Then he soaped her up, and she did the same to him before bringing their slick bodies together.

"I've waited entirely too long to try this," he said.

He was so different from Remy, had such an unusual innocence about him. And yet, he seemed wise, almost world-weary.

They'd used all the hot water before he was willing to get out. Then they had to dress in a hurry so they could make it to the airport on time.

"Stay away from Bastian while I'm gone," he told her. "Give him a wide berth—leave if you have to."

"Should I go to the police?"

"Not unless you're in danger." He put on a jacket and grabbed his bag. "That would antagonize him. We can figure it out when I return."

Ismay nodded and he responded with a grin. But when he opened the door, he tensed and dropped his luggage so he could shove Ismay behind him. There was a man in the yard, just standing there with his hands in his pockets. It took her a second to register that it was Bastian.

"What's up?" Bo asked Remy's brother. "What can I do for you?"

"I've gotten something stuck in the garbage disposal," Bastian said. "I was wondering if you could get it out for me."

Bo picked up his suitcase again. "I hate to tell you this, but I have an emergency at home. I'm flying out today and won't be back for a few days, at least."

"Where's home?"

"Louisiana."

"So… I'm supposed to live without a garbage disposal?" Bastian said.

Bo checked his watch. "I'll text you the name of a good plumber."

"Does my mother know you're leaving?"

As Bo carried his suitcase to the truck, Bastian wandered a bit closer and watched as he put it in the back. "I let her know, yes."

Bastian studied Ismay, who'd followed Bo out and was circling around to get in the driver's side. "I see you've taken over where Remy left off with Ismay."

"Ismay's giving me a ride to the airport," Bo said. "That's all."

Bastian started to chuckle, which quickly crescendoed into the maniacal laughter Ismay had heard from him before. "You're not fucking her?"

Bo pivoted to face his employer's son. "I'm saying you'd better stay away from her."

Bastian sobered instantly. "Or what? My caretaker's going to beat me up?"

"Don't cause a problem, Bastian," Bo said.

"You're sleeping with my brother's fiancée on our property, and you think I'm the one causing a problem?" Bastian asked, then turned to Ismay. "Is Bo better in bed? Or is it just that you like to go slumming every once in a while?"

"Bastian, this is between me and Remy," Ismay said.

"He's definitely going to be interested." Bastian pulled out his phone and began taking a video. "Look what I have here, Rem. Your girl's just spent the night with our caretaker. That's thanks for sending her to an island paradise for a few months, isn't it?"

Ismay could tell Bo wanted to knock the phone from Bastian's hand.

"I'm going to miss my flight if we don't go," Bo said, making an effort to remain calm. "I'll text you that plumber's number. Now, if you'll excuse us…"

"Look at the two of them," Bastian said. "Just like a little couple—already!"

Bo gestured for Ismay to get in, and she climbed behind the wheel as he slid into the passenger side. She had to pull out very slowly because Bastian wouldn't stay far enough away from the vehicle.

Bo lowered his window. "You're going to get yourself hurt if you don't step back," he said. But Bastian, who was still filming, just continued to laugh.

"I can't wait for Remy to get here!" he yelled as they finally reached the road.

Ignoring this latest outburst, Ismay punched the gas.

Bastian watched Bo and Ismay disappear around the bend. Then he went to the cottage and got the key to the bungalow, which had always hung on the inside door of the pantry. Bo thought he could disrespect his employers? He was living in a house *they* provided, driving a vehicle *they* provided, eating food *they* provided via his paycheck. Who the hell did he think he was?

Bastian sent Remy the video he'd taken of Ismay coming out of Bo's house at the crack of dawn looking as though she'd just rolled out of bed. He didn't caption it, didn't explain. Remy would be able to see for himself what was going on.

Letting the screen door slam behind him, he gripped the handrail tightly as he descended the stairs. He was feeling a bit lightheaded from all he'd had to drink the night before and stumbled on the uneven ground as he took the path that led to the bungalow.

Birds were singing and flitting through the trees overhead, and the sun felt warm and mellow as it climbed higher in the sky. This was Mariners at its best. But he couldn't enjoy it. He was dealing with one of the longest stretches of insomnia he'd ever experienced—since Lyssa's death, anyway.

Anger helped override the disorientation he felt and kept him focused as he entered Bo's house. He had no idea what he was looking for. Anything interesting, he supposed. Or he just wanted to satisfy his curiosity about someone whose quiet strength he longed to destroy—because he envied it so damn much. When Bo had come to get Ismay from the cottage, he'd felt no compunction about invading *his* privacy, and Bastian was eager to return the favor.

He thumbed through the stack of books he found piled near the recliner and grimaced. Most were from the library, but there were plenty of others—books on carpentry, building, history, philosophy, even poetry. Apparently, their caretaker liked to read.

"I guess you have to do *something* during the long winter months," Bastian mumbled.

His phone dinged. Pulling it out of his pocket, he squinted to be able to read words that suddenly looked blurry to him.

What the hell is this?

Remy. What was he doing up? It would be three thirty in the morning in California. Isn't it clear? Bastian wrote back, which, fortunately, prompted Remy to call him, because texting was too cumbersome for Bastian at the moment.

"Ismay spent the night with Bo?" Remy demanded. "Is that what you're saying?"

Remy sank into the recliner. "What does it look like?"

There was a long pause. "It's bullshit. When did you take it?"

"Not very long ago. Maybe twenty minutes?"

"She's leaving me for our maintenance man—who doesn't have a fucking dime to his name?"

"She doesn't seem overly concerned about that. Maybe she just wants him for his body." Bastian couldn't help laughing but Remy's silence warned him that he was pushing his brother too far.

"She's just trying to punish me," Remy said, obviously looking to minimize the problem.

Bastian didn't get that impression. Whatever was going on between Ismay and Bo seemed real enough. But he knew his words were too slurred and his brain too muddled for long explanations. "Whatever you say."

There was another pause, then he heard an audible sigh. "Should I come there?"

"Hell, no. What about your exams? Besides, Bo's leaving for a few days. They were going to the airport. Something about a family emergency in Louisiana. Don't worry, bro. I'm looking out for you."

"Like you've looked out for me in the past?"

"Have you looked out for me any better? Anyway, this isn't my fault. If I hadn't come here, you wouldn't even know what was going on."

Remy didn't argue. He seemed too caught up in his own thoughts. "This might be the perfect moment to show up—when he's not around. Better yet, Mom needs to fire his ass. Then maybe he won't come back at all."

"Already tried to get him fired. She called me back and said she wasn't going to let me cost her a good caretaker."

"You're kidding..."

"Nope. He has this sort of strong, silent resilience. It's hard to describe. Women go wild for it."

"He's going to be sorry he ever tried to steal from me," Remy said and disconnected.

Bastian let his phone drop into his lap and rested his head on the recliner to stop it from swimming. He didn't know if Ismay would return to the bungalow after dropping Bo off at the airport. But he sort of hoped she would. He'd love to have her walk in and find him in the living room, sitting in what was obviously Bo's favorite chair.

With any Windsor, paybacks were a bitch.

Ashleigh was trying to reach him. Jack squeezed his eyes closed as his finger hovered over the talk button. He'd been accepting her calls for so long it was almost automatic. But everything that'd happened in the past couple of weeks rushed through his mind, and he didn't think he could bear to hear her voice, knowing it would drag him back into the pit of despair he'd been trying so hard to climb out of.

As soon as the call transferred to voice mail, another call came in. This one was from Ismay, so he answered.

"Good morning!" she said cheerfully.

He ran a hand through his hair. He was no longer sure it *was* a good morning.

"Uh, yeah, good morning," he said.

"Is something wrong?" she asked.

"No. I'm just waking up, so I'm a little groggy. I got your text last night when I got up to go to the bathroom. Did you take Bo to the airport?"

"I did. I was wondering if I should grab some breakfast buns and coffee on the way back, or if you'd rather go out to breakfast."

Clementine had spent the night curled up next to him and the gentle attention she gave him helped him feel better. He stroked her fur as he tried to decide how to return to the place of strength and healing he'd found yesterday. "I say we go out," he said. That would give him less time to think and he'd be with Ismay, who helped buoy him simply by being who she was.

"Okay. I'll come grab you," she said. "I've got Bo's truck while he's away."

"That'll be convenient. After breakfast, should we go to the police about that duffel bag?"

"Not yet. Bo made me promise I wouldn't do anything to antagonize Bastian while he's gone."

"I guess there's no rush. I mean...hopefully there's not."

"Bastian was right outside Bo's door this morning when we were leaving for the airport, looking pale and drawn. He claimed he wanted Bo to fix the garbage disposal."

"At that time of morning?"

"Yeah."

"Was he drunk?"

"*Something* was wrong with him. He's unraveling."

"Great," he said sarcastically. "Just what I want to hear after learning about a stash of women's underwear hidden in a freaking wall."

"Hopefully, Bastian will lay off the booze and get some sleep."

He thought about telling her that Ashleigh had tried calling, but there was a notification that she'd left a message, and he decided to listen to that first. "I hope so," he said. "I'd better get in the shower."

As soon as she said goodbye, he navigated to his messages and braced for the sound of Ashleigh's voice. Part of him didn't want to hear from her ever again; he especially didn't want to let anything set him back right now. But curiosity prevailed.

"Hi, Jack. I just... I haven't heard from you in a while and wanted to see how you're doing. I heard you'd left town, but no one will say where you are or how long you'll be gone. About the car, my dad said he'd give me some money to help while

Jess and I get on our feet, which is so nice of him. My mother and siblings won't even talk to me. Neither will some of your family, by the way. I ran into a few of your brothers at the gas station. When I tapped on the window to say hi to William and Oliver while Hank was paying the cashier, they—" Her voice broke. "Never mind," she said quickly and hung up.

Jack didn't realize he had tears streaming down his cheeks until one dripped off his chin. *I shouldn't have listened to that*, he thought.

He sat there, staring at the wall, his heart aching with the loss of someone who'd been everything to him. But a new emotion had stepped out of the shadows—pity for what *she* was feeling. She wouldn't have left him if she were happy, he realized. She had the right to love and be loved as deeply as almost everyone craved.

He lifted his phone to type his father a text.

Please tell everyone that the best way to help me is to be kind to Ashleigh. I can't add any other emotion to what I'm feeling right now, if that makes sense.

He wiped the tears from his cheeks as he waited for a response. It was still early in Utah, but Buzz got up early, and after checking his watch, Jack knew his father, who lived a life of routine, would be having his usual breakfast of hot oatmeal and raisins with toast, prepared and served by his mother. That meant he'd have his phone with him and would be reading the news.

It does make sense. Forgiving her is the best thing you could do—for both of you. And we need to forgive her, too.

Jack sent a thumbs-up emoji. His dad didn't like a lot of emotion. Jack had often lamented that he was more like his mother and unable to control or mute what he felt.

Clementine snuck under his arm and batted a paw at his

phone. She didn't like the loss of his attention. He set it aside to lift her in his arms and rub his chin on her soft fur. But when she wiggled to get loose and jumped down again, he sent a text to Ashleigh.

> Thanks for making the car payment. The transition is going to be rough on both of us, but I hope you'll be happy. Honestly. I'm sorry about William and Oliver. My family won't mistreat you again.

Somehow just writing that brought back the lump in his throat, but he managed a nostalgic smile as he set his phone aside so he could get ready to go out for breakfast. He would get through this, and no matter how hard it turned out to be, he'd do it without destroying the person he'd cared about so deeply since they were both in their teens.

After all, what was love if not that?

29

Bastian woke up hours later. He'd slept. Thank God! It had been in Bo's recliner, which was ironic enough to make him chuckle, but he'd finally been able to give his mind and body a rest.

His stomach felt sour. He hadn't been eating enough and the alcohol had left him dehydrated and shaky. But at least his thoughts were clear. He'd been afraid he was losing his mind, was terrified he'd wind up in an institution, where Remy had long said he belonged. The memories of Lyssa had triggered some sort of mental relapse…

Getting up, he stretched before checking the time. It was six thirty in the evening. Damn. He'd slept for nearly twelve hours. No wonder he was hungry…

Maybe he'd see what was in the cupboards. As far as he was concerned, Bo owed him a meal. The healthy food Ismay had left at the cottage didn't tempt him. Surely, Bo had some good ol' processed staples.

He sifted through the cupboards and refrigerator and ultimately took out some hamburger and buns from the freezer to have alongside a baked potato with sour cream.

He got it all started, then wandered around the house, trying to satisfy his curiosity about Bo. Who was he? What made him tick? Why was he content to live alone and stay year-round on the island when it could get so damn lonely?

The bathroom held the usual toiletries. Bastian shaved with Bo's razor, used an extra toothbrush, and put on his cologne. Then he went through Bo's drawers and medicine cabinet.

No condoms anywhere. That was interesting.

No drugs. Not even a little pot. No medicines, either. That was interesting, too.

The rest of what he found was pretty standard—and boring. Bo wore boxer briefs. He didn't have a lot of clothes, but he'd taken some with him, and what was left was folded neatly in his drawers.

Had he been in the military?

Possibly. His Spartan existence kind of suggested it. Bastian was tempted to dump out his clothes and leave them in a mess on the floor, but that was a little too flagrant.

There weren't any condoms in the nightstand, either—just an e-reader. "Jesus," he muttered. "Do you care about *anything* except books?"

Where had he gone to college? Bastian wondered. Somewhere in the south? Apparently, he had family in Louisiana…

The bed had been made, but when Bastian brought one of the pillows to his nose, he thought he could smell Ismay. There was definitely perfume on the pillowcase, but he'd already guessed they'd spent the night together. It'd been all too apparent when they'd walked out of the house this morning.

He was planning to return to the kitchen so he could finish his dinner when he realized what was wrong. Bo had no personal effects. No pictures of his mother, father, siblings, or any family. He had no letters or documents lying around. His house had none of the mementos most people would add, not even a single photograph of him with a dog or a friend.

Beginning to search more earnestly, looking for anything that might reveal some weakness or vulnerability, Bastian used his hand to check under each drawer, in case Bo had taped something there.

Nothing.

He dragged out the weights Bo kept under his bed, so he could search there.

No luck.

It wasn't until he lifted the mattress that he found something that wouldn't normally have been there. A wallet had been shoved there, pushed way into the middle.

At first, Bastian didn't think much about it. It could be that Bo had stuck it there to hide it in case someone broke in. But he'd just left town. If this was the wallet he used on a daily basis, wouldn't he have taken it with him?

Shoving the mattress farther so he could reach it, he flipped it open. Finally, he'd found pictures, but only a few. One was of Bo when he was about ten with what looked like a little sister, one was of Bo, more recently, with an old man, and the last one was a pregnant woman from possibly the '90s.

There were also a couple of credit cards and a driver's license.

Bastian almost closed it and tossed it back into the middle of the bed. He didn't think it was any kind of big revelation, but then he realized Bo would've needed his ID to get on the plane. So why'd he leave it?

He pulled out the driver's license. It'd been issued in Louisiana and was expired by nearly a year. Nothing unusual about that. Plenty of people held on to an expired license for several months in case they lost their new one.

But then Bastian's heart began to beat a little faster. Something was up, all right. The driver's license had Bo's picture with a different name. It didn't say Bo Broussard, it said Beau Landry. And when he took a closer look, the credit cards did, too.

Why?

Grand Isle sat at the end of Louisiana Highway 1, about fifty miles south of New Orleans. It was the only inhabited barrier island in Louisiana, and as far as Bo was concerned, there was no other place like it. Some of the families who'd lived here for generations, including his uncle Chester and his grandparents before they passed, claimed they'd never leave.

Today, there were only about a thousand locals on the island, down from thirteen hundred not many years ago, and that number was continuing to shrink. Those who remained were determined to keep fighting the wind and the waves that were slowly washing away their beloved home.

Climate change would eventually win, which made Bo sad. He loved Grand Isle almost as much as Chester did. He was just more pragmatic. Plus, he didn't want to stay in a place where so many people believed he was guilty of the crime of which he'd been convicted.

Half a dozen chickens pecked in the dirt beneath the weathered stilted shack where Chester had finished raising him. Once Bo got out of his rental car, the smell of the earth and trees brought him back to the days he'd walked around barefoot wearing the same dirty jeans and often no shirt as a young teen. Back then, he'd always had a fishing rod in his hands. His uncle had taught him to fish as soon as he'd arrived on Grand Isle, and he'd loved it.

A calico three-legged mutt Chester had found roaming the island, foraging to stay alive, while Bo was locked up, stood from where he'd been sleeping at the front door and started to bark as Bo climbed the stairs.

"Hey, boy." At Bo's suggestion, Chester had named the dog Long John Silver—an ode to the one-legged pirate captain in *Treasure Island*. "You been taking good care of Chester?" he asked the dog and was surprised to hear a human voice answer from inside the house.

"*I've* been doing that."

If the weather was warm enough, the door stood open—there was no air-conditioning—and today it was a humid eight-five degrees. The shadows created by the porch were too deep and dark for Bo to be able to see who was talking. But he recognized the voice.

Matilda.

Straightening, he considered driving straight back to the airport. But now that he'd come all the way from Mariners, he had to see the old man. With Chester's age and failing health, for all Bo knew, it could be the last time. "Why didn't you tell me you were going to be here?" he asked.

"Would you have come if you knew?" She pushed open the screen door from the inside and stood in the opening, and he caught his first glimpse of his younger sister in fourteen years. Her face was rounder but she was pretty as ever with her hazel eyes and dark wavy hair falling below her shoulders. She looked older than thirty, though. They'd both had to grow up fast.

"Probably not," he admitted. "So you baited the trap by acting as though Chester needed me? Why?"

"Because it's time we made our peace."

Again, he felt the impulse to walk away. This discussion was fraught with too many emotional landmines he'd sooner avoid. "There will never be a time. What sister turns on her own brother?"

Her knuckles whitened on the door. "He was our father!"

"He killed our mother!" he nearly yelled.

She winced as though he'd struck her. "I didn't believe that then. Still, more bloodshed didn't make it right."

"I didn't shoot Dad! He deserved a bullet. I won't say otherwise. But all I did was go over to talk to him, to tell him that even if the police couldn't charge him, *I* knew the truth. I knew what he really was. He didn't like hearing it, but he was alive when I left."

Lifting her chin, she glared at him defiantly. "So you think someone else came along?"

"I think when he realized he wouldn't get away with what he'd done, he took his own life."

"With *your* gun."

"It was *his* gun, Tilly. One of several Mom hid from him when he moved out because she planned to sell them. It was her only way of getting some money, and I took it with me after she died and I moved to Grand Isle. Yes, I brought it back with me, stuffed in my luggage as I hitchhiked to Tampa, and had it at the apartment. But *he* used it after that. You must believe that now, tricking me to get me out here. Why? What's finally convinced you?"

She opened her mouth, closed it again, then covered it with a hand as tears filled her eyes. "As an adult, I just… I see things differently—things I couldn't accept back then. Things Dad did. Aunt Marva has told me more about Mom and Dad's relationship and how he treated her when they were together—the extramarital affairs, how miserable she was, his refusal to give her the divorce she was begging for, and then how he drained their bank account when he did finally leave. All of it."

Marva was their mother's sister, but even she had stood by Tilly during the trial. "If Marva was aware of all that, why'd she turn on me, too? The whole damn family did! Except Chester. He was the only one on my side."

"We all knew how you felt about Dad, how angry you were. You took a gun to his apartment, for God's sake!"

"I took that gun because I wanted to give Mom the justice she deserved! But I realized once I got there that going to prison for him wasn't worth it—which is *so* ironic now, right? I told him what I thought of him, then I threw the gun at him and left." Matilda knew that. She'd heard it in court, when she testified to nearly crashing into him as she arrived at the apartment complex and he was tearing out of the parking lot. But this seemed to be the first time she was actually listening.

Closing her eyes, she shook her head. "I'm sorry. I—I couldn't believe he'd take his own life and leave me when I needed him the most." Her voice fell to just above a whisper. "I thought he loved me."

She'd been blinded by loyalty to a man who didn't deserve it. On some level, Bo had understood that and already forgiven her. He just couldn't have her in his life. She'd been young, just sixteen, but he'd been only two years older and had never felt more alone. Family, friends, neighbors—everyone—had rallied around her and turned their backs on him, probably because Matilda had stayed in Florida when Bo moved to Grand Isle. With Uncle Chester's help, he'd spent eight years pressing the police to look more closely at their father, Clint, certain he was to blame for their mother's death, but unable to prove it.

"The only person he loved was himself," Bo said. "And I waited year after year for the police to do their job. They knew it was him but couldn't prove it beyond a reasonable doubt. The one thing I'd been living for, the one thing that could make the loss we'd suffered tolerable was justice for Mom. And yet I—*we*—were going to be denied even that."

"If only I'd come home earlier that night," she lamented.

"Then you'd know I didn't do it. But that's the only thing that would've changed. Mom would still be dead, Tilly," Bo said. "Dad's where he deserves to be."

"After that night, I was left without either parent," she said as the tears that'd been filling her eyes streamed down her cheeks. "I was so hurt, so angry..."

What Matilda had done was wrong, but she'd acted on what she believed at the time. They were both victims of a man who didn't care enough about them to curb his own selfish desires. All the heartache they'd suffered stemmed directly from the night their father took their mother's life.

At least Bo had chosen to live with Chester. From ten to eighteen, he'd been as happy as a kid could be, under the circumstances. Although he'd been waiting for closure, he'd run wild and free on Grand Isle, and Chester had looked out for him and treated him well.

Matilda, on the other hand, had chosen to believe in their father, who hadn't deserved her trust. Clint had had both the opportunity and the motive. A witness could place him near the house the night their mother was shot and killed, even though he'd at first claimed to be out of town. He'd had access to a firearm, even though the police could never find it. Bo had even heard him tell their mother he'd kill her if she ever started seeing another man.

Bo pinched the bridge of his nose with one hand. He'd tried desperately to leave the past in the past.

But he and Matilda would continue paying a price for what his father had done as long as Bo continued to hold a grudge.

"Bo?" Chester yelled from inside. "Bo, that you?"

The old man was shuffling through the living room, trying to reach the front door.

"Yeah, it's me," he called back.

"Well, you don't say!" Chester exclaimed. "It's about damn time! Tilly, don't just stand there, invite him in."

Matilda held the door open, but Bo hesitated. He knew if he went inside, the wall he'd built to keep her out would crumble. She'd become part of his life again.

But maybe that was for the best. Maybe it was time he tried to forgive and forget. Although there was no changing the past, he could change the future.

Hadn't their father cost them enough already?

The TV droned in the background as Bastian sat on the couch with his laptop. Ever since he'd found that driver's license tucked between the mattresses in the master bedroom of the bungalow, he'd been digging up information on Beau Landry, and after three hours, he felt fairly certain he'd figured out what was going on.

The links that'd populated his screen were mostly newspaper articles about a young man—eighteen-year-old Beau Landry—who shot and killed his father because he believed the man had killed his mother eight years earlier. He was tried, convicted, and sentenced to twelve years in a Florida state penitentiary, but he'd been living in Louisiana at the time he shot his father.

Except for the name, everything fit the Bo he knew. The caretaker his mother had hired was close to or the same age as Beau Landry. He was associated with Louisiana, just like Beau Landry. And he had Beau Landry's driver's license and credit cards.

Bo Broussard *had* to be Beau Landry, but Bastian had yet to come up with a good enough picture to prove it, at least to others. He'd been able to tell from the driver's license he'd found that Beau was Bo, but that picture was so old it barely looked like him. And the only other picture he'd found so far was of Beau sitting with his lawyers in court, which was partially obscured. It took searching through several more links to find one that was clear enough to determine if the two men were absolutely the same—and then it was unquestionable.

As soon as he found it, Bastian rocked back and laughed. His mother had hired an ex-con—a *murderer.* She'd been thrilled to get someone as capable as Bo Broussard, and she was naive enough to believe he'd never lie about his past.

"This is too much," Bastian said, still laughing. He took a screenshot of the picture and grabbed the links of several of the articles he'd found online and sent them to the "fam chat," which included both his parents and his brother.

It was Remy who reacted first. What is this?

Bastian couldn't help feeling smug when he typed, Our caretaker.

Remy: Bo Broussard?

Bastian: You mean Beau Landry, the ex-con and murderer?

Remy: How did you find this?

Bastian: Does it matter? It's real. Look it up for yourself if you don't believe me.

A message appeared from their mother. Bo has been lying to us?

Bastian steadied his computer on his knees so he could type again. From the beginning...

Annabelle: You're saying Bo murdered his father?

Bastian: That's exactly what I'm saying.

Remy: He came to Mariners after spending twelve years in prison?

Bastian relished the opportunity to find fault with their mother. And then you hired him, Mom, he wrote. Didn't you do a background check?

Annabelle: I don't know how to do a background check, Bastian.

Bastian: Maybe you should've hired someone.

Annabelle: How was I supposed to know he wasn't who he said he was?

Mort's first message appeared. We can't have a murderer working for us. Only God knows what he'll do. We need to fire him.

Annabelle: Do you think he's been stealing from us?

Bastian: Not that I can tell, but you never know. He certainly isn't trustworthy.

Annabelle: I should've fired him when you told me he entered the house in the middle of the night! You need to stay away from him, Bastian. I'm going to call the police.

Bastian: And tell them what? That he lied about his background? They aren't going to do anything about that.

Mort: Just fire him, Anna. I'll start asking people I know on the island for recommendations so we can get a replacement as soon as possible.

Annabelle: I should've known he was too good to be true. He seemed so solid and dependable! I'm shocked!

That would teach her for taking Bo's side over his, Bastian thought. She deserved to be mortified and embarrassed, so he wasn't going to be too quick to accept her apology.

Remy: I have his number. I'll fire him for you.

After the video Bastian had sent his brother this morning showing Ismay coming out of the bungalow with Bo at dawn, no doubt Remy would enjoy being the one to let him go.

Annabelle: No! I don't want you to make yourself a target. If he's violent, who knows what he might do?

Bastian: Poor Ismay. He's fooled her just like he fooled you.

Annabelle: We need to make sure she stays away from him. Should I call her and explain? I sent him to the cottage when she was there alone in the storm, for God's sake!

Remy: Why don't you do that? Considering the situation, it might be better coming from you. I'll talk to her after.

His mother put a thumbs-up on Remy's response before Bastian wrote: Remy, when you fire Bo, tell him I'll box up his stuff and ship it to Louisiana. That way, he won't even have to come back here.

Annabelle: Be careful. He could be dangerous. We don't want any trouble—we've been through enough.

Remy: Don't worry, Mom. I'll make sure he leaves us all alone in the future.

Annabelle: It's hard to believe he's actually killed a man. My God, what's this world coming to?

As far as Bastian was concerned, Bo shooting his father wasn't any big thing. Under those circumstances, he would've done the same. As it was, he sometimes dreamed of what it would be like to inherit his parents' fortune early. Then he'd never have to work another day in his life.

30

Ismay had been waiting for the other shoe to drop all day. She knew Bastian wouldn't let what'd happened this morning go. He'd tell Remy and possibly his parents and do what he could to get Bo fired.

She didn't care if the Windsors were mad at her. She'd gone too far with Bo, knew that she could never go back to Remy. The fact that she was missing Bo, although he'd only been gone a day, and felt a mild sort of relief that she no longer had to deal with Remy, said a lot. She cared about Remy as a human being, and maybe they could somehow remain friends, but she was no longer in love with him. The separation had probably happened slowly over time, but enough distance had crept between them that it was obvious at last.

The question was…how did she feel about Bo? She couldn't be in love with him. Everything was too new. When she first started seeing Remy, it'd been exciting, too. She'd thought she was in love. But after she moved in with him, the shine had quickly worn off as he began to take her for granted.

She checked her phone, hoping to hear that Bo had arrived safely in Louisiana, but she hadn't received anything from him. Unable to wait any longer, she sent him a message.

You safe? All good with your uncle?

It took a moment, but she got a response.

He fell and hurt his shoulder. His arm's in a sling, but my sister is here taking care of him. He's going to be fine.

Any word from Remy? she asked.

Not yet. He's not bothering you, is he?

No. Jack and I had a great day looking for shells and sea glass on the beach, napping in the sun, eating, and watching movies.

Good. I'm happy all is well.

He said he'd finish the fence tomorrow, so don't worry about that. Where are you in Louisiana?

She was still waiting for a response when a call came in. She hoped it was Bo but saw a number she didn't recognize. She probably wouldn't have answered it, except she thought he might be calling her from someone else's phone. "Hello?"

"Ismay?"

The female voice sounded somewhat familiar. "Yes?"

"This is Annabelle Windsor, Remy's mother."

Ismay immediately thought of the truck she and Jack were driving and wondered if using it was going to get Bo in even more trouble. "I'm guessing you've heard from Bastian…"

"Yes. I'm sorry you felt he was acting erratically—"

"He *was* acting erratically," she insisted.

"Maybe so, but I'm calling to let you know that he's not the one you have to be afraid of."

Ismay pictured the duffel bag and its contents. "What are you talking about? *Remy* isn't safe?"

"It's *Bo* who's dangerous, Ismay."

"You don't know what you're talking about. Bo is—"

"You know he's a murderer, right?" Annabelle broke in.

Ismay started to laugh. "Oh, my God! No, he's not! That… that's outlandish!"

Annabelle remained unruffled; she merely sounded sadly adamant. "Apparently, he's duped you, just like he duped me."

The fact that Annabelle wasn't backing off sent a chill through Ismay, but she still couldn't believe it. "He hasn't *duped* anyone—"

"Check your texts," Annabelle interrupted again. "I just sent you a picture of his driver's license under his real name. Do a Google search on that and see what you come up with. I'm sorry I ever trusted him, that I exposed you to a man like that. I—I should've done a background check. I just never dreamed…"

Ismay didn't respond. Eager to see this "proof" Annabelle purported to have so she could shoot it down, she navigated to the picture that'd just come through. It was a driver's license, all right—one with Bo's picture as a much younger man and the name Beau Landry.

This *had* to have been doctored, she told herself. She was intent on finding the flaw in what Annabelle had sent, so she told Remy's mother that she'd get back to her and hung up and opened her laptop. But when she typed *Beau Landry* into Google, the links that appeared made her skin prickle.

Son Kills Father, Claims He Murdered Mother

Son Secures Justice for Mother Eight Years After Her Death

Beau Landry Gets Revenge on His Own Father

Beau Landry Sentenced to Twelve Years

Jury Empathizes With Boy Who Lost Mother, Goes Easy on Landry

She squeezed her eyes shut. She didn't want to see what she was seeing, didn't want to believe it. But Bo had told her his mother had been killed. The timing matched. One article even mentioned that he'd been living in Louisiana with his great-uncle after his mother was killed. Too many details fit with the little she knew of Bo. And now she understood why he hadn't been more forthcoming…

The article that shocked her the most was titled *Sister to Testify Against Beau Landry.* That had to have been excruciating for him, but even that fit with what she knew.

Ismay dropped her head in one hand. She'd been so caught up in what was inside the duffel bag she'd found, what it might mean about Remy. Now she wondered if it was *Bo* who'd hidden that stuff. He was in and out of the cottage; he could easily have stashed it anywhere he liked.

But that didn't explain the picture of Lyssa. How would he even have known her? And why encourage Ismay to go to the police?

Some details fit, others didn't. Her head was spinning. But Bo was an ex-con. There were too many articles to deny it. And although she ached for him, losing his mother when he was so young, she had to wonder if he was truly capable of shooting and killing someone. Did he have that kind of rage inside him?

It was possible…

What kind of person, exactly, had she trusted?

Suddenly ice-cold, she could scarcely breathe. She'd made love to Bo. She'd thought of almost nothing but him ever since. She'd trusted him over Remy and Bastian.

And how did she feel now? Shocked. Betrayed. Hurt most of all. Surely, the Windsors' retribution would be swift. They'd fire him, of course. But maybe they'd spread the word about his background around the island, so he wouldn't feel comfortable returning and wouldn't be able to find work even if he did. She could even see them threatening to alert any future employer, which would make the coming years incredibly difficult—unless he could find a way to disappear again.

Setting her computer aside, she pulled the lap blanket from

the arm of the couch over her and curled up as she stared blankly at the opposite wall.

Her phone dinged again. She thought it might be Annabelle, trying to confirm that Ismay had found the articles backing up her claims. But Ismay didn't want to read whatever message she'd sent, let alone respond to it. She didn't want to hear from Bo, either. Right now, she had no idea what to say.

Remy had tried calling him twice in the past fifteen minutes. Bo had silenced both calls; he had no interest in talking to Remy. If the Windsors had something to say to him, Annabelle or Mort could reach out. But he'd sent Ismay three texts since she'd asked him where he was in Louisiana, and she hadn't responded. That made him wonder if something was wrong…

Bastian better not have done anything to her. The fact that he'd stolen a pair of Ismay's underwear—and that he had a collection of other panties in that damn duffel bag—scared the hell out of him.

Everything okay? he wrote to Ismay.

Again, she didn't answer. Maybe she'd fallen asleep. It was an hour later on Mariners. But she'd asked him a question…

Remy was calling again after not leaving a voice mail, so Bo decided he'd better see what was going on.

Because Uncle Chester and Matilda were sleeping, he got off the couch, where he'd made himself a bed for the night, and stepped out via the screen door before hurrying down the stairs to the path he knew so well from his childhood. It led to the water, which was exactly where he wanted to go. Then he wouldn't disturb his family. Nor would they be able to eavesdrop. "'Lo?"

"Bo? It's Remy."

He could hear the gentle lapping of the waves against the shore, see the thin smile of a half-moon overhead and the water far out on the horizon lined with silver. "I know."

"I have to admit, I'm shocked. I had no idea who you really were."

Bo stopped walking. Apparently, the day he'd both feared and dreaded had arrived. After finally establishing some stability in a place he enjoyed, without too much fear that his past would catch up to him, he was coming face-to-face with the truth he'd been trying so hard to hide. "How'd you find out?" he asked.

"You're not going to play dumb? Deny it?"

"I'm assuming you have it on good authority."

"I do. Bastian came across that wallet you hid between the mattresses, Beau Landry."

"I don't suppose it'll do any good to say that Bastian had no business snooping around in my things..."

"You can complain about that to the police, if you want," Remy said. "But if I were you, I'd stay away from them."

Bo turned to face the water. "Why? I've served my time. I'm not even on probation. And I plan to speak with the cops, anyway, when I tell them about the duffel bag I found hidden in the wall of your old closet." It was a lie—Ismay had found the duffel bag, not him. But he preferred to leave her out of this, if he could. He didn't want to give Remy a reason to target her. And now he had nothing to lose.

"What are you talking about?" Remy sounded leery.

"You're going to pretend you don't know?"

"I don't remember any duffel bag," he insisted.

"You'd remember this one," Bo said. "It was filled with women's underwear, some cheap jewelry, and a picture of Lyssa Helberg."

"What the fuck are you talking about?" he exploded. "You have no idea what happened that night. I don't know anything about a bag of panties."

"Really? Because it was right there by your notebook. Nice sketches, by the way—if you have violent, twisted fantasies that would turn a decent person's stomach."

"You couldn't even guess what I fantasize about."

"The contents of that duffel bag would give anyone a pretty good indication," Bo said.

"That duffel bag—and what's in it—must belong to Bastian. It's not mine."

"Oh, of course. He just hid it in your room."

"You're fired, you know that?" Remy shouted. "Bastian will box up your shit and send it. Don't ever set foot on Mariners again."

Bo gripped his phone tighter. "You think you own the whole island?"

"I might as well. You'll be sorry if you come back," he said and disconnected.

Bo sighed as he stared off into the distance. No wonder Ismay was no longer responding to him.

What the hell was he going to do now?

Jack never thought he'd be the one doing the comforting, but when he woke up the next morning, Ismay was still on the couch in her clothes, with nothing but a lap blanket to cover her and balled up tissue all over the floor. When he gave her shoulder a gentle shake, and she opened her eyes, he could see tear tracks on her cheeks, and she immediately broke down again when he asked her what was wrong. Because she was trying to stop from crying and was then crying too hard to answer him, all he could do was put his arm around her to console her. And when she finally calmed down enough to tell him what'd happened, he couldn't believe it.

"That *can't* be true," he said. "I feel like I know the kind of man Bo is. He's not a murderer."

"If anything could push someone to that kind of violence, it would be justice for his mother," she said.

He had to agree with that, but still… It was hard to believe the man who'd been kind enough to take him in so he wouldn't have to pay for a hotel, which he couldn't really afford, and had tried so hard to look out for Ismay could be guilty of shooting anyone, regardless of the situation. Bo had lied about his identity and his background, so whether or not he was guilty of more, Jack could understand why Ismay would be distraught. He'd watched the attraction grow between them, knew they'd been getting closer and that Bo was largely the reason she was suddenly so decisive about being done with Remy.

She showed him Bo's unanswered messages on her phone. "Do I tell him I know? What do I say?"

"I wouldn't say anything until you're ready. Take some time. Then ask him whatever you honestly need to know."

"Why bother?" she said, her voice sounding nasally from all the tears. "We don't have a future together, anyway."

Jack hated to hear her say that. He was as shocked by what he'd learned as she was, but there was something about Bo that made it difficult to just…cast him aside. No matter what he'd done, Jack felt he'd earned more of their trust, respect, and loyalty than that. "Issues like this can be complicated," he said.

"What does that mean?"

"It means we don't know what was going through his mind at the time. Or for that matter, what really happened. Are you even sure he did it?"

"He was convicted. He served twelve years."

"That's not always the same thing," Jack said. "What'd he plead?"

"Not guilty."

"Maybe he isn't. A lot of innocent men go to prison."

"Who else would've done it?"

"I don't know," Jack said, "but he deserves the chance to explain. Don't you think?"

"I guess, but what if he *did* do it? I mean…we'd all like to mete out justice when we feel someone has wronged us. But we can't…"

"I'm not making any excuses for him, Is. I'm just saying the man we've come to know is a good man. I firmly believe that. Don't you?"

She grabbed another tissue to blow her nose. "I do," she admitted. "But is that because it's what I want to believe? Am I being stupid? Naive? Foolhardy?"

Jack shook his head. "I don't have those answers. But I will say he's done all he can to look out for you—and he's put himself on the line to do it."

Her gaze fell to the carpet.

"What's happened since you got here is probably the reason he's been found out," Jack continued. "I know that wasn't intentional on your part, but I'm sure Remy's parents have fired him. Or they will. That means he has no place to live. Starting over with a record isn't easy, which is probably why he lied about his identity in the first place."

She wiped her nose as another tear fell. "I can't stand the thought of him being without the things he needs. Or feeling rejected. Or unloved."

"Then that should tell you something right there."

She massaged her temples. "I have a terrible headache."

"Then go back to sleep while I finish the fence. We can talk about this later."

She caught his arm. "You're not going to finish the fence knowing Bo probably won't even get paid for it!"

"He might get paid for it. I hope he does. Either way, I said I'd finish it, so I want to follow through. You get some rest, and we'll talk later."

"Jack, I'm just…trying not to ruin my life by falling in love with the wrong man."

He gave her a gentle smile. "I know. But given all these tears, I think it might be too late for that."

Remy was coming to the island. He was forgetting about his big exam, said he'd have to take it later, during his residency.

Bastian knew he couldn't be happy that Ismay was making it necessary for him to drop everything and come to Mariners. But Remy could never take no for an answer.

Bastian sat in the Jeep and surfed the internet on his phone while waiting for his brother's plane to arrive. At last, Remy came walking from the terminal and climbed into the passenger side of the Jeep. "Finally!" he said as he slammed the door.

Bastian started the engine. "Rough flight?"

"Aren't they all? I hate air travel."

"Where do you want to eat?" Bastian asked.

"I don't want to eat. Take me to Honey's. That's where you said Ismay and Jack are staying, right?"

Bastian blinked at him. "You've got to be starving."

"I ate in Boston on my layover. And if we wait any longer, they might go to bed."

Bastian checked his watch. "At ten?"

"I want to talk to her, Bastian," Remy said. *"Now."*

"If she won't answer your calls or your texts, what makes you think she'll let you in?"

"It's easier to ignore a call or a message than someone banging on your door," he replied.

Bastian was hungry, but he knew better than to insist on eating first. He didn't want to start this visit off on the wrong foot. Taking Remy head-on was never the right thing to do. "Fine. We have to get the keys to the truck Bo left with them, anyway," he said and drove out of the parking lot.

The lights were on at Honey's, and the truck was sitting in the drive. It appeared as if someone was home. But when Remy went to the door and knocked, no one answered.

Bastian lowered his window. "Let's go eat. We can deal with this tomorrow," he yelled, but Remy shook his head.

"No way," he said. "We'll deal with it tonight."

•

31

Ismay spotted the Jeep in the drive before Jack did and grabbed his arm.

"What is it?" Jack said, lifting his head.

"Bastian's here."

"Oh, shit." He peered through the trees that partially concealed Honey's house and scowled. They'd slipped down to the Windsors' private beach and spent the past forty minutes enjoying the mild spring evening while they talked about so many things—their upbringing, their parents' life view, letting go of Ashleigh, getting a condo or apartment together in Los Angeles, Ismay's engagement to Remy and their subsequent breakup. And Bo. Mostly Bo. Ismay hadn't responded to his last text from over a day ago, and he hadn't tried to reach her again. She assumed he knew she'd learned the truth. The practical part of her—the part that was most like her father, she supposed—warned her to let him go. To leave things as they were. There were plenty of other men in the world who hadn't experienced what he'd experienced and with whom she'd never face such difficult questions.

But she couldn't stop thinking of him and didn't want to walk away, despite what she'd learned. She'd never felt so strongly about anyone else. She at least owed it to him to decide if she believed his version of events, didn't she?

"Let's go back to the beach," Jack said, stopping. "I don't want to deal with Bastian."

"He's probably come to get the keys to the truck," she said, trying to guess the purpose of this unwanted visit. "I say we give them to him and be done with him. We don't need the truck—we can always walk or Uber. And then he'll have no reason to bother us."

With a shrug, Jack started walking toward the house again. "Yeah, might as well get it over with."

Prepared for a hostile encounter, Ismay squared her shoulders as they approached the vehicle, but there was no one sitting inside. Because she and Jack hadn't planned on being gone more than a few minutes, they hadn't bothered to lock the house, and she got the distinct impression Bastian had let himself in. She could see why he might feel free to do that with the bungalow. His family owned that. But Honey's house? It came as a shock that he'd go so far.

"What an assuming bastard," Jack muttered just before he opened the door. But it wasn't only Bastian who was in the living room. Remy was with him.

Ismay felt her jaw drop. "Remy! What are you doing here? What about your exam?"

"I decided I can take it during residency when we're both in LA. We don't have to be apart, not with so much going on here." He'd stood when he saw her and was coming forward as if he expected her to fall into his arms.

She put up a hand to let him know that wasn't going to happen, and he stopped about three feet away. "Nothing's going on here. Not anymore."

His thick dark eyebrows slammed together. "You're not answering my calls and texts..."

"And you know why..."

"I think you're making a big mistake," he said.

"Breaking up with you?"

"Yes! You're trading a physician who could give you a great life, everything you could ask for, for an ex-con who probably doesn't have two nickels to his name. He has no family to speak of, either—just a history of violence. Do you really want to tie your future to his? He can't take care of you like I can!"

What Bo had been through was terrible, and he probably had some deep scars that would inform his worldview. But maybe his past had taught him a few good things, too—made him humble and kind and more aware of what really mattered in life. Maybe, unlike Remy, he wouldn't take so much for granted. At least he seemed capable of true feeling. With Remy, she'd never connected on a deep level, not like she had with Bo, especially when they were making love. Bo had made her feel that those moments were precious beyond measure.

Bottom line, Bo made her feel valued, and she wasn't sure any feeling could be better than that. "I don't need anyone to take care of me, Remy. I'm an attorney. I'll be fine. And you're not so innocent yourself."

Remy stiffened. "What are you talking about?"

"Your affair with Sam, your so-called study partner, for one. The underwear in that duffel bag in the wall of your closet for another. And the cheap jewelry. Where did all that come from?"

His eyes began to glitter—with anger, she supposed. He wasn't used to anyone calling him out on anything, especially her. She typically did what she could to avoid a fight, because he was always willing to go further than she was. "I still can't believe you didn't ask me about it," he said. "That you took it to Bo instead?"

"I was pretty freaked out. I still am."

"I had nothing to do with that," he said. "Until you mentioned it, I had no idea it even existed!"

"It's gone missing, so I figured it had to be Bastian's, especially because a pair of my underwear suddenly went missing, too. Only he could've taken that stuff. But now that I think about it, maybe he took my underwear to upset me or scare me. Lord knows he likes to get under people's skin. It's possible he was even imitating you. But I don't think he'd leave that bag in your room. Why would he leave it outside his control? And it was with *your* notebook. So what'd you do—tell him to get it for you?"

"I didn't tell him anything." He whipped around to face his brother. "Did you put that stuff there?"

Uncertainty flashed across Bastian's face. He looked cornered, frantic. But he quickly masked those emotions. "I don't know what you're talking about," he insisted.

"You *have* to know." Jack joined the conversation even though he'd been making an effort to stay out of it. "You're the only one who could've taken it—and Ismay's underwear."

"It wasn't me," he said. "I didn't take either one!"

Remy's eyes narrowed. "Bastian, if you're up to your old tricks—"

"Stop it!" Bastian broke in. "Shut up, or you'll be sorry!"

Ismay didn't know what that meant. Was she wrong? Did those things belong to Bastian or Remy? "One of you is very sick," she said. "You should seek help."

"It's not me," Remy said emphatically. "According to my mother, you're willing to believe Bo didn't murder his father, even though he was convicted of it and served time, and yet you won't believe I didn't stick a duffel bag of underwear in my closet?"

Ismay rubbed her forehead. She couldn't say who had done what. But she knew one thing. Bo was the man she wanted. "Forget it," she said. "This isn't even about that."

"Then what's it about?" he asked. "Why have you broken off our engagement?"

The memories of everything they'd shared over the past three years flashed through her mind as she looked at him. A certain nostalgia came with it. They'd had good times and bad. But when she thought of going back to Remy—she knew that wasn't the path she wanted to take. "Because I'm in love with someone else," she replied.

He looked like she'd slapped him. "You've only been here a short time!"

She got the keys to the truck from the kitchen counter and gave them to him. "I know," she said. "I can't explain it. But I can't deny it, either."

"You're making a big mistake. Huge!" he snapped and might have pushed her on his way out if Jack hadn't yanked her to one side. "This isn't over," he added.

Bastian looked surprisingly rattled as he followed his brother outside. "This isn't going to end well," he muttered.

"All you have to do is leave us alone, and it'll end fine," Jack called after them. But they didn't respond. They didn't bother to shut the door, either, so Ismay could hear both engines when they flared to life and reached the front stoop in time to see Remy squeal the tires of the Jeep as he backed out of the drive and went flying down the road.

When his phone dinged, Bo glanced down to see Ismay's name pop up with a message. But he didn't dare read it. He couldn't take having her turn on him, making him feel the way Matilda had made him feel fourteen years ago, as if he had no chance of being heard, let alone believed.

When Ismay didn't respond to him the day he was fired, he almost blocked her—not because he didn't want to hear from her but because he was afraid he'd never hear from her again. If he blocked her, he'd never have to know. He thought it might be easier that way.

But he couldn't bring himself to go through with it, couldn't quite extinguish the hope that he might've established enough credibility with her that she'd give him a chance to explain.

She didn't know him very well, however, so he was asking for a lot, probably more than he had a right to expect. Most people believed the worst when they heard someone had been convicted of murder. If he hadn't been through what he'd been through, maybe he'd be like everyone else. He *had* assumed a fake name and lied about his past. He was guilty of that, which didn't exactly build his credibility.

Still, he hadn't murdered anyone and would always want the people he cared about most to believe him.

He let her text go unread for the rest of the day. Matilda was cooking up a storm and storing meals in the freezer, so Chester could heat them up after she was gone. And Bo was repairing all the dry rot around the dilapidated house and painting. They'd both been busy, but they had dinner with Chester every night, and after Chester went to bed, they'd sit out on the deck and talk until late. Despite having his past discovered by the Windsors, which meant Ismay had learned about it, too, the past three days had been a time of healing as he and his sister put things right between them. But they didn't have too much longer to be together, especially with time alone. Her husband was bringing her two boys—five and three—to Louisiana over the weekend to meet him. Then Matilda was going home with her family.

Bo figured he'd stay on Grand Isle until Chester's arm healed. Then, after his belongings arrived from Mariners, he'd try to find another job in another place that held more promise. Fortunately, he'd saved most of the money he'd earned working for the Windsors. Since his housing and vehicle had been covered, and he lived a simple life, he hadn't spent much, only what he'd needed for food and basic necessities.

"You were quiet at dinner tonight," Matilda pointed out after Chester said good-night and shuffled down the hall, and they once again settled into the chairs on the deck.

Bo had been consumed by the text he'd received from Ismay—was constantly thinking about it while putting off actually looking at it. He was afraid she'd sent a reproach of some kind. She had a right to be angry. He'd slept with her without telling her who he really was, but he didn't want to ruin his memory of that night by spoiling it with accusations and anger or the news that she was going back to Remy.

"Just tired," he said. He hadn't told her that he'd assumed a new name or been fired. He didn't see the point of going into all that. Although she knew his time on Mariners was over, he'd just told her he was tired of doing maintenance work for rich people and was going to move on in search of something else after he left Louisiana. She'd been trying to talk him into moving to Tampa, where she lived, ever since. But he could never go back to Florida. Florida held too many memories.

Almost an hour later, Matilda's phone dinged with a text, and she lifted it to show him. "I can't wait for you to meet the boys," she said.

Bo smiled at a picture her husband had sent of her children hamming it up in their pajamas. He'd never dreamed Matilda would be eager to have him around her kids. It was proof that she finally believed he was innocent—and that felt even better than he could've imagined. "You think you'll have any more children?" he asked.

"Maybe one. I'd like a little girl." She set her phone aside and took another sip of her beer. "What about you? Would you like children one day?"

Bo had finished his beer thirty minutes ago. "If I can get anyone to marry me," he joked.

She didn't laugh with him. She studied him for several seconds, then said, "You'll find someone. And whoever you settle down with will be lucky to have you."

"There isn't much to recommend me."

She looked pained when she said, "I'm sorry for my part in that. The more I've come to know you these last few days, the more I realize how wrong I was to believe what I did."

"Let's not relive it," he said. "It happened, it's over. We have to salvage what we can from the wreckage and move on."

"I know. It's just..." She groaned. "You lost twelve years of your life because of me."

"We don't know that. I had the motive and the opportunity, and my fingerprints were on the murder weapon. I probably would've been convicted either way." What she'd said to the jury certainly hadn't done him any favors, but he'd been far more hurt by the fact that she'd refused to believe him about what really happened that night.

"Thank you." She reached out to take his hand. "Thank you for understanding and forgiving me in spite of everything," she said and gave his hand a squeeze before getting up to go to bed.

Bo stayed on the deck alone, listening to the cicadas as he held his phone in his hand, both longing to read Ismay's text and dreading it. Finally, when the hall light snapped off and he knew Matilda wouldn't come out again, he drew a bolstering breath and navigated to the message that'd held his heart and mind hostage all day.

> I'm sorry it's taken me a while to process everything that's happened. I wanted to be sure of how I feel before I said anything. Now I hope I'm ready because I can't wait any longer. I miss you too much. And I want to tell you that I have no idea what happened the night your father died, but deep inside, I know you're a good man—and that's all that matters to me. I hope what we had, though new and untried, was worth enough to you that you'll come back.

He'd prepared himself for so much worse he almost couldn't absorb the meaning of those words. He read her message three times before the pressure on his heart and gut eased—so much that he suddenly felt light as a feather—and he turned his face up to the moon and smiled. He'd gotten twelve years in prison he didn't deserve. Now he was getting the chance to continue a relationship with the most beautiful woman he'd ever met—beautiful in every sense—which was probably something he didn't deserve, either.

Life could be inexplicable, totally unfair and cruel and yet exquisite and fleeting and gorgeous at the same time. Ismay had far less reason to believe in him than the family and friends who'd turned their backs on him when he was on trial. But against all odds, she was still there, and she had her hand outstretched.

But could he take it? What did he have to offer someone like her?

"Any word from Bo?"

After having breakfast in town, Ismay and Jack were slowly walking around the island to the public beach closest to Honey's house. They could've taken an Uber, but the exercise was good for them, and the long lazy days ahead removed any sense of urgency. "Not yet," she replied.

"But you wrote him last night?"

"I did. After you went to bed." She took out her phone and showed her brother the message.

He smiled as he read it. "That's nice. It must've felt good to receive that. I'm shocked he hasn't written you back."

"I took a while to decide how I feel. He deserves the same courtesy."

He stopped to remove a small rock from his flip-flop. "Are you afraid he won't come back?" he asked as he straightened.

"Terrified," she admitted. "Especially because Remy's been texting me like crazy, telling me I'm making a big mistake—never mind his cheating," she added with a roll of her eyes.

Jack started walking again. "He's not taking no for an answer?"

"Not so far. He insists things will be different back in LA.

He also told me Bastian packed up Bo's things and will be shipping them to Louisiana."

Jack frowned. "That suggests Bo isn't coming back."

She stared at the ground as they walked. "Yeah. There'll be nothing left for him here."

"Except you," he pointed out hopefully. "At least if he comes back, you'll know why."

"I guess," she allowed.

He adjusted his sunglasses. "What will you do if he doesn't?"

"There's not much I can do," she replied. "I'll try to stay in touch for a while, but he has to want me badly enough to make the effort and be willing to take the risk. And I'm not convinced he does."

He gave her a lopsided smile. "He'd be a fool to miss out on someone like you."

"After what he's been through, maybe all he wants is to lick his wounds. He might not be ready for a relationship." As much as it hurt to admit that, it was a stark reality she had to face. Maybe it was easiest to remain closed off, so he couldn't make a mistake or get hurt again.

"All you can do is let go and hope he comes back," Jack said, but then he grabbed her arm and jerked her to a stop. "Ismay..."

She looked up to see Remy and Bastian coming around the bend in the Jeep, probably going into town. "Just ignore them. Act like you don't even see them," she muttered, and he fell in step beside her as she started walking again. But she was glad he didn't look away like she did, because a second later, the Jeep swerved toward them going full speed, and he had to throw her to the side so she wouldn't be hit.

She landed so hard that she skinned her hands and knees, but at least they hadn't been seriously hurt. Jack landed on the ground next her and his hands and knees were also skinned.

"What the heck?" he cried, jumping to his feet. But Remy

and Bastian were already well beyond them, heading down the road toward town as if nothing had happened.

"Remy just tried to hit us!" Jack cried, as if he couldn't quite believe what'd occurred.

Ismay got up and dusted the tiny rocks out of the flesh of her hands and knees as she tried to process the fact that the man she'd been planning to marry could've killed her with that kind of impulsive, reckless behavior.

"Remy and Bastian are dangerous, Is," Jack said. "I'm not sure we can remain on the island. Remy seems like the kind of man who thinks if I can't have her, no one can."

"We can't leave," she said. "What about Honey? We told her we'd look after her house and her cat."

"We'll have to tell her it's not safe for us, not with Bastian and Remy around."

"I think we should go to the police before we do that."

Jack gestured at the blood appearing on some of their scrapes. "About this?"

"About all of it—this, the duffel bag, the picture of Lyssa, Bastian's alarming behavior, Remy's possessiveness..."

"You know the Windsors have a lot of influence here."

"I know. When Lyssa died in that fire, they stepped in to make sure Remy and Bastian walked away without any consequences." They might try to do the same now, but it was high time someone fought them for the sake of truth and justice. "But I'm an attorney, Jack. I believe in upholding the law."

He scowled before finally relenting with a sigh. "O-kay," he said with a heavy emphasis on the second syllable. "We'll try that. But if it doesn't work, I'm getting you off this island."

32

When Ismay left LA to come to Mariners, the last thing she could've imagined was waiting in a police station to talk to an officer about Remy. But she felt strangely empowered, as if she was finally drawing a line after all the little slights and other evidence that he wasn't being as good to her as she deserved. Cheating aside, they hadn't been fine for a long time. Maybe they'd *never* been fine, and she just hadn't known him well enough to realize it.

"You look nervous," Jack said as they waited, sitting in cheap plastic chairs just inside the main doors. "You okay?"

"It's not every day you have to go to the police about your former fiancé," she whispered.

"I hope this doesn't make things worse..."

He was worried about what Remy and Bastian might do in response. So was she. But she didn't get the chance to agree. The female officer at the front desk called her name, and she and Jack stood at the same time.

"Detective Livingston can see you now."

"Detective?" Ismay echoed. "We...we're only here to file a police report."

"You said you had a complaint against Remy Windsor, is that right?"

She nodded.

"Then you might want to speak to the detective."

Ismay exchanged a glance with Jack before they were escorted to a small office that contained files and stacks of paper piled on almost every horizontal surface. A medium-sized man, probably in his fifties, with a sprinkling of gray in his dark hair, a jacket that didn't quite go with his slacks, and a dated tie was just clearing off two seats so they'd have a place to sit down.

"Thanks for coming in," he said, turning to shake hands. "What can I do for you?"

"I'd like to file a report," Ismay said and started with what she'd found in the wall of the closet, showing the detective the picture of Lyssa she'd taken on her phone and telling him why she didn't have other pictures—that the duffel bag had been gone when she went back to get it.

"This is alarming," he admitted, frowning as he passed her phone back. "You said the duffel bag was in Remy's room?"

"Yes," Ismay confirmed. "In his closet, right by his notebook."

"That notebook isn't necessarily proof the bag belongs to Remy. It was Bastian we arrested on a Peeping Tom complaint when he was in high school."

Ismay gripped the arms of her chair. "He was peeping in windows?"

Livingston sighed before replying. "Charges were dropped and nothing ever came of it. I was afraid it might lead to bigger problems. A lot of Peeping Toms progress into..." He waved his hand. "Well, never mind. But it's been so long now I'd almost forgotten—until today."

"That gives me the creeps," Ismay said, "especially because he stole a pair of my underwear when I was staying at the cottage—I'm almost positive of it."

"And what about the picture of Lyssa Helberg?" Jack asked. "Does anyone really know what happened that night?"

"The boys had a huge fight, possibly about Lyssa. Things got physical, which led to the fire. Witnesses said Lyssa wasn't in the living room when it happened. She didn't get out in time. I don't think they meant to kill anyone."

It still freaked Ismay out that Bastian had stolen a pair of her underwear—especially since he had a history of peeping. "So… what do we do about Bastian taking *my* underwear?"

"I'm going to have a talk with him to see if he can explain where your underwear went and where all the other underwear came from."

Jack scooted forward. "Um, that worries me a little—given that they just tried to run us down before we came here."

They showed the detective their scrapes and he rubbed the beard growth on his chin. "Sounds like I need to talk to his brother, too. Were there any witnesses?"

Jack shook his head and explained where it happened, that the bend in the road kept them out of sight.

"Then they'll probably deny it. But… I'll do what I can. Those boys have run unchecked for too long."

His reaction to what they'd told him didn't provide much comfort, but Ismay thanked him and kept her mouth shut until she and Jack were out of the police station and in an Uber on their way home.

"What do you think?" she asked Jack.

"I'm nervous," he admitted.

So was she. Going to the police had felt like such a bold, decisive move—as if that was "the answer." But now that they'd been there, Ismay realized how limited the police response would most likely be. Even if she was able to parlay the visit into a restraining order, would she be able to get one against both twins? And what did that do for the women whose underwear were in that duffel bag?

Nothing.

She feared their visit would turn out to be ineffectual, or worse—that it'd make Bastian and Remy angry enough they wouldn't miss the next time they saw Ismay and Jack walking down the road.

The police were at the door. When his brother yelled up to him, Bastian struggled to return to consciousness, but it wasn't easy. He'd finally fallen asleep at six-thirty this morning; it felt like he'd barely closed his eyes.

Lifting his head, he squinted to be able to see the alarm clock on the nightstand. Nine-twenty. Three hours wasn't nearly enough sleep.

"Bastian? You coming?"

Bastian managed to bark out a yes. Then he dragged his tired ass out of bed, rubbed his face, and stared at himself in the mirror over the dresser as his sluggish mind caught up with what was happening. The police were here? *Why?* Was this about yesterday, when he and Remy had seen Jack and Ismay walking along the side of the road?

Surely, Ismay wouldn't have gone to the police. She had to know better than that…

"Bastian! Come on!" Remy yelled.

With a curse, Bastian pulled on a T-shirt with the basketball shorts he'd worn to bed and headed out of the room. He needed to be sharper to deal with the police. Being questioned for hours about the fire back when Lyssa died—it was all so traumatizing. Then there was the Peeping Tom complaint. That had been a close one. Bastian knew he had to be ready for anything. But Remy had no patience.

"What is it?" he bellowed as he descended the stairs.

When his brother had said *police*, he'd thought he'd find an officer in uniform at the door. But it was Detective Livingston wearing his cheap rumpled sports coat. Seeing him sent fresh alarm through Bastian. He remembered how unimpressed Livingston had been with the Windsor influence and wealth.

"I'd like a word with you, if you don't mind," the detective said when their eyes connected.

"I haven't done anything wrong," Bastian said.

Livingston smiled blandly. "Then you have nothing to worry about."

He had plenty to worry about. "Do I *have* to talk to you?"

"If you want to be sure I get all my facts straight," Livingston replied.

Bastian told himself he was overreacting. There wasn't anything his mother couldn't take care of. "Fine. Come in," he said, and as soon as the detective had taken a seat in the living room, he added, "What's wrong?"

Livingston pulled a pad and a pen from his pocket. "This might take a minute. Why don't you sit down, too?"

Bastian chose a side chair, but Remy remained on his feet and said, "I don't think it should take very long at all."

Livingston's eyes narrowed as he considered Remy's response, but he started the interview anyway, and directed his first question to Bastian. "Your brother tells me you grabbed the wheel yesterday when the vehicle you were in nearly struck Ismay Chalmers and her brother Jack Chalmers, who were both on foot, about a mile from town."

"What? Wait—Remy was driving!" he cried but knew he'd spoken too soon when Remy sent him a dirty look.

"I *didn't* say that, Detective, and you know it," Remy clarified. "I said it was an accident, that Bastian was reaching for his drink in the middle console as I took the corner a little too fast, and he fell against the wheel."

"So it was just bad timing," Livingston said.

"That's right," Remy responded.

Bastian could feel his heart beating in his throat as he glanced at his twin brother, who was, as always, completely calm and self-assured. Nothing bothered Remy. He'd acted the same way the night of the fire.

"And did you stop to see if they were okay?" the detective asked.

"No," Remy replied with a shrug. "I could tell they were okay. I could see them in my rearview mirror."

"How thoughtful of you," Livingston said.

Remy chuckled humorlessly. "Maybe it wasn't thoughtful, but you can't charge me with not stopping to see if someone I didn't even hit was okay."

"You're right," Livingston said. "But what about the duffel bag that was in Remy's closet?"

Bastian caught his breath. By now, he knew he was supposed to follow his brother's lead, so he waited for Remy to answer.

"I don't know about any duffel bag, and I'm sure Bastian doesn't, either," Remy said.

Bastian knew he wouldn't be believed quite as easily, but he quickly agreed. "Remy's right."

Livingston was openly skeptical. "There was just an empty hole in the wall…"

Remy threw up his hands. "I guess so. I don't even know about that. I'm not here that often. I've been going to UCLA for the past ten years. I've hardly been on the island since high school. If there was a duffel bag in the wall, maybe it belonged to the contractor who did the renovations. Or Bo Broussard."

Bastian got the impression Livingston was tempted to laugh. "You're pointing your finger at the caretaker?" he said. "Essentially telling me the butler did it?"

"In this case, that might be true," Remy explained. "Maybe you're not aware, but Bo's real name is Beau Landry. He has a record. Shot and killed his own father."

Obviously shocked by this statement, Livingston looked up from his notes, where he'd just written Bo's real name.

"You can do a background check if you don't believe me," Remy added.

Rocking back, Livingston crossed his legs. "And yet your mother hired him to take care of the property?"

"She was unaware of his history at the time," Remy said. "She just found out—and fired him."

"I see. So he served time for murdering his father—a very different kind of crime—but you think he's been stealing women's underwear? How would he have a picture of Lyssa in that bag if he didn't come to the island until…two years ago, was it?"

"I wouldn't know," Remy said.

"You don't think it's relevant that Bastian has a history of peeping on women?" the detective asked. "And that a pair of your ex-fiancée's underwear has gone missing in his company?"

Remy took a step forward. "Who said her underwear's gone missing?"

"She did," Livingston replied.

"That could've been Bo, too," Remy said. "She was having an affair with him while I was in LA trying to finish up my boards."

Livingston nodded. "Ah, the real reason he was fired."

Bastian could tell the detective was really pissing off Remy when a muscle began to twitch in his brother's jaw.

"Look, I know you don't like us," Remy told Livingston. "Maybe you have some chip on your shoulder when it comes to the upper class. But I will tell you this—you have no proof, and continuing to accuse us of crimes we didn't commit is going to cause *you* more trouble than us."

Livingston stiffened. Bastian feared Remy had gone too far, but there was nothing he could do, not without making the situation even worse.

"I'll keep that in mind and get back to you after I investigate this more thoroughly," he said through a clenched jaw.

The detective left immediately after that. Bastian waited until he saw his plain brown sedan pull down the drive, then turned on Remy. "What the hell?" he cried. "Why'd you piss him off like that? Now he's going to come after us for sure—and by us, I mean *me*!"

Remy shrugged. "Don't worry about it. There's nothing he can do."

"So what's the plan?"

Bo hadn't realized his sister had come out of the house. When he heard her voice, he turned from where he stood at the water's edge, watching the sunset, and mustered a smile, even though he wasn't eager for company. He'd been deep in thought, trying to decide what to do about his future. More than anything, he wanted to return to Mariners, to see Ismay again. But by now, word of his past would have spread, so he'd have to face all the people he'd deceived. The locals gossiped about everything. Ivy at the library would know. Honey would know if she was home—thank God she wasn't, because he cared about her opinion. So would the contractor he'd helped on the cottage renovations. The grocery store clerks. And Remy and Bastian would be right there, just down the street from Ismay and Jack, antagonizing him whenever possible.

But none of that had to do with the real reason he was hesitant. Although returning wouldn't be *comfortable*, he cared enough about Ismay to run the gauntlet. The problem was that he didn't believe she could be truly happy with someone like him, and he didn't want to get his hopes up only to have them dashed.

"You're thinking about Ismay," Matilda said before he could answer.

Last night, while they were sitting on the porch, he'd opened up for the first time and shared a little about his dilemma. He still hadn't told her he'd lied about his background and been caught and fired. He didn't plan to ever tell her that because it didn't matter now, didn't change anything. But he had let her know he'd met a woman he cared about and would have a hard time moving on without her.

Then don't move on without her, she'd replied.

She made it sound so simple. Her words had been ringing in his head as he finished painting the house today. But every time he convinced himself to take her advice, he backed away from the decision. Why would Ismay, someone who had everything a man could want in a woman, ever settle for him?

"I'm always thinking about Ismay." He didn't see any point in denying it.

She picked up a seashell and threw it into the Gulf of Mexico. "And?"

"I think she's better off without me."

"Really?" she said, as if she couldn't believe all his thinking had brought him to that conclusion.

"It makes the most sense," he said.

"To whom?" she responded. "To you? Of course, it does. Because that's the safest route. Then you don't have to risk your heart, risk failing in the relationship that's most important to you."

"I'm looking out for *her*," he insisted.

She rolled her eyes. "Sure, you are."

He scowled. "What's that supposed to mean?"

"She's a big girl. Why don't you show her enough respect to let her look out for herself?"

He glared at her. "You realize there's only a very small chance this would end well…"

"I realize you have *no* chance if you refuse to even try," she said. "What are you afraid of exactly? Losing her? If you don't go back and let her know you care, you'll lose her for certain, right?"

He squeezed his forehead. "Damn, you're hard on me."

He could tell she knew he was joking when she put her arm around him and briefly rested her head on his shoulder. "That's what sisters are for," she said. "I'd better get back to the house to check on Chester after his shower."

He chuckled to himself as he watched her go. He was glad he'd come home. It was the best thing he could've done. And maybe she was right. Maybe he was doing himself a disservice even thinking about walking away from someone like Ismay...

A text message came in on his phone. He checked it and laughed out loud when he saw that it was from his sister.

Go back to Mariners, you big dolt.

He'd pretty much decided he'd hate himself for the rest of his life if he didn't, but it was the message that came next, almost right on top of Matilda's—this one from Jack—that sealed the deal.

Remy and Bastian tried to run us down in the Jeep yesterday, so we went to the police about that and the duffel bag. Not sure it was a wise decision.

Bo cursed. He believed the Windsor twins were dangerous.

I'll get there as soon as I can, he wrote back. No way was he going to leave Ismay vulnerable to the Windsor twins, not even with Jack around to protect her. Jack had never seen anyone who was truly evil, not like Bo had.

That meant Uncle Chester would have to get along on his own for a few days after Matilda left, but the old man was doing better all the time. Bo would also miss meeting his brother-in-law and nephews, but he'd make sure he had another opportunity soon.

33

You went to the police? How could you?

Ismay had been staring at Remy's text for probably three minutes. She was sitting in The Human Bean, a coffee shop that always had a lineup and was located beneath a trendy art gallery.

She'd considered blocking Remy. His messages had devolved into angry missives that made her wince. But she was hoping he might say something she could take to the police. Detective Livingston had warned her not to engage with him if she thought he might be dangerous. But she couldn't help responding to this.

What'd you expect me to do? You almost killed me and Jack two days ago!

That was Bastian! He pulled on the fucking wheel! He thought it was funny to see you two scatter.

And you didn't stop or do anything about it?

I could tell you were okay. I'm sorry. But it wasn't me! I have a demented brother. I've told you that before.

You never told me he was arrested as a Peeping Tom! You let him come stay with me at the cottage without even warning me.

That was years ago. He didn't do anything to you, did he?

He stole a pair of my panties, which is creepy and weird!

I'll get them back for you.

I don't want them back! Something is seriously wrong with him, so if you can tell the police anything, you should come forward.

You're telling me to rat out my own brother?

I think he might be a danger to those around him, Remy, so what choice do I have? You're going to be a doctor. You, of all people, should understand why that sacrifice might have to be made.

"What are you doing?"

Startled by the interruption, Ismay looked up as Jack put down their drinks and took a seat at the small round table. "Texting Remy," she admitted.

"What? *Why?*" he said, immediately alarmed.

"He seems almost…conciliatory today. It's as if he still thinks there's a chance I'll take him back—as if he never tried to run us down or send me all those mean messages."

"My question still stands," Jack said emphatically. "Why are you responding to him?"

Because she could sense an opportunity. It was a slim opportunity, but it might be their *only* opportunity… "I'm thinking we play into his delusion, get him to believe he'll come out of this just fine as long as he's transparent about what he knows.

Something has to give, Jack. I don't think the police are going to be able to do anything about Bastian otherwise."

Jack took a sip of his latte while studying her over the rim. "But you don't really think Remy would ever tell on Bastian..."

"If I can get him to believe I might come back to him, he might..."

Jack winced. "I'm not sure I like the sound of that."

"He's going to get away with it. It's not like they live here year-round, which makes the detective's job that much tougher. What about the women who owned that underwear? Had he been peeping at them? Breaking and entering and fondling their things? Or doing something even worse? All it would take is for Remy to get Bastian to say where those panties came from. Then the police could follow up from there."

"But that's such a long shot..."

"Not if he thinks that by throwing Bastian overboard, he can save himself. If Remy continues to protect his brother, they'll both forever seem suspicious. But if he makes it clear it was Bastian, he can protect his own reputation. And Remy cares more about his image than anyone I know. He's always trying to prove he's smarter or better than the next guy."

"I almost feel sorry for Bastian, growing up with that," Jack muttered.

"Except Bastian's insufferable himself."

"They both have issues."

"So if I can drive a wedge between them, and I think I know how to do that, it might be just what we need." She went back to her text chain with Remy.

Either way, I'm going to the newspaper early tomorrow morning.

For what????

To tell them everything I know.

Wait! No! Everyone on the island knows my family.

Jack scooted closer so he could read what was going on. "You're playing with fire," he murmured.

Ismay ignored him. She had a feeling this might work…

I'm sorry, but if there are women who are missing underwear, or who've had an encounter with Bastian that wasn't quite right, maybe they'll come forward.

Are you kidding me? The whole island will think I'm the pervert if you say you found that duffel bag in my closet!

I have to do what I think is right.

That's bullshit! I love you, and this is what you do to me? Don't you care about me at all anymore?

Of course I do. This isn't easy for me. But I have to be able to live with myself.

She saw the dots that signaled he was writing something appear and disappear twice, but nothing came through.

"He's thinking about it," Jack said, looking tense. "What will he decide?"

She shook her head. "He and Bastian have spent their lives blaming each other for one thing after another, even Lyssa, right? We just need Remy to do it one more time…"

Finally, she received his response.

You can't do this to me. Or my parents.

I don't want to, believe me! But if you can't get Bastian to tell you where he got every single pair of those panties, you'll force my hand. I'm an attorney. What do you expect?

You're saying if I tell you where they came from, you'll keep your mouth shut about where you found the duffel bag?

Once Livingston has that information, I won't say a word—I'll stay out of it completely.

She held her breath, then added, I'm just trying to do the right thing. As hard as it is, I would hope you'd want to do the right thing, too.

He's my brother.

If he's peeping in windows or breaking and entering or whatever, he has to be stopped. Let's get him some help before it gets worse.

You're not going to let this go.

I can't.

She got nothing from him for probably five minutes. Then Remy wrote, Fine. I'll see what I can do.

Ismay felt her eyes go wide. She set her phone down and tried to take her first sip of coffee, but her hand was shaking from the adrenaline pumping through her, so she put it down again. "I think he's going to do it."

The first thing Bo learned when he landed on Mariners was that Bastian Windsor had been arrested. Jack had texted during Bo's flight to say that Ismay had convinced Remy to come forward, and what he'd told the police must've been meaningful because Bastian was already in custody.

Bo couldn't help thinking of Annabelle, who was probably on her way to the island with an expensive attorney in tow, determined to go to battle on behalf of her son. He would've texted her to offer his condolences, but he hadn't heard from her since Remy fired him, and he was afraid she'd assume he was gloating.

He wasn't. *She* wasn't to blame for Bastian's actions, and he knew how mortified, embarrassed, and heartbroken she had to be. He believed part of the reason she overindulged her sons was to remain relevant in their lives. He got the impression she wasn't fulfilled in her marriage. Mort was always so busy. She needed something or someone to cling to.

How did she do that? he wrote back, referring to Ismay. He'd told Jack not to tell Ismay he was returning. He wanted to talk to her in person. Only then did he feel he'd be able to determine if coming back had been the right decision.

She didn't go back to him, did she? he wrote and held his breath, waiting for the answer. If she had, he'd get up in the morning and take the first flight he could get back to New Orleans, and all the money he'd spent to return to Mariners would be a waste. He'd also feel like a fool.

No. He's pressing her about it, especially now that she knows he wasn't responsible for the stuff in that duffel bag. But she's stuck on another guy I know. ;)

Bo felt a smile stretch across his face as he read Jack's answer. He was still smiling when he released his seat belt and got his bag down from the overhead bin. It was after eleven o'clock. Because he'd booked his flights at the last minute, he'd had to take a circuitous route to Boston and had barely arrived there in time to catch the last flight of the day to the island. Before leaving Louisiana, he'd booked a hotel here in town so he'd have a place to stay when he got in. He hadn't planned on bothering Ismay tonight. But if Jack was up, maybe she was, too, and Bo suddenly couldn't wait any longer to see her.

Is Ismay with you?

She is. There's no way we could go to bed right now. We're busy celebrating.

At Honey's?

No, at the Starfish Beach Bar.

That place was on the other side of the island, much closer to the cottage than downtown, but he could easily grab an Uber…

He read Jack's message again, the one about Ismay being stuck on *another guy* and used his app to call for a ride.

Ismay felt as if a huge weight had been lifted from her shoulders. Livingston hadn't been able to tell her much, but he had indicated that what Remy had shared with him was specific and significant and should be enough to get a conviction—hopefully followed by some counseling. Several of the women whose panties were in that bag knew Bastian, but they'd never had any kind of contact with him that would give him access to their underwear. That meant he'd been breaking in and stealing it—and had probably been watching them, too. Some of them were locals, even older women, but others had been tourists who'd visited the island while he was around.

"To think I was staying in the cottage with him," she said to Jack with a shudder. "I can't believe Remy let that happen, knowing what he knew, but I'm going to keep my promise to not go to the papers."

"Didn't he say he was surprised by the duffel bag? That he hadn't thought of the Peeping Tom accusations in years?"

When he'd called to tell her he'd gone to the police, he'd explained all of that. But still… "He did, but I told him Bastian tried to get in my room!"

"Even if he knew Bastian had a problem with women, he probably thought—because you were his fiancée—you'd be exempt."

She held her wineglass loosely in one hand. "That's a hell of a gamble to take. I'm still freaked out."

"I don't blame you." He put down his soda and waved off the waitress when she asked if he wanted another. "I think he's expecting you to come back to him now that you know he's innocent."

"I haven't promised him that, but I did tell him I'd meet him for breakfast in the morning, and that we can talk. It'll be the first time we've had an open and honest conversation about our relationship since I left LA."

"What do you think he'll say?"

"I'm guessing he'll want to salvage what we can during the next two months, before his residency starts, or he wouldn't have asked to see me."

"Are you tempted?"

She pursed her lips as she examined how she felt. "No," she decided. "Not even a little bit. Whatever happened with Bo... It changed me. I can't go back."

He crossed his legs out in front of him. The bar was getting busier as the night wore on, so he had to talk louder to be heard over the crowd. "Remy won't like that answer."

"He generally gets what he wants. But not this time."

"Maybe I should go with you."

"I'll be fine. It was Bastian who pulled on the steering wheel. I feel bad I ever doubted Remy."

"Have you heard from Bo?" Jack asked.

Her heart suddenly felt heavy as she shook her head. "You?"

"Just a few lines when I told him about Bastian."

She finished her wine. "What'd he say?"

"He wanted to know if you're going back to Remy."

"And what did you tell him?"

"That you're holding out for him."

She gasped. "Jack! I hope you didn't! I've given him plenty of time to respond, and he hasn't. He's obviously not interested."

"You don't know that," he said.

"It's becoming clear."

Jack was startled by something happening behind her. Then a huge smile appeared on his face. "Oh, yes I do," he said.

"What—" she started to say but turned to look over her shoulder at the same time—and saw Bo walking toward her, carrying a bouquet of flowers.

"Sorry these look a little sad," he said as she stood up and he handed them to her. "The street vendor by the airport was closing and didn't have a lot left to choose from."

She didn't care if they were weeds. He was back. "What are you doing here?" she asked.

He grinned. "Well, you see, there's a girl on Mariners that I just couldn't leave behind."

He was saying exactly what she wanted to hear. But she still had one question she had to ask him. "Did you shoot your father, Bo?"

He shook his head. "No."

She knew that subject would require a longer conversation, but not when Jack was around and not tonight, when she was happier than she'd ever been. She put his flowers on her seat before throwing her arms around him. "I knew it," she breathed into his ear.

Then he kissed her, and everyone in the restaurant started to clap, including Jack.

Annabelle stood on the patio of the apartment they'd recently bought in Hudson Yards, staring down at the lights of the busy Manhattan street far below her. Everything looked so tiny from her perspective—the people and cars were almost like ants as they zipped about. She knew what was happening on Mariners and that she should be rushing around, throwing clothes in a suitcase and catching a flight to the island as soon as possible. But she hadn't moved from the patio for hours, since she'd received

Bastian's call. She hadn't even gone in to get a coat, despite the fact that it was growing colder and colder as the night wore on.

Mort wasn't home from work yet. She'd tried to call him so she could tell him that Bastian had been arrested. She needed his advice, his support. But these days there was none of that to be found. She'd only been able to reach his voice mail. When he finally came home—*if* he came home—he'd say he'd been intent on whatever he was working on at the office. But it was almost midnight. She knew the truth, knew he was seeing someone else—maybe a string of women. He hardly bothered to hide it anymore. She'd probably be looking at a divorce soon, she realized, and what a mess that would be.

Regardless, she couldn't continue to dwell on the sad state of her marriage. She had a bigger decision to make. Did she allow Bastian to take the fall for Remy? Or did she tell the truth?

She tried to imagine the future if she came forward—the difficulty she'd continue to have with her "no good" son. Even if she got Bastian out of jail, he wouldn't change. He'd still be far too self-indulgent, wouldn't take hold and work, wouldn't thrive.

And if she didn't come forward? If she let him take the punishment Remy deserved? Remy had the intelligence and drive to make such a difference in the world—make her proud to call him her son. He could go on and become a doctor. And why not? Bastian would only have to serve a couple of years, if he got prison time at all. With a good lawyer, he might not get much more than a few months in the county jail.

But she knew that duffel bag didn't belong to Bastian. Just hearing about it had told her Remy hadn't stopped the behavior for which Bastian had almost been charged last time. And he'd just turned on his brother *again.* That he had no compunction about doing that, even at this age, was an alarm she couldn't ignore.

Annabelle closed her eyes as an errant tear wandered down her cheek. She should've come forward years ago. Set things right.

Maybe, had they sought counseling, Remy could've changed. Instead, she'd stepped in to erase that whole Peeping Tom incident, hoping against hope that it was just a phase, an aberration from his regular behavior that he would conquer with a second chance—or at the very least, he'd learn his lesson from what had almost happened to Bastian. He had so damn much promise!

But that wasn't all of it. There was what she'd heard Bastian scream at Remy several years ago. He'd insisted Remy had shoved Lyssa into the bathroom so hard she'd fallen and hit her head on the tub, and that was the reason they'd started to fight. It was also the reason Lyssa hadn't gotten out of the house alive.

Annabelle had chosen not to believe what she'd heard that night. The boys always said terrible things to each other. But she knew, deep in her gut, that it was true.

Her cell phone rang. She looked down to see her husband's picture on the screen, but she ignored his call. She knew he'd want her to sweep it all under the rug again. He was largely the reason she'd done that last time. Appearances were all that mattered to him. They had to protect their name, his legacy. But she'd been better than that—once.

She pushed the button that would send his call to voice mail. Then she looked up the number for the Mariners Police Department, and when someone answered, she asked for Detective Livingston.

Ismay sat at The Charles W. Morgan, a restaurant that served fresh seafood in the evenings but also offered a weekend brunch. It was a fancy place, an expensive place, just the kind Remy liked. But she wasn't sure she'd be able to eat anything. She was too nervous.

She'd spent last night at the hotel with Bo, since he'd already prepaid for his stay, and she wanted to get back together with him as soon as possible. He didn't like that she was meeting Remy, said he didn't trust him and tried to talk her out of going.

But she felt she owed it to her ex-fiancé to meet with him and tell him how she felt, so he'd know there was no chance of a reconciliation and could move on without looking back.

It was a courtesy she would've appreciated if the tables were turned. But he was running late, and he wasn't answering her texts.

The waitress stopped by her table. "Can I get you another mimosa?"

"No, thank you. My, um, friend will be here soon."

She smiled as she walked away, but Ismay knew she had to be growing impatient and checked the time on her phone. Remy was usually punctual. So where was he?

He there? That text came from Bo.

Not yet. Maybe he's not coming, after all.

I'd like that. Then you've done your part by giving him the opportunity and it can be over. This is the jerk who almost ran you down. Even if it was Bastian who pulled the wheel, he should've reacted differently afterward.

Bo had a point. But he didn't understand how moody Remy could be.

I'll wait five more minutes and then leave, she wrote back, but when she glanced up, she saw Detective Livingston crossing the restaurant, coming toward her.

Putting down her phone, she shifted in her seat. "Hello, Detective."

He gestured at the chair across from her. "Do you mind if I sit down for a moment?"

She twisted around to look at the entrance of the restaurant, but still didn't see Remy. "No. Of course not."

"Remy won't be coming to meet you for breakfast, Ismay," he said. "He's been arrested."

She felt like he'd just tossed a glass of cold water in her face. "Wh-what for?" she stammered.

"His mother called me late last night. And what she had to say changed everything."

"What do you mean?"

"It was Remy who was doing the peeping way back when, even though Bastian took the blame. With identical twins, it can be hard for witnesses to get the details straight. But she got him off, so she didn't think it would matter which boy it was. Then you found that duffel bag in Remy's closet, and she knew the behavior hadn't stopped—it'd only grown worse."

"But… Remy wasn't even around when that duffel bag was removed from the closet. How could—"

"He asked Bastian to get it for him," he interrupted. "He was mad that Bastian made you move into his room and was afraid you'd find it."

"And Bastian did it? Why didn't he say no?"

Livingston shook his head. "Why do brothers do a lot of things?"

"You believe him?"

"I do. Bastian even showed me a text where he wrote back *I got it. It's in the attic.* And that's right where we found it early this morning."

She set her napkin on the table. "Wait! You're saying Remy was going to let Bastian take the blame *again*?"

"He felt his brother didn't have anything to lose."

"While he was about to become a doctor," she said, catching on.

"Exactly. That's why he thought his mother would go along with it again, too."

"You've got to be kidding me! What about my underwear? Why would Bastian take them unless—"

"He claims that was just bad judgment, a small way to get back at Remy for cheating with Lyssa. He was planning to have

Remy find it in his things, so he'd think the two of you had become…sexually intimate."

She gaped at him as she tried to absorb this information. "I—I can't believe it."

"I don't blame you. But it's clear Bastian both loves and resents his brother. It's complicated, and we'll probably never completely understand it."

"So…did Bastian pull on the steering wheel when he saw me and Jack on the road?"

"I don't think so. He claims Remy swerved right at you, and I, for one, believe him."

Strangely enough, so did Ismay. She'd suspected it all along; she'd just let herself be talked out of it. "Why would his mother come forward now?"

"They were young back then. She convinced herself peeping was somewhat normal for a boy of that age. But the duffel bag and all the underwear inside it, as well as something Bastian yelled at Remy about Lyssa one night, finally convinced her that Remy has a serious problem."

Ismay was almost afraid to ask. "What'd he yell?"

"She claims that Bastian was screaming at Remy for *killing* Lyssa, that Lyssa was yelling at Remy the night of the party, trying to get him to leave Bastian alone, and Remy lost his temper and shoved her so hard she hit her head on the bathtub."

"Why were they in the bathroom?"

"She was crying. Bastian went in there to comfort her, and Remy followed them, causing trouble. The two boys started throwing punches and they nearly fell down the stairs. Then they stumbled into the living room, where they broke a bottle of tequila and eventually knocked over a candle."

"And Remy's been able to live with that?" she asked.

"That's the other reason his mother came forward. As smart as he is, she knows he doesn't feel the empathy and guilt he should."

Ismay stared at the elegant white tablecloth. "And I almost married him," she murmured.

"You're a nice girl. I'm glad you didn't. Now I'd better go. I just…wanted to let you know not to expect Remy to show up for breakfast."

Ismay thanked him, then, stunned, sat at the table for several minutes after he left—until the waitress came by again. "Are you sure you wouldn't like another drink?"

"No, thank you. My plans have changed. I'll take my check now."

Once she received the bill, she paid it and hurried outside, where the sun felt reassuringly warm on her face.

Did he show? Another text from Bo.

No. I'm on my way back. And you're not going to believe what I have to tell you, she wrote.

But she paused before walking the two blocks to the hotel. She wanted to take a second to text Annabelle; she had the number from when Remy's mother had called her to advocate for Remy not too long ago.

Thank you.

EPILOGUE

One year later…

Bo sat back as the waiter brought his meal. He would've preferred a more casual restaurant than the upscale steakhouse in the Beverly Wilshire Hotel. But Annabelle Windsor was staying in the hotel while she was in California, so it was convenient for her. Ever since Remy had been arrested, and Bo had finally reached out to tell her he admired her for making the right choice and knew how difficult it must've been, she'd stayed in touch with him by calling and texting occasionally. She'd even sent him a Christmas gift. Considering he'd lied about his background when he applied to take care of the cottage on Mariners, it was an unlikely relationship, and yet it seemed to be growing stronger over time. He could tell she was incredibly lonely and eager for true friendship—or maybe, as Ismay thought, she was hoping to fill the hole Remy had left in her life since he refused to have any contact with her now that he was at the Souza-Baranowski Correctional Facility in Lancaster, Massachusetts. When she came forward with the truth, the media coverage surrounding the case had dredged up far more alarming things than a bag of stolen underwear. Although the prosecutor was never able to prove that Remy had caused the death of Lyssa Helberg, three different women—one on Mariners, one in Brooklyn, and one in California—had accused Remy of drugging them before having sex with them.

When Annabelle first called Detective Livingston, she probably hadn't expected her son to get any real prison time. She'd just felt she had to step forward to save Bastian, who was innocent. But the case grew very quickly, and it soon became apparent that the duffel bag Ismay had found was, indeed, evidence of a much bigger problem. Ismay still couldn't believe she'd almost married Remy and often marveled over how her life would've gone if not for the storm that'd made her search his closet.

"Can I get you anything else at the moment?" the waiter asked after delivering their plates.

They both said they were fine, the waiter left, and Bo tasted his wild French sea bass. "This is delicious," he said.

Annabelle smiled. "So's my lobster ravioli. I'm glad you could meet me today. I've been anxious to hear the latest. How are you and Ismay doing?"

"Better than ever."

"You're still in that condo you rented with her brother in Burbank?"

"We are. It's only a two-bedroom, so it's not big, but with the prices in LA, we had to be careful. At least it's not far from the beach, so the three of us have had a lot of fun, and it's only temporary. Jack has plans to get his own place in the next year."

"When you and Ismay get married..."

"Yeah. We haven't set the date yet. We're not in a huge hurry. At the moment, she and I are pooling our resources and putting them toward building her practice. But we'd like to have a baby in the next couple of years and plan to marry before then."

She took a drink of her cappuccino. "Well, you know you're welcome to come back to Mariners and use Windsor Cottage for your honeymoon, if you'd like. It hasn't been easy to replace you—I still feel terrible for firing you—but I've finally found an older couple who are living in the bungalow, and they're doing a decent job so far."

"That's a very nice offer, but Mariners might be a little weird for Ismay, considering the cottage's connection to Remy."

"Of course. I can certainly understand that."

"Do you know how Honey's doing?" He'd checked on her a few months ago and all was well, but he hadn't done so lately.

"The neighbor? I think she's doing fine. She's already friends with the new caretakers." She added some salt to her food. "What ever happened to Jack's wife, by the way? Did she stay with Jessica?"

Bo was surprised she remembered so much of what he'd told her over the phone during the past twelve months. "They're still together and seem to be happy. They moved to Salt Lake about three months ago and are more comfortable there. It's only an hour away from Tremonton, so Jessica's kids get to see their father and grandparents and cousins on a regular basis, but that hour makes a big difference when it comes to local attitudes and acceptance. She and Jack are officially divorced, and he's starting to date a little, but he talks to her every once in a while. Despite everything, they're friends."

She speared a piece of lobster in her pasta with her fork. "Is Jack still working for the same building contractor you are?"

Bo swallowed a bite of wild rice. "He is, and we've had plenty of work."

"Building homes in Santa Monica..."

He nodded.

"And how's Ismay's practice coming along?"

He told her about some of their marketing efforts, Ismay's first clients, the referrals she was starting to get, and their hope that her practice would continue to grow. "It's going well. She's an excellent attorney," he said.

Annabelle's smile widened. "You're so proud of her."

He felt slightly embarrassed that he was *that* transparent. "I am."

"It's wonderful you're together. I'm glad something good came out of all that happened last year."

"Me, too," he said. "How's Bastian these days?"

She made a face that indicated Bastian would always be Bastian. "He's still working with his father," she said, using her fingers to make quotation marks around *working.* "But having Remy out of his life seems to be good for him. Knowing what Remy did to Lyssa and almost taking the fall for him with that Peeping Tom complaint were screwing him up. He's seeing a therapist now, and I'm optimistic that he will do better with time."

"And now the big question." Bo put down his fork. "What about you?"

"What about me?"

"Last time we talked, you were thinking of leaving Mort."

Her smile wilted. "I've asked him to go to marriage counseling with me. He claims he will, but he hasn't so far, and if things don't improve, I will leave him eventually."

Bo thought that was long overdue, but he knew these things took time, and she'd been dealing with a lot. "Is he still seeing other women?"

"Probably. But it is what it is, you know? During the past year, what happened with Remy took center stage. Now I'm trying to get myself into a healthy position and help Bastian. In other words, I'm putting out one fire at a time," she joked.

"You're doing great," he told her. "Any word from Remy?"

"None. He refuses my visits, never calls, never writes. He even sends back my letters." She lifted her chin. "But he's my son. No matter what's wrong with him, I'll always love him. So I keep writing him and trying to believe he'll come out of prison a better man."

He'd only gotten ten years and could be paroled before the

end of his sentence. He wouldn't even serve as much time as Bo had. "Prison can either make or break a person."

"Knowing what you've been through, and that you're such a good man, gives me hope." She made a little hand gesture. "I know it was different with you, that you were innocent, but...a mother's hope springs eternal, I guess."

Bo couldn't help thinking that his father had robbed him of ever having a lunch like this with his own mother. But he had Ismay, Matilda and her boys, who had just come to Orange County to go to Disneyland, and Uncle Chester, who was finally back to full strength. Now he had Annabelle, too, who was eager to have another *son* to love. "What would life be without hope?" he said, and her smile returned.

★ ★ ★ ★ ★